He came to stand behind me. Gently, he cupped my elbow and turned me, so we were face to face.

"Claire," he spoke softly but his tone was stern. "Are you suggesting one of your own family would do something this atrocious?"

Tears welled once again. Angrily I wiped them away. "You of all people should know sometimes even those we care about can do the most evil of things."

He took a swift intake of breath. "You're right," he agreed. "Someone did not want anyone reading your mother's journals. But their actions bring only greater significance to their contents."

His fingers pressed into my arm and in his face I saw the reflection of what I imagined was on mine.

"Whoever did this will pay." My voice was almost a growl.

Ivan nodded. "Claire. This is the start of something very dangerous."

"It may be," I said. "But whoever this person is, they underestimate the abilities of a woman. They underestimate me."

The Secret of Darkwater Abbey

by

Jude Bayton

This is a work of fiction. Names, characters, places, and incidents are either the product of the author's imagination or are used fictitiously, and any resemblance to actual persons living or dead, business establishments, events, or locales, is entirely coincidental.

The Secret of Darkwater Abbey

Contact Information: author@judebayton.com

Cover Art by *Diana Carlile*

Print ISBN 978-1-955441-13-1
Digital ISBN 978-1-955441-14-8

Published by redbus llc 

Dedication

To my favourite Ivan – the inspiration for this story, and to Keith, Ollie, Max and Princess.

To Jezz Strutt-Sperry, Rhona Harding and Sarah Wilkom, my fellow Brits – who bring a little bit of England into my life when I need it the most.

Acknowledgements

Ally Robertson, and Diana Carlile. I'm so lucky to get to work with you both. Thank you for everything.
To Sheila Dawn Smith, thanks so much for those sharp eyes, and great advice.
Finally, to my readers. Thank you for all your continued support. I hope you enjoy the story.
Jude

Chapter One

England, Wednesday, September 17th—1902

I WAS SEVEN YEARS OLD WHEN my father died, but sixteen when Mother finally told me the truth. It was not a heart attack which had killed him, but the rope of the hangman's gibbet.

To say I'd been livid, furious with her for the long deception was an understatement. It mattered not to me that she steadfastly claimed his innocence. The burden of my fury and shame changed my life and challenged the imperfect relationship between us.

How I disliked our mundane existence. Adding the awful revelation of a sordid family secret fuelled my ardent desire to leave home and forge a path of my own. I was determined to be independent and self-sufficient. Unlike my poor mother, whose life had been ruined by scandal.

I had accomplished my dreams. Grown up and left Hampshire, then ventured to foreign shores as a nurse in the service of my Queen and country. Only to return to England recently as a widow, and now an orphan. For Mother had been interred in the local cemetery not a month hence.

My loved ones were all dead and buried. Mother, here in Hampshire, and my darling George along with our tiny daughter, Sarah, buried in a grave thousands of miles away under the relentless South African sun.

Tears filled my eyes. I pushed away the half-emptied trunk as though it burned my hands, getting swiftly to my feet. Enough digging through the past. I had a sudden, desperate need to get outside into the fresh air.

I hurried past the adjoining row of cottages before anyone could venture out to greet me. Since arriving back from the African continent the previous week, I had been inundated with a feeble mix of both well-wishers and nosey parkers.

To her neighbours, Mother had been an enigma, a mysterious recluse. It was little wonder, for she had spent years in hiding. Consequently, my return home aroused much interest and a curiosity I could well do without.

The narrow lane abruptly forked, and I turned away from town, preferring instead the company of flora and fauna. I'd walk near the woods and let the fresh, pine-scented breeze sift the nagging worries from my troubled mind.

Yorkshire born and bred, I'd nevertheless spent my formative years in Hampshire, where Mother took us after the death of my father. Three years ago, I'd departed England. Bound for South Africa, and a career in nursing, I'd left my mother, Jane, awaiting my eventual return.

It seemed a lifetime ago when I signed up for the journey to Cape Town. Mother had been extremely proud of my becoming a nurse but did not want me so far from home.

"Why must it be Africa and not a London hospital?" she'd asked, voicing her fear of my working in close proximity to the battlefields of the bloody Boer War. Certainly, there was danger out there. But I was young and ambitious, driven to atone for the sins of my father by an innate desire to help those who suffered, and perchance save lives.

Little did I know it would be the last I saw of her.

When my ship sailed from Southampton to Cape Town, Jane Shaw was a woman still in her prime, barely fifty-one years of age. Yet three years later as the steamer carried me back to England and our much-anticipated reunion, fate had stolen my mother from me. When the Castle Liner docked in Southampton, she had been in the ground almost a week, and I'd brought my broken heart back to an empty home.

My shoulders sagged under the weight of unhappy meditation. With a sigh, I stopped to peer over the hedgerows at the Galloway cows chewing lush, green grass in the nearby field. Their gentle eyes contemplated me, and I envied them their easy contentment.

Walking on, Nature's lucid colours were my canvas, vibrant today under the unusually generous September sunshine. Light bounced from every blade of grass and glittered under a picture-perfect indigo sky. How could there be such perfection when my life spun like an eddy in a muddy pool?

With Mother's passing, there were legal matters demanding immediate action necessitating my travelling up north. Plans were already in motion for my immediate future. In three days, my personal possessions would be packed up and sent on ahead to Yorkshire and the furnished cottage put up for sale.

I'd accepted my uncle's generous invitation to join

his family, the Mannings, at Darkwater Abbey, in the North Yorkshire Dales, the place of my birth. Many years had passed since I'd been to the familial home, bought by my grandfather, where Uncle Simon, and his daughters, Nicolette, and Vivienne, still resided. It promised to be an excellent opportunity for a brief respite. A place to mull over my options now I was alone with an undetermined path to follow.

I owed my uncle a great deal of gratitude. It was he who travelled to Hampshire in my absence to oversee Mother's funeral. I only wished I had been there to pay my last respects.

Mother always thought highly of my uncle. Simon Manning had married her only sister, Charlotte, and then become Father's partner in the family textile business. It was Uncle Simon she had turned to after Father's untimely death.

I had fleeting memories of Mother being inconsolable. Losing a husband had devastated her. But I'd been a child. One day my father was there, and then suddenly he was gone. Before my eighth birthday, Mother whisked us away to Hampshire. When I would ask why we'd left our home she'd claimed Yorkshire bore too many painful reminders of my father's absence.

At sixteen that had changed. I finally understood Mother had run away. Fled the gossip and scrutiny of those who knew her and the ugly stain of death tainting our name. My pride took a blow.

And now I was to travel back to Darkwater Abbey and see Uncle Simon. He, who was so kind to me on my intermittent trips there—unlike my cousins, who delighted in tormenting me at every opportunity.

Had Vivienne and Nanette known what really happened to my father? Perhaps they did now, but surely not back then. For the two of them liked nothing better than putting me in my place. They'd have taken great delight badgering me about him. The truth must have been kept from them as it had me.

I cast my mind back to earlier this morning, when the discovery of Mother's trunk had initially thrilled me. Delving through her personal items was like uncovering buried treasure. Items of clothing which still carried her scent, Lily of the Valley. A golden locket with a tiny image of my father inside, which I had instantly put around my neck. All the letters I'd sent from Africa, tied up neatly with a blue ribbon, and five small books which had been her diaries.

It was a tiny Aladdin's cave, that trunk. A balm to soothe away the pain of losing her, right at the very moment we were supposed to be together again with old grievances forgiven.

When my hands touched a large, thick, brown envelope, they stilled. I assumed it would be some type of documentation. Perhaps records of our births and other legal papers. I was horrified to find it stuffed with newspaper clippings of a heinous deed done and one best forgotten…a hanged man receiving his punishment. '*Murderous Villain Pays the Ultimate Price for the Death of Mr Keith Delahunt,*' read the headlines. The murderer's name emblazoned across the front page belonged of course to my father, Thomas Shaw.

****

His manner of walking caught my attention as he navigated the steep staircase down to Platform One at

Southampton Station. My trained nurse's eye could not help but notice the man favoured his right leg. An injury or affliction? I'd seen every kind during my time in nursing.

I lost sight of him at the bottom of the steps whereupon I was drawn into the swell of others onto Platform One. I kept moving. The platform teemed with people. Travellers, meandering like schools of fish, avoiding one another with surprising dexterity considering the confines of the area.

The air, damp with a promise of rain, hung onto the unpleasant odour of coal fumes and grease, with the occasional respite of pleasant wafts of coffee, coming from a tiny café in the near vicinity.

Intent upon escaping the melee, I navigated a passage through the throng, where I knew the end carriages of the train would be accessible when it arrived. There was no place to sit, the few benches positioned along the platform being already occupied.

While waiting, I absent-mindedly glanced around at people of every description and walk of life. Most of the finely dressed folks were far from where I stood. They would be travelling in the first-class compartments at the front of the train.

Amongst the hum of conversation from other passengers I detected the lilt of foreign tongues close by and looked around. There, sprinkled like a dash of spice on plain fare, stood a small group of East Indians, dressed in bright, colourful saris. No doubt they were recent arrivals come direct from the port of Southampton.

At my end of the platform, I spotted the man I'd noticed earlier. Standing apart from the rest of us, surrounded by at least five stacks of wooden crates, he became the object of my scrutiny.

The gentleman had what I called a military bearing. Dressed in a dark grey travelling suit—his posture, straight and erect, bore the tell-tale sign of authority. As I watched, he called out to a porter, his tone commanding, with an assertiveness allowing no question.

What on earth was in all those crates?

Thank goodness my trunk had been sent on ahead. I'd brought a single valise, and one of the porters had taken it off my hands when I'd got to the station. I carried a small reticule containing my few valuables, including a small derringer I never travelled without.

A series of whistles suddenly pierced the air, and like a genie emerging from a lamp, my train chugged slowly into the station. Steam hissed from the engine like an irritable dragon, and the brakes squealed like banshees until the locomotive came to a halt.

I expected the train to be busy, not having originated here. But I was surprised how full it actually was, even this many carriages back. As we pulled away from the station, I passed through the remaining cars, still in search of a vacant seat.

It was not until reaching the last passenger coach before the freight carriages that I finally found a place. By coincidence, the gentleman I'd noticed earlier was in the same compartment, no doubt wanting to be close to his crates. Absorbed in a newspaper, he did not look up as I took the open spot across from him. But the younger man sitting next to him ogled me quite rudely, grinning like an ape. He even had the impertinence to give me a cheeky wink.

I glowered back at him and quickly put a stop to his scrutiny. After my years nursing military men of every character, I was not intimidated by a silly flirt.

The wheels of the train glided smooth as skates over ice, and not five minutes later the city lay behind us. Settling back, I glanced at a matronly woman sitting beside me, who sighed in slumber, her jaw loose and slack. She'd spoken a few friendly words when first I'd sat down and then promptly fallen asleep. Even the flirtatious man had closed his eyes.

Silence reigned, the quiet broken only by the occasional rustle of a newspaper page and the clickety-clack of the train tickling the tracks. As the carriage rocked gently along the railway lines, my body relaxed. The rigidity of my joints and bones sagged against the cushioned seat as tension deflated. I leant my head back and felt my eyelids grow heavy.

THE BANGING OF A DOOR sliding shut brought me instantly awake. My eyes flew open to see the younger man leaving the compartment. The train was slowing down, and I gathered we must be approaching a station. I glanced to my left. The lady who'd been sitting beside me had gone. My goodness, how long had I slumbered?

My remaining companion, the gentleman, had put down his newspaper and currently regarded me with no particular expression upon his face. He obviously saw my consternation and addressed me for the first time.

"The next station is Doncaster," he said.

I gave a sigh of relief. "Thank you. It would have been awful if I'd missed my stop."

His eyes, on the blue side of grey, studied me intently. "Are you going to Leeds or all the way through to Skipton?"

"Skipton," I answered. "And you?"

"The same. You needn't worry then, for the train goes no farther than that. The ticket collector will be sure to wake you."

He looked close in age to me, perhaps a little older, with a face most would consider handsome. His thick hair shone a pleasant shade of brown with highlights that the sun had bleached, as was the well-trimmed light beard and moustache. A gentleman by dress and manners, his physique boasted health and he had the build of a person used to yielding a plough rather than a pencil. His hands looked as though they had worked hard.

He spoke again. "I deduce from your accent, you're not a Yorkshire lass?"

"Oh, but I am. Born in Yorkshire but lived in Hampshire most of my life. And you, sir? I detect no northern burr in your voice either."

"Sussex," he said. "Near Brighton. Though I've lived in Yorkshire since childhood, I'm still considered a foreigner by all and sundry. At least you can claim real pedigree." He smiled, and for a moment I was captivated at the change brought by that slight shift of expression. The severity of his countenance was eradicated. His eyes softened and there was something most appealing about them.

"I suppose I can," I said. "I do have family there. In fact, I go to stay with my uncle. And you, sir? How long have you resided in the north?"

"A long time. My father worked in the textile industry and moved us to Leeds when I was but a lad. Then we settled in Starling Village, not four miles away from Skipton."

It was my turn to smile. "Why, it appears we have a similar destination. I am bound for Starling also. Our family home is just beyond the village. Darkwater Abbey. You must know it?"

The smile slid from his face and his eyes darkened. He frowned. "Tell me, are you by chance a Mrs Claire Holloway?"

How did this stranger know my name? Caught off-guard I could not answer. Instinctively I stiffened, not caring for the sudden shift in atmosphere. I observed the hard set of his jaw, a flash of malevolence in his eyes. Was I in some sort of danger? Uncomfortable at his abrupt change in manner I steeled myself, sat straighter and looked at him directly, unflinching. My grip tightened on my reticule, grateful for the weapon concealed there.

"Yes, sir. That is my name. Yet you have me at a disadvantage, for I do not know yours. How then are you acquainted with mine?"

His face hardened even more. His eyes cold. "I live at Darkwater Abbey. I am Ivan Delahunt, married to your cousin, Nanette Manning, these past two years. Your uncle, Simon Manning, is my father-in-law."

A vague memory stirred of Mother mentioning Nanette's marriage in one of her many letters. But in the midst of my turbulent life, I'd paid little heed to the news. Truthfully, I'd completely forgotten my cousin had wed.

I caught my breath. Not with embarrassment at my slip in etiquette, but something far worse. This man's identity was utterly disconcerting.

I was astonished. My mind aghast at the sound of

his name…*that* name. Ivan Delahunt. Delahunt! The words resounded again and again, like loud clanging bells in my head.

No wonder Mr Delahunt was unhappy making my acquaintance. The man had every reason to detest me. After all, it had been his father who had died at the hands of mine.

Chapter Two

I FOUGHT FOR COMPOSURE. I could not blame his sudden disparagement. In his shoes, I would undoubtedly feel the same. Yet though unfortunate and tragic, whatever transpired between our parents decades earlier had no bearing on the present day—we'd been children back then.

I recovered my senses. "Mr Delahunt. I find myself in a very awkward position indeed. I've recently returned to England from a long stay overseas, only to find my mother, Jane, buried, days before my ship docked. With my situation so quickly altered, and without other family, it was at my uncle's behest I travel directly to Yorkshire, where I am to attend to some business matters. However, I must tell you when I accepted Uncle Simon's invitation, I was unaware of your position in his household. That I neglected to remember your marriage to Nanette, and her married name, is an oversight on my part that I can only attribute to circumstances beyond my control. I have been abroad a while, and in truth paid little attention to the news from England during my absence. Had I not been so preoccupied these past days and realised who you were, I should have reconsidered my options and never travelled north. Inadvertently and without realising it, I have placed us both in an unfortunate situation. I am sorry for it. I certainly do not wish to cause any unpleasantness."

His face relaxed slightly at my sincerity. I was not lying. Had I known this man lived at Darkwater Abbey, I should have gone elsewhere.

He cleared his throat, then his eyes fastened upon mine. "For my part, I apologise for making you uncomfortable, Mrs Holloway. I have been out of the country this past month and was not informed of your coming, nor of your mother's passing, for which you have my sincere condolences. I was unprepared to meet you. Please forgive my rudeness and poor manners."

Polite words, yet I did not believe him. The tension in the space between us was palpable. But if the man pretended to ease the hostility between us. I would play along. There was little choice really.

"Do not apologise sir. We find ourselves together with no forewarning. It was wrong of my uncle not to apprise me. I am rather unsure what to say under these circumstances, other than this. You might deem it inconsequential, but my mother never shared our unfortunate history until my sixteenth year. Until then, I was ignorant of the shocking facts. For I was but a child and have no memory of it at all."

"Would that I could say the same." His eyes met mine with a mix of anger and sorrow.

I flinched. "Mr Delahunt. This is awkward already, and I have not even arrived at Darkwater Abbey. I shall leave the train when we reach Leeds and not go on to my destination. I'll send word to Uncle Simon that my plans have changed—"

"No," he said bluntly. "I do not wish you to do that. Please excuse my behaviour on the grounds it is only the surprise of meeting you which brings the past unexpectedly before me. As you say, you were but a child, and the actions of our families do not cast aspersions upon the children. I don't wish to be the catalyst for your changing any premade plans. I imagine Simon looks forward to seeing you after such a long time. He has spoken much about you and your own losses. Again, I apologise for my rudeness."

We stared at one another, assessing. Were we to be adversaries? Then he looked away and glanced out of the window, while I struggled with my quandary.

Mr Delahunt was right about one thing. My father's actions had nothing to do with me, nor should I be accountable for them. With this thought in mind, I made my decision.

"Then I shall continue on to Darkwater Abbey," I stated, drawing his attention once again. "But if my being there brings any discomfort, Mr Delahunt, I ask you tell me at once, rather than treat me as an unwelcome guest. Do you agree?"

His eyes narrowed as he mulled over my remark. Then he gave a curt nod. "You have my word, Mrs Holloway."

There settled an uncomfortable quiet. After a few moments I began to feel uneasy once more. This would not do. I sought to make conversation.

"How fares my cousin, Nanette?" I inquired. "It must be ten years since I saw her, or her sister. Uncle Simon came and visited Mother periodically, but he never brought the girls. Is Vivienne also wed?"

Mr Delahunt shook his head. "Vivienne is in no hurry to do anything. She spends a great deal of time with her sister. Nanette's health continues to decline, and Vivienne endeavours to keep her spirits up." Was that a note of disdain in his voice?

"I am sorry Nanette is unwell. I remember her being frail as a child." That was putting it mildly. Nanette had been cossetted and spoiled. She used her exaggerated frailty as an invincible weapon, and even back then I'd questioned its legitimacy. Vivienne, a year older, had long lived in Nanette's shadow. What a shame nothing had changed there.

"Simon has spoken of your escapades in Africa, Mrs Holloway. England will seem tame by comparison. I have heard much about your nursing our brave men fighting the Boer. The suffering of my wife will seem inconsequential in light of what you've witnessed from the bloody battlefields."

I did not wish to discuss my time in Africa. It was too painful. "England is a welcome return for me, Mr Delahunt. As for my cousin's ailments, it is wise not to compare hers to another's. It seldom helps the situation."

A strange look came over him as he stared at me, reading beyond my words and into my thoughts. Before I could remark, the sound of the ticket inspector's voice rang out down the carriage.

"Next stop Leeds. All passengers for Leeds leave the train at the next station."

****

During the last hour of our journey, Mr Delahunt excused himself and left to check on his belongings in the freight car. I was utterly relieved to see him go. My nerves were frayed and my mind stewed.

Dear God. How was it that the very name I had just read on the newspaper clippings in Mother's trunk had now been personified by the son of a dead man—a man killed by my father?

And what of Uncle Simon? Why had he invited me to share a home with Mr Delahunt, a man whose life had been irrefutably damaged because of my father's actions?

My mind sought to put it to rights. Why had my uncle not realised I would be uneasy living in the same house as Mr Delahunt? But then, the man had wed my cousin. We were, in effect, now family.

Oh, what a blasted mess. I should have known better and allowed myself time to settle back into life in England, stayed in Hampshire a while before making rash decisions. Too late now. I had sold Mother's house, sent on my possessions, and essentially rendered myself homeless.

For the immediate future, I would be dependent upon Uncle Simon's charity until Mother's estate was settled and I inherited her majority in Parslow Mill, the family company. The money from the sale of our cottage would not be available until after probate. Until then I had little income

There was nothing for it but to carry on as planned. I'd assess my level of discomfort residing at Darkwater Abbey after a few days, and not hesitate to leave should the need arise. If I left, Uncle Simon would have to help me financially. After all, we were business partners now.

Convinced I was completely in charge of my destiny, I resolved to make the best of a bad situation. When the train eventually slowed on the approach to Skipton and the end of the line, I gathered my belongings.

I reminded myself if I could keep my head whilst

working next to a battlefield, I could certainly cope living with the Mannings and the Delahunts. Yet in war, one easily identified the enemy by their uniform. This was not the case any longer. I would have to be on my guard.

****

A carriage and a large box-cart from Darkwater Abbey awaited outside Skipton Railway Station. Mr Delahunt kindly walked me over and introduced me to the coachman, Gibbons, a giant of a man with hands the size of shovels and a deep, gruff voice. The bearded brute quickly located my valise, picked it up as though it were the weight of a book, and secured it to the back of the conveyance. Whereupon Mr Delahunt tipped his hat and bade me a safe journey. Gibbons and I departed, leaving him to supervise the loading of his wooden crates into the cart.

Only mid-afternoon, yet a distinct chill gripped the Yorkshire air. I pulled my wool coat tighter and stared out of the window. This time of year, the Dales could be fickle. There might be radiant sunshine over the grassy hills and valleys, but in an instant the clouds could scud in and chase the warmth away.

Weariness plagued me. My joints and muscles protested after two weeks of relentless work. I'd arrived in England after a long voyage across the world, to be met at the port by Mother's solicitor. From there, I'd gone straight to Hampshire and packed up the cottage.

Even with many misgivings about staying with my uncle and cousins, the prospect of both emotional and physical rest at Darkwater Abbey, seemed paramount to my wellbeing. It had been such an awful, turbulent year. How I craved a little peace, and time to heal.

And yet look at my current situation. I had not even arrived at Darkwater and already walked into quite the predicament. Well, it was too late to do anything about it now. I must proceed as planned and stop worrying. "Don't borrow trouble," Mother had always said. For once, I'd heed her words.

With that in mind, I stared out of the closed window at the splendid land of my birth. I'd seen much beauty in the world. The expansive plains of Africa and rugged, spectacular coastline of Cape Town. Yet the beautiful British landscape surpassed them all in my heart.

As the carriage clipped down the well-trodden road, I became engrossed with the rolling landscape of windswept hills, and lush, sloping dales we passed through. I devoured nature's painted canvas with greedy eyes. From the heights of soaring limestone crags to the depths of secret chambers, hidden in clandestine labyrinths down below. Ah, but there was magic here, and its majesty resonated within me, whispering through my veins. Here I was indeed a native. The Dales were in my blood.

Yet back in my birthplace my memories were vague, having left at so young an age. Those I had of my time in Yorkshire were colourful, kept alive by infrequent visits over the years to see my relatives.

Of my grandfather, Arthur Parslow, the founder of the family business, I had no recollection at all. He had died when I was three years of age. But Grandmother's kindly face shone clear in my mind, along with pretty Aunt Charlotte's, Mother's sister.

My grandmother, Mabel, lived only a handful of years after her husband's death. Aunt Charlotte had followed her mother to the grave a few months later. We attended their funerals though Mother had already moved us to Hampshire.

It saddened me to think of those long departed. Growing up, whenever I thought of my father, it was like peering through a morning mist. I'd often wondered at that. For in contrast, my emotional memories of him were unambiguous and gratifying. Papa loved me as deeply as I loved him, this I knew without a doubt. Yet somehow his clear image was always just slightly out of reach.

I suppose the trauma of his dying made my memories thin, perhaps to protect myself. Though the secret of his wicked deed had been kept from my innocent ears for a long while, on a deep psychological plane I must have detected something important was being withheld—I had been an astute child.

I reached for the locket I'd yet to take off since discovering it amongst Mother's things. The miniature inside was all I had of him.

A horse whinnied, bringing me back to the present. We were nearing the turn towards Starling. The journey had seemed short after the thousands of miles I'd already traversed these past weeks.

Overhead, pale clouds darkened, ominous with intent. Sure enough, as the carriage reached the outskirts of Starling, so the rain commenced. Not a heavy downpour, thank goodness, but a miserable drizzle.

We passed through the centre of the pretty village which was much as I remembered. A succession of limestone buildings and cottages, small shops and two taverns. I saw little obvious change since my last time here, but we were past it before I could blink. Now a jolt of anticipation ran through me. I was almost at the culmination of my journey.

After a turn at the crossroad, the horses sensed they were close to home and a warm stable, and the carriage suddenly picked up pace. My face pressed against the cool window and my breath quickened. Then all at once, there it was.

Darkwater Abbey.

Built on the ruins of an old Abbey which had burned to the ground hundreds of years earlier, Darkwater featured in many local tales. Haunted, according to some, by the priests who had lost their lives in the raging fire.

Darkwater exuded character. The rugged grey stone of the aged Tudor manor blended into the leaden sky, its edges blurred by thickening rainy mist. Marooned, encircled by a brimming silver moat, the building itself was a tiny island.

I stared at the manor. Hidden away, nestled within ancient valleys and dales, my mind found it easy to conjure up unfathomable tales and stories. And as we drew nearer, each rotation of the carriage wheels seemed to turn back time.

Our gait slowed, but my heart raced.

We came to a halt in front of a narrow stone footbridge, the only access to Darkwater Abbey. I stepped out quickly, heedless of the drizzling rain, mindless of everything but the place I had once called home.

It was good to be back.

If a building could look weary, then Darkwater Abbey was exhausted. After four hundred years and a thousand seasons, it had earned every crack in the stone, every inch of moss and ivy clinging like limpets to the masonry. Though Tudor in origin, since then, each subsequent owner of the manse had added something of their own personality to the place. Darkwater Abbey was neither one thing nor another, but an amorphous, unapologetic building.

Yet that eclectic design of the manor endeared it to the onlooker. Three wings in the shape of a 'U', with the main entrance situated on the east wing, as opposed to its centre. And that only accessible by a walled, narrow pedestrian bridge crossing the moat.

Several outbuildings were situated a little farther down from where I stood on the lane. Stables, cowsheds, even cottages where the servants were housed.

I stared at the familiar ghastly gargoyles which greeted all visitors, perched atop stone plinths on either side of the bridge. Their bulging eyes wicked and weather-beaten, watched all who approached as they guarded the only entrance to the tiny islet.

In my youth, the deep moat had frightened me for it seemed vast as an ocean. Now I easily understood why. A child could imagine shapeless, ghoulish creatures, lurking under the tangled water weed, down in the dark, cold, depths.

Vivienne had delighted in telling ghost stories at bedtime all those years ago. Invariably they involved a monster living deep among the wet rushes—one with an appetite for young boys and girls.

Now, the water conjured up ugly memories of my recent past. Thoughts I ran from during daylight which returned uninvited in my dreams at night.

I passed the demonic gargoyles and quickly crossed the bridge. I walked towards the tower room, wondering if anyone watched from behind stone-mullioned windows. My eyes focused upon the great nail-studded oak doors on the far side so I would not look down at the cold, dark water.

Soon I should see my uncle. How would it be after so much time and so long away? Today would be about reuniting with a family I had never been close to.

My confounded nerves began to get the better of me. What an odd homecoming this was. For though I'd many memories of being here I'd never come alone, only with my mother. The sudden twist of pain in my heart took me aback. I desperately missed her.

But all thoughts evaporated as the large oak doors swung open wide, revealing my Uncle Simon, who seemed to completely fill the space.

"Claire!" He called out with such genuine pleasure in his voice, I forgot everything that had tormented my thoughts these past days and rushed into his embrace. He held me close for a few moments and I hung onto him like I would a buoy in a raging sea.

Gently, he released me.

Uncle Simon was close in age to my mother, yet he did not resemble a man nearing his fifty-sixth year. Tall in stature and of strong build, he exuded good health. Simon boasted a thick thatch of silver hair and dark eyebrows, emphasising the brilliant Dresden blue of his eyes. Though I would not consider him handsome in the romantic way, he was striking. Coupled with a pleasant countenance, it was surprising he had remained a widower for so long.

"Claire," he said, his voice thick with emotion as

he stared at my face. "It does my heart good to see you after all these years. I am so pleased you have come." He tucked my arm in the crook of his and led me through the doors. "Come along. Let us take refreshment while they bring in your belongings. There is much for us to talk about."

Ancient wooden floorboards squeaked in protest as we went inside and turned to the left down the carpeted hallway. Nothing had changed. The corridor, dark and narrow, bordered with ancestral furnishings and hanging tapestries, seemed more like a tunnel. Until one stepped into the drawing room.

It was like the sun rising and chasing away night. This room, like all the other main rooms, was lit by a kaleidoscope of colour from light refracting through the beautiful stained glass. It was a feature in every window of the ground floor. I used to think I lived in a fairy kingdom. The pretty colours magical to the eyes of a child.

I followed Uncle Simon into the drawing room, the heart of the home. Wherever one cast their eyes there was something of beauty. A low ceiling supported thick, solid timbers overhead. But the eye was instantly drawn to the magnificent stone fireplace, as large as the carriage I had arrived in. This ceiling to floor marvel displayed masonry of such artistic merit, one questioned if Michaelangelo had visited Darkwater Abbey, so adroitly had it been carved.

High up in its centre, the family's heraldry was proudly displayed, flagged either side with different shields depicting many familial allegiances over the past four centuries. There was even a rendition of Satan himself, being overcome by a band of angels in celebration of good triumphing evil. Appropriate in a home named Darkwater Abbey.

The fire grate was large enough for three people to stand inside and currently held a welcoming roaring fire. The room smelled of lavender, pipe tobacco and burning logs.

Uncle Simon gestured for me to sit on a well-worn settee, patterned with the red and black tartan of the Stewart clan. He did not sit himself but went to stand before the fire where he studied me intently.

"My dear Claire. It has been too long since you last visited." His expression became pained. "Please accept my condolences for the loss of our Jane. She was an exemplary person, and I counted her as a lifelong friend. I am sorry your return to England has been so distressing." He looked at me pitifully.

My pleasure in seeing Uncle Simon surprised me. Having lost so many near and dear, I reasoned it was the relief of finally being with someone from my family after so much time. I thought of Simon as a father figure, a constant presence, albeit from afar, throughout my entire life.

I smiled at him. "Thank you for your kind words about Mother and for seeing to her internment. It was a sad return home, especially receiving the horrid news while still at sea. My one concession is that she did not suffer, and her end was swift."

Uncle Simon's expression became grave. "It was a shocking accident. Unfortunately, the streets of Southampton teem with pedestrians, cyclists, and conveyances of all description. Traffic is unruly. In a single moment, tragedy can occur, changing lives forever. As you say, Jane would not have expected what came to pass, and that is one thing to be thankful for."

I did not wish to dwell upon my mother's death, nor that it had been under the wheels of a coal cart. I changed the subject.

"Speaking of family," I said. "By strange coincidence, I found myself sharing the same train compartment as your son-in-law, Ivan Delahunt. He was most surprised to learn I was coming here."

Uncle Simon had the grace to look slightly embarrassed. "Indeed? Ivan has been away for some time. Had I known his plans to return to Yorkshire coincided with the same day as your arrival, I would have told you to be on the lookout for him. It was an oversight on my part. But how fortuitous you've already met, for he is the only new addition to our family here at Darkwater Abbey."

I heard the rattle of china and turned to look. The door to the drawing room stood wide open, and as I recognised a familiar face, my heart swelled.

"Tibbetts? Is it you?" I beamed with delight.

"Ah, here is our tea." Simon moved to sit at the opposite end of the settee. I watched as Tibbetts placed a tea tray on the low table in front of us.

The middle-aged man straightened up and gave me a familiar crooked grin. "Why 'course 'tis me, Miss Claire. A fair bit older and with less hair on't head, but same Archie that fetched you in fra' dales for supper."

Poor Tibbetts, a lowly stable lad back then, had borne the brunt of watching out for me on my many escapades. He was of low birth, but I held a high opinion of the man. Here was an ally. Thank goodness he was still at Darkwater Abbey.

"That will be all, Tibbetts. You may leave us to pour." Uncle's dismissive command put an end to our chat. Tibbetts gave a slight nod of his head, gave me another grin, and left us.

Uncle Simon poured two cups of tea and handed me mine. I took a sip, finding it wonderfully refreshing. My mouth was parched from the long journey.

I placed the cup back in its saucer. "I am pleased to see Tibbetts still here. I see he's escalated his position with you. I always thought him a decent man."

"Yes. He is a good fellow, and we are fortunate to have him. He was promoted to an indoor jack-of-all-trades after we lost so many staff. People in the village are all seeking work in Skipton nowadays. There is more money to be made in the factories, shops, and mills like ours, than there is being a domestic servant." He frowned, then took a sip of tea.

"I believe it is the same everywhere." I set down my cup. "By the way, I am sorry to hear Nanette's health is still precarious. Mr Delahunt told me while on the train."

Uncle Simon shrugged. "You know how it is with your cousin. She has long suffered a weak constitution. I had hoped marriage would change that, but it seems it is not to be the case." There was no judgement in his voice, but Simon's face displayed obvious disappointment. "I despair I shall ever have grandchildren. I have one daughter who ails, while her sister, Vivienne, seems determined never to wed. I cannot tell you how many suitors the girl has had, yet she will pay them no mind whatsoever. Vivienne is far too comfortable living here. She enjoys the companionship of her sister more than she should." He took another sip of tea and set it back down, then lifted an arm and draped it casually along the back of the sofa. He studied me with a serious expression. "Look, my dear. I hate to start your visit by talking about this, but I fear it must be said. You'll hear about it from someone."

His tone sounded foreboding. "What is it, Uncle?"

He gave a heavy sigh. "Oh, nothing to worry about, but a bit of bad news. Just yesterday, some poor fellow had a seizure and dropped dead just down the road from here."

"That's terrible. Was it someone you knew?"

He shook his head. "No. Constable McNabb said he was walking from the village and most likely a visitor to the Dales. We often get ramblers around here. Of course, I was called out, along with the doctor. Fellow took a nasty turn." He turned a smile on me. "McNabb is sorting it all out, but in light of all you've dealt with lately, I wanted you to hear it from me."

"Thank you. That was most considerate." It was. I had much sympathy for the man's family, whoever he might be.

"So other than a bit of bad news, very little has changed at Darkwater Abbey. While in contrast you, my dear, have travelled the world, witnessed a bloody war, and had a multitude of events take place. I wonder how have you coped with everything at so young an age?" His tone softened. "You are a marvel, Claire. I wish my own girls had half of your drive."

"All things considered, I'm doing as well as can be expected. But if you don't mind, Uncle, I'd rather not talk about my time in Africa. At least not yet. I would much prefer contemplating the future. It shall be a balm for my mind, staying at Darkwater Abbey. I take great comfort being in a place that is both familiar and special." I turned to look at him. "You and my cousins are the only family left to me now Mother has gone."

Simon reached over and gently took my hand in his. The warmth of his skin soothed me. He looked at me with great affection.

"Yes, dearest. We are your family. I want to help you in any way I can. You need rest, a good dose of healthy Yorkshire air, and regular walks upon the Dales. That will strengthen your spirits and have you feeling better in every way."

"Papa?"

Simon quickly released my hand and got to his feet. "Look, Vivienne. 'Tis your cousin Claire. She has finally arrived."

Chapter Three

I STOOD UP TO GREET SIMON'S daughter. When had I last seen Vivienne? At least eleven years ago, when I'd been fifteen years old. She and I were a year apart, but there had never been any love lost between myself and the younger Manning sister. I'd always found Vivienne sly and underhanded. She kept me on my guard.

The woman approaching me was no longer a child. Her features had matured. Vivienne wore a dark green day dress over an ample, well-rounded figure. Her blonde hair was swept up in an artful chignon, her eyes, blue as her father's, stared intently at me, taking in every detail.

In my grey travelling skirt, matching jacket, and no hat, I looked drab in comparison. Vivienne stared unabashedly at my hair, cut in a bob no longer than my chin. Most of the European nurses had lopped off their long tresses within a week of arriving in the sweltering African climate. Who had time for toilette when there were wounded men to tend? After three years, I found I preferred the length, and kept it thus.

"Claire," said Vivienne with little warmth. "Why, Cousin, I barely recognised you. Welcome back to Yorkshire. My, but you seem quite…different." She turned to her father. "Do you not agree, Papa? Claire has such an exotic look, with her short hair and such brown skin."

And there it was. Vivienne being her typical feline self. A masterful little dig concealed in a complimentary tone. I ignored the comment. I cared little for maintaining an English complexion and gave not a whit if I freckled.

"It is wonderful to see you again too, Vivienne. Your father was just telling me all the news. I am surprised to find you still living at home. I always thought you'd be the first to marry and fly the nest. Yet I see Nanette beat you to it." I kept my tone pleasant but returned her sting. I'd no intent upon hurting her feelings. But she needed to understand however she spoke to me, I would respond like mindedly.

Her mouth pinched, Vivienne passed by to take a seat in one of two armchairs facing the settle. She gave a dramatic sigh. "Unfortunately, it is difficult for me to leave home, when Nanette faces so many challenges with her health." Her eyes travelled to her father who had resumed his seat, as had I. "Besides, who would care for dear Papa? He can barely keep the few servants we have as it is. And none have his best interests at heart more than his own family." She settled back in her chair looking directly at me. "Papa tells me you are unsure of your next situation. I am very sorry about dear Aunt Jane. She was always extremely kind to me. I take it you plan to stay on at Darkwater Abbey for some time?"

Remembering my new acquaintance in the train and our sensitive situation, I quickly replied. "I doubt it. A few weeks, perhaps. Just long enough to settle Mother's estate and see a few other legalities are in order."

"Ah," said Uncle Simon. "As to that, we have an

appointment with the company solicitor this Friday to finalise the transfer of Jane's Parslow Mill shares into your name. Once you are made fully aware of your expected income, it might influence the decisions you make going forward." He smiled warmly. "Of course, you are welcome to stay on here. It is your family home as much as it is ours, and you are at liberty to remain at Darkwater Abbey permanently should you wish. We would be delighted to have you join us here. Wouldn't we, Vivienne?"

Father and daughter looked at one another. I did not imagine the glint in Simon's eye as he willed Vivienne to agree with his welcoming invitation. The hesitation for her reply was pronounced.

"Of course, Papa. Whatever you say," Vivienne said sweetly. Then abruptly, she got to her feet. "I am sure cousin Claire is tired from her journey and would like to refresh herself. Shall I take her up now?"

Simon rose as well. "Yes, my dear. Thank you."

VIVIENNE SAID VERY LITTLE as I followed her up the curving stairs. When we reached the first floor, she turned to the right, leading us into the west wing. This too was familiar and unchanged since my last visit to Darkwater Abbey. The floor was covered with a stretch of dull red carpet, the walls decorated with so many hanging pictures of various subjects, you could barely see the whitewash behind them.

There were three bedrooms in this part of the house. This I knew because this wing had been our living quarters years ago. On our subsequent visits, Mother and I always slept here.

Vivienne led me past my old room to the end of the

narrow hall until we reached the last bedroom. At last, she deigned to speak as we stepped into the chamber.

"Your bedroom is riddled with damp, so I have put you in here."

This had been Mother's room. A corner room which jutted out from the main building with windows on three of the walls. Here were views of the back of the house and the centre courtyard. They brought in light from outside, relieving the darkness from the centuries-old wooden panelling.

I loved the rich colours and intricate patterns in the wood grain. As children, we had always enjoyed exploring all the manor's rooms, because there were so many hidden cupboards and compartments behind cleverly concealed panels. It made for a great game. There were many wonderful hiding places all over, especially the priest holes down in the cellar.

Every room in Darkwater Abbey had its own impressive fireplace. Though none as grand as the drawing room hearth downstairs, they were all still individually fascinating. Each one differing from another. Mother had always loved this fireplace for its beautiful stonework of flowers. The upper part, ornately decorated with coloured mosaic stones, was dominated by the White Rose of York, in recognition of Yorkshire's volatile history, and the family's patriotic allegiance to their county. The manor was richly steeped in history everywhere you looked.

Anchored in the centre of the room stood a large bed covered with a rich purple spread. The massive wooden headboard stretched all the way up to the ceiling. Like the fireplace, it too was lavishly carved, but with interesting geometric designs. At the foot of the bed, my unopened trunk awaited. It had probably arrived yesterday.

In one corner, a thick curtain hung to hide a small bathroom. A mirrored dressing table and chair completed the sparse furnishings. The walls were devoid of paintings. Back when we lived here, there had been many, mostly of Mother's family, the Parslows. I must ask what had happened to them.

Vivienne walked over to where a small iron handle protruded from the panelled wall and pulled. "Here is the wardrobe for your clothes, Claire," she said. "Let me know if there is anything else you have need of. Mellors, our maid, will bring some fresh towels presently." She bestowed a look upon me of veiled dislike. I felt extremely unwelcome. It was time for me to be more direct.

I faced her. "Vivienne, you seem unhappy with my arrival. Have I done something to upset you? You do understand I am only here at your father's bidding? There is business to conduct, as you know."

She flushed. I had put her on the spot. Would she deny it, or explain her attitude towards me?

Vivienne sighed. Walking over to the side of the bed she sat down and brushed imaginary wrinkles out from her skirts.

"All right, Claire. I'll admit it. When Papa told me you were coming to stay, I was not pleased. Things at Darkwater Abbey have been very unsettled of late. I have much on my mind at the moment. My sister's behaviour is getting rather erratic, thus affecting her relationship with her husband. Consequently, the atmosphere in the house is uncomfortable, to say the least. Papa spends all day either hiding in his library, or in the Skipton office, pretending everything is normal. But it is not. Nanette lives on her nerves, and I am at my wits end what to do with her."

How unlike Vivienne to sound so defeated. In that moment I felt a great deal of empathy.

I joined her on the bed. "I'm sorry. It sounds as though you have your hands full. Vivienne, I don't wish to add to your burden in any way. If there is anything I can do to help, perhaps share some of your responsibilities, you only have to say."

Ivan Delahunt's face passed through my thoughts and prompted my next words. "My plans are not to remain here long. Once my business is concluded, I shall be on my way."

"Good," she retorted without looking at me. "Thank you for the offer of help. You can sit with Nanette from time to time. That would be one less thing for me to do." She rose to leave. Apparently, that was all my cousin was prepared to say. I watched as Vivienne made her escape.

BY THE TIME MY TRUNK WAS unpacked and my things put away, it had grown dark outside. A rumbling in my stomach reminded me I had not eaten all day, and I wondered what time dinner would be served here at the manor.

I retrieved Mother's journals and the envelope containing all the newspaper clippings I'd found along with an assortment of daguerreotype pictures, and placed them in the top-dressing table drawer.

I'd barely glanced at any of it. After one glimpse at that awful newspaper heading, it had been enough. Besides, there had been too much to do before leaving

Hampshire. At Darkwater, there'd be more time to read everything thoroughly.

I also planned to speak to Uncle Simon about the murder Papa was convicted of. Did he share Mother's adamant belief Father had not been guilty? Framed by another who stood by and watched an innocent man die on the gallows.

What to make of it? I'd been preoccupied packing up the cottage after losing yet another loved one. I would reserve my judgement until I'd had time to read through Mother's journals.

Yet now I was back where the deed had been done, I could discover what really happened all those years ago. I could use the information at hand and look up local newspaper archives from that time, even talk to any of the people named in Mother's journals, if they still lived here.

Of the victim himself, Mr Delahunt, I knew little about him, other than he worked as an accountant for Grandfather's company. There was much for me to learn.

But not today. This evening was a time to take stock of my current situation and be cordial to my hosts. Would Ivan Delahunt be present for dinner? One would think so. Surely he and his vast amount of luggage should have arrived by now.

I changed from my travelling clothes into one of two mourning dresses styled for evening wear I'd brought with me. I'd had them made after losing my husband and child back in Cape Town. Little did I realise I'd have need of them on English soil as well.

The black silk was plain with a neckline cut lower than I might wear during the day. Its bodice was crusted with tiny jet beads, and the pattern repeated at the end of long sleeves.

I glanced in the mirror of the dressing table. I still felt grubby from being on public transport most of the day, but a light wash had refreshed me somewhat.

I studied my face and thought about Vivienne's earlier comments upon my appearance. She was correct. Wearing my hair at this length was unusual in English society, and likely to be looked down upon, even by common folk. But I preferred it this way, for my dark brown hair had always been somewhat unruly. In this style, the natural wave in my hair could be allowed its freedom.

Though my appearance was lacklustre, my light brown complexion from years abroad saved me from looking pale and wan from exhaustion. The colour of my eyes fluctuated from hazel to green, and tonight they looked almost copper.

I chewed my bottom lip reflecting what the evening may hold. Did Nanette feel well enough to leave her room for dinner? I had yet to see my cousin and found myself vastly curious. If she were not downstairs then I would most certainly go and visit her in her room.

I looked at my reflection one last time. "Wish me luck, Mother."

Chapter Four

DOWNSTAIRS IN THE DRAWING room, Uncle Simon sat in one of the armchairs cradling a glass of sherry in his hand. Seated on the matching chair next to him was the gentleman I'd met on the train. Both stood when I approached.

"There you are, Claire," Uncle Simon sounded pleased to see me. "Do come and join us for a sherry before dinner. No need for introductions as you have already met Ivan." He walked over to a side table and poured sherry from a crystal decanter, then returned to hand me the glass.

"Thank you." I accepted the drink and sat on the sofa. Mr Delahunt did not speak. I glanced at him and saw he looked serious. He wore a charcoal grey suit, as though he had just returned from a day at work and was not dressed for dinner.

Outside, rain tap-tapped against the windows. The smell of the blazing wood fire was pleasant, and the room comfortable and warm. I took a sip of my drink and savoured the delicious flavour.

"I trust you are settled in, Claire?" asked my host, returning to his own seat.

"Yes, thank you, Uncle. I had forgotten how much I liked the west wing and the wonderful view of the courtyard. It's nice being in Mother's old room."

"It is rather pretty up there," he agreed. Then he

gestured to the windows of the drawing room. "That's the only trouble with having stained-glass down here. Can't see a bloody thing outside."

"Surely that's a boon?" I said. "You receive plenty of light through the glass yet no one out there can see into the manor."

Mr Delahunt glanced over at me. "And privacy is of the utmost importance when one lives in an isolated house surrounded by a moat," he said with sarcasm.

Simon ignored the comment. He was looking at me with a concerned frown. "I do hope you shall be comfortable here, Claire. I'm afraid you'll have to see to yourself. As I implied earlier, we don't have many servants at the manor anymore. We can barely hang on to the few remaining. Thank goodness Tibbetts has stayed on. We've only a stable hand, cook, and one maid left, and a woman from the village who comes in to do all the laundry. Sorry business it is indeed."

I chuckled. "Goodness, please don't concern yourself about me. I've been looking after myself for a long time now. I've no need for a maid. One benefit of wearing shorter hair is you require no help with its care. Mark my words, before long, women will abandon wearing their hair long."

Simon smiled affectionately. "It looks dashed fetching on you, Claire. But I don't know that it would be for every lady. I should miss seeing their elaborate coiffures."

Mr Delahunt gave what I took for a bored sigh. "Simon, if men had to wear their hair in the ridiculous styles women do, they would have long cut it all off as Miss Holloway has. I say bravo to you, madam. You are a woman ahead of your time."

As I considered his odd compliment, the men rose again as Vivienne joined us. Given our conversation, her timing was impeccable. Unlike myself, she looked the epitome of a true example of the current fashion. Vivienne wore a beautiful silk dress the colour of spun gold. It was expensive and no doubt recently from Paris. Yet for someone of her stature and colouring, it was all wrong. With her blonde hair and blue eyes, I fancied blues and greens would favour her more.

Both men were extremely polite and remarked upon her appearance favourably. She flushed a little and I noticed her eyes linger on Ivan.

Simon fetched his daughter a glass of sherry, and Vivienne sat down at the other end of the settee.

"How does your sister fare this evening, my dear?" Uncle Simon asked.

Vivienne gave a melodramatic sigh. "I fear the damp from the rain renders her achy. Nanette wished to join us this evening in light of Claire's arrival, but she sends her excuses and asks that we try tomorrow instead."

"I didn't see that coming," Ivan said dryly. His eyes were the colour of steel.

Vivienne seemed unaffected by the comment, but Simon bristled slightly. I was not imagining the tension in the house. There was much at play here.

I spoke up. "I am sorry Nanette isn't joining us. I'm looking forward to seeing her again after all this time. Perhaps I could go up and say hello after dinner?"

Vivienne's eyes flashed disapproval. "You must not," she said. "When my sister is in this type of discomfort, she abhors company. Better to wait until the morning when she has had a good night's rest. Then she will be more like the Nanette you remember."

That sounded feeble to me. But who was I to quarrel? I was in no great hurry to see Nanette. Instead, I turned my attention to her spouse. "Mr Delahunt. I hope you were able to fit all of your crates into the cart today. They accuse ladies of travelling with too much luggage, but you seemed to have enough to fill one freight carriage by yourself. Surely you don't have that extensive a wardrobe, do you?" I gave a smile in an attempt to lighten the tension in the room.

He was obviously happy to keep it that way with his quick response. "One must be prepared for any event when abroad. Rain, snow, hot weather, all require different styles of dress." He gave a deep chuckle. "Of course, that's utter nonsense. I have been overseas collecting bolts of fabric for the mill to examine. Although in England our tweeds cannot be matched by any other country, there's much to be learned from our peers. Italy has exquisite fabrics that are used in the making of suits. And of course, no one can surpass the French when it comes to ladies' fashions."

"Have you been gone very long?" I asked.

"More than a month," answered Vivienne for him, then quickly blushed as though realising it was not her place to say. It went unnoticed by Mr Delahunt, but Uncle Simon gave his daughter an odd look.

"You must have travelled extensively?" I persisted.

"I did. Across the continent, from Portugal to the Balkans. Unfortunately, I spent little time in each city, and it was all work and little recreation." He looked at me directly and smiled much as he had in the train earlier that day. It had the same effect as I had noticed before. A slight tilt of his mouth rendered his expression far less severe. I could not decide if Ivan Delahunt was unhappy, or just a mean-spirited person. I imagined I would find out in time.

Tibbetts came to announce dinner was ready, bestowing me with a friendly smile. Simon got to his feet and offered me his arm, leaving Mr Delahunt to escort Vivienne.

The informal dining room was next to the drawing room and a place with which I was familiar as it was an old favourite of mine. Intimate, the room had a scent of linseed oil from the elaborately carved wood panelling. It glowed from years of oil and varnish and from the firelight flickering in the hearth.

Years ago, I'd often hidden in this room during the day. Treading across thick rugs of deep umber, I'd nestle into the comfy cushioned window seat, tucked behind thick curtains. The light always cast such pretty shades in here. As a child I found it magical.

The round table in the centre was set for four. Uncle Simon pulled out my chair and then after I was settled, sat down himself. Tibbetts reappeared carrying a large silver tray bearing a soup tureen. He proceeded to ladle soup into each of our bowls and then departed.

My uncle commanded most of the conversation as we ate. He discussed local events in the village, touched upon the subject of the unfortunate man who'd suffered the fatal seizure the day before. He answered Ivan's many questions about the matter.

Eventually, the subject was closed. Several other names came up, and Uncle Simon paused to ask me if I knew this person or that.

"It is likely I do," I said. "But I am famously hopeless with names. I'll warrant I'd know them in person though."

"Being a nurse, I would imagine a poor memory of names could be considered a handicap with your patients." Vivienne gave a thin smile. "Especially since one soldier must look like any other?" The word 'nurse' had been spoken with great disdain. Her flippant tone instantly affronted me.

"It was no handicap," I replied drolly. "You see, Vivienne, when wounded men are dying in your arms, they do not care if you know their names or not. They are too busy calling for their mothers."

The appalled look on her face told me I had gone too far. Even Uncle Simon's spoon paused in mid-air. Mr Delahunt stared at me with what…respect?

I cared not. With a person like Vivienne, it was important to set the pecking order quickly. She was a bully, and I, no longer the child she could pick on. This was my warning shot from the bow of my ship.

It worked.

****

The remainder of dinner was awkward after my comment. As soon as the last course came and went, so did I. Vivienne was probably relieved to see me go up the stairs.

I slept a deep, dreamless sleep and awoke feeling better than I had in days. Surprising what a full stomach and comfortable bed could accomplish.

I lay in bed long after waking and stared at the ceiling, a myriad of thoughts cascading through my mind. There was much to consider now I had come to Darkwater Abbey. But first things first.

I got out of bed and went to the dressing table, pulled open the top drawer and took out one of

Mother's books. I plumped up the pillows against the headboard, got back into bed, and opened the cover.

When I'd spotted her diaries amongst the other items in the trunk, I was not surprised. A small, red leather-bound book had been Mother's constant companion for years. I remembered many evenings watching her write a note or two in the candlelight, whilst I read one of my stories. I'd imagined she'd written about her thoughts and dreams, or the events of a particular day and what she and I had been doing.

I had not realised there were so many of the books, for they all looked the same. But of course, it made perfect sense. She would not have been able to fit two decades worth of words into one little diary.

This book was dated the same year my father had died, Eighteen hundred and eighty-three. I read the introduction.

I write this account to record the absolute truth of what happened on the night Keith Delahunt was murdered. My story is in direct conflict with the events that were purported to have taken place that night, according to a court of law.

My claim is an honest one. My husband, Thomas Shaw, was not guilty of committing the foul act of murder. In these pages, I will attempt to explain why.

I paused. Poor Mother, devastated by Father's death, she'd been terribly pre-occupied by the circumstances around the events of that awful time. I could feel the pain in each of her words and it broke my heart. Having lost my own husband, I now understood her sorrow was insurmountable. That she had loved my dear papa was obvious. It must have been impossible for her to accept he could be capable of murder. I struggled with that myself,

I set the book down. I was not in the right frame of mind to read her emotional and personal observations. Instead, I retrieved the envelope from the drawer and returned to bed, whereupon I pulled out several newspaper clippings Mother had collected.

There were quite a few, all dated from the year prior to my father's death up until a few weeks after he had been executed. I shuddered at the very thought of such heinous words and deeds. Yet I was determined to learn more about my past. My mother's words would be invaluable, but what was being said about Thomas Shaw by the press would be concise and direct. I began to read.

Keith Delahunt was an accountant who worked for my grandfather, Arthur Parslow. When Grandfather died, my father and Uncle Simon took over the running of the mill, which had been his fervent wish.

Upon my grandfather's death, the ownership of Parslow Mill was divided between Arthur Parslow's two daughters, my mother, Jane, and her younger sister, Charlotte. Of course, neither sister held official positions at the mill, but both their husbands had assumed operations. According to this report, the mill thrived under their direction.

The first article stated that my father, Thomas, had apparently been confronted by Mr Delahunt about possible fraudulent activity with the mill's accounts. Mr Delahunt supposedly had been overheard accusing my father of stealing money, even suggesting Father might be having an affair out of wedlock and using the money to finance that relationship.

Later that night, my father had allegedly gone to

meet his paramour. Delahunt had followed him to that location, a church graveyard, intent upon proving Shaw's infidelity. The paramour had never arrived. Whereupon Delahunt confronted Thomas Shaw, and in a fit of rage, my father had shot him.

I swallowed the acid rising in my throat. Affair? What affair? This was news to me. Mother had never mentioned this. But then, she seldom wanted to speak about the past with me for it was too painful.

After she told me the truth about Father's demise, Mother refused to allow his fate to be discussed. We tiptoed around our dark secret as though it were a cavernous hole in the ground we might fall into. I accepted the stain on our family name and understood why she had taken me and fled Yorkshire, where the awful deed had taken place.

I read on.

The paper reported a gunshot being heard by the local Catholic priest, who happened to have a guest dining with him—the village constable. Both men rushed outside to find Thomas Shaw bent over the dead man, who'd been shot through the heart. My father was arrested immediately.

I put down the paper and chose another. This story was similar but did not mention anyone overhearing an argument between Papa and Keith Delahunt. This account focused upon the trial, with an illustrator's rendition of my father standing in the dock. I stared at the sketch on the paper. At once the face of my father formed in my mind. My heart ached and tears burned my cheeks as I remembered his smile, the kindness in his eyes.

Yet here he was portrayed as a vicious killer. I

baulked at the ugly words. Papa had been a gentle soul, a kind man, and a generous employer. This portrayal of him was all wrong. But as I read the report of the trial, how the evidence damned him—his gun, his motive, and finally, his discovery by a member of the constabulary and the church, it was strong proof indeed.

The testimony of an alleged mistress helped seal his fate. The man I loved and cherished was portrayed as a deceitful, manipulative man. A man who would commit murder to keep his dark secrets.

I set the paper down upon the bedcover. What I'd read seemed totally surreal. It was too hard to take in, an abomination to accept. Yet my mother had never swayed from her belief in his innocence. Why?

And what had I thought at sixteen, when Mother finally told me the dark, secret truth about Papa's death? I had been shocked. Appalled and angry. With her, with him, with everyone.

I'd refused to speak of it, think of it, contemplate it in any way. I pretended those dreadful events had never occurred. From that day forward I'd buried my head in academics, until I had the credentials to forge my own path and get away from the country which had condemned my father to an early grave.

But what about now?

I glanced back at Mother's diary. I had so many questions and wished she were here with me to answer them. Jane Shaw was a strong, intelligent woman. I could not see her clinging to my father's innocence for two decades if he had betrayed their vows. She would never have countenanced infidelity. Yet though her husband had died for a horrendous crime, she had never stopped loving him.

If only we could talk now. I was not the self-centred woman who left England three years ago. Maturity would have guided my relationship with Mother. We could have been so much closer than when I left her behind. Thinking about that saddened me.

Now I was confused and so unsettled. To understand my mother's theories about Keith Delahunt's murder, I would need to read through her journals, one by one. Would I be able to comprehend the events of twenty-one years ago when something so awful happened and changed the course of so many lives?

Standing up, I went to peer out of the window at the solemn, grey sky. In the distance sprawled the smooth swell of green hills dipping and climbing as far as the eye could see. I sighed and watched my breath fog up the window.

There was the winding road leading from here to the village, and for a moment I thought about the poor soul who'd lost his life somewhere down there. Did he have a daughter waiting for him to come home?

Home. A word I seldom used anymore. But after everything that had happened in my lifetime, here I was, back at Darkwater Abbey. I'd come full circle. All I loved and cherished were lost to me now, and only memories remained. My mother, the victim of an accident. My husband and daughter, cruelly killed in a tragedy. My Papa, executed by the Queen's hangman. Each one of them beyond my help, for I could not change their fates.

Yet as I stood in deep reflection, a small pulse beat in the pit of my stomach. I could not do anything to bring my family back to me, but I could at least try and understand what had occurred more than two decades ago on the night Keith Delahunt died.

At the very least, I owed it to the memory of my mother.

But more importantly, I owed it to myself.

Chapter Five

I BREAKFASTED ALONE. TIBBETTS informed me Uncle Simon and Mr Delahunt had left for the mill in Skipton. I did not mind. It gave me a chance to catch up with the middle-aged butler, who had always shown such kindness to me.

When he came to clear my plate away, I invited Tibbetts to sit and have a cup of tea with me.

"Oh no miss," he said quickly. "I couldn't do that. Wouldn't be seemly, you being 'lady and me 'servant. Miss Vivienne would have me guts fer garters."

I shrugged my shoulders. I didn't care what she thought, but I wouldn't want Tibbetts to get in trouble. I smiled at him as he stood across the table from me. He'd changed little in the years he'd worked at Darkwater Abbey. Despite thinning light brown hair and the laughter lines upon his face, Tibbetts still had a youthful air about him. He must be close to forty by now, I supposed.

"I am pleased to see you after all this time, Tibbetts. I hope my coming hasn't made too much work for you. Doesn't sound like you've much help running the house."

"No, miss. There's nowt to worry about. It's good to see you back home."

What a nice thing for him to say. He'd always been a good fellow. "How have you been?" I asked. "How does your family fare?" I knew his father was long gone, but Archie Tibbetts had an older brother in the Navy, back when I lived here.

"Nothin's changed. Jack's sailing somewhere in't West Indies on't Majesty's pleasure. But he's home soon on leave."

"Is there no Mrs Tibbetts, yet?" I enquired.

"Um, no. No time for that, miss. I spend all me days at Darkwater." His face reddened and he blinked a few times. That spoke volumes. Someone had caught his eye.

I decided not to embarrass him further and changed the subject.

"It sounds as though there has been a lot happening at Darkwater. Uncle Simon told me a man died quite near here. He said it was likely a rambler."

"Aye, you've the right o' it, miss. T'were a sad business. Constable McNabb were here askin' questions. Asked if the bloke stopped by Darkwater."

"Is that so? Had the man been here?" I don't know why I asked, but once I had, Tibbetts looked very uncomfortable. Why was that?

Tibbetts quickly looked away from me and moved the salt and pepper pots into a straight line. "I wouldn't know, miss. T'wasn't in't house." He would not meet my eye, and something about his tone didn't ring true. I should have liked to press the subject, but the sound of footsteps approaching stopped me.

Tibbetts picked up my plate and quickly moved aside, passing Vivienne on his way out.

"Have you breakfasted?" she asked politely, approaching the table. This morning, she was dressed in dark brown, which complemented her piercing light eyes.

"Yes, thank you."

"Good. I came to tell you Nanette feels better this morning and wishes to see you. Can you come up now?"

"Indeed." I rose to my feet and followed Vivienne out of the dining room.

The family lived in the east wing. We ascended the stairs and turned in the opposite direction of my apartments, though the hallway looked much the same as the other.

Vivienne stopped in front of the third door and gave it a light rap.

"Come in," came the answer.

I stepped into my cousin's bedroom and was immediately aware of two things. The room felt overly warm, and there was a strong scent of something rather pungent, a cloying citrus odour.

"Nanette, here is our cousin," exclaimed Vivienne.

Like a small child lost among a sea of pink pillows, Nanette Delahunt sat upright, her pale face an oasis in the silken bedding. Long blonde hair spilled behind her, tumbling past her shoulders and down her back.

"Claire," came a breathy voice. "Oh, but it is good to see you after all these years."

I moved closer, and her small hand gestured to a chair by the bed.

"Please sit with me for a while."

I met her eyes, always so disarming as they were unusual, one blue, the other brown. Then she threw a dismissive glance at Vivienne, who nodded in acquiescence.

"I have some things to tend to. I shall leave you to

talk," Vivienne announced and left the bedchamber.

When the door closed, I spoke. "Nanette, it is lovely to see you again," I said sincerely. "I cannot believe so much time has passed since I was here."

She tucked her coverlet closer and then rested her clasped hands upon her lap. Though Nanette and Vivienne had similar characteristics, she was the real beauty of the family. I'd forgotten how perfectly formed her features were. The cherubic nose and cupid bow lips. Her skin, flawless ivory, untouched by the sun. Nanette's only imperfection was the differing colour of her eyes. The condition was called heterochromia, and it was quite uncommon. Yet the blue and hazel irises served to add to Nanette's uniqueness. She was delicate and fragile. If Vivienne could be compared to an Arabian horse, then Nanette was a unicorn. My cousin was a mythical creature who belonged with the faeries.

"I am so very sorry about poor Aunt Jane," she said softly. "You have had such an awful time of it these past two years, Claire." Her eyes were wide, earnest with compassion. "How you have borne it, I shall never know. But at least you are here with us now. It will do you the world of good, being with family."

I swallowed hard, not wanting to think about my recent past. It would paralyze me. I cleared my throat. "And I see my family has grown. Did your husband tell you we met quite by chance on the train yesterday?"

Her demeanour underwent a swift change. Nanette looked away, and her hands unconsciously knitted together, twisting the covers as though she wanted to strangle them. She gave a weak smile. "He did not," she said softly. "But then we didn't speak last night as I felt too ill. I hope he was pleasant?"

What an odd thing for her to say. "Indeed, he was," I replied. "Though I did not envy him with all his luggage. We didn't talk much as I spent most of my journey asleep."

She gave a small laugh. "Oh my. But it is easy to do for the trains are so comfortable." She spoke as though she rode them regularly. I'd bet she rarely ever left the house.

"They are. But it was more to do with my being tired. Since arriving back from Cape Town, there have been many demands. Frankly it was nice to sit still and do nothing for a few hours."

Nanette sat forward. She reached over and laid a small hand on my arm. "You are here now, Claire. You must relax and catch up with your rest. I understand only too well how exhaustion and fatigue can diminish and wear you down. Being with us will help strengthen your body and your mind. I am so pleased you have come." She tapped my arm stressing her point before letting go of me.

"Never mind me," I said. "How do you fare? Vivienne says you have been under the weather. What ails you, Nanette?" I did not wish to sound impertinent, but I was curious.

She gave a long sigh. Her nimble fingers picked at her covers.

"Doctor Tipton says it is my nerves. He insists there is no physical ailment or disease, although I do not quite believe him. I suffer with terrible headaches and am prone to dizzy spells. Sometimes, I cannot even eat, for my digestion is problematic. These symptoms, all together, can render me weak and tired." She gave a sideward glance at me. “Why, you are a nurse, Claire. Have you heard these complaints before?”

I shook my head. “I’m not knowledgeable about your particular symptoms, Nanette. My skills are limited to physical wounds received upon a battlefield.”

She looked suddenly crestfallen. Feeling guilty, I reached out to grasp her hand with mine. It felt small and soft against the coarseness of my skin.

“But I am here to help in any way I can,” I said encouragingly. “Perhaps I can speak to your physician when next he visits and learn about your condition so I might be of use to you.”

My words were the tonic needed. At once her mood lifted and she bestowed me with a beaming smile. “Oh, thank you, Claire.” Her eyes filled with tears. “You do not know how happy that makes me.”

I stayed for another half an hour while we chatted about the task of packing up Mother’s home and what plans I might have for the future. She looked weary. I promised to return later in the day, then bade her farewell and left her to rest.

****

By mid-morning I paced the drawing room with pent-up energy. I’d thought about going to my room and reading the journals, but I was in no mood to sit still. At length, I went upstairs and retrieved my coat and gloves. I needed to get outside and into the fresh air.

I informed Tibbetts I was going out for a walk and then left the house, mindful not to look at the moat as I quickly crossed the bridge to the road.

It was chilly this morning. There had been a frost, but the sun peeked out from behind moody skies and already brought the promise of warmth. The air, so crisp, stung as I breathed it into my lungs.

On this side of the bridge were the stables, barn and a half dozen cottages for the servants working at Darkwater Abbey. I remembered Uncle Simon saying there were only four servants left. At least they had their own places to live.

I saw no one. They were probably all at work. One of the cottages had a washing line full of clothing hanging out to dry.

Moss-covered rock walls bordered the road I'd come in on only yesterday and divided the fields into a patchwork of greens and dark yellow. A jigsaw of local stone mixed with flat flint, they snaked across the meadows, hugging the contours of the land. The glistening grass, still damp from the morning's frost, were so many shades of green, as varied as an artist's palette of colour.

Again, I felt the strong connection between my beautiful surroundings and my soul. I looked about me, drinking in the vista of lush hills and dales, marvelling at the majesty of nature here. I felt entirely alone in this wonderful place.

As far as I could see, nothing stirred. Not a man nor beast moved. Only the birds were at play this morning. Robins, sparrows and starlings darted though the air, alighting on the rock walls to peck a juicy insect from the blanket of moss. Had I walked in the other direction, I would have seen the herds of cows and sheep grazing in the pastures of Darkwater Abbey.

But this had always been my favourite route, and it was wonderful reacquainting myself with the scenery before me. In the summer, I used to leave the road and traverse through the fields. It was far too wet to do that today. I would content myself staying on the road so I wouldn't get muddy.

I picked up my pace, enjoying the air and feeling the cobwebs in my mind starting to clear. Once I had stretched my legs, I'd be in a better frame of mind to spend the remainder of the afternoon reading Mother's diaries.

This evening, at dinner, I planned to ask Uncle Simon if I might accompany him to the mill tomorrow. I wished to spend the day in Skipton. I'd see Parslow Mill and then explore the town for a few hours.

I realised having worked for many years and being unused to idleness, I'd need an occupation at Darkwater Abbey, or I should go batty. Without a purpose, my mind easily settled on unhappy thoughts and became morose. What work was Mother engaged in at the mill before I was born? I must ask my uncle.

I pressed on, but with no actual destination. I'd walk a while longer and then turn around and go back. I went along my way, mindlessly absorbing the sparse trees, the interesting colours in limestone rocks poking through the ground like the heads of white rabbits.

A horse whinnied and up ahead a small trap came around the bend in the road. A man, garbed in black held the reins. He instructed the horse to slow down, and when they drew level, came to a halt.

He touched the rim of his wide brimmed hat. "Good day to you, miss," came his friendly greeting.

I glanced up and registered the white collar and black cassock of a religious man. He looked quite old, at least in his sixties, with a narrow face hardened by the sharp angles of his cheekbones. The thin hair poking out under his hat was snowy-white, but in contrast, his eyes were black as coal.

"Good day," I replied.

"Now, I don't believe we have met," he said, his thin lips forming a weak smile. "I am Father Lynch, and I'm on my way to Darkwater Abbey. Would that be where you were coming from?"

I detected the hint of an Irish accent. I surmised he might be of the Catholic faith and therefore a priest, not a reverend with the Church of England.

"Indeed," I replied. "That is where I am staying. My name is Claire Holloway. I am niece to Simon Manning."

The priest nodded. He stared at me intently. This happened occasionally, and I assumed it was down to my having a very different hairstyle to that worn by most women. I saw the glint of disapproval shining from his expression. I suppose being a priest, he would be extremely conservative.

"Ah," he said. "To be sure. Simon told me you were expected any day now. And aren't I delighted to meet you. Will I give you a lift back to the house?"

"That is most kind of you to offer, but I think I'll go on walking a while longer."

"That's grand. I'll be on my way then. I'm to pay a call on young Nanette to see how she fares. Perhaps I'll still be there when you return. I should enjoy having some conversation if you have the time?"

His smile broadened, displaying a full set of teeth that were too long for his mouth and slightly yellowed. Then he doffed his hat, made a clicking sound to the horse and tugged the reins. Slowly, the horse moved away.

I turned and watched the vehicle go down the road and gave an involuntary shudder. Intuitively, I had not liked the man. There was something unsettling about him. Was it the tone of his voice, or the slyness of his look?

Just then, the sun appeared between a large gap in the clouds and light suffused everything around me. I gasped in delight and continued on my way.

TRUE TO HIS WORD, FATHER Lynch was comfortably ensconced in an armchair nursing a cup of tea when I returned to Darkwater Abbey. He sat closest to the fire, while Vivienne was across from him on the sofa. Their conversation was low and came to an abrupt halt as I entered the room.

"'Tis Miss Holloway, back from her walk," the priest announced, setting down his cup and getting to his feet in a polite display of manners. "Will you join us for a wee drop of tea to warm the chill from your bones?"

Vivienne remained quiet with a strange expression on her face. Had I interrupted something important?

How odd that the visitor in the house acted as host and offered refreshment. I had no real desire to spend time with either one of them, but curiosity got the better of me. I removed my coat and draped it over the back of the empty chair.

"Don't mind if I do." I helped myself to a cup from the tray and then took a seat facing my cousin.

"How was your walk?" Vivienne enquired with little interest in her tone.

"Refreshing," I said with a smile. "You can't beat breathing in fresh Yorkshire air. I had forgotten how lovely it is here." I took a sip of tea.

"To be sure it is," Father Lynch agreed. "Sometimes the grass turns a Kelly green, and I could swear I was back in Ireland." He gave his toothy smile and I noticed when he did, the skin on his face stretched so thin it was almost translucent. The man was as pale as a stick of chalk.

"Have you lived in England long, Father?"

He nodded. "Almost thirty years now. First in Liverpool, and then I came to Starling Parish in 'seventy-nine. But sure, you won't remember me. You girls at Darkwater Abbey were only wee bairns back then."

"You are right," I replied. "I don't remember much about those days." I would have been four years old, and my cousins younger still. I'd no recollection of him whatsoever. Yet he was here during the time Keith Delahunt was killed. Something tugged at my memory.

"I was so sorry about your dear mother," he said. "Jane Shaw was a fine woman indeed. Always a kind word for all, and a generous heart. She and her sister, Charlotte, were ladies of the first order. Both gone before their time."

He took a sip of tea, and above the cup his black eyes regarded me from underneath thick white brows. It was hard to read any expression in those dark depths. I looked away, turning my attention to my cousin who remained silent.

"If you like, Vivienne, I can spend time with Nanette this afternoon. She seemed to enjoy chatting with me earlier."

She regarded me with a blank expression. "As you wish. I do have a few things I need in the village.

Perhaps you can attend to her while I am gone?"

"I'd be happy to." I set down my cup and got to my feet. "But for now, if you will both excuse me, I have some correspondence to see to."

The priest also got to his feet. He was a thin, wiry man, but unusually tall. The top of my head barely reached his chin, and I was not short myself.

"It was a pleasure to meet you, Father Lynch." I forced a smile to my face, still feeling something unpleasant emanate from him, though he'd been nothing but politeness itself towards me.

He nodded his head. "As it was to see you after all these years. I'm very happy you have returned to your home, as are your uncle and cousins, to be sure."

I took my leave and ascended the stairs. The two of them were speaking once again, but they spoke quietly. I cared not if I was the subject.

Back in my room, I took off my shoes and stockings and got on my bed. The diary lay scattered across the coverlet with the newspapers I'd looked at earlier. I plumped up several pillows against the headboard and picked up the diary but the bold headlines of the newspapers distracted me.

I set down the journal and thought back to earlier that morning. What had I read? I shuffled through the small pile until something familiar caught my eye.

There it was.

'Priest's evidence seals the fate of accused murderer!'

The breath left my body. My heart picked up pace. I lifted the newspaper and scanned the article quickly.

My eyes devoured the words.

'The gunshot was heard by the local Catholic

priest. The good Father was eating dinner with a guest who happened to be the local constable. The two men rushed outside and found Thomas Shaw holding a gun, standing over the dead man who had been shot through the heart.'

There it was. Father Lynch had been living locally during the time of the murder. Surely there was only one Catholic priest in Starling Village…my stomach churned.

Now I understood why instinctively I had not liked the tall, wafer-thin man of the cloth.

His testimony had helped send my father to his death.

Chapter Six

WITH NEWFOUND INTEREST, I set the paper down and picked up Mother's diary. I voraciously started reading where I had left off.

'The night of November 10th is a night I shall never forget and always remember with fear and sadness. This account I give is the truth of what transpired that fateful evening.

My husband, Thomas, had been in Leeds all day and would be home late. When a note addressed to him arrived at the house, it was brought directly to me. The message was from a woman, who identified herself as 'Barbara'. In this note, she asked Thomas to go to St. Michael's and meet her in the churchyard at seven o'clock that very night. That it was a matter of life and death.

I was perturbed. Who was Barbara? And why would a woman seek a private meeting with my husband at night? Although I trusted Thomas completely, this invitation rankled. Suspicious and jealous, I determined to go in his stead.'

I paused. Sitting in Mother's room here at Darkwater Abbey, I could imagine a dark, cold November evening. Someone knocking on the door and giving the servant a note.

I continued.

'It was a frigid night. Tibbetts saddled up my

horse, gave me a lantern, and I went as quickly as I could to St. Michael's. When I arrived, it was almost impossible to see, but the moon was bright, and my eyes adjusted to the surroundings.

I was not scared, for I knew Father Lynch was in his cottage next-door to the chapel, as a light shone from the windows. I looked around for the mysterious woman, but there was no one else to be seen or heard.

The sudden report of a gunshot split through the quiet of night. Startled, I dropped my lantern. My heart beat fast, and I held my breath and listened. There came a thud, as though something heavy had fallen to the ground. Mindless of danger, I rushed towards the noise. As I did, I heard someone running away through the bushes…

When I reached the black shape laying on damp grass between the headstones, the sound of a horse approaching caught my ears.

"Jane?"

It was Thomas, calling out to me. I shouted his name in a blind panic and dropped to the ground to tend whatever lay there.

It was a man.

Without my lantern it was too dark to make out his features, but I knew at once he was not breathing. Suddenly, the warm glow of a lamp illuminated the area, and Thomas was right there behind me. The light glinted on something metal on the grass, and I reached out and picked it up. It was a gun. The barrel still warm.

I began to shake like a leaf in a gale and knew such welcome relief as my husband knelt down beside me. He leaned over the man. "Good God," he said, his voice quavering in disbelief. "'Tis Keith Delahunt. The poor man's been shot."

What happened next is still a blur. The sound of voices. Father Lynch and the constable staring at me as I got to my feet, the gun still in my shaking hand. Their shocked faces as they took in the sight of me and Thomas, a dead man laying at our feet and me holding a weapon.

My darling husband immediately grabbed the gun from me, and I somehow comprehended in that very moment what he was about to do. We were both compromised by what had just happened, and the expression on the constable's face frightened me.

Thomas glared at the priest and the policeman, then uttered four words which would ultimately seal his fate and destroy all of our lives.

"Jane was never here," he said to them both, his meaning plain.

Oh, if only we'd known how those words condemned him. Neither of us realised that in protecting me, he sacrificed himself.'

Dear God, what was this? Did my father believe Mother had shot Keith Delahunt and wanted to stop her from being arrested?

I left the bed and paced the floor in my room. This made no sense. How could my father have shot Delahunt if he was on horseback within Mother's range of hearing, and coming from a different direction?

While Mother had a plausible explanation for going to the churchyard, her curiosity about the note sent to Papa, she'd expected to find a woman there, not a man. So, if not my parents, then who had killed Keith Delahunt?

I paused. Was Mother lying? Had she fabricated this tale in her book? The answer was instantaneous. My mother was incapable of evading the truth. She was as honest as the day was long. Then could someone else have been in the churchyard that night? If so, who? Who was Barbara?

My mind worked furiously to picture scenarios. If this Barbara had been there the entire time, had she really been Papa's mistress, lying in wait to kill him, but accidentally shot the wrong man?

I picked up my own notebook and made a note to find out more about Barbara and her testimony at Father's trial. But it seemed the most likely explanation. My father had been summoned there that night for a reason. Had he been the intended victim? If so, then why was Keith Delahunt the one shot?

I paced a while longer, my head whirled in thought. Father had been an honourable man taking the gun away from Mother. He'd made his intention clear. If anyone was to be mixed-up in a murder investigation, it would be him and not his wife.

What had Papa been thinking? He'd obviously assumed there was another motive at work and this incident had nothing to do with him. I'm sure his expectation was his name would easily be cleared, the real villain caught, and the sordid details uncovered.

Then what had changed the course of justice? And if both my parents were innocent of murder, how had a judge and jury declared him guilty?

Impatient, I went to the drawer to retrieve the rest of Mother's diaries. I returned to the bed, sat back down, and selected her most recent account.

The first entry in this book was dated in July, three

months ago. Quickly, I skimmed through the pages, finding her thoughts were mostly fixated on me and my imminent homecoming.

Mother was genuinely happy I was returning to England—though she lamented my situation and worried about my mental welfare. Tears welled in my eyes as I read words she would never have been comfortable saying aloud. Our relationship had always been strained.

And no wonder. Jane Shaw had lived a life of grief without the man she loved. If Papa had taken the blame for something Mother had done, she would have spent her life inconsolable and unable to live with herself. But Mother showed no sign of this. Instead, she mourned his loss each and every day, but as a woman truly mourns a lost love.

Oh, it was all too horrid.

Confounded and confused by what she'd shared with me all those years ago, now I had so many questions. None which she could ever answer from the grave.

Frustrated, I turned a few more pages. Her last entry had been only a few days after I'd set sail from Africa.

'Today I received an anonymous letter. The postmark was from New York, America. Not knowing anyone living there, I wondered who might write to me. I was eager to read its contents.

Imagine my shock! For this correspondence was from a person who wrote on behalf of a Barbara Harding—the woman who'd lied in court and testified she'd not only been Thomas's paramour, but that he'd been stealing from Parslow's so they could run away together. What a wicked woman.

This anonymous correspondent claimed Barbara Harding had been paid a large sum of money to give this false statement. She had only agreed in order to leave England for America. There, she hoped to find treatment for her sick son, who had polio. That was how she lived with her despicable actions.

Barbara, being gravely ill, now wished to make amends before meeting her maker. This had been weighing upon her conscience, yet she did not reveal the identity of who paid her to lie in court.

Oh, how I wept at this information.

I did not for one moment ever believe my darling Thomas was unfaithful. Now I have proof. I've waited all these years for a miracle, a tidbit of information to unravel the lies and twisted acts that caused my husband to lose his life.

I cannot wait for Claire to come home. I have erred in my judgement to keep all this from her. She has to know the truth of that night. I must tell her my doubts and suspicions so she can help me right the most grievous of wrongs. I know that together we can get to the bottom of this.

I sign off now with a heart slightly less heavy than yesterday. A glimmer of hope has lit within me, and very soon, my own daughter will be back by my side. Together, we will work to clear my sweetheart's name once and for all. We shall finally discover the evil person who sent my dear husband to his grave.'

Tears coursed down my cheeks. Her words, and endearments, unlocked the dam of emotion kept tightly in check since my coming home. The diary fell from my hands, and I turned and pressed my face into the pillows. I could feel my heart breaking into tiny pieces with each sob racking my body.

It was too much. I had lost everyone who meant anything to me. Each person, ripped away without warning, until I had nothing to love, no one to care for, and none who cared for me either.

I was as isolated as this damned house. Not surrounded by a moat, but by sorrow and despair. I had never felt so entirely alone as I did now.

To think, Mother had been so excited at my coming home. Perhaps things between us would have been resolved in our working together to clear Papa's name?

At that thought, my crying slowed, and I gathered my composure. I fumbled for my handkerchief and blew my nose. Tears would gain me nothing. Only actions could change a situation.

I got up and walked over to the dressing table mirror. I stared at my face, swollen and pink from crying. I looked at my eyes, and those of Papa's stared back at me. What was I going to do?

I took a deep breath and let it out. I must pull myself together. This was no time to be weak. What was the truth about the events two decades ago on a cold, winter's night? Was my father really the villain he was made out to be? Were Mother's words an honest depiction of that night or the ramblings of a woman destroyed by the loss of her husband?

Had my father been unfaithful? The initial claim there had been a lover now appeared nullified by the recent letter sent to Mother. If the correspondence was true, then who had paid that woman to testify at the trial? Had my father been framed by an enemy as yet unknown to us?

And what of that strange priest, Father Lynch? Now I knew for certain he was there the night of the murder, for Mother had named him. He'd witnessed what occurred right after the gun was fired.

I would need to talk to him.

First things first. Where was the letter from America? I had not seen anything mixed up with all the newspapers. I picked up her last journal and, holding it by the spine, gave it a hard shake.

A square piece of paper fell onto the bed. I unfolded it. The writing was hard to read but Mother had recorded it correctly, word for word.

Carefully, I folded it back up, but instead of putting it back where I had found it, I decided to tuck it into my own notebook to read again later.

How ironic the past was catching up with me after all this time. Though I'd successfully ignored my family's dark history, it now tapped me upon the shoulder.

Questions lingered and spun through my mind. I knew I could not push them away and pretend it didn't matter. Because suddenly it did. The honour of my father's name had been thrown into the gutter. And if it was unwarranted, then it was my duty to correct an injustice.

But what if Mother was wrong and the letter a lie? If Father had betrayed their marriage vows and also killed a man, it would be devastating to relive such an awful series of events.

I wiped my face with my hands. I was being pathetic. I was a mother who'd lost her child. There was no pain, no anguish, no heartbreak that could compare to the feelings I'd known losing Sarah, and I had made it through, barely. If I could survive that, I could face anything.

It was time for me to know the absolute truth about my family. I would be staying here for a spell anyway. Why not take advantage of my situation and delve into the secrets of the past?

I took one last look in the mirror. My eyes burned, but not with tears. They shone with purpose.

****

The evening was uneventful. Mr Delahunt was absent at dinner, and Uncle Simon regaled us with stories from Skipton. Vivienne said little and mostly toyed with her food. Nanette remained in her room.

I broached the subject of accompanying my uncle to the mill the next day, and he received the idea favourably well. With an agreed time to meet in the morning, I excused myself to have an early night and went up to bed.

My thoughts still stewed. I readied myself for sleep, but my mind would not rest. There was no way I'd find slumber this early. Instead, I picked up the second of Mother's diaries. This journal spoke of my father's trial. Due to the severity of the crime, the hearing took place in Leeds.

As I read the entries, part of me knew a huge sense of relief that I had been so young and kept ignorant of what was taking place. My mother attended every minute of my father's trial judging by the dates in here. She must have taken her book with her and written notes as things progressed.

It was difficult reading. The order of her sentences was at times jumbled—no doubt due to her emotional state. How tremendously hard it must have been for her, listening to the testimonies of the witnesses, especially those for the prosecution.

I learned no new details, other than the constable present the night of the murder had been taken ill shortly after and subsequently died before the trial began. How odd.

Mother endeavoured to capture what was said, but often went into detail about her opinion of statements being made. I'd need a clearer head to understand how the trial actually played out. Perhaps there was a legal record somewhere I could look at?

But there was important information in here. On one page, Mother wrote the names of the two solicitors Uncle Simon had engaged to defend my father. Underneath that was a list of witnesses who had testified, including herself. I copied them all into my own notebook.

I had not given much consideration to her testifying. What had she said? Had she admitted being there that night, regardless of Father's asking the priest not to mention it? What had happened to the constable who had been with Father Lynch?

When I'd looked at the papers earlier, I had not previously read about the actual trial. Now, that had changed. I compared Mother's information to the accounts in the newspapers and found they correlated fairly accurately with one another. The difference in the texts was simply the message being delivered. Mother maintained Thomas Shaw's innocence, while the papers condemned my dear father from the start.

It was not unusual for a wealthy, middle-class man with a good life to lose favour with the public. It was easy, sometimes gratifying, for those less fortunate to throw stones at a person with so much. That any man with such good fortune would risk it all for murder, appalled the unsympathetic masses.

A common assumption was that people with money could buy their way out of anything. It was like waving a red flag at a bull. Thomas Shaw was guilty before he even went to trial.

I paused.

What a muddle. Were my expectations realistic thinking I could learn more, and understand better? After all, mother had struggled with discovering the truth, even though she had been there in person.

Yet the temptation was strong to keep digging, based upon one or two things I'd read. The fact that Mother declared she'd been present that night made me desperately curious. Then, the mysterious note enticing my father to come to a dark quiet place, all alone. What had happened to the note? Did Keith Delahunt receive one as well? Why else would he have been there?

And Papa's actions. Insisting his wife could not be complicit in a murder was the most compelling reason of all. I wanted, needed to learn more. For if that was the truth, then my father was a very brave man. A man willing to forfeit his life for love.

Mother's receipt of the American letter prior to my coming back intrigued me. For what purpose would it serve twenty years too late? It would not bring my father back. I doubted it strong enough evidence to appeal the conviction, even posthumously. There was legitimacy in the claim of a dying person wishing to wipe their slate clean. And if that was true, then it did shed a totally different light upon the damning testimony of the woman claiming to be my father's mistress.

Weren't most men unfaithful? On this matter I took my mother's lead. Her instincts and intuition of her own husband were sharp enough to recognise the truth of that. Mother was no fool. An astute woman, the daughter of a successful businessman, she had been well educated and even worked in the mill offices until I was born.

I could not accept she would be easily taken in by a deceitful husband. So, on this matter I would side with my mother's opinion and take it in good faith.

Then where would I even start? I suppose I had already by writing my own notes. Like mother like daughter. Which seemed rather ironic since I had always thought us opposing poles. Yet it never hurt to put your thoughts onto paper and clear your mind.

And I spent the next hour doing exactly that, until my eyes became heavy with sleep.

Chapter Seven

IVAN DELAHUNT DID NOT CONCEAL his surprise when I joined him for breakfast the next morning. His hand stilled holding the coffee cup next to his mouth, and he frowned.

"Good morning, Mrs Holloway. You are up early." He looked at me as though I had intruded.

"Indeed," I answered taking a seat to his right. "I am going to Skipton this morning with Uncle Simon. I asked if I could join him last night when we dined. I plan a visit to the mill and to do some shopping."

The frown lingered. "Simon has already gone," Mr Delahunt informed me. "He seemed to be in a hurry and didn't mention anything about your accompanying him."

I let out a deep breath of annoyance. "Oh, that will not do," I said sternly. "I set my mind upon going. Perhaps I can take one of the horses?"

Mr Delahunt set down his cup. "That would be unwise. The weather is changeable this time of year. Skipton is far enough away you wouldn't want to be caught out in the elements on horseback. If you insist upon going to Skipton, then you can come with me. Gibbons will be here shortly. If that suits."

Though his offer was polite, I didn't think it given freely. The serious expression showed slight irritation at having to extend the invitation.

I cared not. Bound and determined to get out of the house and into town, I painted on a pleasant smile.

"That is very kind of you, Mr Delahunt. If you're ready to leave now, I can go without breakfast. I should not want to make you tardy."

His face relaxed a little. And I wondered how unhappy he must be to always look so angry and out of sorts.

"There is plenty of time for you to eat. I've no pressing business at the mill which demands you miss your meal. Besides, Gibbon has yet to return from taking Simon." He took another sip of his drink then looked directly at me.

"Mrs Holloway. I know we didn't start off on the right foot, and I'm sorry for it. But as we live under the same roof, at least for the foreseeable future, I feel the need to be less formal. After all, we are cousins by marriage now. I think it appropriate we use one another's Christian names. Do you agree?"

His statement surprised me. I appreciated the attempt to be cordial.

"I should prefer it as well. As you say, we are family. Besides, you and I are the outsiders at Darkwater Abbey. There should be some solidarity based upon that."

His response was a tight smile which I was glad to see. Though it still felt awkward, I did feel a truce between us and relaxed a little.

AFTER BREAKFAST, I WENT UP to my room to get my hat, coat, and gloves. Today I would leave the derringer behind. The only possible threat I could encounter in Skipton would be that of an over-zealous shopkeeper.

Tibbetts saw us off with a beaming smile and asked if I could drop off a shopping list for items sold in a specific shop in Skipton which would be delivered to the house later.

I hastened to follow Ivan across the long footbridge, all the while keeping my eyes trained on his back, never straying to look at the dark, gloomy water in the broad moat. But as I left the bridge, passing the gargoyles, I turned to look back at the house and a movement in one of the upstairs windows caught my eye. I waved. It had to be one of my cousins.

Presently, with the giant Gibbons at the helm, the carriage took off at a fast pace.

A thread of excitement sparked in my blood. I would finally see my family's mill after more than a decade. I shivered in nervous anticipation, but Ivan mistook it for my being cold and passed a rug to drape across my lap. I took it willingly, for it was still early and the air frigid.

The sky was waking up. Grey, with the morning sun concealed behind the clouds, it certainly looked like rain. As we travelled down the road I turned and looked out of the window and saw a spray of wildflowers set against the stone wall.

"They're for the man who died," Ivan said sombrely. "A kind gesture, especially for someone not from these parts."

"How awful to be away from home and die like that. I wonder if he has any family?"

"I don't believe so. I spoke to Constable McNabb yesterday. Turns out the fellow was staying at the Ace of Spades in the village. Of all things he was Australian."

"Australian? He was a long way from home then."

"Seems so. They are trying to find out more about him, but it's my bet he'll be buried here."

A quiet fell momentarily as we both reflected. I did not like to dwell upon death, not after the past few months. I addressed my companion.

"I wonder why Uncle forgot I was to accompany him today. Fortunate for me you were still at home. Thank you, Ivan, for allowing me to come with you. I've only been at Darkwater Abbey a day but felt the need to get out. I am unused to being cooped up." I gave a short laugh. "That's what happens when you spend three years living in tents."

Mr Delahunt sat across from me, assessing me with thoughtful eyes. "You must find it strange being back in this country. What a huge contrast to the lifestyle in Africa. Has it been a culture shock returning to England after living in such a wild place?"

"Yes," I replied. "It's odd, because my first impressions of Africa were of a country still quite uncivilised. Even the cities seemed inadequate in comparison to those of Europe. Yet after some time there, I learned that it does not take architecture, fashion, or even money to become civilised. It takes a nation of people coming together for a common good. Living in another country changes you. It's strange, but now I am home again, I don't really feel like I belong."

He gave a slight smile. "In my opinion, when you leave a place, you can never return to it the same person."

"That is very perceptive," I said. "You speak as though you know from personal experience?"

He chuckled. "Mine don't come close to yours,

Claire. I went away to Huddersfield to attend technical school. After that, I spent a year travelling the continent, researching the textile industries in several cities. It forever changed me. When I returned to Darkwater Abbey, I saw everything from different eyes."

I stared at him wondering about the meaning behind his words. He must have realised, as I had myself, that the world is vast. The way he spoke, there was something in his voice which was wistful. Like it was a lifetime ago.

There was a melancholy about Ivan Delahunt. Small wonder since he'd never known his mother, and the loss of his father would have been extraordinarily traumatic. A shame. He had good reason to be sad.

"Yet you stayed on at Darkwater Abbey? You must like living here."

His expression changed. I could tell he was carefully selecting his response.

"Before I went off to school, I became engaged to your cousin. Though I had the freedom to travel for that solitary year, I was still bound by my commitment to Nanette. There was never any question I would not come back. In addition, my studies were in the production of cotton so that I could be an asset to Parslow Mill. Your family had financed my education and my travels."

I couldn't resist. "And were you worthy of their investment?"

He gave a frown and then a chuckle. "I am not about to say anything to the contrary, am I? I hope I'm an asset. I do enjoy my work. And even though my ideas are, in your uncle's opinion, far too modern at times, my intention is to contribute to the company's success."

"What is your role at the mill?" It seemed a ridiculous question, but I honestly had no idea.

"I am responsible for all the raw materials we purchase. Hence my recent travels. Simon is the general manager and runs all the departments through various supervisors. I also conduct research to determine what our competitors are doing and to stay current with the public's demands. Currently, I am looking into expansion. There's a huge international market that Parslow's is not taking advantage of. It's my goal to change that."

"And let me guess. Your modern ideas do not go over well with the older people working there. Am I correct?"

He nodded. "Indeed, you are."

"It is similar to medicine and methods of nursing. There are two different schools of thought. Traditional medicine is tried and true. Whenever anyone has better ideas or suggestions of how to improve certain procedures, it is almost always met with the more experienced staff baulking. People are easily intimidated by things they don't understand. And that usually includes any kind of change."

"I agree. Simon is fairly progressive in his way of thinking. But he has run the mill for many years and naturally believes he knows best. If time stood still, I would agree with him being the expert. But he is sequestered here in Yorkshire and barely even leaves the county. Therefore, he remains ignorant of what is going on in the rest of the world when it comes to the textile industry. Certainly, he reads and stays current with different reports and studies, but it is not quite the same as being there and experiencing everything first hand."

"I completely understand your point," I said, enjoying our conversation. "I felt the same way while in Africa. Though the newspapers kept the world abreast of the situation, it could not capture what it was really like. You must be physically present to definitively comprehend anything. I think it's marvellous you make a point to get away and investigate what else is happening within your industry."

So engrossed was I with our conversation, I had paid scant attention to our surroundings. We had already arrived in the outskirts of Skipton. There was the grand castle in the distance, and I knew we were headed towards the canal. The thought of the waterway made me shudder. Would it always be like this whenever I was near a body of water?

The horses' hooves clacked on the street as we turned before reaching the town centre and headed towards the mill. Even inside the carriage with the windows closed, the smell of smoke and damp found its way to my nostrils.

The familiar odour brought memories rushing into my mind. Spending time at the mill with Papa. Helping him in his office and being fussed over by some of the mill workers. My, how long ago that was.

My companion forgotten, I pressed my face against the window and peered out. The carriage slowed down, and I saw the familiar building up ahead. My heart skipped a beat. A swell of emotion flooded through me, and a lump formed in my throat.

Parslow Mill. A massive, foreboding, red brick,

three-storey building at the end of the cobbled road, as wide as a small university. At once I saw it clearly. The main building, it's edifice elaborately decorated, and the huge name painted at the top in bold black letters on a white background.

Steps led from the street up to gargantuan oak doors, cleverly concealing heavy factory equipment.

Without seeing them, I knew of the huts and sheds in the courtyard behind, below the towering, belching chimney. The river running. The pulse of water fuelling the pumps, while the steam engine gobbled up coal like a starved man to keep all the equipment running.

"Arthur Parslow was a man of vision," said Ivan.

I blinked. I'd forgotten he was there. I sat back. "Yes, he was. Building the mill was a huge endeavour. Mother spoke of it often after he died. Grandfather really was successful, against all the odds and nay-sayers."

The carriage came to a halt. Mr Delahunt got out first and then gave me a hand as I stepped onto the street, which shone from the moisture in the air and looked as if it had been polished.

Several workers walked to or from the mill. Most dressed in dull clothing. The men wore soft cloth caps; the women hid their hair under scarves. One or two nodded at us as we passed.

And then we were ascending the steep staircase that was the entrance to the mill. At the top was a large stone griffin, a replica of the guardians of the footbridge at Darkwater Abbey. Above it, my grandfather's mantra, *Spectemur Agendo* . 'Let Us be judged by our Acts.' Strange I still remembered that.

Ivan pushed open the heavy doors. At once I felt

the sudden whoosh of hot, damp air, necessary for keeping the cotton intact. You could feel it thick in your chest, the sudden awareness of having to work harder to get oxygen into your lungs. It was cloying and sticky.

We veered away from the entrance to the main floor. I heard the mechanical clatter of spinning mules chomping at thread, even through closed doors. Turning away from the hallway, Ivan led me up a familiar staircase. The first two floors were dedicated to equipment and machinery. The third, to the business offices.

As we reached the top floor of the mill, I took a step back in time. Nothing had changed whatsoever. The walls looked as shabby as they had when I was a child. I doubted there had even been a new layer of paint put on the old plaster. I remember Papa telling me the paint flaked away because the building had to be kept so hot and moist. I'd completely forgotten that fact until this very moment.

This floor was divided into small offices, with the General Manager's being at the end, considerably larger than the rest, and where Ivan led me.

"Your uncle is here, Claire. I'll leave you to it and get to work. If you need anything else, come and find me." His words were courteous, but his expression still solemn.

"Thank you, Ivan. You've been more than helpful. I do appreciate it." I gave a brief smile of gratitude and watched him walk away.

I stepped through the open door. A middle-aged woman with upswept red hair sat at a desk behind a typewriter. A pile of folders stacked next to it. The typewriter keys snapped under her fingertips. She was completely engrossed in her work.

I cleared my throat, and she glanced up, staring at me through thick lensed, round wire spectacles. I stared back. Surely, it couldn't be?

"Miss Buxton?"

The years fell away. I was suddenly a child of six, standing before a much younger, and very pretty, woman. My father's secretary from years ago.

"Is it really you, Miss Buxton? After all this time you're still working here?"

Miss Buxton had not recognised me until I began to speak. Her mouth fell open, and she looked me over with surprise.

"It can't be Claire Shaw, I mean Claire Holloway now. Well, I never." The woman took off her spectacles and got to her feet. She came around the desk to stand before me, hands on hips. "I'd like as not recognise you, lass. My, but you're all grown up. Mr Manning said you'd arrived, but he didn't tell me you were coming up to' mill. Oh, but it's good to see you, lass."

To be welcomed so sincerely warmed my heart.

Miss Buxton returned to her seat. She looked quite well. How old would she be? A few years younger than my mother? For a woman in her late forties, Mary had aged gracefully. Her face was still smooth, and her green eyes sparkled. Her hair, always such a lovely titian shade, had a brassy shine. I suspected she might use henna to keep it red.

"It's a lifetime since I was up here. I remember coming with Father whenever he'd let me. You used to give me paper and pencils to draw when he was busy."

She laughed. "Aye, I did. Have you come to see your uncle?"

"Yes. I was meant to come along with him today, but he left without me. Mr Delahunt brought me instead."

At the mention of Ivan's name, Miss Buxton's mouth puckered. Interesting.

The secretary got back up. "Let me tell him you're here. Then I'll put 'kettle on and make us a nice cup of tea."

"That would be lovely, thank you."

Miss Buxton went through an adjoining door at the back of the room, and I heard the murmur of voices. I stayed put and glanced around. It really did look the same. At least as far as I could tell. The furniture was arranged exactly where it had always been. The same dull pictures hung upon the wall, mostly local scenes. Even the smell was familiar. A mixture of cotton mill, damp, paper, and dust, all mixed up with the scent of whatever oil they used to wipe over the furniture.

Miss Buxton reappeared. "Go on in, lass."

Uncle Simon did not stand when I entered his office.

"Ah, Claire. Come in and have a seat. You must be quite vexed with me. I am sorry. I was in rather a hurry, and I just completely forgot. I'm a creature of habit. I follow the same routine every day." He smiled at me, his bright blue eyes earnest with apology.

"I understand," I replied. "Please, don't give it another thought. Ivan brought me with him, so all's well."

Something rippled across my uncle's expression. What had I said? Odd that both times I'd mentioned Mr Delahunt's name it had elicited a negative response from Miss Buxton, and now, Uncle Simon.

"What do you think about the old place then, Claire? Do you find it changed?"

"Hardly at all," I said happily. "When we arrived, I felt as though I'd stepped back into my childhood. I have such wonderful memories of coming here with Father. I was delighted to see Miss Buxton still working here as well."

"I think Mary has been here longer than all of us. She was still in her teens when your grandfather hired her. That woman knows more about Parslow Mill than anyone. We depend upon her for many things."

"She always gave me a lollipop whenever I'd come to the mill."

"Did you get one today?" Uncle Simon chuckled.

I grinned. "Not yet."

"So, what are your plans? Are you taking a tour of the mill?"

"Not this time. I just wanted to see the building before attending to a few things in town. I've some shopping to do. It's been an age since I've been in Yorkshire and I'm eager to look about. Then I'll come back here. Might I return to Darkwater Abbey with you, or Mr Delahunt, if it suits?"

"That will be fine," Uncle Simon replied. "On Thursdays, I finish here at four o'clock." He glanced at the clock. "It's after nine now. So that should give you plenty of time to do your errands."

Miss Buxton came back in clutching a tray with two cups of tea and a plate of brown cake.

"Who's for a nice cuppa? If you're peckish, I've brought in a few slices o' Parkin."

Chapter Eight

THOUGH TEMPTED TO EXPLORE the mill, I decided to save that for another day. I had an urge to walk around Skipton, do a little shopping and have a day to myself which did not include travel, packing or moving. Here I could wander anonymously. No one would remember me after all this time.

On the few occasions Mother and I visited Darkwater Abbey, we had not come into town. So, it was with great pleasure I walked down to the High Street, stopping to admire the displays in the windows whenever the fancy took me. The morning was still chilly, but some of the clouds dissipated to allow a little bit of sunshine to peek through.

I had no clear memories of the town centre, insomuch as what shops were situated here. But judging by the variety, Skipton must be booming. I knew the cotton industry was doing particularly well, which correlated to the bustling town.

The roads were full of carriages and cyclists, and I even saw one motor car, which was quite interesting. Everyone stopped and stared with fascination, including me. Again, I felt the stark contrast between my new surroundings and the juvenile towns of Africa.

I enjoyed perusing the shops. But surrounded by people, albeit strangers, I became highly aware of being alone. Since my return to England, a cloak of despondency seemed determined to settle about my shoulders, no matter how positive and unmelancholy I tried to be.

I disliked feeling this way. Though I did not chastise my feelings, for they were justifiable, I didn't want to sink deeper into sadness. George, my sweet husband, would be the first to tell me not to mourn, but embrace the joy of life and fill each day with pleasure, knowledge, and experiences.

As if reflecting my morose thoughts, a drop of rain splashed on my face. In the space of a moment, dark clouds had blocked the sun, and a downpour began. Fortuitously, I was close to a tearoom. I ducked inside quickly.

The facility was already quite full. At length I was seated but asked to share a table with two young women, as there were few places left. I agreed. The thought of a hot cup of tea and perhaps a piece of cake far outweighed the inconvenience of sitting with strangers. After all, had I not just lamented the fact I was alone?

Ten minutes later, I nibbled on a large slice of lemon drizzle cake whilst being entertained by the Misses Tipton, who lived near Darkwater Abbey, in Starling Village. I'd heard the name before but couldn't place it.

Hazel, the eldest at nineteen, chattered like a bird, her large grey eyes wide as though she was constantly surprised. While her sister Phoebe nodded in vigorous agreement at everything her older sibling said, with light brown hair bobbing under her hat as though it might tumble down at any time.

They were a likeable duo. Daughters of a

physician, Doctor Tipton, a gentleman in a small practice in Skipton, they were a welcome distraction and thoroughly entertaining.

"I think you very avant-guard, Mrs Holloway," Hazel said, staring at my hair. She patted the side of her head, her locks in an upswept arrangement. "It must be awfully liberating not wearing cumbersome styles as we must."

I smiled at the young, impressionable women. "I cannot recommend it enough. I honestly believe in due course; most women will chop off their hair and wear lengths more agreeable for day-to-day living."

"How terribly modern," echoed Phoebe, her light eyes wistful. "One day I should like to be that way and do whatever I want. See the world, perhaps even have a profession."

"Sister," Hazel gasped. "What on earth are you saying? One cup of tea with our new friend, Mrs Holloway, and you sound quite rebellious. Next, you'll be wanting to join the Women's Franchise League."

The younger Miss Tipton's spine straightened. She held her teacup in one gloved hand and peered over its rim at her sister. "And what if I did. Emmeline Pankhurst has the right of it. 'Tis time women were given the vote, and all the other rights afforded to gentlemen. She—"

Hazel placed her hand upon her sister's arm. "Perhaps this is not the place to air your personal beliefs. You might be overheard, and our father does have a reputation to maintain." She glared at Phoebe, who set down her cup, pouted, but became silent.

"The world is changing rapidly," I said. "Before long, many of the conventions and customs our society has in place will be challenged. Since the Queen's death last year, our King has encouraged a more contemporary way of life. I think it appropriate to embrace change." I looked at Phoebe, she stared intently at me, hanging on my every word. Oh, to be so young and innocent…

I continued. "Becoming an independent woman has many advantages. But with it comes the opposite as well. I have often been treated disrespectfully for being an employed lady. Though my work required months of education and training, I was nevertheless looked upon no differently than a poor chambermaid. One day, women will not be judged so harshly for using their brains, they shall be celebrated as is their right."

"Hear, hear," Phoebe cried enthusiastically, attracting the attention of four matronly older women sitting at the table next to us.

Hazel glowered. "Phoebe," she hissed. "Be quiet."

Phoebe rolled her eyes. "Stop chastising, sister. We are both young and should be ambitious about our futures. Would you rather live in Starling forever? Marry, be submissive to your husband while tending a handful of bratty children as Father Lynch preaches we should?"

That name instantly caught my attention. I set down my teacup. "Father Lynch? Why I just became acquainted with the man yesterday."

"Poor you," said Phoebe, earning yet another disapproving glare from her sister.

I laughed. "I did find him an 'interesting' character."

"That is an understatement," Phoebe blurted. "I don't like him. He's—"

“Enough, Phoebe,” Hazel interjected. “Father Lynch is loved and well respected by everyone. He is a man of God, and you have no business saying anything detrimental about him.”

“It is not uncommon for people to have mixed feelings about public figures,” I said. “I am sure Phoebe means no ill against the man. Often, men in religious or other influential positions will have equal amounts of admirers as they do those who find them unfavourable. I remember disliking one of the doctors who taught me when I was training. But I respected his intelligence, and his medical skills. Yet we agreed upon absolutely nothing. One must keep an open mind with people. Though it isn’t often easy.”

“You can say that again,” Phoebe said dryly. “I do respect Father Lynch in his capacity as a priest, but how does he know what is best for people decades younger than him? He lives in a small Yorkshire village in the middle of nowhere. He expects us to carry on like all those before us who have lived in his tiny parish. While in cities, like Leeds and Harrogate, women are not expected to be mere vessels to keep a family name from extinction.”

I was impressed with the younger Miss Tipton’s speech. At fifteen, she had strong convictions and a solid backbone.

“You are such a hypocrite,” Hazel said with a trace of annoyance in her voice. “You always talk about being independent, but if Jeremy Rotherham asked you to wed, you’d marry him in an instant.”

Phoebe looked vexed for an moment, and then her lips parted into a wide grin. “There you have me, dear sister,” she said. “How well you know me.”

We all three laughed, which drew another glare from our neighbouring table of matrons.

"And who is Jeremy Rotherham?" I asked.

"A friend of Martin's, our older brother. They attended school together, and he's become a frequent visitor to our home," answered Hazel. "He shows my sister a great deal of attention, and she becomes tongue tied whenever he dines with us."

Phoebe did not deny this. Her cheeks grew pink.

I finished the last piece of my cake and dusted the crumbs from my fingers. "You ladies are still young. I shall predict that in due course, you will both change your minds about many things by the time you reach my age." I noticed some of the customers were gathering their belongings and I looked outside.

"Ah. The rain has stopped. I must continue with my shopping. Thank you both for allowing me to sit with you. It was an unexpected pleasure. Perhaps we can meet again closer to home?"

"Oh, that would be wonderful," Phoebe gushed.

"Honestly," Hazel said disapprovingly. "Mrs Holloway shall avoid us if you insist upon being so dramatic about everything."

I couldn't help but chuckle. "I can assure you this interlude has been rather entertaining, Hazel, and I shall look forward to repeating it."

With that, and a final farewell, I left the two sisters at the table. As I walked away I could hear Hazel scolding Phoebe for her behaviour. I smiled.

MY COMPANIONS HAD LIFTED my spirits. I spent the next two hours meandering through the side streets of Skipton where I dropped off Tibbetts' list, bought a few toiletry items, and finally stopped at the post office, where I purchased stationary and some stamps. I planned to correspond with a few of my nursing friends who were still in Cape Town. With the war coming to an end they, like me, would be returning to England.

On my walk back towards the mill, Skipton's great church clock struck three times. My goodness, I had been on my outing longer than I realised. The soles of my feet ached, but I was invigorated from my time outside.

As I approached Parslow Mill, I felt a sense of awe at the sheer enormity of my grandfather's accomplishment. Arthur Parslow had not been wealthy. But what he lacked in funds he compensated for in sheer determination and ambition. He had secured two partners and together they financed the building of the mill. My grandfather had bought both of them out within six years of the mill being in operation. I wish I were more like him.

I arrived back at Uncle Simon's office, whereupon Miss Buxton informed me he was absent, visiting a supervisor on one of the other floors, but would return shortly. She provided me with another cup of tea, and I finally took the weight off my feet and relaxed in one of the two leather armchairs in my uncle's room.

At length, he returned.

"Well, Claire. I am surprised you haven't a multitude of purchases at your feet. Your cousins would have already filled my carriage with shopping by now." He took a seat behind his desk.

"I didn't have need for many things. Just a few items which I readily found. I wanted to re acquaint myself with Skipton after all this time."

"And did you?"

"Indeed, I did. My goodness, how the town has grown. It is truly more like a small city. That speaks well of industry here. I imagine the mill has contributed to the healthy economy."

"We have been most fortunate. Your grandfather taught us how to manage a business successfully and not run it into the ground. His practises work just as well now as they did for him decades ago. No need to change anything."

His words reminded me of the conversation I'd had earlier with Ivan. The younger man's obvious frustration with trying to modernise the mill and meeting some resistance was evident by my uncle's comments. Progress and change were never easy, and I could see Uncle Simon having very strong opinions about what would, or would not happen, under his management of Parslow's.

"Now, my dear. Unfortunately, I have some pressing business to attend to, and I cannot leave early as planned. Therefore, I have instructed Gibbons to take you back to Darkwater Abbey now. He will return for me later. I hope you do not mind?"

I stood up. "Not at all, Uncle. I appreciate you allowing me to interrupt your work. I have had a pleasant time of it and do not wish to disturb you any longer than necessary. I shall get on my way and see you this evening."

Uncle Simon surprised me by coming around the desk and approaching me. Whereupon he placed one hand upon my cheek and touched his lips gently to my other.

"Goodbye, Claire. I am so pleased you have come

home."

I was taken aback by his display of affection. Though he had welcomed me with a kiss upon my initial arrival at Darkwater Abbey, it was not unexpected as he had not seen me for many years. Today, this behaviour seemed out of place with our situation.

Perplexed, I bid him farewell. I thanked Miss Buxton on my way out, then hurried down to the street.

Gibbons leaned against the cab of the carriage which was parked outside the front of the mill. He opened the door and I thanked him and stepped inside. We pulled away but had only gone a few yards when I noticed a man hurrying towards the mill.

It was Father Lynch. His gaunt frame, garbed in black, was unmistakeable. He did not see me pass by, so intent was he on his destination.

As the carriage turned away from the town, I sat back and pondered. How strange that in the two days since my arrival, I had not only met the priest, but read an account of him in old newspapers, heard him spoken off by the Miss Tiptons, and now had seen him visiting my family's mill in Skipton.

Though there might be a likely reason for his being here, it still struck me as odd. Father Lynch was a busy man. He must have parishioners working at the mill with whom he needed to speak. For I doubted he'd have any mill business with Uncle Simon.

****

I did not see my cousins upon my return and therefore retired to my bedroom. It was raining yet again, and the air cold with it. One of the servants had kindly lit a fire in the hearth, and I languished in the comforting warmth once I'd removed my wet things. With my coat hung upon a peg drying, I placed my sodden shoes close to the fireplace. I put away my purchases, then with a sigh, sank down onto my bed.

I was weary, which seemed ridiculous as all I had done was walk around Skipton. But then being tired seemed to plague me much lately. How had I managed to work all those long hours back in Cape Town? I'd never be able to do it now.

I lay staring at the high ceiling. I considered reading more of Mother's journals but did not have the energy.

I yawned. The hour was still early and there was nothing expected of me until dinner. I closed my eyes and listened to the soft crackling noises from the fire.

I AWOKE TO FIND IT ALREADY dark. I fumbled for the matches on the table next to the bed and lit my lamp. The clock over the mantel showed it was nearing time for our evening meal. I had better get dressed for dinner.

Chapter Nine

THERE WERE NO LAMPS LIT IN the small dining room. But then I heard a hum of conversation from the other end of the hall. It seemed we were to eat in the formal dining room. This was a long, thin room with the same wood panelled walls as the rest of the house yet somehow lacked atmosphere. A fire blazed in the hearth, so at least it was warm.

Uncle Simon, Ivan and both my cousins were already seated. My uncle saw me.

"Ah, here she is." Both gentlemen got to their feet.

The table was huge but set for five, all at one end. I took the seat next Vivienne, facing the Delahunts. My Uncle Simon sat at the head of the table.

"Good evening, Nanette," I said with genuine pleasure. "I am so pleased you are dining this evening. How are you?" I thought my cousin looked quite well. There was a slight flush to her cheeks and her disarming eyes were bright.

"Still weak, unfortunately. But I desperately wanted to dine with everyone."

"A nourishing meal will do you the world of good, my dear." Her father encouraged. "Look here. Mrs Blitch has prepared a wonderful roast pork, with her delicious Yorkshire pudding and fresh apple sauce." He stood and began carving the meat. "This'll nourish the blood, I'll be bound." But though Uncle Simon spoke to his daughter, his eyes were fastened upon me. "What say you, Claire? Good, hearty food is just what the doctor ordered."

"Indeed," I agreed quickly. "A healthy diet is the first step to recovery with any malaise."

Uncle Simon sliced the meat and distributed pieces on each of our proffered plates. We helped ourselves from serving bowls in the centre of the table to roast potatoes, fresh carrots, and Cook's delectable Yorkshire puddings, ladled with lashings of rich gravy.

Having missed lunch, I was ravenous. Everything tasted delicious, and I was content tucking into my food, listening while everyone else talked.

As he had the previous two nights, Uncle Simon dominated the conversation. This mainly consisted of the ridiculous prices of raw materials, a couple of troublesome situations at Parslow's, and local political news.

Ivan was quiet. Whenever I looked over at him, he sensed my perusal and lifted his gaze to meet mine. His expression was difficult to read, but I would estimate it somewhere between being utterly bored and having a nagging toothache.

Nanette paid rapt attention to her father. She made the obligatory responses to his opinions, periodically decorating her comments with an attractive giggle.

Vivienne, sitting to my right and closest to her father, remained stoically silent. I noticed her ice-blue eyes examining Ivan and her sister several times. What, I wondered, went on in that shrewd mind?

As a child, Vivienne had always been difficult to read. At one moment, she could be extremely nice, and then she'd coil into a cobra, wounding you with wicked words. Most of us outgrew childhood habits as we aged, but seldom did we outgrow our personalities. Hadn't I already been the recipient of that razor tongue?

Yet Vivienne's behaviour around Ivan seemed far more sedate. Perhaps she held genuine affection for her brother-in-law? I determined she did, but wondered just how fond of the handsome young engineer she was?

"Did you enjoy your time in Skipton, Claire?"

Nanette's question roused me from thought. "Why yes, I did. The town has almost become a city. Though I stayed mostly on the High Street, I was amazed how many shops have opened everywhere."

"Father says we've no need to go to Leeds as often anymore," said Nanette.

"No indeed," Uncle Simon stated, spearing another potato. "Other than specialised items, you can buy anything you want in Skipton."

"Except fine dining, or a night at the theatre," Ivan retorted. "Skipton has gained in size, but unfortunately, not in culture."

"Oh Ivan, must you always be so disheartening?" his wife said, her voice tight with annoyance. "My cousin merely compliments the improvements over time, she does not point out discrepancies."

"Nanette is correct. We'll always want to visit Leeds," continued my uncle, ignoring the unrest. "But it is pleasant not having to travel as far for things, especially in bad weather and such."

"I enjoyed walking around." I attempted to bring the conversation back. "When it started raining, I stopped in one of the tea rooms, as did many others. I shared a table with two young women from Starling Village."

"You don't say." Uncle Simon popped a large forkful of pork into his mouth.

"What were their names?" asked Nannette.

"Hazel and Phoebe Tipton. I understand their father is a physician in Skipton. They were delightful company. I especially took a liking to the younger, Phoebe."

Vivienne deigned to speak. "We know the family. Doctor Tipton attends Nanette."

"Oh," I said. "I thought the name sounded familiar. Nanette mentioned him to me the other day."

"He's quite a good doctor, but the daughters are somewhat silly, and Martin, his son, thinks too highly of himself," she added.

"Martin Tipton?" said Nanette. "Did you not once hold a candle for him, sister? I thought you quite fond of the man." Nanette looked at me. "He is a pharmacist."

Vivienne's colour rose. I knew a moment's pleasure that her sister had delivered a sting as sharp as one of Vivienne's own. I silently congratulated Nanette.

"Actually," began Vivienne, "If you must know, Martin and I went walking once or twice, but he was someone I found terribly uninteresting."

Her cold eyes were on Ivan, who stared at the crystal glass in his hand and acted as though he hadn't heard a word.

It was like watching a play being acted before me. Uncle Simon, happily eating his dinner, while Nanette and Vivienne locked horns. Nanette, uncaring of her husband's attention, while her sister kept seeking it and failing. What was afoot? Were families always like this? Not being brought up in a normal family, I had nought to compare this to. Yet something in the dynamics of this foursome was definitely wrong.

In the quiet that followed, I threw out another topic of conversation.

"Uncle, was that Father Lynch I saw going into the mill when I left this afternoon?"

"Yes, my dear. He needed to speak with me on a matter."

"I see. For a village priest, he seems to have many duties. His parish must be large."

"Not really. It extends a few miles outside the village. But he had other things to attend in Skipton and asked to stop in."

Vivienne spoke up again. She turned to look at me. "Why are you so interested in Father Lynch, Claire? You just met him the day before yesterday."

Because he gave evidence which helped hang my father, I desperately wanted to say. But instead, I looked at her hard face and smiled. "No reason. I was curious."

"He does such good work for so many," said Nanette. "Father Lynch established a school in Starling, Claire. They have a small library and even a choir." She looked over at her father. "Parslow's sponsored the school, didn't they Father? We are rather proud of that." Nanette's eyes gleamed.

My uncle looked pleased with himself. "Yes. The school has been most beneficial. Many of our workers live in Starling. It's given their children an opportunity to learn basic skills. which will enable them as they become adults."

"How so, Simon? The children are sent to work at Parslow's once they reach the ripe old age of ten."

Ivan's comment stilled the room into utter silence.

I looked at Uncle Simon. If his eyes could shoot fire, Ivan would be ablaze.

"Considering the profits of the mill have financed your education and currently pay your wages, I would be less inclined to sling mud, if I were you, Ivan." Uncle Simon's voice was low, but stern.

The two men stared at one another, the tension growing thicker.

"I wonder where Tibbetts is with our dessert," Vivienne said getting to her feet. "Why don't I go and see."

Feeling at a loss of what to say to bridge the awkwardness, I spoke to Uncle Simon.

"What day am I to come and meet with you and the solicitors, Uncle?" It was all I could think to say.

Ivan looked furious. His eyes smouldered with rage. Understandable as Uncle Simon had belittled him. Personally, I had no quarrel with Ivan's statement. I didn't know how many children the mill employed, nor was I familiar with their circumstances. But the dinner table was not the best place to embark upon an argument about child labour.

"This coming Friday, I believe." Uncle Simon turned his attention to me and answered the question.

Vivienne rejoined us and took her seat. "Cook has made an apple pie. Tibbetts will be along with it presently."

Ivan abruptly rose from the table. "Please excuse me. There is something I must attend to." He departed with a curt nod to the ladies.

"Well," muttered Nanette once he was gone from the room. "I don't know what has got into my husband.

It is most unlike him to be so argumentative, Father. I am sorry for his behaviour. Perhaps Ivan is tired. He spends far too much time at the mill these days."

Uncle Simon was not mollified. "That is his choice. But there we are." He gave a forced smile as Tibbetts entered the room carrying a tray with a large pie and a bowl of thick cream. He continued. "Let us not dwell on Ivan anymore. I would prefer enjoying my dessert in peace."

AFTER DINNER, WE REMOVED TO the drawing room where the sisters sat together on the couch, Uncle and I, in the armchairs.

In the firelight, Nanette's face glowed, and I wondered again at her illness, and if it was feigned or real? She looked quite pretty in a lilac dress, her skin pale and smooth. Her hair, swept up in a French knot, was dotted with tiny purple flowers. I wondered how she managed to wear it thus, with no lady's maid on hand. Perhaps Vivienne had helped?

Vivienne, though of similar colouring to her sister had opted for a deep red velvet dress. Sitting close together, their choice of fabric colours clashed violently. I studied them intently. How opposite they were in stature. Nanette, svelte and slim, Vivienne, more matronly and rotund. Yet they were alike in familial looks with the same facial bone structure and features. Vivienne with her father's piercing blue eyes, Nanette with her heterochromia afflicted irises.

I did not resemble my cousins. Our mothers, though sisters, were as different as chalk and cheese. Jane, dark like a Celtic warrior, and Charlotte, blonde as a Viking princess. It was my Aunt Charlotte who'd captured the hearts of the local boys, according to Grandmother, while her older sister, Jane, had been too busy accompanying Grandfather to the mill.

It gave me immense pride knowing Mother had been intelligent and her business acumen respected by her father. What did it matter that she was not the beauty of the family? Yet Mother had given up her career to care for me when I was born, and then the tragedy with my father had finished her. She'd run away to Hampshire, leaving her dreams and aspirations behind.

I wondered what the future would have held for Jane Shaw had the events of that cold November night never occurred. I did not doubt for a moment, she and my father would have run the mill hand in hand.

"Claire?" Nanette asked. "Did you not hear me?"

"Oh, I am sorry. I was miles away."

"I was telling Father that we should host a dinner in your honour, if I am well enough, of course. What say you to that?"

I did not like the idea at all. "Really," I began. "There is no need. I rather like being here incognito, as it were. Please don't trouble yourself—"

"—It is no trouble." The sliver of steel in her voice surprised me. "It's been an age since we planned any entertainment at Darkwater Abbey. Come, Claire, don't spoil it by being a bore. It's not as if I'm planning a ball. Just a small, intimate dinner with a few friends." Her eyes lit up. "We could invite the Tiptons?"

Vivienne gave a groan. "Honestly, Nanette. How can you possibly think their company would be exciting? Those two girls give me the headache. I'd rather go out for dinner in Skipton."

A fleeting shadow of unmitigated anger swept across Nanette's face. In a flash, it had gone. She glared at her sister. "Why must you naysay all I suggest? Our cousin is back in England after years away, only to lose her dear mama. We are all the family Claire has. Why can't we shed a little light into her gloom and introduce her to our neighbours. Where's the harm in that? I am sure you won't be disappointed if Martin Tipton comes along. Some male attention might cheer you, would it not, sister?"

I couldn't keep my eyes from the sparring women. The meek, ailing Nanette had her claws out and they were sharp indeed. Vivienne flinched at the barb. I watched her consider a rebuttal, for she was entirely capable of putting Nanette back in her place. Surprisingly, it was not forthcoming. How odd.

"I shall not have my girls quarrelling, and there's an end to it," Simon interjected sternly. "If Nanette desires a dinner party, then so be it." He gave Vivienne a disapproving glare. "You, my dear, should be only too glad to mix with other young people. It's time you were doing something other than playing nursemaid to your sister and found yourself a husband."

Both daughters were berated into silence. One for being ill, the other for being an old maid. Despite my not being particularly close to either, I felt for them.

"I shall be fine with whatever you suggest," I said to Nanette. "And Vivienne, a dinner in Skipton sounds like a wonderful evening. We should plan both."

The tension dissipated and my cousins relaxed. Uncle Simon poured us all another sherry and returned to his seat.

"Nanette has the right of it. Life at Darkwater

Abbey has fallen into an uninteresting routine. I remember years ago when both of your mothers were alive, the house was filled with laughter and fun. There's been so many unfortunate events that have changed the place. But now with Claire's return, I feel a sense of urgency to reverse it all." He took a sip of sherry and then continued. "Nanette's idea of a dinner party is an excellent way to begin making those changes. Therefore, I propose you go forward with your plans and invite whomever you desire, my dear. Sooner, rather than later."

Nanette beamed with pleasure. "Consider it done, Papa."

Vivienne bristled but remained silent.

"Now then," said Uncle Simon. "Your cousin, Claire, has been an independent, hardworking nurse for many years. Though I wish to see her take time to relax, I'll hazard a guess she is much like her dear mama and will be bored out of her mind within a week, given no occupation."

He turned to look at me affectionately. "Tell me, have you any ideas about what you would like to do? Obviously, you'll come to the mill and attend to some business, but it has been years since you were in the Dales. Are there places you have an interest in seeing?"

I had already contemplated approaching the subject of Mother's journals with Uncle Simon and my cousins. But my plans were to wait until I was more settled and become familiar with the family. Yet he was opening a door of conversation where I could introduce a subject that was somewhat awkward. With Ivan's absence, it would certainly be easier to bring it up. I made my decision.

"Actually, Uncle Simon, there is a matter I should like to discuss with the three of you while we are together. It is a delicate topic, but you are family, and I am comfortable speaking if you don't mind?"

Uncle Simon looked perplexed, but he nodded. "Please, Claire, go on."

"This relates to something terrible which occurred when my cousins and I were but children. It is, of course, the murder committed by my father."

The atmosphere in the room immediately became rigid. My hands twisted in my lap, and I stared down at them, unable to look anyone in the eye lest I lose confidence and stop talking.

"After Mother died it was my duty to go through her possessions, and I came across a great deal of information she amassed over the years, regarding what happened that fateful night when Keith Delahunt died. Apart from multiple newspaper cuttings she had collected, giving their accounts of the murder, Mother had also kept journals for the past two decades, where she recorded her personal observations of what transpired. I have them all."

"I don't understand," interrupted Nanette. "Why should we resurrect something that happened long ago. I might add, a tragedy which almost destroyed our family."

I looked up quickly, meeting her stare, and felt the flicker of anger reach my eyes.

"That is a harsh statement for you to make, Cousin. You, like me, were but a very young child. Therefore, your knowledge of what took place is completely based upon what you have been told."

"And you believe you know more about what

happened?" Uncle Simon asked quietly.

I turned to him. "As a matter of fact, I do."

Vivienne gave a derisive laugh. "Claire, I mean no disrespect, but you were not much older than Nanette and I. What could you possibly know?"

I took a deep breath. "I have an eyewitness account in my mother's journal. It was kept a secret to protect my mother from the scrutiny of the law, but she states very plainly in her writing that the night Keith Delahunt was killed, she was there in that churchyard. She is adamant that there is absolutely no way my father could have killed that poor man."

I ignored the gasps from my cousins. Though I felt the heat from Uncle Simon's bold glare up on my face, I carried on speaking.

"Mother makes it plain that on the night Mr Delahunt died, she was there at the invitation of a note sent to my father. When the fatal gunshot was fired, my parents were nowhere near Mr Delahunt. At the arrival of the priest, who I assume is your own Father Lynch, and the constable who dined with him that night, Father insisted that Mother's name be kept from any statements given to the authorities. It was the ultimate sacrifice to protect her even though she had done nothing wrong. Consequently, it was a decision he made never realising he would be hung for it."

Chapter Ten

THE ROOM FELL SILENT. AFTER a few moments Uncle Simon finally spoke up.

"My dear Claire. Jane spoke of this many years ago." He sighed. "And she testified in court that she had been there. But your father and his lawyers dismissed her statement. Jane was distraught and wracked with grief. She would have said anything to save Thom." He paused in reflection. "Over the years, Jane never spoke of it again, and out of respect for her I acted accordingly. But now you've shared these revelations, and her sentiments, I don't really know how to respond." Uncle Simon took a sip of his sherry. "You mother's version of events questions what we know, and what was said at the trial. I wasn't privy to any of the conversation between Jane, the lawyers and Thomas. But I do know your father was adamant about her name not being dragged through the courts." Uncle Simon suddenly looked weary. "Claire, my dear. None of us here know what really happened on that fateful night. I often think Thomas believed his wife might have done something, and to stop it being discovered he protected her. Yet I can't imagine Jane Shaw ever being capable of hurting another human being. She'd have no reason to harm Keith. Other than his accusation against your father regarding money disappearing from the mill accounts." He leaned back in his chair. "I wish everyone had been straightforward from the beginning. Instead, what happened ultimately took the lives of two men I greatly admired."

"I find this all vastly confusing," piped up Vivienne. "So, what you are saying Papa, is Aunt Jane may have killed Ivan's father, but Uncle Thomas took the blame to spare her life?"

"Not exactly," said my uncle. "There were mitigating circumstances which complicated what happened. Thomas was holding a gun, his own gun, I might add. Keith Delahunt had been shot. Other evidence supported the theory he had a motive to want Delahunt out of the picture."

"What motive was that?" asked Vivienne.

Uncle Simon looked at me for a moment, then at his daughter.

"I don't think we should continue speaking of this, Vivienne. Let it rest for now. The subject is most delicate, and I don't want to upset Claire."

I could tell Vivienne wanted more answers. Her eyes were wide with interest. But she and Nanette remained quiet.

"Thank you for listening to me tonight." I addressed them all. "It had not been my intention to speak of it having just arrived. But being back here where everything changed for Mother and I, I can't seem to think of anything else. I do hope I haven't offended you."

"Don't be silly," said Nanette. "You have every right to speak of your history. Besides, what happened impacts you and Papa, not Vivienne and I. We were all so young then, and I don't think any of us really understood what was happening." She gave an elaborate sigh and then stifled a yawn. "My goodness, this evening has been most eventful. I am feeling rather tired." She glanced at her sister. "Vivienne. Be a dear and come up to my room with me. I require your help with my toilette, if you please."

My cousins bade Uncle Simon and I goodnight and left to go upstairs. I remained seated, staring into my sherry glass, my mind a battleground. Had I erred talking about Mother's journals?

Uncle Simon noticed my discomfort. His warm hand reached over to cover mine. He leaned towards me from where he sat.

"Dearest Claire. Don't fret about your disclosure this evening. Now you're here, we've all the time in the world to discuss the past." He gave my hand a reassuring squeeze and an odd look came over him. He smiled. "And the future."

Drawing back his hand, Uncle Simon emptied his glass, setting the vessel on a small wooden table between our chairs. Then he rose. "Now. I fear I must bid you good evening. It has been rather a long day and I've an early start in the morning. Will you go on up yourself? Or shall you remain down here for a time?"

"I think I'd like to enjoy the fire a while longer," I replied.

He bestowed me with a smile and left me to my own devices.

I was glad Uncle Simon had gone upstairs. I stared at the hand he'd grasped so familiarly. I hadn't liked it. I couldn't quite identify the feeling, but there was something about his being overly familiar which made me uncomfortable. His kiss at the mill, the look in his eyes when he squeezed my hand…and what did he mean about discussing the past and the future? No. It didn't sit right.

His actions did not intimidate me. Years of dealing with soldiers had trained me how to be forceful, blunt, and put people in their place whenever necessary. But Simon was a relative, albeit one by marriage. Why was he behaving thus?

"May I join you?"

The voice gave me a start.

It was Ivan. I had thought him long retired. He was still in evening dress and came into the drawing room to take a seat on the settee.

Our eyes met, and I was glad to see he no longer appeared angry. I also noticed he had undone his cravat and a top button.

"I'm surprised to find you still up when everyone is already abed," he said.

I sighed. "I am not tired. My mind refuses to slow down and give me peace."

He raised a thick brow. "Then you have my sympathy. I am often cursed that way myself." Ivan got up and went to pour himself a sherry. He gestured towards my half-empty glass. "Would you care for another?"

"I'd better not," I answered. "I've probably had enough for one evening."

Ivan returned and sat back down. He seemed pensive for a moment, and then he finally spoke. "Claire, though we barely know one another, please permit me to speak frankly."

I shrugged. "By all means. I don't believe people should be anything but honest."

He took a quick sip of his drink and then cradled

the glass in his large hand. "This evening, I was on my way to rejoin the family after dinner, when I overheard you discussing what happened to my father."

I flinched. It was one thing speaking plainly to the others, but entirely another conversing with the man who had lost his only parent that night.

"Look," he continued. "I think we've formed an understanding that the actions committed decades ago have nothing to do with you or me. Of course, it is awkward and uncomfortable to speak of it. How can you not remind me of my past? But you have no blame in the matter whatsoever. When you shared what you'd read in your mother's journals, it made my ears burn. Even if Simon doesn't believe the importance of her writings, you do. Obviously, for you, it implies the innocence of your father, and that's a huge discovery, if true. Yet can you imagine the implications it would mean for me?"

I nodded. But kept silent.

"If your father was not guilty of killing mine. If your mother was indeed there and saw everything—an actual witness. Then the murderer, the bastard who took my father's life, is still free."

I gasped. Ivan was right. It was ridiculous, but I hadn't even considered it. I'd been wholly intent on the revelation my father had never been guilty.

"That is a troubling thought to consider," I said quietly. "I must admit, finding Mother's journals has been like unearthing an unexploded bomb. I am sure my uncle and others would question the thoughts and notes of a woman bereaved by the loss of her husband. But I do not. My mother was an exceptionally bright woman. Intellectually, she could give most men a run for their money. I know she was inconsolable when my father died—trust me, I have very distinct memories of that. Yet wasn't that to be expected when she loved him so very much. But now I've read her words, I see her distress would be a thousand-fold, comprehending his chivalrous actions were ultimately a death sentence." My throat became thick with sorrow, and I stopped to quickly take another sip of sherry.

"These journals you speak of. Would you be willing to let me read them?" Ivan asked.

I looked at his face. Undeniably handsome though he wore a frown, and his eyes smouldered.

The atmosphere between us changed. We were newly met. Instant adversaries based upon our connected history. But in the last few moments something significant shifted.

My mother's words had the potential to amend what we knew of our pasts. At the very least, they could clarify an event we had not participated in, but one which altered the trajectory of our futures. How strange, but I believed we were on the same side.

I was not ready to let down all my defences. "I'm sorry, but I'm not prepared to let the journals out of my sight. I have no problem with your reading them. I'd just rather it be in my presence."

"I've no quarrel with that. I'd feel the same. All right, can we make plans to meet then?" He glanced around the room. "Perhaps it would be better to conduct our business elsewhere."

He was right. I couldn't say why exactly. Privacy was important. And though the other people living here were my relatives, they were still people I did not know well. Better to be safe than sorry.

"What do you suggest?" I asked. "I'm familiar with the area, but you'd know better than I."

He considered. "Do you remember the location of the old Rosell cottage? It's just down the lane a half mile. You cut through the cow pasture, and the building is up on a rise. Can we meet there?"

"Yes. I know it. But Ivan, I shan't bring all of them, just what's pertinent. The one which speaks of that night in the churchyard." At once I suddenly felt weary. The seriousness of our subject matter had taken its toll, and the sherry enhanced the feeling.

I set down my glass. "I grow tired. I think I should like to retire for the evening if you'll excuse me?" I got to my feet.

Ivan did the same. "Then we'll meet tomorrow? Nine o'clock at the cottage?"

"Yes," I replied. "I'll be there."

I climbed the stairs and reached the corridor where both east and west wing conjoined. I had the odd sensation I was being watched. I spun around, expecting it to be Ivan Delahunt at the bottom of the stairs. But no one was there.

As I turned to walk towards the west wing, I heard the creak of a door hinge from the opposite direction. I had not imagined it. Someone had been watching me. It could only be one of three people. Uncle Simon, Nanette, or Vivienne.

But which one had it been?

THAT NIGHT I DREAMT OF SONWABI beach. The bright blue skies, the brilliant turquoise sea, the little red boat we'd borrowed from our friends, bobbing atop the swelling and diminishing powerful waves.

It had been so calm when we'd set out a couple of hours earlier. Until huge clouds materialised from nowhere as the wind took an almighty breath and then blew it out with great force.

There was George, battling to take down the sails and turn the bow of the boat into the wind, while I clutched our baby close to my bosom. Giving up on the sails, he ran to me, took Sarah, and quickly tucked her inside his shirt, then wrapped his arms around me.

Suddenly the boat was sucked down, while the current gathered strength to form a massive wave. As the sea drew up again, we were pulled helplessly into that huge wall of water…and then came the wave. A shapeless, evil, liquid monster, rising from the depths of hell, and reaching for the heavens above.

Taller than a building, it crashed down, a powerful boulder splintering our tiny boat. Hungrily engulfing everything in its path and scattering it into the water. Liquid hands that plucked us up and then tossed us into the depths.

Swirling in the deep like a human whirlpool. Gasping for air. Eyes stinging with salt as I frantically searched in vain for my husband, my baby. While the rampant energy of the ocean tugged at my skirts and pulled me down.

I sat bolt upright up in my bed, the sheets damp with my perspiration and tears. My breath galloped as though I'd been running. I pressed my lips together and closed my mouth for a few moments to regulate the beating of my heart.

In my chest, the ache of desperate loss throbbed like an open, bloody wound. The sensation so overwhelming, it settled upon me like a heavy iron shroud. I lay back against the pillows and closed my tear-soaked eyes.

This nightmare haunted me. Not every night, not even every week now the months had passed. I accepted it as my penance. Reliving the worst day of my life was the price I paid for surviving an event that had robbed me of the two most precious people in my world.

Yet again this awful dream had dragged me into the jaws of my own private hell. Even awake the scene played on. The memory of pulling off my shoes and my outer skirts, a crazed madwoman, frantically trying to break to the surface and breathe, before submerging once more in search of my loved ones.

But I'd failed.

When they'd found darling George, he still had our sweet baby nestled against his chest, bound inside his buttoned shirt. And there she had stayed. But the current had dragged them under, sucked the breath from their lips, and then eventually delivered their lifeless bodies back to shore.

I'd wailed and screamed when they took me to my husband and child. Their cold bodies lay on the warm sand. Their expressions peaceful now they slept the eternal sleep. My precious Sarah. A tiny angel held forever in her father's protective embrace.

Would that I had been taken with them. But a fishing boat had rescued me. The crew, spying the accident from the shore had braved the elements and rowed out to where our boat had capsized.

Dear God, how I had cried. Sobbed until every cell of my being died.

I'd left my soul on Sonwabi beach. Nothing had

mattered after that.

I brushed away my tears and sat up in bed. I would not go back to sleep this night. Instead, I'd spend the hours until dawn in mental flagellation. Punishing myself for living.

Yet what good did it do? Months had come and gone, and all my tears, my guilt, would not bring my loves back to me.

Such a futile endeavour.

Yet I deserved it.

But tonight, my mind faltered, and instead of losing myself in misery, my eyes were drawn to the silhouette of a stack of books upon the dressing table.

I got out of bed to retrieve one of Mother's journals, but as I passed the window, something flickered in the corner of my eye.

My room was in total darkness, but outside, the moon shone feebly and thinned out the obscurity of night. I peered through the glass, looking down into the courtyard and the small garden. The perimeter, lined with bushes, stood guard. The wide moat just beyond.

There it was again…a faint light appearing and disappearing between the bushes like a firefly. It must be a small lantern, for it was not terribly bright, especially from this distance. Who would be outside at this late hour, neither night nor morning? A servant? Unlikely. None stayed in the house overnight but resided across the footbridge in their own cottages.

The flicker of light emerged near the end of the bushes and turned towards the house. Soon it would be out of range for me to see. But as fortune had it, a shaft of moonlight suddenly glowed brighter, and for an instant, illuminated the figure out there.

I held my breath. Though too far away to see the identity of the person, I was still close enough to tell one thing for certain.

It was a man.

Chapter Eleven

TIBBETTS HAD ALREADY STARTED clearing away breakfast when I came down the next morning. I'd fallen asleep again as dawn rose after re-reading the journal I would take with me to meet Ivan.

Tibbetts was surprised to see me.

"Mornin' miss," he said pleasantly. "Thought you'd supped." He seemed concerned. He glanced at the table; all that remained was a plate of toast and the teapot. "What'll I bring you?"

I sat down. "Actually, I'm not very hungry." I eyed the toast. "I'll eat the toast and that will be plenty. Is there still tea?"

He picked it up as I reached for the toast. "Nay. I'll fetch 'fresh pot." He left the room.

I was eating a piece of toast, thick with blackcurrant jam when he returned. Tibbetts set the pot down and I poured myself a cup.

"Thank you, Tibbetts. By the way, this jam is delicious," I dabbed a serviette to my mouth. "How are you this morning?"

"Well, thank you, miss. By the by, Miss Nanette asks you take luncheon in her room today. I'm to take an answer."

"Oh," I said. "That will be fine. Please tell her I'll be there." I glanced up at the mantel clock; it was quarter past eight. Plenty of time to finish breakfast before leaving to meet Ivan.

Tibbetts moved away.

I stopped him. “Tibbetts. Do you mind if I ask you something.”

He turned to me with a ready smile. “Anythin’ you like, miss, ’cept about me love life.”

I laughed. “No, it’s nothing personal this time.” I beckoned him to come closer so I might speak more quietly.

“Last night I couldn’t sleep. In the early hours of the morning, I got out of bed and happened to look out of my corner window. There was someone out there. I saw a light and a person walking through the bushes, over near the moat.”

Tibbetts’ already fair skin paled, then he quickly composed himself. “Are you certain you weren’t still asleep, miss? Might easily been t’dream.”

“No. I was wide awake; I can assure you. But I can’t imagine who it would have been at such a late hour. I didn’t think it was you or the other servants. You’d all have still been abed in your cottages. It had to be someone from the house. And why were they prowling around by the courtyard? They couldn’t go very far.”

“That don’t make sense, Miss Claire. Out in’t middle of night?” He still looked slightly concerned and almost afraid.

“Tibbetts, what is it? Something’s bothering you. Come on. Out with it.”

His eyes looked back to the door to make sure no one would overhear and then he leaned forward. “I reckon you saw’t ghost. Were it man or woman, miss? Could you tell?”

"It was definitely a man."

He gave a little shudder. "Then't must of been one o' them priests, I'll wager."

"What on earth are you on about?"

Tibbetts gave a long sigh. "Miss knows about t'stories. Fire that killed thirty-three priests. You must remember hearin' tales?"

"Of course I do. But those stories are nonsense."

Tibbetts raised a thin brow. "Miss can doubt, but many've seen spirits wanderin' 'round 'place in't dead o' night."

"Probably after supping a little too much ale," I said dismissively.

Tibbetts shrugged "Say what you want, an' think it too. But there's restless souls here at Darkwater."

"Utter rubbish," I declared. "The Abbey certainly looks like it could be haunted. But you see, Tibbetts, I've never heard of a ghost needing a lantern to find his way around. This fellow had one."

"If you say so, miss." Tibbetts picked up my empty plate, gave me a wink and walked off.

I pondered. Darkwater had many connections to the priesthood. The original building had been that of an abbey and the new house built during the Tudor era, late in Henry VIII's reign. When Henry's daughter, Elizabeth, inherited the crown, so began many bloody battles between Protestant and Catholic. And the evolution of priest holes had begun.

As a child, I'd loved hearing tales about the priests' holes concealed down in the cellar, kept secret and out of the way. That my family home, Darkwater, was famous for having three of them was so interesting.

Mother had taught me about their importance.

Then after we moved to Hampshire, I'd often read the history of them in books from the library.

Priest holes were not uncommon in larger, more affluent homes. During Queen Elizabeth's reign, there were many Catholic plots to remove her from the throne. Consequently, severe measures were taken against Catholic priests in England. They were prohibited to celebrate their rites, to hold mass, or convert an Anglican, or any other to Catholicism, upon pain of death. It was considered high treason. With many of the population avid Papists, priests disobeyed the laws. With priest hunters on the lookout at all times, there came a need to provide safety for the men of God.

In the homes of wealthy Catholic families, spaces were craftily built behind walls and wainscoting, and under floors. The presence of a priest could easily be hidden, and many were saved due to this. I wondered how often they had been used at Darkwater?

I shuddered. What an awful time in English history that was. Thank goodness things were better nowadays. I finished my tea but found myself still thinking about the figure I'd seen in the courtyard.

****

After breakfast, I went upstairs and prepared for my walk. I placed Mother's journal in my reticule, along with my trusty derringer. I'd be silly not to take it with me. Since my days in Africa, I'd become used to keeping the weapon close at hand. In Cape Town, it was to protect me from a sudden attack by a wild animal, or at worst, a Boer soldier. I doubted I had much to fear in civilised Yorkshire other than rabid badger or an angry weasel. But one never knew.

I peeked out of the window, misted from the cold

outside and the warmth of my room. It did look chilly this morning. I'd dress accordingly.

I changed into sturdy walking boots as I'd be crossing through a pasture, then put on my coat and gloves. I gave the fire a few stokes, placing more coals in the grate. It would be nice to come back to a warm room.

I did not see a soul when I left the house. Crossing the footbridge I gave an involuntary shudder. It was silly, I knew. The moat was no ocean. But it mattered not to me. Just seeing the gloomy depths, even stilled as they were this morning, brought visions of my loved ones lost to me forever. I kept my eyes focused on the other side of the bridge and walked briskly.

Wisps of mist floated like fairies in the chilled air and I pulled my coat tight, then turned in the opposite direction I'd taken previously, and set off down the lane.

I reached the stables and saw the doors were wide open, and the scent of horseflesh and fresh straw was pungent and most pleasant. A horse whinnied, and a warm light spread out into the mist. I slowed my gait when I drew level with the door.

Stepping inside, I found myself in familiar territory. I'd always loved horses. And somewhere in the recesses of childhood memories I knew an association between these stables and my father. He probably brought me to see the horses to give them treats.

"Good day to you, miss." It was Gibbons. He was seated in a partially closed off area which housed a table and a chair. I spotted a tin mug, and an open newspaper. The walls were patterned with hooks and nails where various pieces of equestrian equipment hung.

He got to his feet. My goodness he was such a tall man.

"Were you needing transport this morning, Mrs Holloway?" It was the most the man had spoken to me, and I detected a lilting Irish accent. It sounded pleasant, even delivered in such a deep voice.

"No thank you," I replied. "I'm only taking a walk. But I couldn't resist looking in when I heard the horses. Years ago, my father would often bring me in here to see them."

Gibbons looked like the strong man in a circus. Without his coachman's jacket on, the bulk of his arms strained against the fabric of his shirt. Besides the mere size of him, every feature seemed larger than life.

His curly black hair was cut so close, it looked like it had been knitted, sewn onto his scalp and would be impossible to put a comb through. His eyebrows, bushy and thick, emphasised the unusual yellow tint of his eyes. The man had the look of a predator. Instinctively, I felt vulnerable. But the weight of the little weapon in my bag was reassuring.

"You're an Irishman, Gibbons? How long have you been in this part of the world?"

His thick fingers scratched at his dense beard. "About nineteen years now. I came over to work on the canal. But I got hurt and that put a stop to it. Ended up in Skipton an' got myself on at Parslow's. But factory work wasn't for me. I've always liked the horses and working outside 'n all. Mr Simon saw I had a way with the animals, an' gave me this job. I've been lookin' after 'em for fourteen years and some."

He would have come to Darkwater after we'd moved away. On my visits, I hadn't had occasion to meet the man. "If you have to spend hours working, it's much better doing something you like." I glanced at the row of stalls. "Would you mind my coming back another time to look at the horses? I promise I won't get in your way."

His expression softened. I supposed anyone who admired horses went up favourably in Gibbons' estimations.

He gave what might be considered a smile. "To be sure. Come whenever you like, miss. Just don't scare 'em." He pointed to a tin pail by the desk. "There's some apples and such you can give 'em when you come back."

I thanked the man and took my leave.

I passed the carriage house and then the cowshed. The cattle would already be in the fields, leaving workers to muck out the shed.

Going on down the lane I scoured the area looking for familiar landmarks. I recognised the cow pasture where I'd cut through to get to the cottage easy enough. The gate was closed but there was a handy stile next to it one could navigate. This I did, clutching my skirts so I would not get caught up.

A sizeable herd grazed contentedly. Several pairs of bovine eyes paused to glance my way as I walked through thick, damp grass in the direction of a small hill. The family who had once lived here, had put another stile where the pasture met their property. This provided an easy shortcut down to the lane.

I trudged slowly up the hill. The track showing the way had been reclaimed by nature now the family were long gone. At the crest of the hill, I stopped to catch my breath. My goodness, that had taken the wind out of me. I must be more diligent about getting better exercise.

Rosell's Cottage looked sad and neglected. The bones of the dilapidated house stood firm, though weathered, and the glass was gone from the windows. There was no door, for someone had probably stolen it once the place was vacant.

I was early, so I stepped inside what had been the kitchen to look around and instantly spooked a few pigeons up in the rafters. They flapped about for a moment and then settled back down once they realised I was no threat.

There was nothing left inside the house except broken floorboards with twisted weeds reaching through the gaps. Light came in through gaping holes in the roof, and everything smelled damp. Judging by prints in the dirt coating the floor, many animals had visited.

Empty houses always saddened me. It was the melancholy about them. I used to think if I closed my eyes and concentrated, I'd hear the sounds of people who had once lived there. Their voices, their laughter, even their sorrows, forever captured in the soul of the house.

This place had long stood empty. There had been a beautiful girl living here, a girl by the name of Lucy Rosell. She'd gone for a walk one afternoon, never to return. Her frantic parents, and some kind people from the village had spent days searching for her.

Her body had been discovered out by the waterfall at Starling Foss. She'd been brutally murdered and her body picked at by the crows. She was buried in the churchyard. Months later, her parents, so distraught, had both taken a sleeping potion and killed themselves.

Though my recollections of my time living in Yorkshire were scant, I'd never forgotten that tale because it was so tragic. Consequently, nobody had ever purchased the cottage and it had remained empty since.

As a mother who had lost her child, I could understand the Rosells' despair at the death of their only child. The unbearable pain of it.

"Claire?"

I gasped and spun around. I hadn't heard Ivan enter the cottage.

"Sorry," he said. "I did not mean to startle you."

"You didn't. I was thinking about the family that used to live here."

"Yes. A sad business indeed."

"Were you living in Yorkshire when it happened?" I asked. For though I remembered the story I wasn't sure when it occurred.

"We were still in Leeds, I think. But my father recounted the story on one of our visits to Darkwater Abbey."

"Goodness, I've just realised that each time you and I converse, it's usually about a very morbid subject."

Ivan smiled. "I hadn't given that any thought. But you're right. It's rather depressing."

I returned the smile. "Yes. But necessary in this case." I opened my bag, retrieved Mother's journal and held it out to him.

"Start with the part where Mother writes about the

night your father was attacked. I'll go outside and give you a moment to read in peace."

He took the book from me. "Thank you."

I left the cottage and walked around to the front of the building. The view from up here was pleasant.

In the distance I could see the village of Starling, and the Protestant church spire only a mile away. And there was the steeple of St. Michael's, on the outskirts of Starling, this side of the village.

Papa and I had regularly passed St. Michael's on our way into Starling. I remember asking him why we never attended. For some reason, the answer he gave escaped me now.

Revisiting the past was becoming a frequent occurrence since coming back to the dales. Strange, but all the years I'd lived in Hampshire, I'd given Yorkshire little thought. For the most part, reminiscing was enjoyable. But I was not looking forward to the conversation I was going to have with Ivan. Speaking of murder was terribly unpleasant. Considering it involved both of our fathers, it really was quite awful.

I continued walking the circumference of the property, stopping periodically to observe the views from different perspectives. It was a shame no one lived here. It was quite a pretty spot. How lovely it would be to see beautiful flowers growing here, bringing colour and sunshine around a building tarnished with grief.

"Claire?" Ivan called from inside the cottage.

"Coming," I answered and headed back.

The man I had left reading was not the same person I saw when I returned.

Ivan's eyes were troubled and dark. His frown deep, his mouth, a taut line. Prominent cheekbones showed his jaw was tightly clenched.

He held Mother's journal tight in his hands.

"Dear God, I cannot believe what I have just read. Your mother writes so convincingly. What she says about being present that night rings true. The sincerity of her words, the emotion there…it would be difficult to fake. But what does it all mean? How am I supposed to digest these implications she brings to light?"

At once I felt compassion for the man. Before me stood a mature, confident person struggling with the emotions of the child who had lost his father. My heart went out to him.

"It is a great deal to comprehend, and you've every right to be shocked and confused." I stepped closer and reached out to touch his arm. He flinched, and I quickly pulled back.

"Ivan. Calm your thoughts. Take a little time to think. To digest what you've read."

His voice grew menacing. "Think? I have done little else since bloody childhood." He stepped past me and paced the room like a pent-up bull. "Do you know what it's like growing up a pauper? All my life I have lived on handouts given to me by your uncle." He ran his fingers through his hair and kept pacing. "I've appreciated it all—every bit. But even as a child one is aware of pity. Whether it is in someone's eyes, or conversations you hear whispered behind your back. When my father was murdered, there was gossip. Certain allegations made against him, nasty suspicions, seemingly more important than the fact he was dead."

I did not know what to say, so I remained quiet. Ivan paced on. I understood he was trying to walk off his anger and frustration.

"All these years, Claire, I have struggled with my past. Memories of my father are good. He was a kind man, a caring parent, and a hard-working provider. My father held strong principles which he taught me. Keith Delahunt would never steal a penny from anyone. Yet there were suggestions that he'd been stealing money from the mill and intentionally blamed your father. It wasn't enough his life was taken, they tried to take away his good reputation too."

He stopped abruptly and I reached out and grabbed his wrist. This time he did not pull away.

"Ivan. Listen to me," I implored. "You must stop thinking about the past and what you knew. Don't you understand? Now you've read what Mother wrote, surely you see there are possibilities? What if everything we've been told was a lie? Mother's account certainly casts many doubts on what was said to the public, and in court. My father was lured to the graveyard that night because of a note he received from a mysterious woman. But who was the note really from? It was only a fluke my mother read it first and decided to go and meet this person in my father's stead."

I looked up at his face. Some of the anger had gone but he looked as though he'd been slapped.

Ivan waved the book he held, and I let go of his wrist. "You believe everything in here, don't you?"

I nodded vigorously. "Yes, and if you had ever known my mother you would understand why. She was not prone to flights of fancy. Jane Shaw had the resolve and the backbone to be a port in a storm. The dependable person people came to when their lives were intolerable. She was a strong woman. I know her life was falling apart when this all took place, but she wrote those words for a reason. She wanted an accurate record of what was happening as it transpired. That way it would be a true account, and not one subject to cloudy memories."

He stared hard at me. In the light of the cottage, his eyes were the colour of steel. "What about the other journals? What does she write in all of those?"

"A number of observations and thoughts as the years passed. I found the first journal and her last to be the most interesting." I recounted what my mother had written about the letter.

"Do you think it is true?" he said, astounded.

"I have the letter. It bears an American postmark which looks legitimate. A false testimony in a murder case is no small thing, Ivan. It might be enough to appeal the verdict."

"And what do you plan on doing with all this new information? Are you going to show it to your uncle? Do you expect him to do something about it? If you think he'll rake this all up again and ask for a new investigation, you'd be mistaken."

It was my turn to pace. "Oh, I don't know what I think. I came back to England to be with my mother. I did not expect her to be dead before my feet touched dry land. Then, finding her diaries and reading what's in them got me utterly confounded. It would be simple to just forget I've read any of the damn things. But I can't." My voice grew thick with emotion. I stopped just a step away from him and looked at him imploringly.

"Ivan, we grieve for different reasons, but share the fact both our fathers are dead. We were robbed of our parents. Don't we owe it to them to discover the truth?"

I could hear his breath, agitated, troubled.

I continued. "If Papa was wrongly convicted and executed, I want to clear his name. And by doing so, I'll learn more about what really happened back then. For my father to be a scapegoat, the prosecution needed a strong case. Thomas Shaw was a well-respected businessman. It would have taken a great deal of evidence to convince a jury he was a murderer. What better way to do it than to invent a conflict between him and your father."

Ivan did not speak.

"Look. You are a virtual stranger to me, and I don't remember your father. But what I do know is I cannot tolerate lies. If a wrong has been done then it should be righted." I gave a frustrated groan. "The very least that can happen is I discover what's in the journals are just the fanciful dreams of a bereaved woman, even though that letter makes everything so credible. The best that can happen is the truth comes out and innocent people are exonerated of their crimes and the real villain exposed. So, tell me, do you agree with me? Will you help me determine what really took place twenty years ago?"

My heart thudded in my chest as I waited for Ivan's reply. A myriad of thoughts plowed through my head. I hadn't planned any of this. When I set out this morning, little did I know I'd suggest this to the one person who made the most unlikely ally.

Ivan reached out to hand me the little red book. Our eyes met. He stared at me for a few moments as though still deciding his answer.

Then he gave a little nod. "I want to read the other

journals before I commit to anything."

"All right," I said. It was a reasonable request. "You can collect them from me when we get back to the house. There are four others and the newspaper clippings as well."

"Then let's head back. I shan't go to the mill until after luncheon. I have the remainder of the morning free, so I'll read through them now."

With that, we left the cottage and made our way down the hillside, back through the cow pasture and down to the lane. We made no conversation. Ivan had much to consider.

When we reached the stables, Ivan told me to go ahead. He wanted to tell Gibbons he wouldn't need the carriage until after luncheon.

When I reached the house, I went directly up to my room. I felt chilled to the bone from being outside so long.

My bedroom was delightfully warm. I removed my coat and muddy boots and put on my slippers. Ivan would be stopping by shortly.

I glanced over at the dressing table and frowned. I thought I'd left the books there this morning, but they were gone. Had Mellors been in my room and tidied up?

Puzzled, I opened the top drawer where I had been keeping them, along with the brown envelope full of clippings, only to find it empty.

There came a sharp knock at my door. Still flustered, I opened it and saw Ivan standing on the threshold. He took one look at my face and his expression changed to that of concern.

"What's wrong?" he asked. "You look extremely

worried."

"Come in," I said quickly. "I can't find Mother's books."

He strode into the room, his brow furrowed. "What on earth do you mean?"

I pointed at the dressing table. "I had the others stacked up there and the newspaper articles in my top drawer." My throat thickened and I was filled with a sudden sense of unease. "Someone's taken them."

Suddenly there came a loud crack from the hearth. Ivan and I turned at the same time to look at the fire.

"Oh no!" I rushed towards the fireplace. There among the burning coals were remnants of white paper. I saw the red covers of my mother's journals blackened and twisted into macabre shapes, as yet not completely devoured by the flames. Of the newspapers there was nothing to be seen.

Horrorstruck, I turned to look at Ivan. The accusation in his eyes took me aback. Then I realised what he was thinking.

I stepped back from the hearth, anger quickly replacing shock. "Wait a moment, do you think I've done this?"

He glared back at me. "I'd say the timing was impeccable, wouldn't you?"

Fury engulfed me. I gasped in outrage. "How dare you," I said angrily. "I would never destroy all I have left of my father's story." Before I could control myself, my eyes welled with tears. "How can you accuse me after I have tried to heal a rift between our families and search for the truth." I glowered at him. "I thought better of you, Mr Delahunt. Apparently, the feeling is not mutual." I walked to the door and opened it. "Please leave."

Ivan went to the door, but gently moved my hand from the handle and closed it himself. He looked at my face, glanced at the fire and then back at me again. Then he reached into the breast pocket of his jacket and pulled out a handkerchief and handed it to me before going to stand by the hearth.

I wiped my eyes.

Ivan picked up a poker and prodded at what was left in the grate. "I should not have accused you of doing this, Claire. I'm sorry." He moved the detritus around. "I'm not myself today. Please forgive me. I know you didn't do this." He returned the poker to its holder. "The amount of damage already done to the covers suggests they have been burning for some time. Leather takes a while to melt." He gave me a grave look. "But I do not like the implication of this."

I put the handkerchief in my own pocket. I went to stand in front of a window, my head pounding with anger, sorrow, and disgust.

"I don't understand," I said quietly. "Who, in this house, would do such a despicable thing? I've been here three days, and my most valued possessions are now destroyed. Am I living with enemies?"

"I can't answer that," said Ivan. "Just remember, with few staff working here, it is not difficult to enter this house unseen."

I gave a derisive laugh. "Perhaps. Yet it is easy enough to enter my room if one already lives here."

He came to stand behind me. Gently, he cupped my elbow and turned me, so we were face to face.

"Claire," he spoke softly but his tone was stern. "Are you suggesting one of your own family would do something this atrocious?"

Tears welled once again. Angrily I wiped them away. "You of all people should know sometimes even those we care about can do the most evil of things."

He took a swift intake of breath. "You're right," he agreed. "Someone did not want anyone reading your mother's journals. But their actions bring only greater significance to their contents."

His fingers pressed into my arm and in his face I saw the reflection of what I imagined was on mine.

"Whoever did this will pay." My voice was almost a growl.

Ivan nodded. "Claire. This is the start of something very dangerous."

"It may be," I said. "But whoever this person is, they underestimate the abilities of a woman. They underestimate me."

Chapter Twelve

IVAN LEFT TO GO TO THE MILL, but only after convincing me to remain quiet about what had happened—at least until he returned later that day. I'd argued. Furious and full of rage, I wanted to throttle whoever had committed such an unspeakable deed. Yet what he said made sense. Better to plan and strategize than show your hand to an unknown adversary.

I splashed cold water on my face and willed myself to calm down. I'd promised to join Nanette for luncheon and did not want her to see I'd been crying.

At noon, I left my chamber for the east wing. I rapped lightly on Nanette's door and went in once invited.

I'd expected to find my cousin reclining in bed as she had been previously. But to my surprise she sat at a small table near the hearth, vibrant and healthy in a lovely pale blue dress.

She beamed at me. "Claire. Do come and join me."

I took a seat across from her at the little table. There was already a tea tray there and a plate of dainty sandwiches.

I injected a cheery note into my voice. "You look well, Nanette. That shade of blue suits you so nicely."

Pouring the tea, she smiled at the compliment. "Why thank you, Cousin." Nanette handed me a cup of tea. "I'm so pleased you can lunch with me. I wanted to chat without everyone around. I am sorry about the beastly time you had at dinner last night. Ivan shouldn't get so cross with Papa, but they have such differing opinions about the mill."

That was putting it mildly. "No need to apologise," I said reassuringly. "It's better for business to have differing styles of management. If everyone thought the same, we'd still be in the dark ages."

Nanette's eyes shone. "You are so clever, Claire. How I wish I was more like you. I envy your independent nature. In this day and age, you are something of an enigma."

"I hardly think so," I replied. "Women today are striking out on their own. It would shock you to see how many of our fair sex have careers and even live alone. As a matter of fact, if you lived in a city instead of here, you might have employment yourself." This was a blatantly false statement. One look at the fair Nanette and it was obvious she'd be exhausted if she had to make up her own bed.

I sipped my tea. After the events of the morning, the last thing I felt like doing was making small talk with a person I had little in common with, other than our forebears. I would much prefer pursuing whoever burned the journals. The mere thought of it made me feel nauseous.

Meanwhile, Nanette chatted obliviously on.

"It's wonderful you've come back to Yorkshire. I've so looked forward to seeing you. After all, it has been years. As you can probably tell, life at Darkwater Abbey isn't particularly exciting. You've certainly livened things up with your coming. Well other than that poor fellow dropping dead down the road." She stated the fact as though the event were as insignificant as a horse losing a shoe.

"Goodness me," I replied. "It is hardly dull here. Why do you complain? It's not as if you're alone. You've Vivienne for company and, of course, your husband."

Nanette passed a small plate, and I took a cucumber sandwich from the selection offered. I took a bite. It tasted like sawdust on my tongue. I had absolutely no appetite after what had happened in my room.

"Vivienne tries to be amiable. But in truth, she exhausts me. Of late, she has become so moody. Honestly, she's always sulking about something or another. I don't know what's wrong with her."

"It would do her good to get away," I said. "She should be around other unmarried people of her age. Vivienne must get lonesome without company. You have your husband. Uncle Simon has the mill. I expect your sister could use an interesting occupation which does not involve the running of a house."

Nanette rolled her eyes. There was no empathy. "It's not as though I haven't suggested she go away for a spell. I tried convincing her to visit Leeds. We have a mutual school friend living there. Kate is married to a doctor and doing rather well. But Vivienne always declines." Nanette glanced at me. "I think she's afraid she'll miss something if she goes anywhere."

I wondered what that meant. Miss what? Had she not just said it was uneventful here? I forced myself to engage in this mindless chit-chat. "Some people don't enjoy travelling." I looked at my cousin's pretty face. "Anyway, I am surprised you'd want her gone from here. I thought you quite depended on her when you are unwell?"

A frown appeared upon Nanette's pretty face. With a snub nose and dimpled cheek, she suddenly looked all of twelve. "You are right. My sister is good to me when I am indisposed. Nevertheless, she complains about having to help me, even then." Nanette took a sandwich. "But now you are here, Cousin, everything shall be more fun." She nibbled at her food like a rabbit. "In fact, let us plan the dinner we spoke of having last night." Her eyes lit up. "We can invite the Tiptons, Major Baldwin, and Father Lynch, of course."

"The priest?" I could not disguise my surprise. "Why invite him?"

"Oh, Claire. Father Lynch is practically family. He's been like an uncle to Vivienne and I. Frankly, I don't know how Papa would have manged after Mother died. Father Lynch helped him cope with her loss. Over the years he's been all but brother to poor Papa. Besides, it is a lonely life for a man of the cloth. He does not have the luxury of his own family. We always include him whenever there's anything special going on and he's always so grateful."

Father Lynch reminded me of a tall, skinny crow. He'd made an instant, negative impression upon me, which had only increased by my realising his role in Father's trial.

Nanette carried on chattering, "I shall send invitations out today. This coming Saturday will be perfect. I'll speak to Mrs Blitch about the menu and getting some help with the house. I am so excited we shall have company." Her apparent pleasure suddenly faded.

"Is something amiss?" I asked.

"It's Ivan. I do hope he'll be on his best behaviour. My husband tends to be surly whenever we have company. You must have noticed. You are family, and he's not been very friendly, even towards you."

I shrugged. "I cannot blame him for that. I'm a constant reminder of the worst thing that ever happened to him."

"Nonsense," Nanette said. "You could make the same argument about me, my sister, and my father. Not to mention living at Darkwater." She grew thoughtful. "Perhaps that's why he's always so cross." Her voice turned wistful. "Honestly, Claire. Ivan was so different before we married. He was witty, light-hearted, and enjoyable to be around. I delighted in his company."

"What happened to change him?"

Nanette set down her teacup. "I suppose I can confide in you as you're family." A blush spread across her pale face. "It is slightly indelicate to speak of. But due to my weak constitution, it has been advised I should not carry children. I was ignorant of this until after my wedding. Ivan is convinced I duped him into marrying me and intentionally withheld that information. He doesn't believe I was unaware of it before we wed."

I'd expected Nanette to give me some silly nonsensical reason and not divulge something quite so personal. I was somewhat taken aback.

"I am very sorry. That must be a difficult situation to navigate."

"You have no idea," Nanette said quietly. She looked at me with tearful eyes. "Ivan has kept to his own room for many months now. He barely speaks to me at the best of times. I sometimes fancy he wishes I would die, so he can marry another and have the family he so longs for."

Tears spilled down her lovely face as she spoke. I reached across the table to take her hand in mine, at a complete loss of what to say or do.

She looked at me with mournful eyes. "You see, Claire. I cannot divorce Ivan, because of my faith. It would take a special dispensation from the Pope if he would even grant it. It goes against the grain as a Catholic. I have spoken with Father Lynch at length, and he encourages me to make the best of my marriage. But there are times when I fear for my safety." She had become agitated.

"What on earth do you mean? Surely…"

Nanette gave a curt laugh. "It wouldn't be the first time a man has disposed of an unproductive wife. It would be easy enough. Just slip a potion into my drink or my food." She searched my face. "Now do you understand why I live on my nerves? Not only does my health fail me but my mind is tormented with worry."

The conversation had become disturbing. What started as a frivolous chat was now dark and sinister. Across the table from me, my cousin looked as vulnerable and defenceless as a tiny kitten. In turn, she was married to a man devastated and unhappy since a young age.

"You can't really think Ivan means you ill? Have you spoken to anyone besides Father Lynch about this?"

She nodded. "I did mention it once to Doctor Tipton. But he gave me such an odd look I've been loath to bring it up again." Nanette wiped her face and gave a feeble smile. "My goodness," she said flustered. "Look at me. Here I wanted to have a light-hearted luncheon with my cousin who I have not seen for many years, and instead I have turned it into a melodrama of the worst kind. You must forget my nonsense, Claire. Consider it the ramblings of a silly woman."

"Nanette, if you truly feel in any kind of danger, you must not dismiss your intuition." I was having difficulty absorbing her accusations regarding Ivan Delahunt. Yet what did I really know of the man? I pressed my point. "I am sure Ivan loves you dearly, Cousin. But again, I would caution you to speak about your concerns. Talk to your father."

"You are a dear to worry for me," she said sweetly. "I shall consider your advice."

With that, the subject was closed. Nanette retrieved a small notebook and commenced writing a list of potential dinner guests for the coming Saturday.

MY ROOM FELT UNWELCOME now my possessions had been destroyed and my privacy violated. Every time I thought about what happened, a new surge of rage flooded my senses. But it was impotent anger. There was no one to direct it upon, no way of feeling any satisfaction. The only way I could contain the scream of frustration threatening to burst from my lips was to promise myself I would exact my revenge.

Fortunately, I had made my own notes, and my book was still safe. I'd put it away in my bedside table when I hadn't been able to sleep. Getting it out, I glanced through my notes. Though not in my mother's eloquent words, I'd jotted down each significant point she'd written, mainly about the trial. I'd also added her notes about Barbara. So, all was not lost.

As far as the newspaper articles were concerned, I remembered the ones I'd looked at, and while they were still in my memory I wrote the names of them down in my book. Newspapers archived every edition. These could be found if Ivan or I thought it pertinent. Gosh, I'd included Ivan in that consideration.

Before the awful shock of the journals burning, I had been pleased with the outcome of our meeting. Though the relationship was tenuous, I liked the fact I wasn't the only person struggling with the past. Also, two heads were always better than one. With both of us pursuing the same goal, I'd felt a sense of hope. Until I'd come back to the room and seen the damage done.

Nanette's conversation about her marriage disturbed me. The fact she brought up Ivan's dissatisfaction at their situation, and her concerns he might want to be rid of her sounded far-fetched. I'd counselled her to share any fears with her father, mainly so I would not have to worry about her welfare. But though I knew Ivan very little, he did not strike me as someone who would kill his own wife. Yet it did explain a lot about his sullen moods and his melancholy disposition.

I finished writing my notes and thoughts down, including what Nanette had said. I set down my pen and reached for my reticule to empty it on the bed. Mother's first journal, the letter from America and my small gun. I lay my notebook next to it.

Where could I keep them all? It would be tedious carrying these items around. I must find a safe place to hide them. I glanced around the room. There were quite a few hidden compartments behind the panelled walls.

But if they were known to me they were known to many.

I stood up and walked around the room. I ran my hand over the headboard. I peeked behind my mirror. I explored the dressing table and nightstand for a hidden catch or drawer. All to no end.

I pulled the curtain back to go into the tiny bathroom. It consisted of a commode, a shallow tub, and a sink. There was a small cabinet above the sink, and in one corner a little armoire where the towels were kept. Back in the bedroom area, I looked around once more and then spotted the chair.

It was a small chair, in the design of a dining chair. The frame was carved wood and appeared quite old. The seat was a hard cushion, covered in woven tapestry fabric. I sat down. It was rickety. Getting up again, I knelt down on the floor and looked underneath the seat. Nowhere to hide anything there.

I tipped the chair, and the cushion slipped off. It wasn't attached to the chair but rested in a depression especially cut out to fit the seat. A grooved ledge kept the cushion in place. Between the bottom of the cushion, and the actual seat of the chair, it was hollow.

I tipped the chair upside down, and the cushion plopped out and to the ground. I set it back into an upright position, retrieved the two notebooks, the letter and my derringer, and spread them out in the hollow. I replaced the chair cushion, and voila, they were invisible to see.

I was rather pleased with myself. It was a canny spot. Whoever destroyed Mother's journals would think they found them all. They would have no need to search my room again. But if they did, I doubted they would discover my new hiding place.

I looked at the clock. It was barely past three o'clock in the afternoon. Ivan would still be at the mill, as would Uncle Simon.

I took myself downstairs, closing the door behind me. This would be a good time to get to know the servants better. Currently, everyone was a suspect in my mind.

In the kitchen, the cook, Mrs Blitch rolled out a large blanket of pastry, while Mellors stood at the sink peeling vegetables. Tibbetts sat at the far end of the table drinking a cup of tea.

"Miss Claire?" He spluttered the sip he'd just taken. Cook ceased rolling, and Mellors turned to see what was going on.

"Is it all right if I join you?" I asked. I fully respected I was in the servants' domain.

Tibbetts looked at Cook. I did the same. "Hello, Mrs Blitch. I don't believe we have met, but I've certainly been enjoying the delicious meals you've prepared. The apple pie last night melted in my mouth." I pointed at the table. "You have a delicate touch with your pastry."

Mrs Blitch, her grey hair tucked neatly under a white cap stared at me like I was on exhibit at the London Zoo. She blinked.

"Thou's got good taste in pastry then," she said, her voice as low in register as a man's. She pointed the rolling pin in my general direction. "Thou must be young lady from down south. Thou's a nurse just back from t'war?"

"Yes. That's me. I'm Claire Holloway. It is nice to meet you." Gosh, but she looked fearsome. Low browed, broad of face and thin lips. I shouldn't want to be on her bad side.

Suddenly she smiled, but still looked frightfully scary.

"Sit thyself down at table. Tibbetts there can fetch a cup o' tea. Any woman that's nursed a soldier is always welcome at 'table."

I pulled out a chair next to Tibbetts, who was doing as he was told and pouring me out a cup of strong dark tea. He put a dollop of milk in it and a spoon of sugar, then passed it over. I took a sip.

"Oh, that's more like it," I said. "They only drink the fancy stuff upstairs with a slice of lemon in it, but this is much better."

Cook commenced rolling her pastry. "Strong tea'll put lead in yer pencil, my Harry always said. He were soldier in't army, he were. Got a leg shot off, but they saved him. I don't hold much with doctoring, but they saved my Harry, so they did."

"I'm glad to hear it," I said, unsure of the correct response.

"Aye. He come home wi' one leg, and still managed t'run off wi' butcher's wife."

I wasn't sure whether to gasp with shock, or roar with laughter the way she said it.

"Well," I said grimly. "I'll wager he's missing that apple pie."

HALF AN HOUR, TWO CUPS OF tea, and one fresh scone right out of the oven later, I made my way upstairs. My foray into the kitchen had taken Cook, Tibbetts, and Mellors off my suspect list of burning Mother's journals. Mellors hadn't said much, but she didn't look very sharp.

Then who else could have done such a despicable deed? If I ruled out myself and Ivan, my uncle too, for he had been at the mill, that did not leave a very long list of suspects. Only Vivienne and Nanette, or someone who had come in from outside. Gibbons perhaps? He had seen me walk off, but then there might have been others working in the cowshed watching me.

To what end, though? The person in my room had not been a thief. I had little of value, and all I owned was still in my room where I'd left it, I had checked.

None of the workers would have an interest in the journals. But they could do it at another's bidding. Someone was threatened by what Mother had written down.

And what about the figure I had seen earlier that morning, sneaking around outside. Was that connected? I would feel better once I had another chance to speak to Ivan about what happened. Hopefully it would not be too long before he returned.

Chapter Thirteen

DINNER WAS DISAPPOINTING.

Ivan had not returned from the mill but been detained due to an important piece of equipment breaking down. Vivienne stayed in her room complaining of a headache which left Uncle Simon, Nanette, and me.

Having already spent lunch with my cousin, I remained somewhat quiet throughout our meal. Both relatives had no difficulty making conversation. The main topic being that of the forthcoming dinner, planned for Saturday evening.

Nanette read out a list of the invitees to her father. Other than the Tipton family, I had little interest in the other guests. That Father Lynch would attend brought no pleasure. Yet it would be another opportunity to study the man and form a solid opinion.

I did not bring up the subject of my mother's diaries as I had the night before. I couldn't help noticing neither did Uncle Simon. Ivan was right. My uncle would want things left alone.

Our meal passed quickly. And after a sherry in the drawing room, I pled feeling tired and turned in early.

****

Thank goodness the nightmare stayed away, and I awoke feeling refreshed and rested, until I recollected what happened to Mother's journals the day before.

I dressed quickly, anxious to catch Ivan at breakfast. I wanted another chance to speak with him and decide a course of action. Who had burned the books? There had to be a connection to them and the past which only served to fuel my desire to start digging.

But then I remembered Uncle Simon planned to wait for me this morning. We had a ten o'clock appointment with the Parslows' solicitor to go over the transfer of Mother's stock into my name.

My uncle was the only one at the table when I arrived downstairs and was engrossed in the newspaper.

"Good morning, Uncle," I said, selecting a place to sit. "I hope I haven't kept you waiting?"

Uncle Simon set down his paper. "Absolutely not, my dear. There's no hurry at all. I was just finishing up breakfast myself."

I poured a cup of tea, wishing it tasted more like the tea down in the kitchen. I helped myself to a poached egg from a tureen in the centre of the table and buttered a slice of toast.

"Did Ivan resolve the problem at the mill last night?" I asked and took a bite of my food.

"No. According to Tibbetts, he left very early to meet an engineer coming in from Leeds. With a bit of luck, they'll get it sorted out." His bright eyes settled on me. "Today's a big day for you, Claire. You will soon be a shareholder of Parslow Mill. What do you think about that?"

"If I'm perfectly honest, Uncle, I have not had a moment to consider it. Since I arrived it seems every day has been so full I've barely had a moment to myself. I will be pleased to get a better understanding of my situation, financially. I am an unemployed person used to an income. It is strange not having wages at my disposal anymore."

"My dear girl." Uncle Simon's tone was full of concern. "Are you telling me you are penniless? If you have no access to funds, Claire, you only have to say. Goodness, I should have given that more thought. Please forgive me if you have suffered any hardships."

"I did not mean to infer anything of the sort." I hastened to correct his suspicions. "I referred more to my future. Not knowing my real situation, I've been loath to make any decisions, at least for the time being."

"A perfectly sensible outlook, Claire. But please bear in mind that as the head of our collective family, I wish to provide and take care of you. Do not hesitate to mention should you need anything." He gave me a reassuring smile. And again, I had the uncomfortable feeling I'd experienced once or twice with him already. It was not so much what he said, more in how he said it. A familiarity laced his words as though he addressed me as equal to him in rank and age, not as my elder.

He took a sip from his teacup and dabbed his mouth with a serviette. "Right. If you'll excuse me, I've something to attend to upstairs. I'll rejoin you down here in about half an hour. I'll have Gibbons bring round the carriage."

"Of course," I replied, grateful to be left alone.

****

We set off for Skipton with Gibbons at the reins of the trap. The cab was chilly, and both of us were glad of the rugs we used to stay warm.

The weather was a promise of what would come in winter. The biting wind stirred up clouds, thick as lace.

Where there were trees, fallen leaves scattered on the ground like autumnal confetti. Thank goodness it wasn't raining as well.

Uncle Simon was most conversational on our journey. He seemed quite enthusiastic having an audience. He talked a great deal about my grandfather, Arthur, and the legacy he left behind.

"One man's passion went from an idea to the reality that is not only the family mill, but one of the largest employers this side of Leeds. No small feat, wouldn't you agree?"

"Indeed. I can't imagine building a company from nothing to a successful venture. My grandfather must have been an exceptional man. I have few memories, but I learned much about him from Mother. I think both his daughters idolised him. Mother often talked about her time working at the mill. Was it considered unusual for a young woman to work in the family business back then?"

"It most certainly was. Many of the men were resentful of a woman telling them what to do. It put poor Arthur in quite a quandary. But ultimately I suppose he decided the wrath of a daughter far outweighed that of his workforce, and dear Jane won the day."

I smiled at the thought of her bossing people about. "Mother was very intelligent. It surprised me she had so little to do with the family business once we moved away. I think she always missed utilising her mind the way she had done living in Yorkshire. I often wanted to ask, but never did."

Uncle Simon gave a long sigh. "To be truthful there was never a discussion about her discontinued association with the mill. The reason seemed obvious to me. It was all about your father. Jane couldn't think about the mill without your father being in that same thought. I think she needed to separate completely from the past because living with those reminders was unbearable. She and your father were very much in love."

"I suppose that makes sense," I said, though on some levels it really didn't. I would have thought Mother more interested in staying connected to Papa. "I understand her desire to be physically living elsewhere, away from the gossips and tattlers. But she had such a great mind, and she needed an occupation, one to keep her busy all the time." Yet as the words left my mouth, I answered my own query. Mother had kept herself busy by obsessing about Papa's conviction and subsequent death. Judging by her journals, she was always working on theories to prove his innocence.

"Well today we are not living in the past, dear Claire, but stepping into the future. After we've met with Satterthwaite, you'll have a lot to consider."

Uncle Simon smiled at me affectionately. His eyes settled on mine, and the smile broadened. I glanced away first. I recognised something in his look. It was not that of a kindly family member. It was that of a suitor.

We arrived at the offices of Satterthwaite, Chandler & Humphries, Ltd. One in a row of conjoined terraced buildings, housing business establishments. Relieved to escape the confines of the carriage, I followed Uncle Simon up several steps to a large double door painted shiny black. Next to the copperplate bearing the names and distinguishing titles of the solicitors who habituated the building was a bellpull.

Uncle Simon rang the bell, and it was promptly opened by a very thin, young man, dressed in a dark suit. The name Uriah Heap leapt into my head at the sight of him, for he looked as though he'd stepped out of a Dickensian story.

We were led up one flight of stairs and into a grand office, where a gentleman got up and came around his desk to greet us.

"Simon," he said in a welcoming tone as he shook my uncle's hand. "Come in, come in. And here is young Mrs Holloway. Goodness me, after all this time. My, my."

He gestured for us to each take a seat by his desk and returned to his own. I studied him curiously.

Mr Satterthwaite was not a large man, shorter than me in fact. He was small of build, except for his stomach, a large paunch which protruded enough to make it appear he might fall forward. He did not look like a man of law but had the face of a friendly tavern-keeper. With thick, wavy grey hair, matching moustaches, and twinkling blue eyes, Mr Satterthwaite was rather jolly. I liked him on sight.

"Mrs Holloway, or may I call you Claire?" Before I could answer, he went on. "It has been so long since I saw you. My, my. You could not have been more than five or six years old. And now, look at you, all grown up and a lady." He stared at me. "That is a most interesting way of styling one's hair. I expect it is rather modern."

"Ernest," interjected my uncle. "The business at hand?"

"Indeed," the solicitor stammered. "Now, where

are those papers?" He ferreted through assorted piles of documents on his desk giving the appearance of someone rather scatter-brained, yet I knew it could not be so for a man whose name came first in the company. Besides, Parslow's would not do business with anyone incompetent.

"Ah, here we are." He grinned with a display of perfect, even teeth. "Before we get started, would either of you care for any refreshment?"

"No, thank you, Ernest," replied Uncle Simon.

I also declined the offer.

Mr Satterthwaite opened a folder. "Claire, your uncle is aware of what I shall impart to you, because after the death of your grandparents, and your Aunt Charlotte, the terms of the trust set up by Arthur Parslow, your grandfather, were put into place." He gave me another smile.

"Arthur Parslow had no sons. Although both his daughters married, and both spouses were given positions within the company, Arthur stipulated the mill ownership would remain within the blood relatives of his family."

I knew this part because Mother had told me. In a world dominated by men, she had been proud her father had not discriminated against her sex.

"Therefore," continued the lawyer. "When your grandmother died, Parslow Mill was divided between your mother, Jane, and her sister, Charlotte. But not in equal amounts."

That caught my attention. This was news to me.

"As the elder child, your mother received a majority of fifty-two percent of the mill and your aunt, forty-eight. Unusual, to say the least, but I daresay

Arthur had his reasons. One can speculate your mother's interest in the mill from an early age may have influenced Arthur's decision, and I should add it caused no ill-will between the sisters. Charlotte had no interest in the business, naming your uncle, Simon Manning as her representative."

I looked at my uncle. His face was impassive. I addressed the solicitor.

"If I comprehend your meaning, you are saying Mother held the controlling shares of the mill?"

The kindly face smiled in assent. "Indeed. However, those shares have now transferred, or will be shortly, to you, Claire. You will be the larger shareholder of the mill."

It was odd, but I hadn't given much thought to my owning anything. Obviously I considered my connection to the family business, from a financial point of view, how could I not? I imagined some sort of annuity, as Mother had received, which would be passed on to me and provide an undisclosed income. But ownership, controlling ownership?

"Claire, you look flushed. Are you feeling unwell?" Uncle Simon studied me intently.

"I am fine, thank you. But I shouldn't mind a glass of water?"

Mr Satterthwaite picked up a small brass bell and shook it. Within moments, his willowy assistant reappeared.

"Bertram, fetch a glass of cold water for the lady, if you please." The solicitor turned his attention to me. "I take it from your reaction you were unaware of your mother's position with the mill?"

"Completely unaware," I said quietly.

The young man came back into the room carrying a small tray bearing a glass of water. I thanked him. I took several sips, and the cool water revived me instantly. Then I placed it back on the tray. The assistant left the room.

"Shall I continue?" asked Mr Satterthwaite.

I nodded assent.

"When your mother, Jane Shaw, inherited her majority, she chose your father to be her legal trustee. At his passing, she selected Simon Manning, your uncle to take on that role. When your aunt Charlotte Manning died, Simon became the living trustee for both your mother and your cousins, Nanette and Vivienne. It is you three ladies, the grandchildren of Arthur Parslow, who own Parslow Mill in its entirety."

I was stupefied. Truly, with everything on my mind these past weeks, this was all news to me. How ridiculous I had not considered any of this. I felt rather stupid.

"I see this comes as a shock." Uncle Simon addressed me, his face wrought with concern. "But dearest Claire, do not be overwhelmed by the news. It is something to celebrate. For you no longer need to worry about your future. You will be well taken care of, as are your cousins, and I shall continue to work hard in your stead and keep Parslow Mill as successful as it is today."

I looked at my uncle. It was quite the speech. I studied his face, noting the kindly smile, in direct contrast to his posture, which seemed tense. And in that single moment my mind suddenly cleared, and I realised something surprising.

Uncle Simon was worried. It was there in his eyes,

in the tautness of his face. I could guess why. His autonomous position in the company had never changed, nor been challenged. For twenty years he was, essentially, my grandfather's successor, running a business for the women who owned it, without anyone telling him what to do. But like the cold wind blowing autumn into winter, change was in the air, in the guise of me. His niece, an unknown entity who had stepped into the picture. I wondered what he truly thought about that.

"Let us continue." Mr Satterthwaite's voice penetrated my thoughts. "Here are several documents for you to sign." He passed them to my side of the desk. He explained each to me, and I duly signed. There were many. At length we came to the last paper.

"This pertains to the continuation of Simon Manning acting in your stead as trustee. He will continue in the role assigned by your mother, Jane Shaw, to act on your behalf for all business decisions regarding Parslow Mill." He placed the document before me, and I scanned the words quickly. Then I looked up at the solicitor.

"What happens if I do not sign?"

I heard my uncle's quiet intake of breath.

Mr Satterthwaite was slightly taken aback. "My, my. Well, nothing actually happens, other than Simon must discuss all Parslow business matters with you. As the controlling partner, your decision will overrule any he has made on behalf of his daughters' interests."

I set the pen down and turned to Uncle Simon. "If you don't mind," I said, "I should like to reflect upon things before I sign."

Though he tried to hide it, he was greatly put out.

"Whatever you wish, Claire."

"Please do not think I am being disrespectful, Uncle. But I should prefer being totally appraised of my position before making this choice. Mr Satterthwaite?"

"Yes."

"Will you make an appointment for me to return. I would like to consult you on a couple of items before I proceed further. Is that possible?"

The solicitor already had a diary open. "Why certainly," he said agreeably. "Let us say, Tuesday of next week, at ten o'clock?"

"Thank you, that will be fine." I got to my feet, noticing both men looking rather bewildered.

"It was a pleasure to meet you Mr Satterthwaite," I said, as the kind fellow rounded his desk to shake my hand.

With that, I walked to the door, my head held high.

UNCLE SIMON CLIMBED INTO the trap where I waited. He had remained with the solicitor for a few minutes after my exit. One look at his face told me all I needed to know.

He was livid.

His colour was up, his eyes like a raging storm.

I waited. How would he behave towards me? Would he berate me for my refusal to sign the papers?

At times, it amused me the way men overlooked women and their intelligence. Relegated to subservient and sometime submissive roles, we were often abused by men. Especially men in power, who automatically assumed things should always go in their favour. For a female to question their authority, in some cases their tyranny, was tantamount to treason.

Behind my passive expression I watched my uncle struggle to find his composure, lest he give away his true feelings. We had traversed for a few minutes before he finally spoke.

"Now you have had a moment to absorb some of the details, Claire, how do you feel about your situation? You seemed rather surprised by the revelations from Mr Satterthwaite." His mouth was tight, but he forced a weak smile.

"It was a lot of information given in a short space of time, Uncle," It was best to placate him. Pride in a man was everything after all. "I thought it wise to think on things," I glanced up at him and softened my voice. "You are not offended by my not signing the trustee paperwork, I hope?"

"No," he stammered, his face flushing slightly. "Of course not. Why should I be?" He feigned surprise at my question.

"Excellent," I said cooly. "For it is no reflection of my good opinion of you. I just prefer to study the document's wording when I have more time than in the solicitor's office." It was my turn to be fraudulent. "Blame it on the Parslow blood," I said light-heartedly, almost surprising myself with my attitude.

What was wrong with me? Why was I acting boldly? But I knew the answer to that. Control. For so long, my life, my destiny, everything had been out of my own control. Losing George, Sarah and my mother, my world had come crashing about me and I had lost my way. Yet in the space of one meeting, it had been handed back to me. I was in charge of my destiny once more.

"My dear Claire," Uncle Simon said. "I applaud

your interest in the legal affairs of the mill and its direct effect on your situation." He was mellowing towards me, and I realised his change of tactics. "I've no doubt once you have had time to examine the paperwork and the accounts of the mill you will be quite content to let me continue as I have these past two decades. I am family. You have the reins of the business in trusted hands. In time you will see everything works well status quo. As a young woman, there are many other interests far more desirable of your time than a cotton mill." He gave a little chuckle to emphasise the point.

I smiled as though agreeing with his statement. Yet the destruction of Mother's journals, the meeting with Ernest Satterthwaite, and Uncle Simon's recent over familiarity towards me had sharpened my instincts. My guard was up and fully in place.

Although they thought differently, the Mannings knew nothing about me. I quietly studied my uncle as Gibbons drove us to the mill. If my uncle took me for a fool, then he was greatly mistaken.

I was after all, my mother's daughter.

Chapter Fourteen

AFTER RETURNING TO THE MILL, I shared a pot of tea with Mary Buxton, while Uncle Simon went to work. At length, and after a nice chat, I set down my cup and got to my feet.

"Thank you for that, Mary," I said. "It was most refreshing. Now I think I shall find Mr Delahunt. I need a word with him before I leave."

Mary directed me to his office situated near the staircase at the end of the hall. I planned to stop by, but if he was busy, especially after working so late the previous evening, I would not trouble him. I wanted to continue our conversation from the day before.

The office door was wide open, and I peeked inside, but he wasn't there. Hardly surprising. Ivan didn't seem the type to sit behind a desk all day. I passed his room and started down the stairs. As I neared the next floor down, warm, damp air filled my nostrils, and the sound of busy machinery ricocheted against the walls and the ceiling.

Time fell away, and I remembered my hand in Papa's as he walked me down these very steps. I was tempted to venture away from the stairs and look around but decided against it.

The last thing these workers needed was me distracting them and I shouldn't want to get in their way. I would come another day and have one of the supervisors take me on a tour.

As I reached the bottom of the stairs, I met Ivan coming up.

"Hello, Claire. I didn't expect to see you here."

"I've been with Uncle Simon. I was about to return to Darkwater."

In the light of day, the man looked exhausted, and no wonder, for he had been awake most of the night.

"You look done in," I said. "Are you going to stay the rest of the day?"

"No. Everything is working now. I've just seen the engineer off on the train, and I spotted Gibbons waiting here. Perhaps I'll join you and go home. I could use the rest."

I went back up the stairs with Ivan, but stayed out of sight while he let Mary Buxton know he was leaving for the day.

GIBBONS, WAITING WITH THE trap, was surprised to see Ivan with me, but said nothing as we got into the conveyance to go back to Darkwater.

It felt colder after the warmth of the mill, and I pulled the rug across my lap. I told Ivan I wanted to look around the mill but thought it better to wait until I had an escort.

"That was wise, Claire. There's a lot happening on each floor. Some of the equipment is quite dangerous and accidents happen so easily. Perhaps I can show you around the next time you are in Skipton when I've had more sleep."

"Thank you. I should like that."

"You are quite intrigued with the workings at Parslow's. Where did this interest arise from? Is it a sentimental curiosity based upon your childhood?" One eyebrow rose in question.

I hesitated, then decided to be honest. I'd already confided some personal thoughts when I'd shared the journal with him. He was an unlikely ally, but the only one I had.

"That enters into it, naturally. But if you must know, my interest stems from a business perspective."

That got his attention. He sat up a little straighter and some of the weariness dissipated.

"Go on," he said.

"This morning Uncle Simon and I met with Mr Satterthwaite."

"Ah, the solicitors."

"Indeed. Tell me, Ivan. Are you aware of how the mill ownership is distributed?"

He shrugged. "I assumed it was left to your mother and her sister, and then passed onto their legitimate offspring, namely you and your cousins. In fact, Simon said as much. But he's been trustee for his daughters and your mother once she moved away."

"You are correct, well mostly. Except the mill was not divided evenly between Jane and Charlotte. My grandfather recognised Mother's interest in the business, while Aunt Charlotte had none whatsoever. Therefore, he gave the eldest daughter, Jane, the majority."

Ivan was incredulous. "What?"

"Mother owned fifty-two percent of the mill, which has now passed to me."

Ivan stared, still taken aback. I watched him compose himself. "I am surprised to hear this. Yet it makes sense. I've heard stories from the past regarding your father,"

Ivan's discomfort at Papa's mention was obvious. His poor opinion of him rankled, especially now Papa's role in Keith Delahunt's murder was in serious doubt.

"In fact," he continued. "I remember snippets of conversation Father shared regarding Arthur Parslow's soft spot for your father. His business acumen and ideas aligned with Arthur's more than your uncle's did. The fact Jane spent time working at the mill meant she'd understood her father's vision. It seems logical Arthur would pass the real power to the two people he trusted the most."

"Until Papa died," I said. Impulsively I made my appeal. "Ivan, your discomfort at the mention of my father is complicating things. I understand you have had years to hate him, but how shall we make any progress discovering the truth of the past unless you stop being surly whenever I say his name."

His jaw became rigid, his eyes steely. "I'm sorry. But once I feel something strongly, I cannot change my opinion so easily."

I believed that. Though I knew little of this man, he exuded a strength of character which would make him a devoted ally or a feared enemy.

"I can respect your feelings. But to move forward we must pretend we are ignorant of all facts regarding our fathers. We have to come at this as though we stepped into someone else's story. Otherwise we're biased, and what we think we know will overrule our capacity to find the truth."

"I shall try," was all he could promise.

It was good enough for the time being. I picked up the thread of my conversation.

"During my meeting with Mr Satterthwaite, I had many papers to sign regarding the transfer of ownership from Mother to myself. One of the documents referenced Uncle Simon's position as trustee for my shares in the mill, and my agreement for him to continue in that role." I changed tack slightly. "Do you think Simon Manning a fair and worthy manager? Is he liked and respected by the mill workers? I know the question is broad, but being gone for so long, I have no way to gauge anything."

Ivan looked puzzled. His brows knotted and his head tilted slightly as he tried to read between the lines.

"That's a loaded question. How am I to answer honestly? I am essentially Simon's right hand at the mill. If I speak to the negative, it could be construed as my desire to oust him and steal his role as general manager. It I tell you he is the God of cotton, then I would be lying."

"Let me rephrase it then. Has my uncle used his position as trustee to further the development of the mill for the benefit of not only the shareholders, but for the employees as well? Have Parslow's products continued to improve over time? Is our mill considered a good place to work? Does business grow at the expected pace our competitors have grown?"

Ivan grinned. "And here I thought you a nurse. Good grief, Claire. There's no mistaking you've Arthur's blood in your veins." His eyes shone with what I took for admiration, and I was surprised at its impact upon me. Why this man's approval should matter, I knew not. But I was pleased to have it, nonetheless.

"You haven't answered my last questions," I

reminded him.

The grin slid away and his eyes darkened. "All right, I'll give you my honest thoughts because you posed very good questions. Simon is a decent manager. But he lacks vision and runs away from risk. The mill operates exactly as it did ten years ago, which means we do not keep up with our competitors. In the current market, it does us no harm, though we make less profit. But if the industry has a downturn, or when the price of raw cotton escalates, which it will, then I think Parslow's could be in trouble. In addition, there have been many changes in labour laws regarding the ages of children working in the mill. As you saw at dinner the other night, the subject is a point of contention between us as our opinions differ greatly." He fastened his eyes on my face. "There, does that answer you?"

I nodded. "Yes, thank you. When you spoke with me the other day, you hinted as much. It influenced me today when I had decisions to make."

"Decisions?"

I took a deep breath. "I refused to sign the trustee papers giving Uncle Simon the right to act upon my behalf at the mill."

"What?" He almost shouted.

I started in surprise. Ivan Delahunt looked amazed and full of wonderment. He was as excited as a child on Christmas morning.

Laughing, I said, "Calm yourself."

But he wasn't listening. His mind worked furiously. He reached over and grabbed my gloved hands with his, staring intently at my face, eyes bright with energy.

"Forgive my enthusiastic reaction, but Claire, this

is the turning point we have needed, don't you see? With one person at the helm, the mill's been falling behind. With more vision, modern ideas, we can get Parslow's running the way it should be." His declaration was earnest.

He searched my face for a response then glanced down at his hands, still cradling mine. He let go as though they might bite him.

"Forgive me," he mumbled apologetically. "I got carried away in the moment." He leaned back against the seat. "This is such good news. I cannot emphasise it enough. There is much to be done to make improvements, and I do hope you will consider discussing some of those issues with me."

"Absolutely," I said firmly. "Look, I believe Uncle Simon has tremendous loyalty for Parslow's, but you have the vision he lacks. You have my ear—I have the majority. And though I cannot say I shall agree with all your ideas, I will give them more consideration than my uncle has. Therefore, I propose a deal, Mr Delahunt. I shall retain control of the mill for the foreseeable future, but in return, you'll help me discover the real killer of your father."

The excitement in his eyes faded instantly. "I have already agreed to do that."

"Not as passionately as you agree to take away Simon Manning's autonomous role at the mill."

He gave a curt laugh. "My God, you are relentless, Mrs Holloway," he said. "But I applaud your cunning and intelligence."

"Then we shall rub along well," I said with a smile. "Now. If I may, can we talk about the loss of Mother's books?"

I recounted my time with the servants, and my concerns how few suspects there were. "I cannot fathom why Vivienne or Nanette would ever do such a despicable thing, and other than Gibbons, who else could it be?"

"Someone could have got into the house unseen," Ivan said. "They could cross the bridge unnoticed while everyone else was gone. At that time of day, Vivienne was probably in her room, and I know for a fact my wife would still have been abed." His voice tightened when he said the word 'wife'.

I let out a breath of frustration. "But why such a malicious act? Was it because the items were cherished by me? Or could it be the actions of someone threatened by the contents of the books?"

Ivan instantly responded. "The latter, I think. You haven't been at Darkwater long enough to anger anyone. The journals were perfectly safe until you mentioned them to the family."

"Then you suspect my cousins and my uncle?"

"Who else, at this point? No one knew they existed, other than the servants if they overheard us talking, and according to your earlier comment, you don't suspect them. So, that leaves the family, or someone acting on their instructions. Do not complicate your suspicions, Claire. Deal only with the facts."

Ivan was right. Yet imagining one of my relatives doing something so atrocious bridled and opened many questions about their motives.

"All right," I said. "Let's go with your theory. You and I were together at Rosell's Cottage, so we are ruled out—unless you instructed someone else to destroy the books. This I doubt, because it is in your best interests to have the information, as it is mine. Uncle Simon had gone to the mill, although someone could have acted on his behalf—possibly Gibbons, as he has the easiest access to the house. If Nanette or Vivienne were the culprits, it would have been an act of spite and nothing to do with the contents of Mother's journals. All that happened when they were children."

Ivan listened. "Your points are valid. But I think your theory of spite is incorrect. Your cousins carry a great deal of affection for your mother. If their grievance was with you, it would be more likely they would destroy something owned by you, or made by you, for that would make it personal." He paused. "Although it is extremely difficult for me to alter my thoughts after these many years, it does appear something happened regarding my father's death which has been concealed for two decades. Whoever knows that secret, does not want anyone else to find out. That would be because it could implicate them, or someone important to them."

"But what does it all mean?" I asked. "I'm terribly confused. Why would anyone want to hurt your father or implicate mine?"

Ivan shrugged. "Your guess is as good as mine. Usually, heinous deeds are carried out for common reasons—money, power, fear, hate, or love. You only need to look at history to understand that. Yet it's where we must start. For if we learn about the people in our parent's circle of friends and acquaintances back then, perhaps we can put the puzzle together."

"You are right," I agreed. "Instead of focusing on the actual crime committed we should concentrate on events that took place prior to that night." My mind raced. "Would you be able to research the events at the mill back then? If I can dig into my family's past, and you can look into the mill's activity, perhaps there's some sort of correlation between the two."

"It's a sound plan," he said. "We must start somewhere. I shall go into Skipton early in the morning before Miss Buxton arrives and take a look through some of our records."

"And I'll speak to Tibbetts and see what he remembers, although he was quite young back then. And of course, I must talk to Uncle Simon, he might know something."

Ivan frowned. "Be careful there. Just remember that although you are his niece, you are still a stranger. He will be alert and wonder at your curiosity."

"True. But as of today, I'm also his partner in business. I have every right to question anything pertinent to the family and the mill."

"Claire," Ivan sounded concerned. "I say again, be cautious. If your mother is correct, then someone connected to a terrible lie could still be among us and is likely dangerous."

I laughed. "I doubt very seriously my uncle would want to harm me. As a matter of fact, if anything, he's been overly affectionate since I arrived at Darkwater. I don't think he harbours any ill feeling for me whatsoever."

Ivan must have seen something in my face.

"What do you mean by overly affectionate?" His expression showed great distaste.

"Oh, I don't know. He's just been a little too familiar with me as a relation. I feel ill at ease when he looks at me." I recovered myself. I had no business sharing this with Ivan. I gave a weak laugh. "But then I may be reading more into it. I'm at sixes and sevens most of the time. No. I'm sure I imagined it."

Ivan stared at me. "If there is one thing I have learned about you in our short acquaintance, Claire, you don't fall prone to fits of fancy. If you say Simon has made you uncomfortable, there is a reason you feel that. Trust your instincts. After what happened today, surely you realise you pose a threat to Simon's solitary rule over Parslow's. With the controlling shares in your hands, he is no longer the one in power. Unless you sign those papers, you have put him in a very querulous position. Though Simon is a good man, he is still just that…a man. One used to commanding the women in his life, not taking instruction."

The horses picked up pace. We were nearing Darkwater Abbey and the time for conversation was at an end.

I crossed the moat, walking behind Ivan, and almost forgot my discomfort being so close to the deep, murky water. My mind regurgitated Ivan's warning and deep in my belly, a seed of doubt was planted.

I did not know if I could trust my own uncle.

And more disturbing, I was prepared to heed the advice of a man I knew little about. A man with great reason to resent me.

****

I spent the remainder of the afternoon up in my room. My mind worked furiously as I read through the only remaining journal once again and made more notes.

I did not want to dwell on Ivan's comments about my uncle. Yet how could I not? I replayed the scenes where he had made me uncomfortable, re-examined what I could remember of his expression.

At the time I wondered why he was being so friendly; it was rather odd. Uncle Simon might be lonely as he grew older, but there were likely many suitable women in his age group living locally who would welcome his attentions.

I was no fool. After what I learned today I now owned half a mill. But the extent of the monetary value was still unclear. I would meet again with Mr Satterthwaite the following week, and he would go over the accounts with me.

Growing up, we'd lived comfortably but not extravagantly, therefore I assumed the income would be minimal. I would not be rich. Running a mill was costly, with the profits divided between myself and cousins, I would be grateful for whatever I got.

That my having a majority rankled Uncle Simon was no surprise. After all, I was a mere female, and most men considered us inferior, regardless of our intellect. So why had he been so friendly to me? Probably because he wished to maintain his current status at the mill and have the final say on everything. He knew about Mother's shares, obviously.

And what about my mother? A woman who had been respected by all who knew her. Jane Shaw had a presence at Parslow Mill which precipitated her marriage to my papa. It was hard to rationalise her continued separation from Arthur Parslow's legacy based solely on her husband's death.

I could understand her distancing herself physically. But Mother had a sharp mind. It was strange she did not associate herself with the business, even from afar. She had walked away from it all, leaving it in Uncle Simon's capable hands and never looked back.

I leaned against the pillows, pulled up my legs and hugged my knees. The status quo of the Mannings had taken a sudden turn at my inheritance. After two decades of everything being the same, I represented a huge interruption to their normal world.

If the destruction of Mother's journals was anything to go by, I was extremely unwelcome.

My arrival at Darkwater Abbey had made someone very unhappy.

But who?

Chapter Fifteen

DINNER THAT EVENING WAS odd—the dynamics strangely swapped around. Tonight, it was my uncle who was out of sorts with everyone, except whenever he spoke to me.

Ivan had a smile on his face whenever I glanced his way. He even seemed tolerant to his wife as she chattered incessantly about our upcoming dinner guests coming the next evening.

"Oh Nanette," Vivienne said curtly, helping herself to a spoonful of trifle from a large crystal bowl. "Can you please stop blathering on about tomorrow? One would think we've never had anyone here for dinner before, and it's only the same boring people we always see."

"Vivienne, is that necessary?" Uncle Simon said harshly. "Must you be so unkind to your sister when she's making an effort to be social? At least she tries, which is more than I can say for you."

His daughter flinched, and in that moment, I felt sorry for her. Uncle Simon had humiliated her in front of us, and that had been unkind.

"The world would be a boring place if we were all the same," I said. "Some people enjoy being very social and others not so much, me included. I remember Nanette having tea parties with her dolls whilst Vivienne and I were off running about in the fields."

My attempt to diffuse the situation fell upon deaf ears.

"Father is right," said Nanette to her sister. "It wouldn't hurt you to help with the preparations. You know how easily I tire. I wrote all the invitations myself and consulted with Mrs Blitch about the menu."

"My dear, you have outdone yourself," remarked Ivan.

Was I the only person noting the sarcasm in his tone? I looked around, waiting for a response. None came. No one took offence.

Vivenne's eyes shot darts at her pretty sister across the table. "I am no stranger to work, Nanette, as well you know. I spend a great deal of time taking care of many things at Darkwater, which includes tending to you when you are ill."

I swallowed a mouthful of trifle. My cousins both had their claws out and it might be better to stay out of it. I felt Ivan's eyes on me and met his stare. He looked amused with the interchange, sitting back in his chair, quite relaxed. How different he appeared in so short a time. Tonight, he was not the troubled soul I had taken him for, but a cat who had just finished a huge bowl of cream.

Uncle Simon poured himself another glass of wine. His face was flushed, his blue eyes bright as stars. I contemplated my role in his change in demeanour. Obviously my refusal to sign the trustee paperwork still rankled.

Why so much? Pride, I supposed. Because in every other way his situation would remain unchanged. Simon Manning would still be in charge, just not free to do his will. I would have to agree with all the decisions going forward.

"Well don't complain to me about the seating arrangements like you did at our last soiree, Vivienne." Nanette continued to lambast her sister. "If you had the slightest interest in helping, you could have chosen where you wanted to sit."

"You haven't put me with the girls, have you?"

I assumed she referred to the Misses Tiptons.

Nanette chuckled wryly. "Oh, does that not suit? Would you rather sit between Martin Tipton and Jeremy Rotherham?"

Vivienne glowered at her sister, then looked over at Ivan blushing furiously while he seemed unaware of her attention.

"Enough." Uncle Simon slammed his hand down on the table and his plate and cutlery rattled. "After a long day at work, the last thing a man wants is to listen to women squabbling about a blasted dinner party." With that, he got to his feet and scooped up his wine glass, which I noticed was full again.

"I'm turning in for the evening." He smiled in my direction. "Good night, Claire. Please excuse me, but I am weary and should like some rest." He addressed his daughters. "If you two insist on continuing your ridiculous quarrel, I beg you do it quietly."

He walked out of the dining room having not spoken to his son-in-law at all.

"Well," said Nanette indignantly. "I wonder what has upset Papa. He's very out of sorts."

Ivan chuckled. "It's probably something he ate." His eyes found mine and I saw the glint of mischief there. Ivan Delahunt was thoroughly enjoying himself, and I did not blame him. But when I caught Vivienne looking from Ivan and then over to me, my amusement faded. Much to my surprise, she looked as though she might burst into tears.

Nanette rose. “Shall we go into the drawing room?”

The four of us made our way into the comfortable room where a fire blazed in the hearth. Tibbetts was right behind us with a small tray bearing four sherry glasses.

I settled in one of the armchairs. My cousins sat on the settee at opposing ends, while Ivan stood in front of the gigantic hearth, staring into the flames.

“You haven’t said how your meeting went today, Claire,” Nanette said. “I trust everything is in order?”

“I believe so. Mr Satterthwaite was cordial and patient. I’m to meet with him again on Tuesday to get additional details before I can make any decisions about the future.”

“Then you are staying a while, I suppose?” Vivienne asked. Her eyes, so like her father’s settled on my face and she could not hide her displeasure. Why did she dislike me? Not that my cousin was predisposed to be friendly; she had few friends. Yet she seemed particularly affronted by my being at Darkwater Abbey. In that moment I decided if anyone had wanted to burn the journals out of spite, Vivienne was the best candidate.

She was beginning to irritate me. “I am unsure what my plans are, Cousin. Until I know my financial status, I can’t go anywhere.” I raised a brow. “Some of us are not fortunate to have our room and board provided.”

My aim hit the target and she visibly flinched.

But I was not finished. “I cherish my

independence, Vivienne. But there are times in everyone's lives when they need help from their family." I levelled my gaze on her. "And how fortunate I am to have such a family. I would be in a predicament otherwise."

"Well said, Claire." Ivan strode over to the other armchair and sat down. "I am sure both my wife and sister-in-law would be more understanding were they in your current situation. But these lovely ladies have only known comfort, and we must forgive their ignorance in the harsh ways of the world."

I allowed myself a moment of pleasure in having Ivan at my flank to blunt Vivienne's arrow. But one look at her took that joy away. Vivienne looked utterly miserable. And then the penny dropped.

She was in love with him.

Now it came into my head I could not unsee it. I thought she was attracted to Ivan, and most women would be, for he was a handsome fellow. But it was more than that for her. Vivienne was in love with her brother-in-law, living in the same house and seeing him every single day. She was tormented at every turn. Now it all made sense. Her moodiness, her dislike of me, her irritation with Nanette.

How unfortunate. It was not reciprocal. Ivan was not unkind to Vivienne, but nor did he seek out her attention, her opinions. In fact, while I considered this, I realised he treated both of the sisters in the same manner, almost as though they were one.

"Shall you wear black tomorrow, Claire? It would be nice to see you in a colour for our dinner. Do you have any other dresses for such an occasion?"

Nanette's question roused me from thought. "Yes. I

have one or two. My wardrobe is limited. I've only what I brought back with me, and I haven't shopped in years."

"I imagine the fashion in Africa is quite different from ours here," Vivienne said. My cousin had recovered from her vulnerable state and the cat was back. "Do they even follow any current trends there?" She assessed my evening dress. It was the same I had worn every night since my arrival. "Surely everyone must wear thin fabrics because of the heat."

"That is true," I said. "Many of them go about half-naked as it is so hot."

She gasped at my boldness. It had been my intent.

"But surprisingly, Africa is not on another planet, Cousin. In fact, its proximity to Asia is beneficial to the clothing industry. They have the most beautiful fabrics you can imagine. Silks and taffetas, the boldness of their prints in such wonderful colours we never see in Europe. The African style of clothing is exquisite. Honestly, I think them far ahead of us. They dress for comfort, not for show."

"It sounds so exotic," chimed in Nanette. "I envy you your travels, Claire. How I should love to see the world." She gave a little cough. "But my health will not allow it."

"You were well enough in Paris, Nanette," Ivan stated. "Perhaps being abroad was good for you. It gave your mind an occupation other than feeling unwell, and I believe that was very beneficial."

Nanette stiffened. She glared at her husband. "Much has changed since then," she said. "My health has deteriorated this past year. I should feel uncomfortable too far from home."

She then talked about a particular malady, but I found myself not paying attention. Instead, I studied the two women on the settee. Could one of them have crept into my room and destroyed Mother's journals?

Nanette? Delicate and pretty, sweet as syrup, yet not as weak as she wanted everyone to think. There was a strong backbone buried beneath the ailing, fretful woman.

And what of Vivienne? Always in her sister's shadow. A spinster, in love with someone else's husband. She was far more the likely candidate as unhappy a person as she seemed to be.

Yet Ivan's words came back to me regarding my cousins' real affection for my mother. Instinct told me they were not the culprits. But if not them, who?

We finished our sherries as Nanette commanded the conversation, still discussing ailments and remedies. I waited as long as was polite, and then I made my excuses and left the three of them alone. It had been a long day, and I wanted nothing more than my bed.

****

Saturday morning, the house was a hive of activity. Mrs Blitch had help from the village, and several strange faces passed me in the hall when I went down to breakfast.

There I found Tibbetts.

"Mornin' miss," he said. "T'gentlemen are at mill. Ladies are still abed. I'd stay out o' way if I were you, miss. Mrs Blitch is on't rampage. She's a right dragon when company's comin'."

I thanked him for the advice, hurried through breakfast, and then went upstairs to retrieve my coat and gloves. I agreed with Tibbetts' philosophy. I should prefer being out of the way.

It was not warm outside, but the bright sun made all the difference. A walk into the village would be just the thing. I had been back in Yorkshire five days already, and other than passing through Starling, had yet to visit.

By road, Starling Village lay a mile and half away. But using footpaths through the pastures, it was a half an hour on foot.

I was not the only creature enjoying the delightful sunshine. Cows and sheep munched grass in the fields, while birds swooped down searching for grubs and worms. The air smelled fresh, and in the distance I saw cottages, their washing lines full of wet clothes drying in the sun.

The outskirts of the village was marked by the spire of St. Michael's, where Father Lynch made his home and his living. The footpath would take me behind the church at the edge of the graveyard. I hadn't considered this until I reached the chapel, and I gave an involuntary shudder.

Papa was not buried here, but in a grave near the prison where he had been executed. Mother was in Hampshire, and my beloved George and Sarah on the other side of the world. My grandparents and aunt were in a vault, but not here. My family were not Catholic. Yet I still felt a connection to this graveyard, the site where Keith Delahunt had been murdered.

Of their own volition, my feet led me away from the path and onto the gravel which meandered through the cemetery, snaking between headstones. As I wandered past slabs of stone, I read the words carved in memory of those long gone.

One inscription in particular caught my attention. A woman, buried with her newborn son. My heart ached as I read the words, for my baby slept in the arms of her father, and I would never know the touch of either again.

"Mrs Holloway. What a pleasant surprise it is seeing you here at St. Michael's."

I dabbed my eyes quickly before turning to face Father Lynch. My few encounters with the priest had left me with an unfavourable impression. Coupled with the fact that it was he, standing in this graveyard, who had been a witness the night Keith Delahunt died.

"Good morning, Father Lynch. I'm on my way to the village and thought I would read some of these tombstones as I passed by. I don't like to think about anyone being forgotten once they have passed away."

The thin man contemplated my words. He was dressed in his usual black cassock, and a flat, wide brimmed, black hat on top of his thick, white hair. Again, the image of a crow came to my mind. Perhaps I did the poor bird an injustice.

"To be sure, to be sure." He steepled his fingers together. "But in the eyes of God, all the people sleeping here are immortal in Heaven."

I did not respond. My personal relationship with religion was my business, and mine alone. Instead, I changed the subject.

"It promises to be a beautiful day today, don't you think?"

His jet-black eyes looked up at the blue sky. "I think you have the right of it there, Mrs Holloway. And for September, it is most unusual."

"It certainly is. Well, I shall bid you good-day and

carry on to the village. I gather you will be joining us for dinner this evening at Darkwater Abbey?"

"Indeed I am. It is always a treat to have Mrs Blitch's fine cooking. Of course, the delightful company of your family make it all the better. Enjoy your walk, Mrs Holloway, and I shall look forward to seeing you this evening." He gave a curt nod and turned to walk back the way he had come.

Ironically, it was that precise moment when a cloud passed in front of the sun and a shadow fell across the ground. I shivered. I did not like that man. Even with my eyes closed I should have felt the same. Something resonated about him which spoke to my baser instincts. What was it? He was very creepy. Yet it was more than that. Was he dangerous?

The cloud moved away, and sunlight showered across the grass and the aged stones. I set off down the path, the gravel crunching underneath my boots.

Was I becoming too fanciful, allowing my imagination to get the better of me? Was Father Lynch just an ordinary man with a calling into the priesthood? That did not make him evil, in fact, quite the opposite. Since the horrible event with Mother's books, my mind was reaching too far. Everyone had taken a role in the melodrama of my life. I must stop being so daft. Yes, I wanted to dig into the past a little, but I still needed to keep my feet on the ground.

STARLING VILLAGE DERIVED ITS name from thousands of Pendlebury Starlings who made the Dales their home and were famous for their murmurations. When I was a child, Father often brought me to the village to watch the birds—always close to sunset. People came from far and wide to observe clouds of Starlings performing countless aerial displays in tight formations, high in the sky.

It had been fascinating. Thousands of birds flocked together, moving in unison as one body was mesmerising. The shapes they made as they swooped through the air, only to suddenly shift, darting in another direction yet staying en-masse. It was breathtaking to behold.

Papa told me Starlings were the only type of bird to perform such impressive dances. He said there was safety in numbers, and it was a way for the birds to protect themselves from their natural predators, like Peregrine Falcons.

No one knew why the birds picked our village to display their flying skills. They had made their home here for as long as anyone remembered. Consequently, the village had been named for them.

I left the footpath and joined the road. As I crossed over the stone bridge I moved aside to allow two large hay carts to pass. They were pulled by huge drays, the coppers on their bridles gleaming in the sun.

After the bridge, the road forked. To the left was the main thoroughfare through the village and on to Skipton. The other was a dead end, the last building being the old rectory, where my family were entombed. There was always a joke about it being fitting, getting buried at the dead end of Starling.

I chose the main road. I passed the Ace of Spades Inn, one of the oldest establishments in the village, famous for its pork pies and hearty ales. On one of my last trips to Starling, Uncle Simon had taken my cousins and I there for lunch. It was where the poor Australian man had been staying before he died.

I walked along, stopping periodically to peer into shop windows. The village's close proximity to Skipton provided plenty of goods easily deliverable here. I was surprised how modern everything was.

But then the railways and the canals of Yorkshire had opened up the Dales. Anything available in Liverpool could be found in towns even as small as Skipton.

Though Mother usually accompanied me to Darkwater Abbey, she never ventured far from the house. Thankfully she allowed me my freedom to roam and explore.

Being in Yorkshire somehow made Jane Shaw's presence ever stronger in my mind. For had not her feet walked along this very road, her eyes surveyed the same scenery I saw now. The familiar knot of sadness tightened in my stomach. Would it always be thus?

Lost in thought, I wasn't paying attention to where I was going until I accidentally bumped into a lady walking in the opposite direction to me.

"Oh!" she exclaimed, dropping a parcel she had been carrying.

"Forgive me," I said, bending over to retrieve it. "I am so sorry." I handed her back the package. "I hope it wasn't fragile. Did I hurt you?"

The woman smiled, and I realised how very pretty she was. Large, clear brown eyes, thickly arched brows, and a full mouth with straight, white teeth. Her dark hair was swept up into a chignon underneath a felt hat which matched the bronze fabric of her coat.

"No, all is well," she said. "But it is I who should apologise, I was preoccupied looking for something in my reticule. Without my spectacles on, I didn't even see you there. I probably walked into you." She chuckled. Then her face grew serious, and she tilted her head to stare at me.

"Forgive me, but do I know you?"

I shook my head. "I doubt it." I held out my hand. "I am Claire Holloway. I used to live around here but moved away many years ago."

The woman took my hand and held it tightly. How odd. Then to my horror, her eyes filled with tears.

"Oh my," I said. "Are you all right?"

She released my hand and dug in her reticule, pulling out a handkerchief. She dried her eyes. "Forgive me," she said. "I was overcome momentarily when you introduced yourself. Look, my cottage is just down the road from here, would you care to come and have a cup of tea with me?"

I frowned. "Miss…"

"Mrs Daly," she replied. "Oh, I am so silly. You think me a stranger and no wonder you hesitate in replying to my invitation. But my dear, I would love to speak with you after all this time."

Puzzled I asked. "But why? I do not know you, Mrs Daly."

She gave another kind smile. "No, Claire, you do not. But your parents were my dear friends for many years."

Chapter Sixteen

BRAMBLE COTTAGE WAS ONE in a row of small, neat homes on the street leading down to the church. The garden, in its last throes before the real cold set in, still looked well-tended.

Once inside the low front door, Mrs Daly stopped in the kitchen and asked a young woman who stood peeling potatoes if she'd put on the kettle for a pot of tea. Then she gestured for me to follow her into a little parlour.

"Let me take your coat, my dear." I took it off and handed it to her.

She laid it on the back of a chair. "Please," she said. "Do have a seat. I'll be back shortly with the tea."

I did not respond. I'd barely uttered a sound since her initial declaration, when I'd bombarded her with questions until she had stated, "Come and have tea and I shall tell you all about it."

I looked around the modest room.

A small fire burned in the grate and the atmosphere was cozy. Low timbered ceilings and floral-patterned furniture added to the ambience. The small-paned windows faced towards the street, and at the bottom of the garden, passers-by were clearly visible.

It wasn't very long before Mrs Daly reappeared carrying a tea tray which she placed on the sideboard. "How do you take your tea? Milk and sugar?"

"Yes, please."

She brought over a cup and handed it to me, then poured her own before sitting beside me on the couch.

"Now then," she began. "Let me embellish on my earlier remark. I knew both Thomas and Jane Shaw very well when we were young. I was best friend to her sister Charlotte back then and spent many a day at Darkwater." Mrs Daly took a sip of tea and set the cup down on a side table.

"At twenty-three, I married and moved away. My husband, Gerard, was in the Diplomatic Corps, and we were sent all over the world, and didn't get home very often. When Gerard died four years ago, I returned to Starling. Of course, by then, both Thomas and your Aunt Charlotte were gone.

Simon gave me Jane's address in Hampshire, and we corresponded for a while. But Jane never wanted to be reminded of the past, she preferred to leave it behind."

"You're right about that," I agreed. "The whole business with my father turned her away from Yorkshire for good."

"Recently, she had been a little more enthusiastic of our seeing one another again. We corresponded about meeting somewhere neutral, like London." Mrs Daly's voice thickened, and she quickly picked up her tea once more and took a sip. "I was so very sorry to hear about her accident."

"Thank you. It has been very sad. I still can't believe she's gone." I set down my cup and saucer. "How did you know who I was?"

Mrs Daly smiled. "Oh, my dear. You are your mother's double in so many ways, with your father's lovely eyes."

"Did you know him well?"

"Thomas? My goodness, all the girls around here knew Thomas. His family had been here for years. Something to do with coal, if I'm not mistaken. My, but he was such a handsome young man, and so very kind natured. We all set our caps at him. But from the day he met Jane, he was hers. And though I'll even admit to being a little jealous, I could see they were a match for one another. I went to their wedding at Darkwater. Your grandfather, Arthur was proud as a peacock that day. Thomas was the son Arthur never had. It was such a lovely wedding, but it poured with rain, and we all got soaked." Mrs Daly's eyes grew wistful. "Not long after that, I took a trip to London with my aunt, and met dearest Gerard. And the rest, as they say, is history."

Speaking with someone outside my family who knew my parents felt incredibly special. To hear them described in their youth was almost like being there myself.

"What did you think about my father being convicted of murder." I had to ask.

Mrs Daly did not hesitate. "That was despicable and unjust. Thomas Shaw was no murderer. That man was gentle and good. I never believed a word of it, and I know your mother didn't either. The letters she wrote me were full of her quest to get justice for him." Her expression grew mournful. "I should have been a better friend. I should have gone to Hampshire and helped poor Jane with her situation. But I couldn't. I had lost my darling Gerard, and, if I'm honest, my will to carry on. That's why I'd left Singapore and come back home."

I considered her comments. I could not blame her for coming here to lick her wounds. In some ways, hadn't I done exactly the same thing?

"I still have her letters, Claire. Would you like them?"

****

I walked back to Darkwater in a state of deep reflection. In my pocket, I carried a small bundle of letters in my mother's hand. It was kind of Mrs Daly to let me have them. She'd apologised, believing she'd had more than she found, but I assured her I was grateful for anything.

Crossing the moat, I willed myself to stop. Then, holding the railing tightly with both hands, I looked down at the water. The familiar feeling crept over me. My legs felt weak, my throat tight, my pulse rapid. I let go and rushed the remainder of the way to the other side. It was no huge success, but at least it was a start.

Inside, Darkwater was filled with the heady scent of fresh flowers. The staff had been busy. The house looked spotless and everywhere I glanced stood a vase of beautiful stems. Bouquets of roses, chrysanthemums, dahlias and veronicas were on display in a delicious riot of colour.

I darted up the stairs before anyone noticed me there and went to my room. I couldn't wait to read the letters in my pocket.

There were five envelopes, all dated the years I was overseas, which was probably why Mother never mentioned Mrs Daly. I carefully took out the first and scanned the words hungrily. I didn't know what I hoped to find, but Mother wrote of her life in Hampshire and that I had recently gone away to South Africa as a nurse. She sent condolences to Mrs Daly, or Hilary, as she was known, for the loss of Gerard. She wrote about her quest to prove my father's innocence and her lack of supporting evidence.

The next two letters were quite short. Again, she spoke of the travesty of justice against Papa, and the remainder mostly about me. In them, she covered each aspect of my time in Africa. She lamented my being so far away and leaving for so long. In another, she rejoiced at my marriage and the arrival of my child.

There was some mention about them meeting in London soon. I gathered the suggestion came from Mrs Daly.

I opened the last letter, already upset by revisiting the past, just like Mrs Daly had been.

Dearest Hilary.

It is with a heavy heart I write this. I have only just learned my son-in-law, George, and my sweet grandchild, Sarah, have been drowned in a terrible boating accident. I am bereft. I know not what to do. My poor darling, Claire, is all alone, so far away with her heart broken. I cannot begin to imagine how she is coping, and I have written to her and begged her to come home.

Therefore, I cannot even think about meeting you in London as you suggested. I can think of nothing else but my dear Claire and how she fares. I am sorry.

I set the letter down and wiped my eyes. Damn this infernal crying! I could have no tears left, surely.

I got up and splashed my face with cold water. I collected the letters together and hid them in the crevice of the chair.

I couldn't help my disappointment. What had I

hoped to find? Had I expected to read something extraordinary about Papa's case? Why would Mother have written something to Mrs Daly that she had not put in her diaries?

All my buoyancy from yesterday at the solicitors deflated.

I walked over to the window and looked at the courtyard below, then beyond the moat to the sweep of the dales stretching out as far as I could see. My mind was in a muddle of my own making, and it grieved me to be confused. Perhaps I should look through my notes once again, think harder about everything I remembered from the books?

As I contemplated, far off in the distance, a small trap moved along the road towards the village. Even though the person was no bigger than my little finger, I could see exactly who it was.

Father Lynch.

Again, I felt something stir inside. Besides being a witness, could Father Lynch know more about the events of that awful night in the graveyard? He would be here later for dinner. Perhaps it was time I asked him.

****

Tonight, I would humour Nanette and not wear black. Never being particularly interested in fashion, I was content owning a few nice things. I hadn't been lying to Vivienne about the amazing colours and fabric I'd seen in Africa.

Years ago, I'd purchased a length of crimson silk at one of the bazaars and had it made into an evening gown. I'd worn it once, for a regimental affair, the night I conceived my child. George had loved the colour and thought it looked well on me.

Dare I wear it tonight?

I went into the cupboard and took out the dress. It had travelled well. There were a few creases, but that could be remedied by a quick visit to Mellors. She would help me steam them out.

An hour later, my dress was hung up and ready to wear. Mellors, and two young village girls working as helpers for the evening, had sighed over the fabric, exclaiming it looked like melted rubies.

While I was downstairs, Tibbetts offered to bring me up some hot water, and I had been delighted to accept. A bath sounded like heaven. I longed to wash my hair.

Several pails of hot water did the trick, and I languished in the bath until the water turned stone cold. I stood in front of the fire trying not to think about Mother's books while vigorously rubbing my hair with a towel to dry it quickly.

More invigorated than I had been in a while, I wondered at my mood. My skin gleamed from a good scrub and shone from a few drops of scented oil I rubbed onto my legs and arms. I'd bought it in Cape Town; it was subtle with the scent of sandalwood and rose, and I used it sparingly.

I studied my face in the mirror. No English beauty there, especially with my skin still darker from three years in the sun. I had little use for cosmetics, although they were growing more popular all the time. But one of my nursing friends, an Indian girl named Surita, had introduced me to the one item she used. A small pot of black kohl, which I occasionally applied near the lash line of my eyes.

There. I would have to do.

THE ATMOSPHERE IN THE house was charged with excitement. The prospect of company, initially abhorrent, now filled me with anticipation. I certainly looked forward to seeing the Tipton girls once again. They were full of life and very sweet. As for the others, I had little interest, but it would make dinner more interesting than usual.

I arrived downstairs on time. Already, a ripple of conversation echoed around the house. One of the guests must be early, for there was still twenty minutes to go until the appointed time.

"Ah, here is my niece," announced Uncle Simon as I entered the drawing room. He stood before the fireplace next to a much older man. Both gentlemen were smartly dressed in black evening attire.

"Claire, do come and meet our neighbour."

Vivienne was seated on the couch and Ivan and Nanette were nowhere in sight. I approached Uncle Simon. His eyes gleamed as they travelled the length of me, and his smile was radiant.

"My goodness, Claire. You look stunning. The colour of your gown is most becoming, my dear."

His expression went beyond that of a proud uncle, and I wondered if I had made a mistake wearing something so ornate.

"Hear, hear," said the older gentleman. Then added. "Colonel Reginald Baldwin, at your service." He grasped my hand, bowed, and clicked his heels, causing multiple strings of medals emblazoned on his chest to jingle. "Jolly nice to meet you, young lady."

The colonel reminded me of so many older military

men I'd met in the past. Robust, ruddy complected, his hair thin, his moustaches bushy, with thick, grey sideburns. Pale eyes settled on my face.

"I hear you are recently back from the field, eh? Damned brave of you, my gal, I do say. Excellent to have our lovely young women aiding the men right there by the battlefield. Next thing you know, they'll be fighting alongside of 'em, don't you know."

"We are very proud of Claire's accomplishments, but selfish enough to be glad she is home where she belongs." Uncle Simon retrieved a glass of poured sherry from a nearby table and handed it to me. He raised his glass and the colonel followed suit.

"Here's to our nurses," toasted my uncle. We all took a sip of our drinks.

The sound of others arriving in the hallway reached us. Uncle Simon put down his glass and made his excuses to welcome his other guests.

"I expect you helped out some of my old regiment in Africa," said the colonel.

"Which regiment?"

"First Royal Dragoons. They were mixed up in the skirmishes at Lady Smith amongst others. Of course, I wasn't there as I'm too damned old. But wish I could have been. Last action I saw was in the Crimea. Nasty business. Though I did meet Florence Nightingale, damned fine filly. That woman was the toughest soldier I knew. Saved many lives and will forever be a saint in the eyes of the military."

I raised a toast to Miss Nightingale. A woman most revered who changed the course of nursing in England.

"Simon tells me you may make your home here at Darkwater? Wonderful place to live, this. I've been all over the world, but there's nothing prettier than the Dales. Can't beat 'em. You wouldn't do any better than stopping here."

"Where do you live, Colonel Baldwin?" His name was unfamiliar, and I wondered if he was a recent addition to the area.

"Near Malham, not too far from here. My wife's family are local. I'm from Surrey myself. But everybody's dead, including the old gal, and I like it better here than all the hubbub down south."

He stopped and looked over to the doorway where several people were coming in.

"Ah," he said. "Won't you excuse me. Here's Doctor Tipton. I need to speak to him about my gout."

He walked away.

"I see you've had the pleasure of meeting the colonel," Vivienne appeared at my side. She looked out of sorts. Her pale lemon dress made her look wan. Her eyebrow arched. "He's a nice old boy, but don't ever let him get started about the war. You'll never get away." Her eyes flickered over me. "That's a beautiful dress you're wearing, Claire. Quite a contrast to your previous evening attire. But I imagine having to dress in mourning so often has become rather tedious for you."

It was a slap in the face. Even for my cousin, a low blow. My blood boiled. I took a step closer.

"You're a spiteful woman, Vivienne. If you were a mother yourself, and not an old maid, you would understand the agony of losing a child." I knew my eyes burned with anger, and I did not care. "You may mock me. You can insult me. But don't ever remark again about the loss of my child, my husband and now my mother. You'll regret it if you do."

I moved away from her, stunned at her cruelty. I cared not if she was unhappy, lonely, or miserable. Any chance we may have had to bridge the gap formed so early in our childhood, was gone. What a horrible person my cousin had become.

The Tiptons, who had just arrived, were being attended to by Uncle Simon and the colonel. As I approached, he broke off his conversation with the elder Tipton.

"And here is my dear niece, Claire."

I immediately recognised Hazel and Phoebe, who stood with two young men, one who favoured both girls and another, who I took to be a friend of the family.

Uncle Simon made the introductions.

Doctor Tipton had no unusual characteristics. A tall, slim man, with grey hair and a weathered complexion. He was clean shaven and when he smiled, displayed very straight, white teeth.

The doctor turned away from Colonel Baldwin and his gout complaints with some relief. "Finally, I meet you, Mrs Holloway. My girls have spoken of little else since your encounter recently. In fact, it is all I can do to stop Phoebe from running away to go to nursing school in London."

"Father!" Phoebe exclaimed with a note of embarrassment.

"You already know my silly daughters, let me introduce you to the sensible person in our family." He smiled affably. "This is my son, Martin, and his good friend, Jeremy Rotherham."

The two younger men stepped forward. Martin Tipton held out a hand to shake mine firmly. I liked him immediately. Nice looking, with a pleasant smile that reached his eyes. He was dark headed, with a neatly trimmed beard and moustache. I could easily see why Vivienne held an attraction towards him. Although after my recent encounter with her, I determined Martin Tipton could do far better.

His companion, Jeremy Rotherham, was similar in appearance but his hair was jet black. He too shook my hand and appeared quite friendly. Yet I noticed his eyes shifted quickly when Ivan and Nanette finally made their entrance.

My cousin came into the room, and we all faded in her light. Nanette resembled a fairy queen. Her gown, a pale pink, encrusted with rhinestones, twinkled as she moved. She wore her blonde hair in an elaborate bun, ornamented with more of the stones cleverly tucked into the folds of her hair. Nanette was a beautiful woman. In that moment, she deserved to have all eyes upon her.

As soon as they came near, Ivan released his wife, and she sauntered over to our party. I commented on how lovely she looked and quickly moved away.

Ivan helped himself to a glass of sherry, and I watched as Vivienne approached him immediately. He did not look particularly interested in conversing with my cousin, yet her face shone with admiration. If anyone had looked at her, surely it would be apparent to them that she had feelings for Ivan Delahunt. In fact, the most oblivious person seemed to be the man himself.

As I considered the dynamics of the room, Father Lynch made his entrance. In my fanciful musings, in contrast to Nanette, I imagined the room dimmed a little by his coming. The man was like a rain cloud on a summer day, a blot of ink on a clean page. He exemplified what I considered to be something gloomy, a disparagement.

Uncle Simon greeted him enthusiastically. Perhaps they really were like brothers.

The drawing room seemed to shrink with all the guests here. Indeed, there were not enough places for everyone to sit. However, most of the company appeared content standing in groups conversing.

Ivan moved away from my cousin and was now in conversation with Colonel Baldwin who had been abandoned by the Tiptons. Our eyes met across the room and Ivan smiled at me, raising his glass in my direction.

It was so unexpected I smiled back. Then I turned to find Vivienne observing me with a thunderous expression. Although I was not in favour of petty, jealous, behaviour, her dislike pleased me momentarily after her cruel comments to me. Vivienne had no claim on her sister's husband. It was ridiculous. I wondered if Nanette paid it much mind.

Apparently not, for beautiful Nanette held court, perfectly happy standing between Martin Tipton and Jeremy Rotherham. Both young men appeared enraptured by her conversation. She in turn, was like a flower turning its head towards the sun. She basked from their attention.

"Mrs Holloway, or can I call you Claire? After all we are friends." Phoebe Tipton's radiant smile greeted me, and I was delighted to see her. She looked quite lovely in a gown of pale blue. There was such appeal in her eagerness which beamed like a light. She was almost the same age I had been when I learned the truth about my dear papa.

"Of course, you must call me Claire. And yes, you are my first new friend in Yorkshire."

She giggled. "It is so exciting you're here. And I am pleased to bits we've come to dine. We never go anywhere, and I get so bored. There's little to do in Starling."

We both glanced over at Hazel Tipton, who had been cornered by Father Lynch.

"My sister spends most of her time mooning about Charlie Hickson who lives next door, or the next gown she should like to have. I'd rather read a book. In fact, I have just finished reading a fabulous story written by a man called Henry James. He's an American. Father would kill me if he saw I was reading it. But I don't care." She looked triumphant.

I laughed. "It's all very well to be rebellious and push the limits and boundaries of society," I said. "But always consider the impact your behaviour has on those you love. A true pioneer manages to balance both their passion for change and protect the reputation of their families. I have no doubt you are capable of being very sensible. I also believe you shall accomplish whatever you set your mind to as you get older."

"My goodness." Phoebe blushed under my compliment. "You are too kind, Claire. I only hope I can be as brave as you."

"What is this flattery?" Ivan joined us.

Phoebe answered quickly, "I'm telling Claire she is a person I aspire to equal. I think she's terribly brave for being a nurse during the war, don't you, Mr Delahunt?"

Ivan looked very handsome this evening. Dressed

in a black evening suit, crisp white shirt, and dark blue bow tie, he was quite dapper. His eyes sparkled in the light of the room, and there was an ease to his expression that was new. The change in his demeanour was astounding, and I attributed it to the news I'd shared with him about my role at the mill. The man must have felt stifled under the sole rule of my uncle.

"Indeed, Miss Tipton. Claire's a fine example of the role women will take in the future. They've been a resource long overlooked. I hope that shall be remedied sooner rather than later."

"You are such a modern thinker," exclaimed Phoebe with pleasure. "I had no idea. Having a new person here at Darkwater is so thrilling. I can almost feel change in the air."

"What's this?" The familiar voice dampened the conversation instantly. Father Lynch joined our group. "What change is this you speak of, my dear?"

Before she could stammer out an answer, Ivan spoke up. "Phoebe spoke of the changing seasons," he stated, much to our surprise. "She laments the passage of autumn and the looming arrival of a cold Yorkshire winter."

Father Lynch smiled, bearing his unattractive teeth. "Indeed, indeed." He turned his attention to me. "This winter will be hard for you, Mrs Holloway, having spent so much time in warmer climates."

"It is not always hot in Africa," I said. "There are seasons, just as we have here. However, it does not get particularly cold. You are right in saying winter shall be a shock to me. But I'm a Yorkshire girl, Father. I daresay I shall tolerate it."

The sound of a gong rang. Tibbetts stood in the

doorway. “Dinner is served,” he announced.

Chapter Seventeen

MRS BLITCH HAD OUTDONE herself, each course better than the previous. Roasted pheasant with baked apples, freshly dug potatoes and carrots, sweet peas, a rice dish, and other delectable items to complement the meal.

Uncle Simon was seated at the head of the table, the guests interspersed with one another for better conversation. Martin Tipton was seated to my right, Phoebe to my left, and much to my disappointment the person directly across the table from me was Father Lynch.

Martin, Phoebe, and I lost no time discussing subjects mainly about popular books and their writers of note. The siblings shared they frequently visited Leeds but were too poor to spend time in London.

"Father cannot run to the expense," Martin said without a trace of embarrassment. "Life as a country doctor cannot command a lucrative income. Don't misunderstand me, we live comfortably in Starling, but going to the capital is not in our budget."

"I wish it were," said Phoebe wistfully. "It's incredibly dull in the village and not much better in Skipton. I suppose Leeds is adequate, but there is nothing like the prospect of being in London. How I should love to see Buckingham Palace, the changing of the guards. To walk through Regent's Park and see all the notables in society." Her eyes gleamed with excitement. "Imagine going to a musical or taking in an opera." She sighed. "I shall probably not live long enough to do any of that. Father will have me married to a boring farmer and I shall spend my life picking straw out of my clothing."

I laughed out loud. "Honestly, Phoebe. You are so entertaining I believe you could appear on the stage yourself."

"Mrs Holloway," Martin turned to face me. "How have you found it being back at Darkwater? I know you lived here as a child, but you have been gone many years, have you not?"

I nodded. "I left Yorkshire when I was young but visited often to see my uncle and my cousins. Yet it does feel as though I have been away a long time." I glanced at Phoebe. "I have lived on another continent and travelled to London often. Every place has its beauty and allure. But I can assure you, Phoebe, there is not much to equal the beauty and tranquillity of our Yorkshire Dales."

"It's easy for you to say that because you've seen other places," Phoebe said quickly. "Also, you're older than I am and perhaps what makes you happy is very different."

"Sister, don't be so rude." Martin scolded her with a glower.

"I wasn't being rude, brother. I was being honest. Claire isn't old, I just meant that she has seen more than me and had her freedom. I get the odd trip to Leeds and everything else I have to read about in magazines and papers. I should like to see it all with my own eyes. I cannot see anything wrong with that."

Phoebe's attention was then drawn away by

Colonel Baldwin, who sat to her left.

Martin gave a roll of his eyes. "I am sorry my sister gets so carried away and tends to be rather blunt. Please do not be offended by her opinions and observations."

"There's no need to apologise. Phoebe is refreshing, like a cool breeze on a hot day. Her candour is admirable, and she is a very intelligent young girl. Just imagine what she could amount to, given education and experience in other walks of life."

"You're right. I often think a future consisting of marriage and children is not the avenue she'll want to take. It would require a very specific personality to make Phoebe happy and keep her grounded." Martin smiled at me.

He really was a pleasant fellow. With his handsome features I imagine he was well sought after in the village. Vivienne was a fool to let this man slip through her fingers. I looked across at my cousin. Vivienne sat flanked by Father Lynch and Doctor Tipton. She looked absolutely miserable.

Periodically, her eyes landed upon me and then shifted to Martin. She was most displeased with my receiving his attention. Gosh, my cousin was such an unhappy woman, but after her unforgivable comments to me earlier, I would never feel sorry for her again.

"Tell me, Martin, are you to follow your father and become a physician?"

Martin took a sip of his wine. "Good God, no. My interests are in pharmaceuticals. I am greatly intrigued by medicines, especially all the advances that have been made in the past few years. I run Father's dispensary and also attend a college in Leeds for certain lectures, those necessary to keep my wits sharp and to stay current with all of the latest scientific developments."

"There have been many advancements made in the world of medicine, don't you agree?"

"Absolutely. I am sure you have much experience with medicine having been a nurse, Mrs Holloway."

"Please, call me Claire. Yes, more experience than I would care to have had at times. But we were very fortunate. Several of the steamer lines ensured we received regular deliveries of medical supplies. When that is not the case it has devastating consequences for the wounded and sick patients."

"You'll find life a bit different in England, don't you think, Mrs Holloway?" Father Lynch interrupted our conversation. "As a woman who has worked for a living, you'll miss having an occupation. Nursing is a remarkable calling. Returning to a normal life and being a member of society will seem less intriguing, but I am sure you'll get used to it soon enough."

I reluctantly answered. "I doubt it, Father Lynch. Like my mother, I cannot abide being idle. I plan to spend the majority of my time with Uncle Simon and Ivan working at the mill."

The other conversations suddenly faded away. All ears were on Father Lynch and myself.

"The mill?" Father Lynch said. He smiled and his long canines made him look like a wolf. "Now that is unexpected. Do you think it wise? Sure, but a fine lady, such as yourself would be better off leaving that work to the men. Your God-given skills are as a healer. Perhaps you could volunteer your time at the infirmary in Skipton, or even help at Doctor Tipton's surgery for the poor. There's many who would benefit from your experience."

Vivienne's smug face looked my way. I'm sure she was enjoying this. I could feel all eyes on me.

"All wonderful suggestions," I said amiably. "But after three long years tending soldiers, I desire a change. One day I may return to nursing, but for now I'd like to learn more about the family business."

Father Lynch glanced over to Uncle Simon. "Well now, Simon. What are your thoughts on having a young woman working at Parslow's with you every day?"

Uncle Simon looked flushed from wine. "Doesn't matter what I think, Lynch. Claire owns more than half of the company. Apparently, she can do what she damn well pleases."

Vivienne's sharp intake of breath was echoed by her sister's. The colonel blinked a few times, and the Tiptons said nothing.

Father Lynch did not appear pleased with my uncle's response. But he raised his glass to me. "I am sure the mill will be a prettier place with you gracing its building."

I raised my glass to meet his. Our eyes met. His, black and fathomless. But I saw something in them.

Anger.

THE GENTLEMEN WERE LEFT to enjoy brandy and cigars, while my cousins, the Tipton girls and I, settled in the drawing room where coffee was served by Tibbetts.

I remained standing when the others sat down. Even after eating, and drinking wine with dinner, I still could not relax. My mind had yet to slow down. Something in the way the priest spoke to me still rattled. I was a hare, my ears pricked upward, listening for the sound of a wolf.

"Don't you wish we could have a concert to attend," this came from Phoebe who sat between Nanette and Hazel. "Or a play? Skipton is too small for a theatre, and there's not much to do."

"Perhaps you should put on your own play," Vivienne commented drily. "I'm sure Father Lynch would let you use the chapel hall." She smirked.

Phoebe was oblivious of Vivienne's sarcasm. I decided to champion the young woman from my cousin's snide remarks.

"What an excellent idea," I chimed in. "I'm sure Father Lynch would welcome the suggestion. You could even charge admission and give all the money to one of his Catholic charities, Phoebe."

Her blue eyes twinkled with excitement. "Gosh. We really could do it. There are so many plays available to purchase. Hazel and I could go to Leeds and pick one out."

"It could have a Christmas theme," I said. "Father Lynch would like that."

As the Tipton girls conversed with Nanette between them, Vivienne glanced over at me. This time, her look of utter dislike did not even faze me. I smiled malevolently in return.

The men joined us, but Colonel Baldwin quickly begged his leave. He remarked that his gout bothered him, and a warm bed called him home.

Uncle Simon, looking worse the wear from his indulgences of the evening, saw the old man out.

Ivan joined me standing near the hearth. "Have you enjoyed your time discussing the latest fashions and hairstyles with the ladies?"

"As much as you enjoyed your time talking about

politics, money and the price of cotton with the gentlemen."

"Let us not forget gout. Gout was quite the topic."

I chuckled at that. "Then perhaps you had the worst of it."

The Tipton girls now sat either side of their father. All three looked rather tired. Jeremy Rotherham was yet again speaking with Nanette having already monopolised her time at the dinner table. Martin sat in the armchair next to Vivienne, who was busy watching Ivan.

What a tableau we made. Where was Father Lynch?

No sooner had I thought it, than the priest appeared. He clapped his hands to get our attention.

"Simon asks that I make his excuses. He fears the food was a little rich and he overindulged. I encouraged him to get some rest. But he insists everyone stays as long as they like."

"Should I go upstairs and check on him?" Offered Doctor Tipton.

"No," said Father Lynch. "It is just a little indigestion." He came over to where Ivan and I stood. "It has been such a pleasant evening. I hope you have enjoyed yourself, Mrs Holloway, and that you were not offended by my comments earlier. To be sure, I meant no insult about you going to the mill." Again, I wondered why he sounded like the host in someone else's house.

"There was none taken," I lied. "As a man of the cloth you have a calling that will last your entire life. For some of us, the call changes multiple times throughout our lives."

"Well said," Ivan commented. "I think it admirable Mrs Holloway shows such a strong interest in her family's business. Arthur would have been happy to see it. As you said, Claire, your mother was renowned for working with her own father."

"I remember that time," said the priest. "Jane Shaw was a very capable woman. But the workers at the mill weren't happy having a woman in a position of power."

There it was again. Referring to women as though they were inferior.

"It is odd," I said, "that women are encouraged to play lesser roles in today's world. Women have been leaders, rulers and held in high respect as a man's equal. Is it so wrong to allow them the same freedom as men in seeking careers?"

Father Lynch gave me another smile. "It is not any man's intent to suppress another based upon their gender. It is God's word which has carved out the roles and the paths we choose in life. In certain things, a man's talents are less than a woman's, and vice-versa."

"Skills are often learned, or some are naturally present, regardless of gender," Ivan chimed in. "Consider this. In England's history of monarchy, her most successful rulers have been women. Queen Elizabeth the first, and our recently departed Queen Victoria will always be given that honour."

"Indeed." The priest glowered at Ivan. "But they did not rule alone. They had governments, ministers, and the like." He looked at me. "All men."

"What are you three talking about over there?" Nanette sauntered towards us. She really did look lovely tonight.

"The role of women," I replied.

"Oh." Her eyes flickered over Ivan and then the priest. "How boring. I am content with sending the men out to work and enjoying my time at home. I'm not a modern-thinker I daresay."

"Each to their own," said Ivan. "If you'll excuse me." To my surprise, he moved away from our group. He went to stand near the window, and I noticed Vivienne bolt in his direction. I looked at Nanette to see her observing them as well. She turned her attention back to me.

"Claire, I must tell you your gown is absolutely stunning. That deep shade of red is most becoming on you."

"Thank you. I could say the same to you, Cousin. You look like a fairy princess tonight. I've never seen such a pretty dress."

"Both you ladies look lovely this evening." Father Lynch gestured to us. "You do your family proud. Now," he said. "I must away before it gets too late. Thank you for a wonderful evening, Nanette." He took her hand in his before turning to face me.

"And to you, Mrs Holloway. I have enjoyed our conversation immensely. I hope to revisit it soon."

I did not speak but nodded my head in response. The opportunity to ask the priest a few questions regarding the night Mr Delahunt died had not presented himself. It could wait. I was more than glad the man was leaving.

Father Lynch made the rounds before departing, closely followed by the Tipton family. Phoebe lamented their leaving, but she was already sleepy.

"I hope I shall see you again soon, Claire," Martin Tipton said when he shook my hand in farewell.

"Perhaps I might call on you?"

Stupefied by the request I mumbled, "Of course." I watched the family leave the room guided by Vivienne and Nanette, Jeremy Rotherham at her side.

"I think young Martin may have a tendre towards you." Ivan came up from behind and drew level with me.

I turned towards him. "I doubt that," I replied. "But he's very pleasant to talk to."

Ivan downed the remainder of his drink. He studied my face intently. "Come now, Claire. Don't play the innocent with me. One of your best qualities is the capacity to be direct and honest. Spare me the coquettish denial. It does not suit you."

His comment irritated me. "Unlike my cousins I am not interested in the romantic intentions of men. It may surprise you to learn that I have known a great love, and a few flattering words and affectionate glances mean nothing to me."

He had the grace to look apologetic. "I am sorry. I meant no insult, nor slight upon your husband."

I sighed. My annoyance subsided. "No. It is I who should apologise. I was too harsh. Yes, Martin Tipton does like me, but not for myself. He is probably pleased to meet a new face for a change. I did enjoy sitting by him at dinner, but that is all. Now, if you will excuse me, I think I shall retire for the evening. Good night, Ivan."

"Goodnight Claire."

I walked away and out of the room, but I felt his eyes watch my every step.

Chapter Eighteen

A BLOODCURDLING SCREAM had me awake in a heartbeat.

I sat bolt upright in bed, registered the sound was not part of a dream, and quickly got up. It was light outside, but still early. I pulled on my dressing gown and slippers then headed out of my room.

The screaming came from the east wing, and I ran down the hallway arriving in the other corridor to see Ivan already there, a bleary-eyed Uncle Simon, and Mellors, sobbing into her hands.

"What is it?" I said. "What has happened."

The maid pointed at a bedroom door, still ajar. "In…there…"

It was Vivienne's room.

Ivan moved past her and went inside. I followed him.

Still dressed in the lemon gown from the previous evening, my cousin lay on her stomach, one arm draped over the edge of the bed.

I moved closer. Her face was turned sideways on the pillow. Her eyes were open and still. She'd been sick. Dried vomit coated her lips, chin and the pillowcase.

I pushed past Ivan as my nursing instinct kicked in. "Call for the doctor," I said loudly to anyone who would listen. I went to Vivienne and felt for her pulse. I knew there would not be one, and there wasn't. I closed her eyelids and placed my ear next to her mouth. Nothing.

I straightened up and looked over to the doorway. Uncle Simon stood on the threshold, his face ghostly pale, his expression, one of deep shock.

"Is she…is she…"

I went to him and gently took his arm, turned him away and led him back into the hall, closing the bedroom door behind me.

"I'm afraid so," I said quietly. I felt the muscles in his arm grow taut, and his whole body stiffened.

"Come, Uncle. Let us go downstairs and wait for Doctor Tipton."

He allowed me to lead him down to the drawing room. I poured him a brandy and settled him in a chair. He numbly accepted the glass from me but said not a word.

"Miss?" Tibbetts came into the room. "Mr Delahunt's gone to fetch Doctor. I've sent Mellors to her room. Shall I wake Mrs Delahunt?"

"Yes, please." I was amazed Nanette hadn't heard all the commotion. Perhaps she took a sleeping draught? That wouldn't surprise me.

I sat in the chair next to Uncle Simon. He'd already finished the brandy and held the empty glass in both hands which shook uncontrollably. He met my gaze and my heart swelled with empathy when I saw the abject misery on his face. I knew what it was to lose a child. He was devastated.

"My little girl," he said, his voice breaking. "What happened to my Vivienne? How can she be gone?" Tears rolled down his cheeks, and I reached over to take the glass from him and grasp his hand. It was frigid.

"Calm yourself, Uncle. Doctor Tipton will be here soon and will be able to speak to you. He will…"

Another shrill cry came from upstairs and within moments, Nanette appeared. Wearing her night attire, her hair loose down her back, she rushed into the room, collapsed at her father's feet and buried her face into his knees.

"Papa…" she wailed. "Vivienne is dead. Dear God, what has happened to my sister?" she sobbed.

Uncle Simon, roused from the depths of shock by the needs of his other child, rallied quickly. He brushed the tears from his cheeks and laid his hands on Nanette's head.

"Hush, child," he soothed. "Hush."

Uncomfortable and an intruder to such a personal moment, I got up and stole out of the room. Neither one noticed my departure.

I went directly to the kitchen, where Mrs Blitch was busy at the hearth. She heard me come in and glanced over her shoulder.

"Well, 'tis true the mistress is dead?" she asked bluntly.

I nodded.

"Sit down there an' get thou some tea. You've had a nasty shock, lass."

Mechanically I did as she said. The reality of what had just happened seeped into my mind. How was it possible? Vivienne, dead?

The cook placed two large kettles on the stove. "T'will be people in and out all the day. I'll have them girls from t'village back to help out. Get the house sorted for what's ahead." She came over to the table, hands on broad hips. "Thou will be in charge, thou knows. T'other miss won't be worth a shilling, and t'master worse. Priest'll be here before long, an' all. Mark my words. Bloody vulture."

I poured myself another strong cup of tea. I would need all the strength I could get.

****

In the drawing room I sat alone, my mind heavy with thought. How was it that death had followed me, like an unwelcome shadow these past two years? I'd been robbed of a darling husband and precious child. My mother had been snatched away before I could make any amends with her, and now Vivienne.

Poor Vivienne.

My feelings for her were so conflicted. She was unkind, and I could have happily slapped that sarcastic face last night at the dinner party. Disliking her was my prerogative. But I never wished her dead.

Someone had.

BY HALF PAST ONE, I'D become suffocated by the endless succession of people coming into the house. Doctor Tipton, the Funeral Director, and the village girls who came to clean up from the night before, and prepare Darkwater for mourning.

Father Lynch's arrival brought it all to a head—I had to get out. I told Mrs Blitch and Tibbetts I wouldn't be long, and quickly left the house.

The wind was angry today. I pulled my coat tighter. Rain threatened, but I paid it no mind so desperate was I to escape from Darkwater and the miserable commotion there, even for an hour.

Somehow, I'd automatically come back to the Rosell Cottage, though I didn't know why. Even though there was such a sad story associated with this house, there also existed something peaceful as well, and it drew me.

I found a large outcrop of limestone which made a perfect seat. Huddled up in my coat like a baby, I contemplated the lovely green fields, the sparse trees, and the calm cows. There was the chapel spire and the village beyond. The view was remarkable up here.

I realised today marked almost a week since my arrival in Yorkshire, yet it might well have been a month. Each day had brought with it something out of the ordinary.

I mulled over the events of the past week when I spotted a figure leaving the road below, climbing over the stile into the field. Even from this distance I knew it was Ivan. The tell-tale favouring of his right leg and the purposeful walk.

I stayed where I was and watched his approach. Had he seen me leave Darkwater?

He arrived quickly, crested the hill, then saw me and gave a start.

"Claire? I didn't know you were here."

I got to my feet as he drew nearer. "I needed fresh air. It has been a horrible day and when Father Lynch arrived, I made a run for it."

He came to stand next to me and stared out at the vista before us. "Good timing on your part. I was not afforded the chance. The man is in his element at the moment."

"If he brings any comfort to Uncle Simon and Nanette, then he's worth putting up with," I said.

"Strangely he does." He looked at me. "What brought you up here? I don't usually run into another soul."

"You frequent this place?"

He nodded. "It's close to Darkwater, and I like the view. And you?"

I shrugged. "I suppose because of its past. The melancholy draws me for some reason. Though what happened was tragic, there's another feeling I get, like the family are here in spirit, waiting."

"Waiting for justice," Ivan mused.

"Yes. I suppose so."

The wind whipped up suddenly, blowing my coat open. I shivered.

"Come," Ivan said. "Let's go inside the cottage and get out of this cold wind."

I followed him to the ramshackle building, and we went in though the back. It did feel better indeed.

There was nowhere to sit, so we stood. Me by the old hearth, while Ivan stayed near the doorway.

"The world is upside down today," he said. "I'm rather glad you're here so we can speak openly. I'd like to know your thoughts about what happened this morning. About Vivienne."

"In what capacity?"

"Her death. You examined her when we went into the room. Just before I came out for a walk, I spoke with Simon to see what the doctor had said, and I'd like your opinion too."

"It was poison," I stated. "No question about it. The fact she'd been sick, and that tell-tale smell on her lips."

"What smell?"

"A bitter odour of almonds. Potassium cyanide. I saw it happen a few times in Africa. A quick way to die."

Ivan frowned. "How odd," he said. "Doctor Tipton said Vivienne had taken an overdose of laudanum. He says it was suicide."

"What?" I gasped. "That is nonsense. There was a distinct smell about her face which any medical person would recognise. I'm a nurse, not a doctor, and it was obvious to me."

Ivan came to stand in front of me. His brows drew together. "Are you certain about this, Claire? Could you be mistaken?"

"Absolutely not. And what is this nonsense about suicide? I saw no note, did you? Besides, why on earth would Vivienne want to die? In the short time I've been here it was obvious she could be a miserable person, but then she's always been unhappy, even as a child. There is a huge disparity between unhappiness and a desire to end your life."

Ivan's expression registered confusion. "Why do you think she was unhappy?"

I gave a laugh. "Honestly, men are so blind. Seldom do you see what's right in front of your nose. Ivan, how could you not notice? My cousin was in love with you."

"What?" His face grew incredulous. "Don't be ridiculous."

"It's true. I've been here less than a week and I saw it. Vivienne never took her eyes off you."

Ivan took a few steps back. I'd made him uncomfortable. Yet now it had been said he would have to consider it.

He walked back over to the door. "Vivienne was my sister-in-law. I've known her for a long time, but we were never close, not even friends." He was extremely perturbed.

I could almost see him thinking as he reached into his mind to corroborate my opinion. His brow furrowed. He did not want to see it for himself.

"Ivan, my cousin was not an easy person to know. Even as children, I have no memories of her laughing, or having fun. Vivienne was always solemn and serious. If I'm honest, she wasn't very nice. But I attribute that to her being discontent. I don't think she knew how to feel joy. She observed it in others and resented them for it."

"How do you mean?"

I paused, not wishing to speak ill of Vivienne, yet desiring to explain my thoughts. "I think it was difficult for her always being compared to Nanette. Having a younger sibling who is often the centre of attention is hard. There is much conflict when you love a sister and are jealous of her simultaneously."

His eyes were bright and intensely blue. "You seriously believe that? How can you make such observations after only being at Darkwater a few days? I live here, for God's sake, and I saw none of this. I know Vivienne was seldom cheerful, but has it occurred to you that many of us don't spend our lives being on top of the world?"

"That's unfair," I snapped. "And yes, of course I know life is not easy for many people. But there is a huge step between misfortune, unhappiness, and killing yourself."

"And you are an authority on this?"

His words stung. For a moment, we stared at one another, two adversaries in a boxing ring.

"Do not presume to know everything about me, Ivan. I do not for one moment believe I am privy to all your darkest personal feelings."

"Nor will you be." There was annoyance in his voice. Ivan was getting angry with my commentary, mainly because he recognised the truth in my words.

"Look," I said. "Think whatever you wish. I am only trying to make the point that Vivienne has always been dissatisfied with a tendency to be verbally unkind. She has never been any different, yet she was fixated upon you. Regardless of those factors, she was not the type of person to commit suicide. She might have been bitter about her lot in life, but she was not despondent."

He still disagreed. "And you feel qualified to make that statement? More qualified than Doctor Tipton?"

"I don't suggest that for a moment. What I am saying is this doesn't feel right. I've relied on my instinct as a nurse for several years. You might think it nonsense, but it has never failed me before. I don't think my cousin killed herself."

"Then what are you saying?"

I glanced up to meet his eyes. "I think someone poisoned Vivienne."

"You cannot be serious."

"I am. And once you think about it a while longer, you'll come to the same conclusion."

He shook his head. "Now you're being overly dramatic. Reading your mother's journals and the conspiracy you think is there has turned your head. You are wrong, Claire. Vivienne Manning was an unhappy woman who had reached the end of her endurance for reasons only known to her. I'm only sorry none of us recognised her fragility and helped her before it was too late."

I watched his handsome face as he spoke. The Ivan I had started to know was hiding somewhere behind his actions. This man sounded more like the child who had lost his father. Vivienne's dying had likely brought back many repressed memories and emotions. It was futile to press my point any longer.

I pulled my coat tighter. "I must go back and check on Uncle Simon," I stated, eager to get away from our conversation.

"I'll see you back at the house," Ivan said. "I shall remain here for a short time. I want to clear my head."

I nodded my understanding and went to the doorway. He stood in front of it yet did not step aside to let me pass. I looked up and our eyes met. His were troubled and sad. He stared at me for what seemed like minutes, and then without saying a word, stepped to one side and let me by.

Chapter Nineteen

ACCORDING TO TIBBETTS, the priest had issued orders for his deacon to oversee Sunday morning's mass so that he could remain at Darkwater to assist my uncle and watch over Nanette. Apparently, the three of them had been sequestered inside Uncle Simon's study most of the afternoon.

Thinking about Father Lynch, I was reminded of Mrs Blitch's comment about him being a vulture. She wasn't far wrong. I'd seen plenty of them in Africa.

Relieved not to have seen the man, I freshened up in my room, still out of sorts, especially with Ivan, who I'd considered an ally and someone with faith in my judgement. Was he right to doubt me? Vehemently I decided he was not. My suspicions of Vivienne's death were no flight of fancy. I was not mistaken by what I'd witnessed.

Upon my examination, I had immediately smelled the bitter odour of almonds on her skin. My speculation of why she died might be obscure to Ivan, but I was not wrong about the method. Then why had Doctor Tipton said differently?

Was I really a conspiracy theorist? Did I read malevolence and evil in all I encountered? Absolutely not. Yes, I might be jaded about many things based upon my own unfortunate experiences, but I was not a fantasist. Watching young men die from horrific wounds in a foreign land had put paid to that.

When I returned downstairs, I ventured into the kitchen to find several faces I did not know. Mrs Blitch, fully in command of the mayhem, barked orders to her helpers, who scurried about preparing what I assumed to be different types of food for the upcoming days. She spotted me and came over.

Wisps of grey hair escaped her cap and she looked weary.

"Ee, but I'm that tired already, lass," she said. "We've help in from t'village as thou can see, but there's much to take care of."

"Is there anything I can do to help?"

"Nay, but I thank you." She paused as a dark-haired woman of middle age called over to the cook asking a question.

"Lass, I've got to tend t'work," Mrs Blitch said by way of apology to me and went to see what the woman needed.

I left the kitchen, not wanting to get in the way, and went back upstairs to the family's part of the building. Passing Uncle Simon's study, I heard the low murmur of voices coming from inside. Perhaps Father Lynch was praying with my family.

Vivienne's door was closed, naturally. I opened it slowly. Her still body lay on the bed, draped with a large white sheet. Tendrils of yellow silk poked out beneath the crisp white of her cover. I assumed someone would be coming soon to wash and lay her out.

I cast my eyes about her room, vaguely remembering it from past times. It was much like all the others here, spacious, the walls covered in dark panelling. Large windows faced the front of the house with a small settle and desk situated close by for a good reading spot.

The cupboards were concealed behind the panelling as in all the bedrooms, but Vivienne had other furnishings in here. I was drawn to a tall, sturdy set of bookshelves, stacked with a variety of books and an assortment of small ornaments. I glanced over the titles, many, favourites of my own. There were a few figurines, some shells, small rocks and other knick-knacks of no particular interest.

I moved on to a writing desk in the corner near the window. Here lay several magazines, mostly discussing fashion and other feminine topics. There was a solitary wide drawer, and without hesitation I opened it. What was I looking for? I did not know. Perhaps for some insight into who my cousin really was.

Inside the drawer were writing supplies, paper, pens, ink and a blotting paper. I moved things around, disappointed there was nothing of interest here. But what had I expected to find? Dissatisfied, I glanced around the room.

Vivienne's reticule lay on top of her dressing table. I grasped the bag and quickly peeked inside. A handkerchief, a pencil, a purse with a few coins, and a piece of paper. I expected it to be a reminder of a purchase needed the next time she was in the village.

It was folded. I opened it up and read the sentence with great interest.

"*Come and see me as soon as you can get away without being seen-HD.*"

Who was HD?

I heard the creaking of floorboards. Someone was

coming down the hall. I hastily stuffed the paper into the pocket of my skirt and put the reticule back where I had found it, then went to stand by Vivienne's bed.

The door clicked open, but I did not look around. Somehow I already knew who it would be.

"'Tis God's will to call his favourites home early," said Father Lynch, coming to stand beside me, his hands clasped together as though in prayer.

There was a pause.

"Then he is a cruel God," I said bluntly.

I turned my head to look at the gaunt man. His head was bowed and his hands together in prayer.

"Tell me, Father. Doesn't your faith demand a person who has taken their own life be denied a Catholic burial in consecrated ground?"

His black eyes narrowed as he stared at me.

"I did not think you an expert upon Catholicism, Mrs Holloway." He sounded annoyed. "However, there is certainly something to what you say." He glanced back at Vivienne's still form. "But if you believe that is the case here, then you are greatly mistaken. Vivienne must have accidentally taken too much of her sedative. The poor wee thing fell into a deep sleep she could not awaken from."

I struggled not to blurt out the many things I wished to say. Instead, I held my tongue, for what good would it do me anyway? Of course Father Lynch would never disclose someone in the Manning family's good standing had killed themselves, even if that were the truth. The scandal would be terrible. But what made my mind spin was that I believed Vivienne had been murdered. Someone had tried to make it look like suicide, and the doctor had lied about the cause of death.

Nothing was as it seemed.

The door opened again behind me. This time, it was Nanette. She came to stand next to the priest and he gently placed his arm about her waist as though to hold her up. At once I felt like an intruder. These two people were closer to my cousin than I had ever been. Quietly I turned and left the room. They wouldn't even notice I had gone.

I hurried straight to my bedroom, went inside and quickly locked the door, relieved to be away from Vivienne's room.

Pulling out the note I'd found I read it again. HD? Who had those initials? I retrieved my notebook from its hiding place, sat on the bed while I scoured through the pages. It did not take long. There it was. I read the entry made about meeting an old friend of my parents who had given me some letters. Hilary Daly.

An unlikely pair of friends indeed. What were Vivienne and Hilary going to talk about? And why the sense of urgency? My interest was piqued. Why did I get the sense that all was not as it appeared at Darkwater?

I glanced at the clock. Was there time to go into the village today? Probably. But it might be inappropriate after what had just occurred. I couldn't leave to converse with others on the very day Vivienne had died. It would be disrespectful to my uncle, given the loss of his daughter. I'd better wait a few days.

I hid the note with my other belongings, and with a reluctant sigh, went downstairs.

****

The rest of the day passed without incident. Two

women from the village came to tend to Vivienne. I helped choose an outfit for them to dress her in as Nanette was inconsolable. They would wash and dress her, then lay her out.

During the remainder of the afternoon, several callers came to express their condolences by leaving flowers and messages for the family. Everyone was told the same story. Vivienne had died in her sleep.

I spoke with them all, for Uncle Simon was upstairs, and Nanette had long since gone to her room. Ivan was absent the entire time. I doubted he was still at Rosell's Cottage. Surely he hadn't gone to Skipton and the mill?

At dinner, I sat alone, half-heartedly picking at a plate of steak and kidney pie. Tibbetts chatted with me briefly, but he too was exhausted from such an emotionally tiring day. I encouraged him to go and eat with the others in the kitchen.

I pushed my half-eaten food away and poured myself a glass of wine.

Ivan came into the dining room. "Mind if I join you, Claire?"

"Of course not. I should be glad of the company."

He took a seat directly across from me, then helped himself to a slice of pie, mashed potatoes, and peas. Without speaking, he ate several bites of food.

I poured a glass of wine for him and passed it over.

"Thank you." He took a hearty swig and set the glass back down. "I've just returned from the mill," he said, "and I haven't eaten a bite all day."

"I can tell." I raised a brow. "I'm surprised you went there today of all days. Nanette has been cloistered with her father and the priest. She's still upstairs in her room crying."

"And let me guess, you think me unfeeling as I seemingly abandoned my wife in her time of grief?" He was almost smiling. His eyes glinted.

"Something like that," I replied, topping up my wine glass.

He took a last bite, then wiped his mouth with a serviette. "You should not judge without having all the facts, Claire. I may not be a wonderful husband, but I am sensitive enough to understand my wife needed consoling. It was she who did not want me here."

"She was likely upset."

"I presumed her state of distress would elicit a certain type of behaviour, and I insisted upon remaining by her side. But she asked me to leave, preferring the company of the priest and her father." He smiled. "See. You have judged me unfairly."

I raised my glass to him. "Then you have my full apology, Ivan." We both took a sip of wine.

"If you must know, I called a meeting at the mill early this afternoon with all the supervisors and shift managers. I wanted to prepare them for Simon's expected absence so the mill would run smoothly until his return. Everything will be in place when the workers show up in the morning."

I regarded him. "My, you certainly are loyal. I'm sure Uncle Simon will appreciate your being so responsible." I still thought Ivan shouldn't have left the house and been gone all day. "But it would have been nice if you had stayed here to greet the constant stream of visitors who came today offering their condolences. I didn't know any of them and have probably been quite rude."

He contemplated what I'd said. "I am sorry. That was thoughtless of me. I was so focused on the mill it didn't dawn on me I could be of use here. Please forgive me." He sounded earnest.

"It is not me you should ask forgiveness of. It is Nanette."

He bristled immediately. "I don't think that's any of your business, Claire. What goes on between your cousin and me, doesn't concern anyone but us."

"I would agree with you when circumstances are normal. But currently, they are far from it. A member of the family has died. There is much to be done, to be organised, and Uncle Simon is incapable of doing anything just now. He's a broken man."

Ivan leaned back against his chair and his stare levelled on my face. "I take it you have decided we need to rally together as a loving family to get everyone through an unexpected tragedy?"

"Something like that," I said quietly, aware of the sarcasm in his voice. "Look, I can't help but feel things aren't right here. I wish I could articulate better, but I can't. My instincts keep reminding me that all is not well. And by the way, I want to talk to you about a lady I met in the village named Hilary Daly. Do you know her?"

"Yes I do. She's a nice person. We've sat next to each other at dinner a few times. Why do you ask?"

"Because this morning I was in Vivienne's room, and I discovered a note she'd received from Mrs Daly."

"Were you snooping?" He seemed amused.

"This isn't funny, Ivan," I said. "I think my cousin died in suspicious circumstances, and I want to find out if I'm right. It's not a game. This is a life. And if you don't want to take me seriously, then I'll stop speaking to you about it."

He at least had the grace to look ashamed. "Again, I am sorry. I do not cope well with death. It brings back too many memories. I find it difficult being in this bloody house at the moment, and I am out of sorts."

"I understand. I could say the same. I've lost the three people I love most in the world in the past eighteen months. If I can cope, then so must you. Perhaps I am being ridiculous. I know my imagination is very colourful and at times I read more into situations than necessary. But you seem to forget I have also been a nurse for many years, and there is an extra sense we develop when people are ill, a perception which guides us sometimes even to save a life. After reading my mother's journals, then coming to Darkwater only for my cousin to die days later, I believe there's every reason to feel suspicious and have concerns. If I am barking up the wrong tree, then what harm has been done? In the event I am actually onto something, perhaps another life could be saved, and someone evil can pay for the harm they have caused."

Ivan gave a long sigh. His face relaxed and his tone softened. "I must agree with you. You are correct on all counts. As you say, it hurts no one to be inquisitive and put your fears to rest." He sat forward and poured himself another glass of wine, then reached over to top mine up. "All right, what do you want me to do?"

"The note sent from Mrs Daly had a sense of urgency to it. She asked Vivienne to call on her as quickly as possible."

"I didn't know they were friends," Ivan remarked. "I never go to church, but the rest of the family and Mrs

Daly attend St. Michael's together. Have you told anyone else about it?"

"No, not yet. I think it better to keep it to myself for now. As soon as propriety allows, I shall go and visit Mrs Daly. I want to ask her what she referred to in the note in case it could be connected to my cousin's death."

"It does seem rather cloak and dagger, Claire. The likelihood of someone wanting to harm Vivienne is slight. A few sharp words and unpleasantries do not warrant murder. And to my knowledge, she seldom went anywhere where she might encounter the type of person who'd show her violence."

"Perhaps," I said. "But everyone has secrets, Ivan. You and my uncle spend your days far away from here. There are minimal servants at Darkwater. You might be surprised what you find out about your sister-in-law."

He regarded me for a moment. I could tell he thought I was being melodramatic. I didn't have the strength to keep arguing my case to him. It had already been a long day and I felt drained.

I took a sip of my drink and set the glass down. "I think I shall retire early tonight. It has been tiring and tomorrow will be no better."

"I'll remain at Darkwater, Claire. The supervisors can manage the mill for the next few days. Although I shall look to you for direction, I promise to be of help going forward."

"Thank you, Ivan." I was so relieved.

As I bade him goodnight and made my way upstairs to my room I was surprised how much better I felt knowing he was going to be here.

Chapter Twenty

THE CHAPEL WAS FULL. There were so many faces, most unknown to me. I assumed not only were they friends of my uncle's, but villagers, and some workers from the mill. I'd even spotted Mr Satterthwaite as well. It did my heart good to see all the warmth and support for my devastated uncle. He was an absolute wreck, broken by the loss of his eldest daughter.

The mass was long and drawn out. Father Lynch stood proudly in his pulpit, and the entire time he spoke I envisioned a large crow, standing on its perch. After a short while, I'd become lost in my own thoughts, mechanically standing and sitting when required.

We were in the front row. I sat at the end, with Ivan to my left. Though my relationship with Vivienne was precarious, I could not help but shed some tears. She was my cousin after all, and we shared the same Parslow blood in our veins.

After the mass was read, we stood around the graveyard in the pouring rain and fierce wind. Those holding umbrellas fought against the strong gusts threatening to wrench them out of cold, numb hands.

Father Lynch finished the ceremony, and we each took our turn throwing dirt into the grave. I stood solemnly, watching everyone pay their last respects and then slowly pass Uncle Simon, Nanette, and Ivan. I hung back—a stranger to these people.

Glancing at the open grave a shudder passed through me. I was transported back to another time, another graveyard where my two loved ones now rested.

I forced my thoughts in another direction. That of my cousin and the strange circumstances of her death. Still convinced Vivienne had not taken her own life, I planned to visit Mrs Daly the very next morning. I had not noticed her presence in the chapel, and it would be hard to identify her amid a sea of black umbrellas.

At last, the service was over. Everyone slowly drifted away, no doubt anxious to get somewhere warm and dry. I left ahead of the family so I could oversee that which awaited our guests at Darkwater.

I arrived to a flustered Tibbetts, and Mrs Blitch who was quite hot under the collar.

"That blasted girl from t'village never showed up to help wi' the food," she cried. "I'm not finished wi' sandwiches, and them cakes need icing."

"Let me help," I said, taking off my wet coat and hat. "Show me what to do and I'll get it done."

The older woman was too flustered to argue. Within a few minutes I was quickly making cucumber sandwiches and neatly chopping off crusts while Cook iced her cakes. Tibbetts and Mellors ran up and down the hall, taking plates of food and decanters of drink into the large dining room.

When Tibbetts announced, "They're here," I took off the apron I'd donned, wiped my hands, and hurriedly went into the drawing room to help receive our guests.

Uncle Simon and Nanette sat together with Father Lynch on the sofa. Here, they graciously received what seemed like droves of people offering their condolences and sorrow at the loss of Vivienne. As I observed, I wondered if any of them really knew her. Judging by the curiosity shown at the interior of the house, I suspected some of the guests were being nosy and just wanted to take a look at the interior of Darkwater Abbey.

"How are you holding up?" Ivan joined me where I stood near the window. He'd been a great help since that night at dinner. His attentiveness to Nanette and my uncle had enabled me to help organise everything else.

"Well enough, thank you. Though I am more than ready for it all to be done with." I glanced at Father Lynch who seemed to be in his element, while my family sat close to him diminished by their loss. Uncle Simon looked bereft and Nanette looked drugged.

"Has Doctor Tipton given Nanette something for her nerves?"

Ivan nodded. "Some sort of sedative. She was so distraught we couldn't calm her down."

We both surveyed the room. I recognised Colonel Baldwin and the doctor who were engrossed in conversation. I'd already seen Phoebe, Hazel, and Martin earlier. They were stood in their own group with two other younger people I did not recognise. There were a few from the mill, Mary Buxton, whose titian hair made her easy to spot. Then, out the corner of my eye I saw Hilary Daly.

"Look," I nudged Ivan with my elbow. "There's Mrs Daly. I shall go and speak to her at once. Come with me," I instructed. Without waiting for his answer, I made directly for the woman.

Mrs Daly chatted to a lady I did not know. I

walked up to them both. “Mrs Daly. How kind of you to come.”

The unknown lady took a step back and allowed me to command the conversation.

Hilary turned large brown eyes to look at me. “Mrs Holloway. Please allow me to express how sad I am at this tragic loss.” Her heartfelt words were kind.

I gestured to Ivan standing close by. “I know you are acquainted with Mr Delahunt.”

“Mrs Daly.” Ivan nodded politely. “Thank you for coming today. I know the support of the community means a great deal to my wife and father-in-law at this difficult time.”

Mrs Daly began a commiserate speech and I tuned it out while contemplating what to say to her. Though Vivienne’s death was made public, the true cause had been kept within close quarters. As far as everyone was concerned, she had died in her sleep from an unsuspected heart ailment.

I waited for the lady to finish speaking, then addressed her. “Mrs Daly. I wonder if I could ask a question?”

The other woman moved politely away.

“Of course, my dear. What is it?”

“Whilst sorting through my cousin possessions, I found a note you sent recently, asking that she come and see you with great urgency. Might I ask what that was in reference to?”

Mrs Daly blanched. “Oh, that.” She took another sip from her sherry glass, her eyes shifting from one thing to another as she obviously searched for an answer to conceal whatever the truth had been.

“I believe it was to do with one of the charities we

fund at the church. Vivienne and I oversee the annual fete and bake sale. It was probably something like that."

"Mrs Daly, you are a terrible liar."

She gasped.

I continued. "It was no such thing. That note implied concern. It had nothing to do with how many cakes you'd have at a sale. Tell me," I said firmly. "What was the real reason?"

Her dark eyes lowered. She would not meet my gaze.

"Mrs Daly," Ivan interjected. "Please do not be upset by Claire's question. There is nothing amiss. We want to ensure Vivienne's personal business is settled on all fronts. It is easier to ask people directly rather than read through all her diaries and ledgers."

I looked at him with admiration. He had boxed the lady in at the mention of diaries that probably didn't exist.

Mrs Daly still looked quite pale. She took another sip of her sherry. Her gaze darted between Ivan and myself. Flustered, she finally spoke.

"I am sorry," she said. "But I really can't remember. Now, if you'll excuse me, I should like to speak with your uncle and cousin." With that, she brushed past us. She did not head towards the sofa where my family held court, but straight to the door.

I watched her stride out of the room, but then felt someone's attention settle upon me. I scoured the room quickly, and there met a steady obsidian gaze.

Father Lynch stared at me, his black eyes fastened on my face. I turned around so he could only see my back.

"The priest is keeping an eye on my actions," I said

to Ivan who still faced him.

"He watches everything that goes on around here," Ivan retorted. "Sometimes I think he runs this village. He seems to have his hands in everything going on in Starling."

"I don't trust him," I blurted out. "There is something about the man I find unsettling."

Ivan smiled at me, the mischievous light back in his eyes. "Don't tell me," he said. "It's that damnable nurses' instinct again."

"Touché," I said with a chuckle. "There, you have me."

We parted ways to mingle among the guests and thank them for coming back to the house. Uncle Simon and Nanette remained seated, and it was only polite for us to speak in their stead.

At length, the last of the company made their way out. It seemed late in the day, although it was only four o'clock in the afternoon. Outside, the rain still fell in sheets, the clouds grey and black, sailing low across the sky.

Uncle Simon had taken Nanette upstairs while our guests were leaving. I wandered into the dining room and gathered up dirty glasses and plates to place on a tray and carry into the kitchen.

"And how do you fare, Mrs Holloway?"

Reluctantly I turned. I hadn't heard the priest come into the room.

"I am manging well enough, Father Lynch." I endeavoured to sound polite. I really wanted to tell him to go away and let me get my work done.

He walked over to the table. "You and Mr Delahunt did admirably well today. It was good of you both, helping with the guests. I fear both Simon and Nanette are taking this very hard." He gave a sigh to show his concern, but his eyes were cold as a snake's.

I forced myself to sound agreeable. "Thank you. I think we all tried to do our bit today. It was kind of you to stay with Uncle Simon and Nanette. I was pleased to see so many people attend the service and show their support. I am sure it meant a great deal to him."

"Yes. In times like this, sometimes God cannot ease all the suffering. Our fellow man can help fill the loss." He smiled at me. "How are you bearing up, my dear? My attention has been so focused upon Simon and Nanette, I feel I have neglected my duties by not ensuring your welfare."

He stared at my face, his, a mask of concern. Though I didn't believe it was genuine. Something about this man kept me on my guard.

"I am doing well," I said quickly, almost too quickly. I took a step away from him and placed my attention to collecting a few more plates. "Of course, I am terribly saddened by what has happened. Though I was not close to my cousin, she is family, and I have known her most of my life."

"It is especially difficult when a person dies at such a young age," he said quietly.

My hand stilled.

"Indeed," he continued. "The unexpected death of those we not only love, but anticipate having in our lives for years to come, is the hardest loss of all. You, my dear, have unfortunately known how unbearable it feels. I understand your child—"

"Let us not speak of it," I snapped, turning to look at the priest. "It is only right to think of what is happening now, Father. The past has no significance today."

"I disagree," he replied, demanding my full attention again. "You see, the events of yesterday control how we behave today. You are a perfect example of that, my dear."

I felt my cheeks growing warm. I stopped what I was doing. "I beg your pardon?"

"Oh, I mean no disrespect, Mrs Holloway. You have suffered more than many with the loss of your loved ones. I think your true vulnerability is hidden beneath a very brave exterior. You appear to the world as a strong woman, when really I believe underneath it all you are broken. Rather like building of a house on swampy land. Your capacity to cope with all your experiences lies on shaky ground."

I was furious. "Tell me, Father. What do you base these suppositions upon? You have known me barely five minutes, yet you deem to think you understand who I am?"

His countenance changed at my tone. The compassion drained away from his face and a muscle clenched in his cheek.

"I have no suppositions," he declared in a low voice. "But I have ears and eyes. You've barely been back a week and already things are in turmoil. All because you are unsettled and still emotionally scarred from your experiences in Africa."

"What?" I gasped. "How dare you speak to me like that. Again, I remind you, you know nothing about me."

"My dear," he cajoled. "'Tis not my intent to upset you. Only to point out that which I see in front of me.

You have come back to Darkwater and spoken to your family of events that took place when you were a child. It has upset your uncle deeply, being reminded of a brutal time in your family history. And I think it is all based upon your unwillingness to accept the death of your mother, so close on the heels of the death of your husband and daughter."

"Enough," I said loudly. "I shall not listen any longer. Your incorrect opinion of me means nothing. The conversations I have with my uncle are none of your business. My interest in the past is to discover the truth. My mother knew a wrong had been committed, and she devoted her life to reveal the true events of the night Keith Delahunt was killed. As a man of God, I would think you on the side of right, yet you seem opposed to my continuing something she began."

He was getting angry. He struggled to maintain his composure, but there was no disguising the shine of irritation burning in his black eyes.

"What's going on in here?" Ivan strode over to where I stood, almost shaking with rage. "I could hear your voices out in the hallway."

Father Lynch's expression changed quickly into that of concern once again. "Mrs Holloway and I were discussing the effect of grief upon us poor humans. I was trying to offer comfort where I could." He glanced at me and then back to Ivan. "But I must get on my way. It has been a long day for us all, and I still have many duties remaining in the parish. If you will excuse me."

Before either one of us could respond, Father Lynch made his escape. I waited a moment until I knew he would be gone from the house.

"I hate that man," I said.

Ivan frowned at me. "Are you all right, Claire? What on earth just happened between you and the crow?"

His use of that word broke through my anger and diffused it somewhat.

"That man had the audacity to berate me for bringing up the past to Uncle Simon. He said I was emotionally imbalanced because I'd lost my husband and my child and now I had come to Darkwater I was making things very unsettled. He was basically telling me to stop poking my nose into what happened to your father and blaming me for upsetting my uncle."

"What nonsense," Ivan said. "The man's an idiot. Just because he's taken a few vows he is not an expert on the psyche." His eyes searched my face. "Don't let him upset you. His opinion is bias and slanted. He's just annoyed you've upset the dynamics. It wouldn't surprise me if Simon had complained to him about your having the controlling vote at the mill. Don't forget, his church is reliant on the financial support of this community. The lion's share comes from the mill."

"Well, he's not going the right way about getting my support," I said angrily. "Quite the opposite."

"He's a priest, Claire. He's old fashioned and set in his ways. Men like that think women have no place in business. Ignore what he said and stop letting it anger you."

"Easier said than done." I began to gather up the dishes once again.

"Here, let me help you," Ivan said. He began collecting up the crockery, and together we carried trays down the hall. We repeated the action several times, until all the dishes were in the kitchen and the food collected and put up.

Mrs Blitch, Mellors and Tibbetts worked hard. The plates and glasses were washed and dried, and the food put in the cold storage room. Ivan and I were at Cook's bidding. He helped dry dishes, while I covered up the food.

With so many helping hands, we made short work of the task. Mrs Blitch put the kettle on the hearth and invited us both to sit and have a cup of tea.

Outside, the rain still poured down. It was lovely and cozy in the warm kitchen and I was happy to stay put.

At length, Mellors went up to her room to get off her feet, while Ivan, Cook, Tibbetts and I sat around the long wooden table drinking strong tea and eating slices of lemon drizzle cake which Cook produced from a large tin. It was mouth-wateringly delicious.

"Mrs Blitch, this is the tastiest cake I believe I've ever eaten," Ivan exclaimed, much to Cook's delight. "And the tea is outstanding."

"That's what I told her," I piped in. "It has such a strong flavour, and it tastes good with milk and sugar."

"Thou'll make me head swell, Master Ivan, wi' all flattery."

I looked at the cook and grinned at the softening of her features. Her eyes sparkled under Ivan's praise. I could tell at once Mrs Blitch liked him, and for some reason it pleased me.

Tibbetts, sitting across from me commented. "Did I tell you, Miss Claire, our Jack's coming home Friday for a few weeks' leave."

"Jack? That is good news. It's been an age since I

saw him. The last few times I visited Darkwater, he was away at sea. I'll have to come and visit him."

There commenced a discussion of the many countries Jack had visited. By the time we finished chatting, the tea was drunk and there was little left of the cake to put back into the tin. We each took our used plates to the sink.

"They'll not be a dinner put on the night," said Cook. "Mr Manning said they'd more as like stay up in t'rooms and take a tray. So I've made a pot o' stew and there's a fresh loaf besides. I'll take 'em up before I leave for 'night."

"Thank you, Mrs Blitch," I said gratefully, relieved I wouldn't have to dine with the others. We were all tired and been in company too long.

"Will you eat in your room?" Ivan asked.

Mrs Blitch spoke before I could answer. "If thou wants, I'll leave pot on t'hearth keeping warm. Thou can take it off later once you've both supped,"

"Excellent," said Ivan. "That's what we'll do." He glanced over at me. "I've enough cake in me to keep going for a couple of hours yet. Want to meet in here at about seven o'clock for dinner?"

"That will be fine," I agreed.

We both thanked Cook and left the kitchen. Ivan returned to the drawing room, but I went upstairs. I was weary, and an hour or two by myself was just the remedy.

Chapter Twenty-One

THE STEW DID NOT DISAPPOINT. We both ate a full bowl of the delicious meal along with hunks of crusty bread.

Our conversation was light-hearted as we ate. It had been such a morose day after all. I talked about old memories of when I lived at Darkwater, and some of the scrapes Tibbetts had helped me out of.

"He's a good man," Ivan said. "He's stayed loyal to the family when he could easily find a well-paying job elsewhere. The mills and factories are always looking for men like him."

"I'm surprised you haven't lured him away to Parslow's."

Ivan grinned wolfishly. "I tried. But he declined."

"Good for him," I said. "He's much better off being here in the fresh air than cooped up in that hot, sticky mill."

"You're right about that. I've been doing some research about how we can make the air healthier for our workers. It's a dilemma difficult to remedy. We need warm, damp air so the cotton won't split and fray, but I know keeping the atmosphere moist is bad for the lungs."

"Is there anything to be done?" I'd seen people with horrid lung conditions when I trained in London. It was awful watching a person struggle to take a breath. It was accepted that textile mills were unhealthy places to work. There were still not many laws governing working practices in factories, let alone people to enforce them.

"We've installed fans and done much to suck out all the polluted air, but it isn't enough. The carding room is where the air gets contaminated by dust. The visible fibres can be dealt with easily enough. Some of the men even put a wad of clean cotton in their mouth to stop anything being breathed in that way. But it's the invisible particles we can't see that does the most harm. There is work being done to try and trap the dust where it forms in the machines, before it reaches the air, and exhaust it out through tubes into containers, or vent it outside."

"That sounds like a wonderful solution. I would like to learn more about the workings of the mill, especially the health and safety aspects of how things are done."

Ivan looked pleased. "I am glad you're taking such an interest, Claire. Simon is focused upon the business side of things. The welfare of our workers costs money, and that never goes over very well."

"It is crucial to a successful business," I said. "If Parslow's can provide good safety measures, they will always have a workforce." I stopped, realising Ivan was staring at me. "What is it?"

"I was thinking how much I enjoy our conversations. We never seem to run out of things to talk about. Considering how awful I was when we met on the train last week, I am taken aback at how glad I am you've come to Darkwater. Vivienne's passing has placed a dark cloud over us—God knows it is tragic. Yet despite that, I can honestly say that you're coming home has made it a better place." Ivan raised his glass of water, "Here's to being back home, Claire."

I lifted my glass, and we reached across the table to clink them together.

"Well, this looks very cozy." Nanette stood in the doorway watching us. "A quiet dinner for two?"

Her accusatory tone made me feel guilty, although I knew not why it should.

Ivan looked over his shoulder at his wife. "Nanette, come and join us. We have just finished eating and were discussing the mill."

Nanette walked into the kitchen dressed in her night attire with a pale pink silk shawl wrapped around her body. Her beautiful hair spilled down her back, reaching to her waist, but it was messy and tangled, as though she'd been sleeping already. As she joined us, I noticed her gait was off, and I recognised she was under the influence of some medication. What it was I did not know. The next time I was in her room I would have to look through her pills and powders.

"Have you eaten anything this evening?" I asked once she'd sat down next to her husband.

"I don't know," she said, her words a little slurred.

"Let me get you something then." I got up.

"No," she said loudly. "I don't want anything. I just want to go to sleep, but I keep dreaming about Vivienne."

I sat back down again. "Did Doctor Tipton give you something to help you sleep?"

"Yes. It helps me fall asleep but doesn't stop the nightmare from coming back." She began to cry.

I understood the ache she must be feeling in her heart. "Perhaps it would make you feel better if you weren't alone?" I suggested, looking over at Ivan to take the cue.

"It would." Nanette looked at me expectantly.

I waited to see if Ivan would speak up, yet he said nothing. I was aware my cousin still stared at me expectantly.

"Claire," she said in a quiet voice. "Please stay in my room tonight. I cannot cope on my own." Her voice broke and tears slid down her cheeks.

Ivan remained conspicuously silent.

"Of course I will," I said in a rush, then immediately regretted it. Yet how could I deny her request? Her sister was dead, and she was distraught. It was the least I could do.

I got up. "Come then, it is late. Let us go upstairs." I looked at Ivan and did not hide my annoyance. "Don't forget to check the hearth and tidy up before you go to bed. I promised Mrs Blitch."

He nodded but did not say a word. I led Nanette up the stairs.

WE LAY SIDE BY SIDE IN HER large bed and I listened as she spoke about Vivienne. Nanette alternated between fond reminiscences and sobbing in misery. I don't know what time it was when she finally slept, but it was close to dawn.

****

At some point, Uncle Simon knocked on the door and showed some surprise seeing me there with his daughter.

"She could not sleep," I whispered. "She asked me to stay." I quietly got out of the bed and stole out into the hall leaving him to sit with her while she slept on. I still wore my funeral attire from the previous day and could not wait to change.

At length I washed and dressed then hurried downstairs to eat breakfast. As expected, I ate alone. Outside the rain still beat down. It had not let up since the day before. Did the moat ever overflow? The thought made me shudder.

Tibbetts brought in a pot of tea, and we exchanged pleasantries.

"Thank you for all the hard work yesterday," I said. "Everyone did a really good job."

"Least we could do for t'master and yerself," he said. "'Tis a rotten shame this house has seen so much sadness."

"I agree. But at least you have something good to look forward to with your Jack coming home."

"Aye. I'm that pleased, Miss Claire. Been too long since he were in't Yorkshire. Will you come see him Saturday fer tea?"

"I should like that very much."

With that, Tibbetts left me to finish my breakfast.

THE HOUSE LAY QUIET. Ivan probably hurried off to the mill at first light, and as far as I knew Nanette was still abed with her father standing guard. I was at a loss of what to do. The house seemed so gloomy, but it was even worse outside. The rain came down so fiercely I had no desire to venture out there.

I walked about the place, in and out of the rooms, reacquainting myself with furniture, objects and paintings. Darkwater had so much history. Any building of this size standing for three centuries would have many stories to tell.

I did not go down to the cellar. It was always dark and dreary, there among the wine caskets and other stores. Besides, with all this rain it would be cold and musty. Oh, how I wished the weather wasn't so awful. I could have gone into Starling Village and spoken with Mrs Daly once again.

Why had Hilary lied about the note? To what end? I was determined to find out and quickly. But only if it would ever stop raining.

Defeated, I wandered up to my room. I paced about for a while. I looked at my notes and re-read the letters from Mother to Mrs Daly. Nothing held my attention. Finally, I grasped one of the books I brought with me from home, an old copy of Jane Eyre which belonged to my mother. I took it with me and settled on my bed.

It seemed such a waste of time lying down reading, when there were things needing attention in the house. But Darkwater was not mine to run, nor did I have a desire to be the mistress here.

I found the place I had last stopped reading and quickly got lost in the story.

A massive thunderclap boomed, and I woke with a start. For a second I lay still trying to remember what I was doing. Then I realised I'd fallen asleep reading, and no wonder. My night had not been a restful one.

Reluctantly I got up and went to look out of the window. The rain still threw itself against the ground as though in a fierce temper. The sky was dark grey, the wind blew hard and wait…the moat was full.

Alarmed, I scanned the area. I was not mistaken. Water lapped over the banks of the moat, blurring the division between it and land. I quickly put on my shoes and went downstairs in search of my uncle.

I found him with Tibbetts, standing at the top of the cellar steps looking down while discussing the situation.

"I saw the moat," I said, coming to join them. "Does the water usually get this high?"

Uncle Simon paused speaking and looked at me. "We often get this much rain, just not in so short a space of time. The ground is too saturated to drain, and so it will flood."

I was alarmed. Visions of us sinking under water danced through my head.

"Don't worry," my uncle said reassuringly. "The house is safe. We are high enough it won't get to us, or cover the bridge, but the cellar might flood a little."

That calmed me. "Will you empty it?" I asked.

"No," he said. "It would be too much trying to move the barrels. We'll bring up some of the wine bottles just in case, but nothing else can get spoiled except the stonework."

With that, Tibbetts went down the steps, and we formed a short line. Tibbetts passed bottles to my uncle, halfway up the stairs, who in turn passed them to me, whereupon I placed them in a tidy row.

We had quite the collection going, when the front door opened with a torrent of cold air revealing Ivan, soaked to the skin. It was early in the afternoon, and I was surprised to see him home so soon. He explained it straight away.

"I thought Gibbons better get us back before nightfall. We'd not find our way back in the dark, and I didn't fancy staying in Skipton overnight." He pulled off his coat and began removing his sodden boots.

Uncle Simon, hearing his son-in-law's voice came

up from the cellar.

"What are the roads like?" he asked.

"Bloody treacherous and flooded," Ivan replied. "Gibbons did a grand job getting us back here. The horses were spooked, and we almost threw a wheel." He then realised something was going on as the cellar door was wide open and wine bottles were standing on the floor of the hall.

"What's amiss here?"

"Damn cellar's starting to let in water," my uncle said irritably. "We're leaving the barrels but bringing up bottles of wine, so they don't get mould."

Ivan moved towards us. He passed by me and offered to take a look. He disappeared down the stairs and I heard him converse with Tibbetts and Uncle Simon. After a few minutes, all three came back up the stairs.

"I'd not worry about it yet," said Ivan. "Even if you try and drain the water, it won't do any good for there's nowhere for it to go. It's like bailing it from a ship in the ocean with a hole in the bow. We can't do much until the rain stops."

"We'll keep an eye on it," Uncle Simon said. "I don't think it will come anywhere near the steps. The cellar is quite large, and it would take a great deal more water to fill it."

"I agree," Ivan said.

I was glad he was back from the mill. Somehow having him here was more reassuring than I cared to admit. Though I was usually a capable person, the water unnerved me after almost drowning. My uncle was a dependable, intelligent man, but he was still not himself and I lacked confidence in his abilities.

Ivan went up to change and I ventured into the kitchen. Mellors had already been sent home. Mrs Blitch decided to remain at the house. She had a cot in the larder where she planned to sleep rather than go out into the elements. I hoped the cottages were not in danger of flooding. They were a ways down from the house and moat, but still under threat.

Mrs Blitch fixed a Lancashire hotpot, and the enticing smell of the casserole filled the kitchen. It was past luncheon, yet not time for dinner, but I suggested we supped anyway. Tibbetts set the table and then went to inform the family we would eat early. He got a nice fire going in the small dining room.

By the time we reassembled, it was almost five o'clock in the afternoon. Ivan had changed into dry clothes, and much to my surprise, Nanette came down to join us.

"Hello, my dear," Uncle Simon said to his daughter, clearly pleased she was downstairs. "Come and sit down. There's some hot food to take the chill off you."

Nanette sat, and we joined her. She looked tired. Below her eyes, dark smudges looked like pale bruises, and her complexion was almost the colour of milk.

Tibbetts carried in a tray bearing a large pot and a basket of thick white bread. He set it down, and Uncle Simon waved him away.

"We'll serve ourselves, man. You go downstairs and sup with Cook. We can manage on our own."

I was pleased my uncle was being so considerate. Tibbetts gave a brief nod and left us to our meal.

We handed our plates to Uncle Simon, and he spooned lashings of casserole onto them. The food looked wonderful, steaming into the cool air. It was full of thick chunks of beef, carrots, onions, and green beans, in thick gravy, with soft slices of potatoes laid out like rooftiles on the top. The bread, fresh and still warm, made the butter melt upon contact. It was light and soft, with a crisp crust that flaked as you bit into each piece.

The men seemed to be enjoying their meal as much as I. But Nanette toyed with her food. She pushed a piece of meat around with her fork, whilst staring at her plate.

"Are you not hungry, Cousin?" I asked.

She shook her head.

"My darling," said her father. "You must eat a little. I don't want you falling ill or becoming anaemic once again. You know how weak that makes you."

Nanette glanced up at her father, then looked at me. Reluctantly, she speared the meat onto her fork and ate it.

Ivan watched his wife and I studied his expression. He looked at Nanette as though she were a complete stranger. It was so very odd. There was no anger there, no dislike. It was an apathy and indifference which I found quite disturbing.

Suddenly a strange sound erupted from down the hall, as if something heavy had fallen and crashed to the ground.

We all stopped eating and turned our heads towards the doorway. A moment later, Tibbetts appeared.

"Mr Manning, sir," he said. "The water's got into the cellar and rotted out some of the plaster. It's knocked down part of a wall."

Ivan and Uncle Simon got up to follow him, and I did likewise, my curiosity aroused. They hastened down the cellar steps, and I went right behind them. I wanted to see this for myself and determine whether or not we were in any danger from the elements.

As I drew closer to the bottom of the cellar stairs, I smelled the murky moat water. I stopped before reaching the last few steps as I saw the water level would soak my shoes. The men had not been concerned, for they were already sloshing through puddles of dark water, Tibbetts leading the way with a bright lantern.

Boldly, I took another two steps downward and stopped. This was far enough. I peered to see what they were doing.

Ivan was talking about the composition of the plaster that had come loose causing a gaping hole where the wall met the ground, now pooled with moat water.

"The plaster that's come away looks different. I'll warrant it was added at a later date than the rest. You can see the difference in the texture as well as the colour."

"Best we leave it alone," said my uncle. "It's only a small part of a priest hole. They're hollowed out and the seals are weaker because of it. Let's wait for the water to recede before we attend to it."

The men seemed to be in agreement and turned to come back to the stairs when there was a loud rumble as more of the lower wall fell in chunks onto the water-covered floor.

Ivan paused, then turned back to take another look at it with Tibbetts holding the light high. "The wall is top heavy," he announced. "The rest of it will fall away eventually." Then he peered into the gap created by the collapsed plaster. "You're right about it being hollow, Simon. Must be one of those…well I'm damned," he suddenly exclaimed. "Tibbetts, come closer with that light," he shouted.

"What is it?" I called out.

In the gaslight I saw the shock on Ivan's face as he turned in our direction. My heart pounded in anticipation.

"There's something in the priest hole," he said. "It's a skeleton."

Chapter Twenty-Two

WE SAT IN THE DRAWING room drinking brandy. Even Tibbetts had been pressed by Ivan to take a sip, and he had done so, though he was certainly uncomfortable.

Uncle Simon looked dazed and flushed from the alcohol—he was on his second glass. Nanette sat quietly on the sofa by her father's side while Ivan and I sat across from them in the armchairs.

"Poor fellow," said Ivan. "He must have been there a long time. It's been centuries since they hid priests down there."

"Was there much of him left?" I asked. In truth, had it not been for the water, I'd have gone to look myself. I'd seen plenty of bones and skeletons in my time.

"No," Ivan replied. "Some tattered fabric, maybe a few wisps of hair. We'll look again tomorrow if the rain lets up. The priest hole is raised from the level of the ground, so hopefully the water won't get near it."

"I'll have to send for Father Lynch," Simon said. He sounded odd, and I guessed it was the brandy. "Gibbons will fetch him first thing."

"This house is full of death," Nanette said, having remained silent for so long. "What's another set of bones after all?"

"That's enough, Nanette," Uncle Simon snapped. "I'll not have you being so flippant."

My cousin set her glass down and got up. "Fine," she retorted with annoyance. "I am most fatigued. I shall go on up to bed at once. You might find a pile of bones interesting, but I can assure you I do not."

With that she walked away and over to the stairs. What odd behaviour she exhibited. But then that was Nanette. One moment a terrified baby and the next cold as ice. Perhaps the brandy had caused an effect upon her as well as her father.

Ivan got up and strode over to the windows. He opened the latch on one side and pushed the glass pane open so he could see outside.

"It's too dark to see much," he said. "But the rain has let up quite a bit. There's a good chance by morning it will come to an end." He closed and locked the window. "If we get too much rain, it's going to impact the deliveries tomorrow as well."

"You might not be able to get to Skipton in the morning," said my uncle. "No use getting the carriage stuck in mud."

"You're right. We'll be short a few workers due to the road conditions as well. Confounded weather."

"At least *you* don't have to travel on foot," I commented. "I can't imagine what it is like walking out in this rain."

Uncle Simon got up and refilled his glass. "I think I'll go up now," he said sounding weary. "I shall see you both in the morning."

We bade him goodnight.

Ivan went over to the hearth and stoked the fire. The flames responded by dancing a little higher. He came and sat back down, this time on the sofa so that we faced one another.

"Quite the evening, wouldn't you say?" he said, leaning back against a cushion.

I nodded in agreement. "What a strange week it's been. It seems like one thing after another. First the diaries, then Vivienne and now this."

"It does bring a new meaning to having skeletons in your cupboard."

"That was awful," I said. "You shouldn't mock the dead."

"You're right," he acknowledged. "As for the diaries, to be honest, all of that slipped my mind after Vivienne died. It is easy to stop thinking when a person loses their life."

"She didn't lose her life, it was taken."

"We don't know that for certain, Claire."

I met his stare. "I do. How can you possibly not see how strange all these events are. All families have their problems and secrets, but Darkwater has too many. First, look what happened with our fathers. Then, years later, all the evidence I own questioning what happened in the past, mysteriously gets thrown into a fire. Vivienne dies, and now you discover a skeleton hidden away in the cellar. You have to admit it's all rather bizarre."

Much to my surprise, Ivan laughed. "Darkwater isn't an appealing place for a holiday," he said, another laugh escaping him.

I glowered at him. But seeing his enjoyment, the release of so much pent-up pressure dissolve into merriment was contagious. I joined in, giggling like a silly girl. We must have looked foolish, two grown people chuckling like children.

Presently the laughter died away.

"I needed that," said Ivan. "This house has been so full of tension, it's been hard to relax, even during the night. I'll be glad when the weather improves so we aren't trapped inside."

I took a sip of my brandy, languishing the warmth spreading through my mouth. I had a sudden thought. "I must re-schedule my missed appointment with Mr Satterthwaite. I spoke with him at the funeral and told him I'd be in touch. Tomorrow, I intend to pay a call on Mrs Daly if the rain eases up. I want to find out the truth about the note she sent Vivienne. She definitely avoided explaining it yesterday."

"We'll have Father Lynch to put up with first," he warned. "Simon will get him here at first light. If the body is that of a priest, at least Lynch'll know what to do regarding its removal and burial."

"How morbid," I said. "Perhaps I can sleep late and avoid seeing him."

"That's harsh, Claire. How can you dislike a man of God? Surely that's not allowed?" He grinned like a fool and against my better judgement I responded by doing the same.

"I can't help myself; he disturbs me. At first I thought it was just his look… that mealy face and those stern black eyes. But it isn't that. I sense something in the man that doesn't ring true to the role he plays. I can't quite explain it; it's a feeling. And it must be mutual, for I know he dislikes me too."

"Ridiculous," Ivan said. "Father Lynch is everyone's friend. Well, except mine. I'm on the bad list right next to you." He raised his glass. "Here's to popularity."

I raised my own and sipped the last drop. I put the

empty glass down on the table. "And on that cheery note, I am off to bed myself. It will be a busy morning, I've no doubt, and then I'm away to Starling Village to see about that note."

"I'm not far behind you," said Ivan, standing politely. "Let's hope we both sleep well tonight."

Our eyes met and held a beat longer than they should have. Something inside me shifted. Quickly, I looked away.

"Goodnight, Ivan." Without another word I left him standing there.

****

When I came down the next morning my head throbbed though I'd slept very well, both factors likely from the brandy I'd consumed. I went in to the dining room to eat a light breakfast, and the first thing I noticed was sunlight coming through the stained-glass windows. It had finally stopped raining. That meant Ivan would have been able to go to the mill. For some reason the thought disappointed me.

I drank a cup of tea, and as I half-heartedly ate a piece of toast, I heard Uncle Simon talking and then the undisguisable sound of Father Lynch. Curious, I wiped the crumbs from my hands and left the dining room to see what they were up to.

From what I could hear, the two men were already down in the cellar. They were speaking quietly now, probably in deference to the poor mite left down there to die. I shuddered. What a ghastly thought. Then I descended the stairs.

There was another man down there with them. He saw me first and gave a start. He was clergy, judging by the robes he wore. This time I stepped into the cellar.

The water had already receded, although there were strands of weeds and dirt sticking to the floor.

"Claire, what are you doing down here?" Uncle Simon seemed surprised to see me as I joined the three men. Father Lynch who was leaning into the cavernous space, stepped back.

"Mrs Holloway, this is no place for a lady such as yourself. You should return upstairs," Father Lynch said sternly.

"Don't be daft," I replied. "I'm a nurse, Father. A few bones don't scare me. Besides, I can be of help."

He was not pleased. I saw him glance at Uncle Simon for support, but none was forthcoming. My uncle looked unwell.

"Are you ill this morning, Uncle?" I asked with concern. He likely had the same sore head as I from drinking too much brandy.

"Fine, my dear," he said quickly. "But thank you for asking."

Father Lynch spoke up. "Mrs Holloway, allow me to introduce you to my right-hand person, Deacon Wirral."

The clergyman, a short, skinny man, barely looked old enough to use a razor, never mind be in the church. He nodded in my direction and picked up a very large carpet bag lying at his feet. I determined they planned to remove the skeleton and place it in there.

"Are you taking the body?" I enquired. "Should we notify the authorities it has been found for their records?"

"No need, Claire," said Uncle Simon. "I am the judicial authority here, and Father Lynch the religious delegate, so it will all be duly noted."

I moved to stand behind them as Father Lynch and Deacon Wirral got to work.

I could see where the wall plaster had rotted out and crumbled away, exposing the space behind it. But the actual opening of the priest hole was cleverly concealed. A large piece of timber intersected the wall which appeared to be a beam to support the cellar. But the piece of timber could be lifted at the bottom and became a doorway as such, allowing a narrow gap a person could slide through, to the other side.

Father Lynch lifted the beam and exposed the gap, and the deacon stepped through. We could only see half of the man as some of the wall remained intact, but I could tell it was a space large enough for possibly three people standing close together.

I peered over the men's shoulders but couldn't see very much other than what looked like a femur. "What is in there?" I asked. "Are there any personal belongings?"

"Claire, please stop asking questions," Uncle Simon said.

"There is only the body," said Deacon Wirral. "It is bound up in a blanket," said the cleric. "And it is intact. We shall need a stretcher of sorts to remove it in one piece for burial. The bag is too small."

"How odd," I said. "Why would you hide in there wrapped in a blanket?"

"Perhaps the Priest Hunters came in the middle of the night?" Father Lynch said. "I'm sure they would want the element of surprise. If you were disturbed from slumber to hide for your life, you would grab whatever was closest and hurry."

"Yes, of course," I agreed. "Poor fellow. If he was

a priest from back then, he's been here a few centuries."

"I don't doubt it," said Father Lynch. He turned to Uncle Simon. "We shall have to return later today with means of transportation."

"If you can fetch something to lay the poor fellow on," Uncle Simon said, "Gibbons can use our wagon to bring him to you."

"Excellent," said the priest as his man rejoined us. "Now, let us be off." Father Lynch gestured with open palms for me to exit the cellar ahead of them. I wanted to take a closer look, but decided it was wise to go along with him.

We ascended the stairs. Father Lynch and his young deacon excused themselves to go and find a stretcher of sorts.

"Only a place like Darkwater could have something like this happen," I said after the men had gone and Uncle Simon and I were in the drawing room.

"What do you mean by that?"

I frowned as I watched him pour a glass of sherry. It was only mid-morning. "I didn't mean anything, Uncle. It's just typical for something odd to occur here. Darkwater Abbey has so many tales about it, and now we've added to its history."

My uncle took his drink and sat down. "I don't mean to be so surly, my dear. I'm just in a bit of a muddle with Vivienne—" He broke off.

"I understand." I resisted the impulse to go and comfort him. I hadn't forgotten his recent tendency to be over familiar with me. "There is no need to apologise after everything you've been through this week. Let me know if there's anything I can do to help."

"Thank you, dearest Claire." His eyes fastened on me and grew wistful.

We talked for a while longer, and then Uncle Simon went up to his study. He stated he would come back down whenever Father Lynch returned.

After a few minutes, I walked over to the cellar door. I lifted down the lantern hanging inside the door and lit it, then carefully made my way back down the stairs.

My curiosity outweighed my fear. I wasn't scared of anything being down here, although I hated rats, it was being under the ground and so close to the moat which worried me. I had visions of the walls caving, and water rushing in a torrent to drown me.

I stood before the priest hole and pushed on the lower part of the timber to make the space for entry. There was no locking device visible, so I would not get stuck. I squeezed through the gap into the small chamber tucked behind.

Thank goodness the light was bright. I stood in a small area that had been crudely carved out of the stone cellar. My hair brushed against the ceiling, and I realised it had been made to accommodate priests in the Tudor era, when people were much smaller than they were today.

The skeleton lay half-sitting, propped up against the end wall. I hunkered down to see it at a better viewpoint.

As the cleric said, the bones were encased in a blanket or wrap of some sort, long degraded by time. It was impossible to tell what it had been, or indeed its colour after being shut away for so long.

I studied the skull. The jaw hung slack. There were

several teeth missing. This would indicate age perhaps, or economic status. Boldy, I reached forward and touched the blanket which covered the shoulders. Surprisingly it did not fall apart as I thought it might but slid down to reveal the ribcage and spine.

The person had not been large, but as I already surmised, sixteenth century folk were not. I looked over the bones.

"Who were you?" I whispered. I looked over the shoulder span and cast my eyes down to the pelvic area and pondered. How odd there was only a blanket on the bones. Did priests sleep naked? Surely not. Could this body have been someone other than a priest? Murders were likely more common in Elizabeth's reign, so it might have been anyone.

I leaned forward to pull the blanket back to its original position so no one would know I'd been snooping. As I did, the light from my lantern caught something and it glinted. I narrowed my eyes. What was that?

Something had fallen through the sternum and onto the dirt floor. Very gently, I reached between the top two ribs, and grasped it with my nails, almost dropping it as I brought it closer to study.

It was a rusty old necklace, the chain broken. I held the lantern over my palm and saw the pendant was a tiny green shamrock, no larger than a raisin. A shamrock? I didn't think that was a symbol of the Catholic faith.

I don't know what came over me, but I did something dishonest. I slipped the chain into my pocket. I cannot say why, other than I was compelled to do it. Then I made sure the skeleton was as I had found it and climbed out of the priest hole. I quickly went back up the stairs, extinguished the lantern and hung it back on the peg.

I walked past the stairs as a knock sounded on the door. I went to open it and there was Father Lynch, already back with his assistant by his side. The deacon had a bolt of thick canvas with rope handles clutched in his hands.

"Mrs Holloway." Father Lynch showed his long teeth in a smile. "We've a stretcher to take the poor wee soul away from his tomb and give him a decent burial."

"Please come in, Father," I said, the necklace burning in my pocket as a reminder of my deceit.

The men came inside and were quickly joined by Uncle Simon, who'd heard voices and descended the stairs.

"Have you brought all you need to take it with you this time?" he asked, still pale and looking worse the wear.

"Aye, we have," said the priest.

"Then let's get to it," my uncle said.

This time, I did not follow them into the cellar. Instead, I went upstairs to my room and hurriedly pulled the chain from my pocket. I stood by the window, laid the necklace on my palm and examined what I'd found.

It was a cheap piece of jewellry, hence the tarnished chain. I also thought the shamrock was probably metal as well, with remnants of green paint that would have been quite pretty a long time ago. There was nothing about it which looked Tudor in design at all. In fact, the chain itself was too modern to be as old as that. In those days they would have worn pendants on threads of cord I should have thought.

Again, I felt the strange sensation that something else was at work here. Was there? A body closed up inside a priest hole was not a normal occurrence. But how long had it really been there?

I touched the tiny shamrock. It was too pretty to belong to a Catholic priest, wasn't it? I sighed at the question. For if those bones didn't belong to a man of the church, then whose were they?

Chapter Twenty-Three

I KEPT TO MY ROOM THE remainder of the morning until the priest and his deacon left with the cart. Then I told Tibbetts I was going into the village and offered to pick up any supplies or post any letters while I was there. I'd written a short note to Mr Satterthwaite, asking if I could call upon him the following Monday, which warranted a trip to the post office.

Cook asked for one or two items from the grocer, and I set off with my basket towards the village, carefully watching my step. After so much rain it was very muddy.

The air was chilly, but the sun shone brightly and tricked you into thinking it was warm. I passed the cow fields and Rosell's Cottage, lost in thought. There were so many things to think about, my mind skipped from one to the next like a game of hopscotch. And somewhere in all of my thoughts were George, my darling Sarah, and the face of Ivan Delahunt.

Why he had popped into my mind escaped me. I liked the man despite our differences. Our minds were attuned on several topics and conversation was always lively in his presence. Yet what of his relationship with Nanette? Their marriage was unhappy, and she had hinted he frightened her, yet I did not feel convinced.

I spotted the St. Michael's spire, and the image of Father Lynch was sobering. I picked up my pace, eager to bypass the chapel without being seen.

My first stop in the village was at the post office, where I bought stamps and sent off my letter to the solicitor. I went into the grocer's and purchased the items Cook asked for, and then turned down the lane towards the Anglican church in the direction of Mrs Daly's house.

I reached the neat garden of Bramble Cottage, went down the path and used the brass knocker to announce my arrival. I heard someone coming, and the door opened to reveal Hilary herself on the threshold.

"Oh, it's you," she said sullenly.

"Hello, Mrs Daly. May I come in for a moment?" I did not care if she disliked my coming. I was determined to start getting some answers to my questions.

"Well…I…"

"I won't take much of your time. Please?"

She blinked and let out a sigh. "Oh, all right. Come in."

We went into her small front room as we had before, only this time, there were no refreshments offered. She gestured for me to take a seat, which I did.

"Thank you for seeing me, Mrs Daly. I think you know what I want to talk about."

"If it's that silly note, I've already told you it was nothing."

I had intended upon being nice and polite, but my good intentions dissolved instantly. "Mrs Daly. I know you are being dishonest, and I am surprised at you. I thought you an honourable woman, like my mother. Yet you intentionally choose to withhold information which could be relevant in finding out what happened to my cousin. Why are you doing this?"

Much to my shock, her eyes filled with tears. She pulled a handkerchief from her pocket and dabbed at them.

I waited for her to regain her composure. "Come, Mrs Daly, why are you so scared to speak about this?"

She took a deep breath and let it out. "Vivienne was struggling with something and I was trying to counsel her." The tears came again. "I had no idea she was so unhappy, that she planned to take her own life."

"You don't believe she died in her sleep as the coroner declared?"

"I do not," she said, wiping away a stray tear. "For she had been debating over a decision which would impact her life."

I was intrigued. "What decision?"

The older woman wiped her eyes. "I cannot tell you. It was told in confidence."

"Mrs Daly, your confidence means nothing now. Vivienne is dead."

She flinched at my intentional bluntness.

"Please tell me," I implored. "It must be important if it became a matter of life and death." I was being dramatic, but I *had* to know the truth.

"How can it matter, Claire, when it is too late."

I snapped. "How dare you decide the relevance of my cousin's troubles."

"I decided nothing. Vivienne endeavoured to make a life decision which she found incredibly difficult. So difficult, she chose to take another way out."

"No, you are wrong," I blurted. "My cousin didn't kill herself, nor did she die in her sleep. She was murdered."

Her gasp was audible. Mrs Daly's brown eyes were huge, her mouth open in shock. "Whatever do you mean, murdered? Why the doctor—"

"I do not care what the doctor said. I know what I saw with my own eyes. I am trained to quickly assess a person's medical situation from my years in a field hospital where time is of the essence. And I tell you, from my experience, Vivienne did not die by her own hand."

Mrs Daly flopped back in her chair, her hand resting on her heaving bosom.

"This cannot be true," she gasped.

I was alarmed at her reaction. I had expected surprise and denial, but Mrs Daly was having a physical response.

"You must calm yourself, madam," I said quietly. "Take several long, slow breaths and try to regulate your breathing." She had gone so pale; I worried my conversation had affected her heart.

I got up and went to her chair. Kneeling in front of her, I took both her hands in mine and squeezed them in a regular rhythm. "Come now, breathe along with me."

I took long breaths and eventually she joined me, until her trembling ceased, and her colour came back. I got up and returned to my seat.

"Are you feeling better?"

She nodded. "Yes, thank you."

"Mrs Daly. I implore you to tell me what Vivienne was talking about. There is a chance it could be something serious enough to get her killed."

Again, she looked horror-struck. "No," she said. "It isn't like that. It was a personal matter the poor girl suffered with."

I thought of Ivan. Did her affection for him torment her? "Was it something to do with feelings for another? An unrequited love, perhaps?"

"Feelings, yes, but not those of a romantic nature."

"Then what?" I pushed. "Please tell me the truth."

"All right," said Mrs Daly, her face set in stone. "If you must know, Vivienne was ready to leave the faith. She wanted to stop going to mass and renounce her religious beliefs."

That was unexpected. I sat back and digested what she'd said. Her faith? That made no sense. Vivienne wouldn't be murdered for no longer being Catholic. How ridiculous.

"That's it?" I said. "Are you certain there was nothing else?"

"No, that is all it was. And before you ask, I could not say anything because it might have affected her burial at St. Michael's; she could have been excommunicated. That would have broken Simon's heart."

This did not quite add up. I stared at my hostess. Was she telling me the truth? I got the impression she was, yet the way she looked at me, I felt Mrs Daly wasn't saying everything.

"Tell me. If Vivienne was struggling, why would she talk to you and not Father Lynch?"

"You must not say anything about it to Father Lynch," she said vehemently. "Nor Simon, for that matter. You cannot mention this to anyone."

Dear God, the woman looked terrified. How so? This was not the Inquisition. People could worship however they chose.

"You're not telling me everything, are you?" I

accused.

Hilary Daly levelled her gaze on mine. "I am telling you all I can," she stated.

I knew then, I had gone as far as I could with this woman for now. Just her omission of facts and details told me there was more to this story than I would learn today.

I got up. "Thank you so much for your time, Mrs Daly. I wish you well." I turned to leave.

"Wait," she said before I had gone very far. "I want to tell you more, but if I do, it will put me in a very compromising position. Please give me time to think on it."

I nodded. "On your conscience be it," I said, and walked out of the door.

****

When I arrived back at Darkwater, it was already late in the afternoon. I wondered if Ivan would be back. I wanted to speak to him about my chat with Mrs Daly and get his thoughts about the necklace I had found too.

The discovery of the skeleton interested me for many reasons which I wanted to discuss with him. The fact there had been bones buried in the house did not faze me whatsoever. Bones could not harm you. People did.

Gosh, there were many loose threads for me to tie together. I'd arrived here determined to carry on Mother's dream of clearing my father's name and hadn't got far at all. In fact, I'd learned very little, and in the process lost all but one of her journals. It peeved me to think whoever had done it thought they'd been so clever.

I crossed the moat, marvelling how I was growing

used to it, even full as it was after all the rain. I entered the house and heard conversation coming from the drawing room. I bypassed it quickly, going straight to the kitchen to give Cook her wares.

"Thank you, lass," she said, taking the items to put away. "There's company in't drawing room. Thou should go and join them. Tibbetts'll bring you a fresh pot o' tea."

I thanked Mrs Blitch and did just that.

"Claire, I'm so pleased you are back." Phoebe Tipton came to greet me, her eyes shining with pleasure. "I thought we'd missed you."

"I didn't know you were coming," I said.

Hazel and Martin were there also, talking to Jeremy Rotherham and Nanette.

"We thought you might like getting cheered up," said Phoebe. "It's been a rotten time for your family. Father said company is a healthy distraction." She reached out and touched my hand. "How are you really? I know you must be awfully sad."

Phoebe was clumsy with subtlety, but her heart was in the right place and I appreciated the genuine concern.

"Yes, it's hard to accept Vivienne is gone forever. But I think we're rallying."

Tibbetts arrived with a fresh pot of tea, and I busied myself with that, refilling cups and then pouring one for myself. Phoebe seemed reluctant to leave my side and provided a constant source of chatter.

"Hello, Claire," Martin said coming to join us. "I hope we're not intruding coming over and visiting unannounced, but we wanted to make sure everyone was doing as well as possible."

"Your family are most thoughtful. It is good to see

fresh faces."

"I'm just glad to get out of the house," Phoebe said. "How did you fare with all that nasty rain? At one point Father thought the river was going to burst its banks and flood the village."

"Our moat flooded," said Nanette, who came to take a seat in one of the chairs, closely followed by Jeremy. Goodness, the man was her shadow.

"Some of the water got into the cellar, but it didn't hurt anything," I added.

I did not mention our macabre discovery down there. Neither did she. Was that intentional, or had Nanette already forgotten the skeleton?

"I bet your cellar is creepy," commented Phoebe. "After all, Darkwater is the oldest house around here, according to Father Lynch. Imagine all the things that have happened here over time."

"Honestly," Hazel admonished her sister. "You have too vivid an imagination. Why you always have to make everything so blasted dramatic, I'll never know."

"Sister, our lives would be boring were it not for Phoebe's constant observations," laughed Martin. "There is never a dull moment in our house, Claire."

"I can believe that." I smiled at him. Martin returned the gesture and his eyes lingered on my face for a while. I looked away quickly, not wanting to encourage him.

"Women certainly have the propensity to change the balance of a home. Some ladies light up a room by their being present." Jeremy Rotherham gave this surprising speech and we all turned to look at him.

The young man stood directly behind where Nanette sat, leaning against the back of her armchair as though standing sentry. Nanette, fully aware she was the subject of his compliment looked rather pleased with herself. I was surprised his flattery had cracked through the veneer of her despondency. But being maudlin would not bring Vivienne back.

"It is important to be happy whenever one can," Phoebe stated. "We all have but one turn upon this earth. I'd prefer to spend mine being positive and affable, not sad and miserable."

The group fell quiet at her comment. Phoebe had not realised her reference to having one life was slightly indelicate due to the recent death in my family. Nanette's expression turned glum.

I tried to change the subject. "Phoebe," I asked. "When were you last in Leeds?"

The young woman immediately launched into a story about her visit there, and eventually the others resumed their conversation. We continued until the clock chimed five times and Martin Tipton declared they should take their leave.

There were cheery farewells made, and as I watched the girls and Jeremy cross the bridge, Martin hung back and then came to my side.

"Claire," he said, his brown eyes kindly. "If you should ever be willing, I would so enjoy an afternoon walk with you, or something of that nature. I have enjoyed our conversations whenever we've met. Would you at least think about accepting my company in the near future?"

Inwardly I groaned. I liked the young pharmacist very well, as I liked Tibbetts and Mrs Blitch. But there was no attraction there for me. My heart was still full of my darling George, and no man could usurp his memory.

"Martin, I am honoured you think well of me, as I do you. But I'm afraid I am not comfortable spending time with anyone at the moment. I do hope you understand."

He gave me a curt nod. "Of course. Please forgive me." Then before I could say another word he hurried across the footbridge to join the others for their walk back to the village.

I went back inside the house where Uncle Simon had joined Nanette.

"You were gone a while," said my cousin with narrowed eyes. "I take it Martin asked you to go walking with him?"

I did not bother denying it. "As a matter of fact, he did."

"And?" said Nanette.

"I told him I would rather not."

"Wise girl," Uncle Simon said sharply. "You are too good for the likes of the Tiptons."

Nanette was shocked at his retort. "Papa? Why would you say that. Claire is a nurse, and Martin also in the medical profession. They would make a good match indeed."

"Nonsense." Simon would not have it. "Claire is leagues ahead of a lad like that. She is far too genteel and sophisticated for a village pharmacist."

Nanette looked me over in an appraising glance. "Hmm," she said. "Perhaps you're right."

"I am in the room," I reprimanded them both. "I am not a side of beef to be discussed. Suffice to say I am not in search of a partner, regardless of them being a suitable or unsuitable match. So, there's an end to it, I beg of you."

Uncle Simon came over to where I stood near the hearth. He still looked tired, and his complexion was ruddy and unshaven. Much to my surprise, he reached over and cupped my chin in his palm.

"You, my dear, are a diamond. As such, only a man with good taste can understand how a gem should be cared for."

Was the man drunk? I moved my face so his hand would fall away. I could feel Nanette staring at us both and my face felt flushed. Again, my uncle had stepped across the unspoken divide between family affection and romantic innuendo. I did not like it at all.

I moved away from the hearth. "As our company has departed, I shall go up and change for dinner."

I did not wait for their response but set off for the stairs, trying not to break into a run.

SAFELY IN MY ROOM I RUBBED my washcloth roughly over my face. I felt unclean. I brushed my hair and dried myself, then went back into the bedroom to stand before the window as I was wont to do whenever in thought.

Coming to stay at Darkwater had been a mistake. I should have taken rooms in Skipton. After all, that would have been conveniently close to the mill, which was the main reason I had come here in the first place. Yet it was not an option at the time. Family obligation and funds saw to that.

I reminded myself in two days I would meet with Mr Satterthwaite without Uncle Simon being present. I'd enquire about my actual financial status. Perhaps I could afford a place of my own? After meeting with the solicitor, I would go to the mill and see about spending some time there each day.

I desperately needed an occupation. If I remained shut up at the abbey with Nanette for company, I should go off my head. Idleness did not suit me, and never had.

It had been a pleasant distraction seeing the Tipton family today. I so enjoyed Phoebe, and I'd rather liked chatting with Martin until he'd shown more than a platonic interest towards me. Between Martin and my uncle, I was slightly off-kilter.

I lay back on my bed, folded my arms behind my head and stared at the ceiling. What a strange assortment of people lived around here. Mentally I went through a list of them, and other than Phoebe and Ivan, none elicited much interest from me. I chose not to reflect upon Mr Delahunt's impression for long, as there was something perplexing about the man.

I considered my new situation as a mill owner. It dawned upon me that the acquisition of wealth in my near future might be alluring to a young pharmacist like Martin Tipton. The thought was disturbing, and the next more so, when I aligned the very same reasoning with the unwarranted attention coming from Uncle Simon. What a horrible notion. But there could be a nugget of truth in there somewhere.

My arrival had certainly made me the proverbial cat among the pigeons. I had deposed Uncle Simon who was no longer the sole controller of the mill. Now he had to answer to me. Goodness, how unsettling, being here and such an instrument of change.

There was too much to contemplate. Yet since my arrival at Darkwater it seemed no sooner did a puzzle present itself than another arrived in tandem. It had all begun with Mother's journals. Oh, how it infuriated me, when all I desperately wanted was to reconcile the burning of her books. The guilty party should be held accountable.

And then what of Vivienne? All and sundry were happy to accept Doctor Tipton's verdict of my cousin's death. Yet I was convinced she had died from ingesting cyanide. Could it have been self-induced? I doubted it. Vivienne would have left a note. She was the type who'd have taken great care about how she'd be found, focused upon the detail, the tragedy. So was it murder? I was convinced it was. Then it followed that we were all in danger. But from whom? And what motive would anyone have to kill my cousin? This was Darkwater Abbey, not the blasted Houses of Parliament.

I wished Mother was here with me. That clever brain, her no-nonsense approach to life. Together, we would have discussed everything. Worked though the nonsense and found answers. Instead I felt alone and almost vulnerable, my only ally being Ivan. And him barely known to me. It was terribly frustrating.

I took the shamrock necklace from my pocket, held it up in one hand and studied it as it dangled above my face. Another puzzle. A woman's cheap necklace buried with a skeleton; a body long dead, forgotten and left to rot.

Recalling seeing those sad bones, there was something odd about them which niggled me. When I tried to place what it was, it moved out of my grasp. I couldn't remember exactly, but it was something learned many years ago in training and in reference to identifying gender from skeletal remains. There were subtle differences between male and female, and I was having trouble recalling what they were. The necklace was probably a woman's but that did not mean a man might not have it as a keepsake.

I got up and put the necklace in the hidey hole under the chair seat. Soon, Ivan would be home for the evening, and I was determined to catch him and share what I'd found today. If he was absent, then I'd be sure and talk to him in the morning before going to tea with Tibbetts' brother, Jack, home from sailing the seas.

I changed into my black dress for dinner, then hung up my skirt and blouse. I'd go downstairs early and see if Ivan was there.

Chapter Twenty-Four

"CLAIRE," IVAN GREETED ME as I joined him in the drawing room.

He stood before a blazing fire, and judging by his dress he must have recently arrived.

"I'm just in from the mill. The evening has turned very cold, so I'm thawing out my bones before changing." He watched me cross the room. I did not want anyone to overhear our conversation.

"There's something I want to tell you," I said quietly. 'I found a—"

From the doorway, Uncle Simon announced. "Now there's a good. hot fire." He headed straight towards the sideboard and picked up the sherry decanter. "Anyone care for a drink?"

I quickly stepped away from Ivan. "No thank you."

Uncle Simon filled a glass and then went to sit in his usual spot.

"If you'll both excuse me," said Ivan. "I shall go up and change." With that he left us alone.

I took a seat on the sofa. My uncle looked at me fondly, and I studied his expression. His eyes, usually such a penetrating blue were dull and bloodshot. His skin appeared sallow and his mouth downcast. The loss of a daughter had taken a considerable toll on him.

"How are you this evening, Uncle?"

"The better for your company, my dear," he said

with a feeble attempt at a smile.

I hid the shudder rippling through me. Then I took myself in hand. I must stop focusing on his strange behaviour towards me and instead try to understand what he was about.

"Do you think you shall return to the mill on Monday?" He had been home all the week.

Uncle Simon gave a long sigh and shrugged his shoulders. "It is my intent to try, Claire. But I make no promises. Ivan tells me he has everything in hand, and so I do not worry about productivity. Yet the workers need to see the head of the mill present as much as possible. My being there exerts the authority needed to ensure the work gets done and there's no slacking."

What a pompous man. "Surely with Ivan and your supervisors there it's enough to keep everything flowing smoothly."

"That is a matter of opinion, my dear. After all my years at Parslow's, I think I can be the judge of that."

At that juncture, he changed the subject. By the time Ivan re-joined us it was time to go into dinner.

Tonight, it was the three of us. Uncle Simon was very talkative and this increased as the wine glass was refilled.

Later, when we returned to the drawing room, my uncle was red-faced and slurring his words. When he spoke directly to me, his demeanour became affected, his manner overly familiar, and I found both greatly embarrassing. Ivan stared at me whenever Uncle Simon did this. Why? Did Ivan expect a reaction, or was he commiserating with me?

As time passed, I counted the moments until Uncle Simon would leave us and go to bed. The hour grew late, and I desperately wanted to speak to Ivan before the night ended.

Fortunately, the wine and sherry finally took a toll on my uncle. He got unsteadily to his feet, made his excuses, and bid us both a good night. I waited patiently for him to ascend the stairs before speaking.

As though understanding my intentions, Ivan came to join me on the sofa. "Now, Claire, what is it you want to talk about?"

"I went down to the cellar today."

"Whatever for?"

"I suppose you could call it maudlin curiosity? I just wanted to see the skeleton for myself."

"And?"

I reached into my pocket and pulled out the shamrock necklace I'd brought down with me. "Here," I said. "Take a look at this. I found it with the skeleton. It had dropped to the dirt as though it had fallen from the body's neck."

Ivan threaded the rusty chain through his fingers and studied the pendant. "This doesn't look much like a religious artefact." He looked up at me and grinned. "I don't think I've ever heard of a religious order called The Shamrocks."

"Very funny. But don't you see how this changes things? We automatically assumed a body in a priest hole must be that of a priest. But what if it wasn't? What if the bones are the remains of an ordinary person?"

"What difference does it make?" said Ivan. "Considering the time the skeleton has been sequestered in the priest hole, I don't find it relevant. Now, don't misunderstand me. I'm not making light of a loss of life. Rather that it has been potentially more than two centuries since the unfortunate soul was trapped down there in the first place. We wouldn't have a clue how to identify them. And after all this time I doubt anyone is looking for them either."

"All right," I agreed. "That's a fair point. But what proof do we have that our skeleton is ancient? Being trapped in the cellar in such a damp environment has affected the remains and even slowed down decomposition. You could tell that by the condition of the blanket, or whatever the fabric was, and now, the necklace."

Ivan took a sip of his drink and then levelled his gaze on me. I stared back. There was no doubting the man was handsome. His features were so well matched, his eyes intelligent, but also holding a depth one could tumble into. I liked that he was masculine, though not in a bullish way. It was obvious he'd engaged in physical labour at some point in his life, as well as using his brain.

Guilt snapped me out of it. What was I doing? How could I ponder any of these facts about a man when I still loved my darling George?

"Well?" asked Ivan.

I came out of my trance. "I'm sorry, can you say that again."

"I asked how you would be able to prove the age of a skeleton?"

"I'm not sure there is an accurate way, although I know there are scientists with methods. I believe whenever they find bones, they look for other clues around the discovery. For example, bones found near Roman artifacts indicate they're Roman."

"That isn't going to help us here," Ivan said drolly. "All we have is some old fabric and a necklace."

"Did you notice anything about the blanket?" I wished now I had paid it more attention, but I was so preoccupied with the jewellry on the ground. "It looked like it had been quite a dark colour, and it didn't rot away when I touched it. Don't you think it would have disintegrated if it was centuries old?"

"I suppose so. Claire, aren't you getting a little carried away with this? The poor fellow's been carted off and will have a wonderful burial, courtesy of Father Lynch, whether the man was Roman Catholic or not. And there's an end to it."

"I wasn't here when they took him away. I went to see Hilary Daly."

"What for?"

"To ask about the note she sent to Vivienne. Remember? She wasn't being honest about it when we confronted her at the funeral."

"What did she have to say this time?"

"Not much in the beginning. So I got a little harsh, I'm ashamed to say. But she told me Vivienne had started questioning her faith. She was considering leaving the church."

"That's no small thing in this family. Simon's connection to Father Lynch is strong. He wouldn't countenance his daughter breaking her ties with him or the church." Ivan looked thoughtful. "Both girls have grown up with the priest practically being their uncle. It's all they know."

"Mrs Daly was worried my uncle or Father Lynch would get wind of it. She didn't want it to affect Vivienne's burial, so she kept quiet."

"She showed good judgement there, at least."

"That's not all, Ivan. Mrs Daly alluded to there being more to tell but was either forbidden or too frightened to say another word. My guess was it was the latter. She promised to think about it and let me know."

"How ridiculous," said Ivan. "Why do women play such silly games? Better to be blunt and get it over with. This teasing of information is unnecessary. My guess is she has nothing of consequence to say. I shouldn't give it another thought, if I were you."

I sighed. "I take offence at your comment that women play silly games. What of all your warmongers? Those are the worst games of all and played by men. Really, Ivan, we shall not have much of a friendship if you continue to behave in such a superior manner when it comes to the difference between sexes."

He had the grace to look guilty. "Forgive me. That was rather biased. You are right. I suppose I have been on the receiving end of being kept out of conversations, especially between Vivienne and Nanette. Your cousins were quite adept about sharing only half the information whenever I asked a question. I should not paint all the fairer sex with the same brush."

"Apology accepted,"

Ivan knocked back the rest of his drink and set his glass down on the table. "Mrs Holloway, I am too tired to bicker with you any longer, so I am off to my bed. We shall have to continue this conversation at another time."

With that, he gave me an exaggerated mock bow and left me sitting in the drawing room.

I sat back against the settee and stared into the

dying flames in the hearth. Was my imagination really working overtime and my mind too unsettled to grasp anything?

I got to my feet and extinguished the light, keeping a small lamp to see my way upstairs. I yawned, the prospect of a warm bed suddenly quite appealing. Even though I could hear the wind whipping through the trees outside, the house stayed surprisingly warm. No doubt because of its thick walls. The Tudors certainly knew how to build houses.

In my room, I turned the lock in the door as I had since the episode with the journals. Tibbets had set a fire before leaving for the evening. He did this in all the bedrooms, and it made for a cozy welcome.

I set down the lamp and went about changing into my night attire. As I hung up my dress, I noticed the curtains were not yet drawn, and I went to close them to keep out the draught. I pulled one heavy piece of fabric across, and as I went to pull the other, I saw a light flicker outside in the courtyard.

I paused, then quickly extinguished my own light to see better outside. I peeked through a gap in the curtain. There it was. Just like the previous time, a thin light weaving through the tree line at the edge of the courtyard. Who was it out there?

Boldly, I quickly reached for my coat, slipped on my boots, and hurried out of my room and down the stairs. I rushed through the kitchen to the back of the house and the door to the courtyard, unbolted it, and let myself out.

Without a lamp to light my way it was dark, but my eyes adjusted enough so I could see where I was going. Instead of crossing the centre of the courtyard and being visible, I took the same route as the figure I had seen, through the tree line and out of direct view.

Where would this lead? Darkwater was marooned on a tiny island, so would I not just arrive at the front of the house? And where had the figure gone?

I pressed on, trying to ignore the freezing bite of night air which penetrated my coat and thin cotton nightgown.

Rounding the corner of the courtyard's perimeter I saw a flicker of light going towards the moat. The person carefully went down the sloping bank where it would surely meet the water. I reached the edge of the trees, close to the bank and stopped, staying hidden in the dark.

The figure reached the moat, and I heard a splash of water. My heart sank. Had they fallen in? I craned my head out away from the tree trunk, reluctant to let it go as my heart raced. I was too close. The smell of murky water filled my nostrils. It was coming to get me and soon would cover my body, my head…

Stop…stop…stop…said the voice in my head, pushing away the hysteria threatening to engulf my mind. I bit my lip, the pain of it distracting me from panic. Gingerly I released my hold of the tree trunk and stepped away from cover, closer to the bank.

There it was again, a gentle splash. And then to my relief, I saw the shadow of a small raft, moving across the moat, someone kneeling down, guiding it with a long pole. I dropped to the ground and made myself small as I observed its short journey across the moat.

In a flash it reached the other bank. The figure nimbly stepped onto land, set down the lantern and tethered the raft. Then they picked up the lamp, and in one split second I saw the glint of blonde hair.

Nanette.

I ARRIVED BACK IN MY ROOM, shivering and frozen with cold. I took off my boots and coat and scrambled under the bed clothes to warm up.

What was Nanette doing, leaving the house so late at night? And why the secrecy? Of course, the obvious answer was she must have an assignation. But where? And with whom? It was unsafe for anyone to be out so late, but especially a woman.

Did it have anything to do with the man I had seen out there not long after I'd first come to Darkwater?

I lay in bed puzzling over my cousin's strange actions, but ultimately sleep won the day, blurring all the questions from my thoughts.

The dream came that night.

Vivid. Frightening. Heart wrenching.

I awoke with a cry on my lips, my face wet with tears. I turned on my side and held a pillow tightly against my chest, a pathetic replacement for the feel of my baby, or my sweet George's touch. I curled my legs up close to my stomach, buried my face in the pillow and cried myself back to sleep.

THERE WAS FROST ON MY window the next morning and I could see my breath in the air. Grateful I had nowhere to go so early, I dressed warmly, adding a thick cardigan to my usual attire of skirt and blouse, then left my room to go down to breakfast.

I saw Tibbetts on my way to the dining room.

"Jack's right looking forward to seeing you today, miss. Said he might even t'shave so he don't scare you."

I laughed. "I'm to come this morning, is that right?"

"Aye," he said. "Twixt ten and eleven, if it suits."

I carried on to the dining room where Ivan was eating alone.

"Good morning. Mind if I join you?"

He looked up with a smile, "Only if you don't eat all of the bacon."

In that moment, I saw Nanette again, slipping onto the raft while she thought her husband slept. A rush of guilt assuaged me. Should I say something? Or did the man already know?

I recovered myself. "No fear of that this morning. I'm having porridge. Hopefully it will warm my bones." I took my usual seat and poured a cup of tea.

I was grateful for the warmth coming from the fireplace. I ladled some porridge into a bowl, added a dash of sugar and a splash of milk.

"What are your plans today?" asked Ivan. "More detection I presume?" There was a mischievous twinkle in his eye.

I ignored the insinuation. "I am going to Tibbetts' family cottage to visit his brother, Jack. He's home on leave from the navy. I haven't seen him since childhood."

"You are on good terms with that family, aren't you."

"I am. When I was younger, Tibbetts was the stable lad. It often fell on his shoulders to find me whenever I went missing out on the dales. I made his life quite difficult. Over the years I visited Darkwater, he was always nice to me and made me feel welcome."

"Unlike your cousins, I'll be bound."

I did not respond. It wasn't worth acknowledging. "And what about you, Ivan. Are you off to Skipton, even on a Saturday?"

He swallowed a bite of toast and gave me a quizzical look. "Of course. Where else would I go? The mill will be running and there is plenty of work to be done."

I had a thought. "Have you had an opportunity to look through any of the mill's old records yet?"

He nodded. "I have picked my moments but haven't found anything of interest. I shan't give up though."

I thanked him. The man could never be called lazy. "Do you ever enjoy anything recreational that does not include work? Like going to the park? Watching an opera, attending the theatre?"

He shook his head. "Not anymore. I used to take Nanette into Leeds periodically, but she no longer wants to go."

I could tell the memory saddened him.

"Then perhaps it is time to plan a trip there. It might be the tonic everyone needs."

He did not look particularly enthused with the idea.

"I doubt it would be seemly so close to a family loss."

"Oh." Of course he was absolutely correct. It would be a huge breach of etiquette. Uncle Simon would never countenance it. "Forget it," I said, and continued eating breakfast.

I finished the porridge and helped myself to some toast and blackcurrant jam. "I am going to Skipton on Monday. I have an appointment with Mr Satterthwaite to go over a few legalities. Once I have finished, I'd like to come up to Parslow's and get the official tour, if you have time?"

Apparently, anything to do with the mill would capture Ivan's interest.

"I'd be glad to show you around." He considered for a moment. "Wouldn't you prefer Simon took you?"

"No," I said quicker than I meant to. "I'd rather it was you."

Ivan didn't comment, but I could tell he'd caught my quick refusal. Well I didn't care. I did not feel a need to explain myself.

Ivan finished his breakfast and pushed his plate to one side. "Speaking of the mill, it's time I made my way there." He got to his feet. "Please excuse me. I hope you have a wonderful time seeing your old friend today."

"Thank you."

****

Tibbetts' cottage was set back off the main road, down a bumpy dirt track. It had been in his family for many generations, and as I neared the building I saw it was still in surprisingly good repair. Tibbetts must take care of the place, even though he spent most of his time at Darkwater and stayed at the servants' cottages.

A thick plume of smoke puffed from the chimney, and I looked forward to getting out of the cold morning. I rapped the knocker on the green painted door.

It was opened almost immediately to reveal a swarthy complected man who looked every inch a sailor. From his sun darkened, creased face, to the hooped ring through one earlobe. He was bald as a coot.

"Miss Claire. Why I'd not know you, for look how

growd you be."

"Hello, Jack," I said, delighted to see a face from my past.

He pulled the door wider. "Come you in, lass. It's right chilly out there the day. I'm already pining to get back t'south and some sunshine."

I followed him inside and felt a rush of warm air.

The cottage was basic. A small living area with a kitchen, and most likely two rooms upstairs. But it was very cozy.

Jack gestured for me to take a seat at a small kitchen table, where he had tea things laid out and ready. He placed an old iron kettle on top of the stove to boil water, then took a seat himself. Jack was a large man and dwarfed the chair.

"Me brother told me about 'appenin's up at Darkwater. Ee, but that's right bad news about t'young lady."

"It has been horrid," I agreed. "My uncle and cousin are desolate. It came as quite a shock."

"I imagine so. T'lass weren't very old. P'raps she had a nasty turn, one o' them seizures, or a tricky heart. Still, long as it weren't painful, poor mite." His light brown eyes settled on my face. "Archie told us 'bout your mother. Now that pained me greatly. Jane Shaw were a fine woman. Always looked up to her, I did. Shame she got taken so early."

His eyes softened as he spoke about my mother. It occurred to me that Jack being several years older than his brother, had been close in age to Mother. He likely knew her quite well.

"In all honesty, Jack, it feels like death has followed me around." I swallowed, unsure why I was speaking of this to him. "First, my husband, George, and my darling daughter, then my mother. I came up to Yorkshire hoping to get away from bad news, and some poor man had just died right outside Darkwater. Now Vivienne."

Jack got up as the kettle steamed. He filled the teapot before putting the kettle back on the hearth. He sat back down. "That's a lot for you to bear, miss, an' I am sorry for you." He frowned. "Archie told me of the fellow droppin' dead over near the moat. Said t'were a stranger from Australia."

"Yes, a rambler, I believe."

"Rambler?" Jack stirred the tea and then poured it through the strainer into our cups. "Don't seem normal to me. An Australian in these parts, taking a walk on a chilly day, all alone." He handed me my cup. I poured a splash of milk into it and took a sip. It was as tasty as Mrs Blitch's tea.

"What makes you say that?"

He took a hearty gulp of his own drink. "Australia is a long way from here. If a fellow comes all way t'Yorkshire, he must be coming back home t'family. No reason otherwise."

He had a point. "Do you know of anyone with relatives who emigrated to Australia?"

"Nay." He shook his head. Then he paused. "But now I think on it, I remember years back, t'was a woman come here. Well, Archie brought her t'cottage. Let's see, your father were still alive, so it's back twenty year at least. Yes, that's the right o' it. This woman had shown herself at Darkwater for some reason I can't recall, an' Archie brought her back here to me dad, an' she took some refreshment and food wi' us." Jack took another sip of tea. I could almost see the cogs turning as he searched for the memory. Then his face cleared.

"I've got it now," he said, pleased with himself. "This woman, fer she weren't no lady, was drunk as a sailor on payday. Archie brought her here, 'cause he were worried she'd fall in t'moat, she were that drunk. Me dad fed her, and I come home an' found them having a nice chat.

"I'd a strange feeling I'd seen her before but weren't sure where. It took a bit, but once she were talkin' about being from Liverpool, an' her job working on t'stage actin' an' dancin', I remembered where I'd seen her. I'd been at one of t'pubs we go to when we make port in Liverpool an' watched her in't play, more than once."

"What an odd coincidence," I said. "Did she know you?"

"Course not," said Jack. "She were on'stage, and me, a punter. But she were a pretty girl, easy to recall that kind o' face. She had a look of a lass I'd gone walkin' with years ago."

"I see." Although I didn't really. What this woman had to do with anything was beyond me. Still, Jack was enjoying telling his story, so I carried on listening.

"Any road, she were gabbing about this and that, still touched with the booze. She told us she lived with her granny in Liverpool. Said she had a brother, but he'd run off to Australia to make his fortune. Once he got there, the silly bugger had only gone and stolen some cows an' got in trouble with the magistrate. Sent to prison for a long time, he were, but always wrote to t'sister. Odd how that popped into my head all of sudden. I suppose it's that this deadun were Australian."

"Did the woman go back to Darkwater?" I asked, wondering who she was there to see.

"I'm sure she did. Hopefully sober. You know, I kept a look out for her the next time we docked at Liverpool. But she weren't with her troupe no longer, and I were sorry for it. Nice lass, really, though I can't think of her name." Jack's face screwed up as he searched his past.

I topped up my tea. "With a bit of luck they'll identify the poor fellow they found. His family's probably wondering where he is.

"Aye," said Jack, still preoccupied with his thoughts. "I've got it," he said, beaming. "She went by the name Milly, nay, Molly. Cheeky face, and hair as yellow a buttercup. I took her as Irish, an' said so which made her laugh."

"Did she not speak with a Liverpool accent then?" Honestly, Jack must have held a candle for this woman.

"Aye, she did. But it were the necklace made me think it."

"Necklace?"

"Aye. T'were unusual an' it caught my eye. It were one of them good luck charms. That leaf the Irish always have. It were a shamrock."

Chapter Twenty-Five

THE REST OF MY VISIT WITH Jack was a blur. He spoke of his most recent voyages to exotic lands, while my mind spun with what he'd shared.

I finished my tea, and after a while thanked him and made my excuses to leave. He would be home the better part of a month, and I said I'd come back and visit again.

I hurried back to Darkwater in search of Tibbetts. I flew across the moat, searching the house until I found him in the boot room, polishing Uncle Simon's shoes.

He looked up as I came into the small room off the kitchen. "Did you see our Jack?" he asked.

"I did. He looked very well. We had a cup of tea and a nice chat. While I was there, he told me about something that happened a few years ago, and I'd like your version of it, if you don't mind."

Tibbetts frowned. "There's nowt wrong is there? Our Jack hasn't said something to upset you, miss?"

"No," I quickly reassured him. "Nothing like that at all. He just recounted a story." I repeated the tale Jack Tibbetts had told me, adding, "Jack said you saw the woman here at Darkwater. That no one was home and so you took her to your father?"

Tibbetts paused, holding the polish rag still while he thought for a moment.

"Aye. That were the right of it, miss. The woman

were drunk an' worse for wear. I weren't much more than a lad meself, but I were worried she'd topple in t'moat. She'd come to see Mr Manning, an' he were at mill. So I took her to me dad and left her there."

"Did she come back later?"

"If she did, I n'er saw her. But then I didn't work in t'house. It would be the old staff who could tell you, an' them are long gone now."

"Do you remember what the woman looked like?" I was curious if both Tibbetts boys would say the same thing.

"Not clearly, for it's been a long time, miss. But it seems she had yellow hair, a bit like Miss Nanette's. She were pretty, but rough about the edges with a mouth like a dock worker."

"Jack mentioned she wore an interesting piece of jewellry. Does that ring a bell?"

"That's an odd question. Funny though, cause I'm not one to notice ornaments on people, but now you bring it up I do remember something green on a chain. I couldn't tell you what it were."

"Did you think it odd that someone like this particular woman would call for my uncle?"

"Nay. It weren't unusual for folk looking for work to stop by. Either wanting a job here at Darkwater, or at mill. Why? What's so special about this lady?"

"Nothing," I said quickly. "I just found it interesting, that's all. From what your brother said, he'd seen her performing on stage in Liverpool. It was just a good story, I suppose. I'll let you get on with your work. Thank you, Tibbetts."

"Course, miss Claire."

MY MIND BUZZED LIKE A BEE. I stopped in the kitchen and helped myself to a cup of tea, which I carried upstairs to my bedroom. I went in, locking the door behind me. From the hiding place in the chair, I gathered everything together, except for my gun, and placed the items on my bed.

Mother's only remaining journal, my notebook, Hilary Daly's letters, her note to Vivienne, and the necklace. What an odd assortment I had collected.

I placed the journal and the letters together; they were connected through my mother. The note to Vivienne was specifically about her and a desire to break away from the church and whatever else Mrs Daly had refused to tell me.

And then the necklace. An important discovery if what the Tibbetts boys remembered was true, and why wouldn't it be? I reached for my notebook and pencil and wrote down a few items.

The necklace belonged to an actress named Molly who had come to Darkwater looking for my uncle. She was from Liverpool and an actress in the dockland area. After leaving old Mr Tibbetts, her whereabouts were never known. But somehow, what appears to be her necklace is found in a priest hole, along with a skeleton, in the cellar here at Darkwater.

The ominous meaning was not lost upon me. I continued writing.

Jack remembered meeting this person, and she spoke of a brother sequestered in an Australia jail. Twenty years later, an Australian stranger has a seizure and dies on the road to Darkwater.

It was too coincidental. Molly and the stranger must be connected somehow.

And what of the skeleton? Was it really an artefact from the Tudor era? Or could it be the remains of a woman from Liverpool? Somehow, the skeleton of a priest from Elizabethan times was not disturbing. But the thought of another body lying there for twenty years produced a very unsettling feeling.

Another death. What about my cousin and her unexplained demise? Why had Doctor Tipton falsified the death certificate? Was it an honest mistake, or intentional? Was her fate connected to her desire to leave the Catholic church and Father Lynch's flock? Surely that was no reason to die, whether by your own hand or another's.

What of Nanette? Why had she left the house under the cover of darkness? Was she meeting a lover?

It was no good. Too many things were happening without explanation. It was time for me to start asking questions. And I knew exactly where to start.

****

"I hope you don't mind me interrupting," I said to Nanette, who lay like a forlorn princess on her bed. My nurse's eye had quickly taken stock of her condition. Her colour was healthy, and she did not look unwell. Nanette was having one of her good spells.

"In truth, I am glad to see another face. I have been in my room far too long. I've been feeling somewhat lonely." Her strange eyes searched my face. "I am lost without my dear Vivienne, simply lost."

I bit my tongue. It would do no good to blurt out what I really wanted to say. That she was unkind to her sister, that she had not been shut up in this room but gadding about in the dark of night.

"Times are challenging, Cousin. Life is so

unsettled at the moment. Uncle Simon is inconsolable. And then the horrible discovery in the cellar."

"Oh that," she snapped, no longer forlorn. "Some old Tudor priest. Hardly surprising in a house this old. I'm glad they got rid of it though, A bit creepy having a body underneath the house."

"Yes," I agreed. "By the way, did you hear about the poor fellow who died right before I arrived? An Australian, here on a ramble, but had a seizure and dropped dead just down the road from here?"

Nanette frowned. "I heard something, maybe from Father or Tibbetts." Her eyes narrowed. "Why do you ask?"

"Curious, I suppose. They do say things always happen in threes. Poor Vivienne, this fellow and then the bones in the cellar."

"How morbid you are," Nanette stated. "Can't you think of something a little cheerier to talk about? You are not improving my mood, Claire."

I leaned back in my chair and levelled my gaze on her face. "There is something else, actually. I think I might have seen a ghost."

Nanette sat bolt upright, her face alight with interest. "Never. Oh, do tell, Cousin."

I smiled. "I've seen a shadowy figure down in the courtyard, late at night. Not once, but twice. A shape who floats between the trees bordering the moat at the back of the house. I can't see them clearly as it's so dark, but they always have a dim light with them, and I can see where they are going."

I watched her face intently. Nanette struggled to keep her expression that of a person intrigued and shocked, but I could read the guilt there as plain as if she wrote it in letters upon her forehead.

She gave a nervous little laugh. "Oh Claire, you are joshing me. What a lot of rubbish. You've been listening to the servants. They're always speaking of ghosts because of the abbey that burned to the ground before the house was built in its stead." She leaned back against her pillows and picked at an imaginary thread on the counterpane. "You must have imagined it."

"No, Nanette," I said calmy. "I imagined nothing. I saw someone, or something out there on both occasions."

She did not like my tone. "And I disagree. It was probably a trick of the light. Surely you don't believe in ghosts? Not a down-to-earth gal like Claire Holloway."

I stared at her. "Absolutely not."

Her eyes met mine. I did not go on because she read what she needed to know just by looking at me. I saw her mouth tighten. She blinked, then licked her lips.

I'd completely unsettled her. She understood I'd seen her.

I got to my feet. "Well, I must go. I've an errand to attend to in the village. I'll leave you to rest." I gave her a caring smile which she did not return.

AS I WALKED IN THE DIRECTION of Starling Village, I knew a moment of guilty pleasure. Even though plain words had not been spoken, it was cathartic confronting Nanette. My cousin irritated me on so many levels. She was nice to me, but below the surface lay a woman who was skilled at being unkind whilst hiding behind a veil of ill health and helplessness.

Sometimes you could tell a person's true nature by

the way others behaved around them. In my cousin's case, both her husband and father walked on eggshells around Nanette. One, catered to her imagined ailments. The other, pretended she wasn't there.

Yet for a person with ill-health, Nanette somehow managed to rally when it was time for a social engagement, or if young Rotherham was around. Could that have been who she slipped out to meet?

I reached St Michael's and on a whim diverted my journey. I'd stop at the vestry and call upon Father Lynch. My mind chomped at the bit to get answers to so many questions which plagued me. Who better to start with than the crow.

I spotted the young deacon I'd met the other day. He was studiously pulling long weeds away from one of the mossy headstones. I greeted him and enquired after the priest but was told Father Lynch was away attending one of his congregation who was unwell. I thanked him and continued on my way.

The road leading to Mrs Daly's cottage was busy this morning. It was a Saturday, and though some folk still worked, there were many who did not. I nodded as I passed by other village women, who gave shy glances in my direction.

I was still a few houses down from Mrs Daly's, when I saw her front door open, and much to my surprise, Father Lynch walked out into the front garden. My impulse was to stop at once, which I did.

There was nowhere to hide; this was a street of cottages, and I could not trespass into a stranger's garden. I turned around and walked in the opposite direction, back the way I had come. At the first opportunity, I stepped inside a shop, peering out of the window to the street, waiting for the thin man to pass by.

In due course, I saw the gaunt figure lope past. I quickly purchased a pennyworth of liquorice to pacify the shopkeeper who had been watching me and then set off for Mrs Daly's at a fast pace.

Hilary Daly looked tired. She had invited me in but with reluctance. I wondered if the priest had been the cause of her exhaustion.

"Thank you for seeing me," I said. "I'm not trying to be a pest, but there are so few people I can talk to. I have so many unanswered questions."

"People don't like questions, Claire. You have to understand. I know you think you belong here, but to everyone you aren't local. You're a stranger who has yet to earn our trust. Why would anyone confide in someone they don't know?"

I gave a heavy sigh. "Then what do you suggest I do? I have come home to Darkwater and the mill as it's my duty to carry out my grandfather's wishes. Yet my home feels uncomfortable, and I am unwelcome. To cap it all, upon my return, my cousin dies. The family seems satisfied that she killed herself; the public believe what they have been told, and I disagree with both theories."

"You still think Vivienne was murdered?" Mrs Daly whispered.

"I do." I looked hard at the woman, her brown eyes wide and frightened like a deer. "And I think secretly, you agree with me. So please, won't you stop hiding information once and for all, and tell me everything you know before someone else gets hurt."

Much to my amazement, the older woman buried

her head in her hands and let out a heavy sigh.

I did not speak.

A few moments passed. Presently, Mrs Daly raised her head. She reached for a glass of water standing on a side table and took a long sip.

"I know you mean well, Claire. But you must understand, things are not as they seem here."

"What do you mean?"

"When I came back to Starling Village, I realised it hadn't changed much in twenty years. Except for our church."

"How so?"

Mrs Daly stared down at her hands, clasped and resting in her lap. "In the past, the wealthiest landowner, or the highest judiciary carried the bulk of power in the area. By that I mean they could do what they wanted at a lesser risk than most. Have a greater influence over the events of the village and so forth. When I left Yorkshire, that power was held by your grandfather, Arthur Parslow. But when I returned after many years away, the power had shifted to another. This person had harnessed all the control. He used his ability and position to lure people into his way of thinking, his way of believing, until they were blinded, unable to see through his methods. Led like children, deaf to the truth, and faithful, even to their detriment."

"What are you saying, Mrs Daly? You're speaking in riddles." I did not understand her point.

Her eyes met mine. "There are things you do not know, Claire. It is better you remain ignorant so that you draw no attention to yourself."

"What are you talking about? Who wields all the control?" I was getting fed up with her wool gathering.

I needed answers. I raised my voice.

"Mrs Daly, I have had enough of this nonsense. I want you to speak plainly to me once and for all. Who is this powerful person you speak of? Is it my uncle?"

"No," she whispered. "Father Lynch."

I stared at her. "The priest? That's ridiculous." But even as the words left my lips, I knew she spoke the truth. For in the short time I'd been home, the man had been in the middle of everything. "Why the priest? What hold does a man like that have over the people in his parish?"

"I cannot really explain it, Claire. But Father Lynch is a force to be reckoned with, and your uncle is his most loyal supporter."

I took a moment to absorb her statement. It did add up. Since my return, whenever anything of importance had taken place, the first person my uncle turned to was the priest. Why? Uncle Simon had always been strong and dependable. It was he Mother leaned upon during the worst time of her life. It was Simon she relied upon to run her share of the mill so we had income to live on. How then had the balance of power been shifted?

"If you are being truthful, how does Father Lynch maintain his control?" I could not imagine someone like Ivan being told what to do by a priest.

"It isn't quite that straightforward. Father Lynch can only assert authority over people belonging to his church. Most of the parishioners attend out of their sincere religious beliefs. However, there is a smaller, private inner circle he spends extra time with, on evenings where there is no mass in the chapel. One known only to a select few."

"What? Like a secret society?"

She nodded.

I was still dubious. “And how do you know this?” I asked.

Mrs Daly’s pale face reddened. “Because I am a member.” She hesitated. “And so was Vivienne.”

Chapter Twenty-Six

"WHAT?" I SAID IN SURPRISE. "Then tell me more about this group. What is its purpose? How is it different from normal worship? I don't understand." My mind was spinning.

"It is complicated, Claire, and I cannot explain it in a way that would make sense to a person outside of the group."

"Then I suggest you try, Mrs Daly. Because I shan't rest until I discover what really happened to my cousin. I'll even go to Father Lynch if I have to. You obviously think there's a connection between Vivienne's death and this society of yours, or you wouldn't be so upset."

She shook her head. "It isn't that straightforward."

I stood up. "Then I shall go directly to the source."

"No!"

She shouted so loudly I sat back down. I fixed her with a glare. "Then you had better start talking, Mrs Daly."

"All right. But I'm worried you will get the wrong idea."

"Tell me." I'd had enough of her dithering.

She let out a deep breath. "Father Lynch is well-respected by his parishioners and the diocese. I am a practicing Catholic, and I have no complaints about the way he supports those under his watch. Several years ago, he formed a small group of what he refers to as 'The Order of the Believers', who meet separately every week to conduct a different kind of worship.

"Our group looks to Father Lynch as our natural leader, rather than to the cardinals or the Pope. His teachings go beyond those of the Catholic church, hence he still ministers, but in the group, our belief system goes far deeper, more in tune with our world. On a different level, one might say."

I thought she sounded completely batty, but now was not the time to challenge her views. I needed information.

"You're saying Vivienne belonged to this order, but had changed her mind and wanted to leave?"

"Yes. She'd been struggling with her views for some time. She felt she could not live according to the vows we took as believers."

"And you think that a strong enough reason for her to have taken her life?"

Mrs Daly stared at me, her face wracked with concern. "Yes, I do. You see, Claire, to bec[illegible] brethren of the believers, one has to accept the teachings and lifestyle requirements of the group without question. That she could no longer fulfil her role would have caused a great deal of confliction for Vivienne, even caused a rift between her and her family."

"The family? Why do you say that? Are they in the order too?"

"Yes. Not Ivan, but Simon and Nanette. They would have been very disappointed with her decision." She wrung her hands. "When Vivienne came to me for counsel, I failed to help the poor girl with her dilemma, and then look what happened."

Mrs Daly obviously felt some responsibility for Vivienne's ultimate demise. Now I understood why she had acted so strangely, even if it made no sense at all.

"Mrs Daly. You must not place any blame upon yourself for what happened to my cousin. Her death had nothing to do with you. Stop punishing yourself. It is not worth it." I stood up to leave. I'd had enough of this conversation. It all sounded perfectly ridiculous to me. I wanted some time to digest what she'd said. My thoughts were all a muddle.

She rose also but grabbed my arm with both of her hands. "Claire, I have broken one of our vows even speaking to you about The Believers. If you repeat anything I have told you, I shall be in great trouble with the group. Swear to me you will not tell another soul what I have shared with you today. Father Lynch—"

"Why was the priest here today?" I interrupted. "I saw him leave your cottage before I arrived."

"Did he see you?" She sounded scared.

"No. I hid until he passed by. Why? Are you not allowed to speak with me?"

"It is not that," she said quickly. "Under the circumstances, it would be better he not know we communicated at all."

"And what about my uncle and my cousin? Am I supposed to feign ignorance with them?"

"It would be for the best."

"Does Ivan know about your order?" I couldn't resist asking.

She shook her head. "I doubt it. Claire, I cannot stress the importance of keeping this quiet. Father Lynch has worked hard to make our order survive. You must swear to me you'll not say a word."

Her eyes looked frantic, and her fingernails dug into my forearm.

"I swear it," I said, mainly to calm the woman and because I suddenly felt the cottage was closing in on me. I wanted to get out of there at once.

I wrenched my arm from her clasp, simultaneously bidding her farewell, and hurried out into the fresh air.

Walking back to Darkwater I could not stop the myriad of thoughts whirling through my head like a murmuration of starlings. The daily life of these people on the surface seemed uncomplicated, yet beneath what the eye saw, lay a complex web of secrets and truths. I had scratched the surface of a scab and made it bleed.

As I passed St Michael's, on a bold whim I decided to try for Father Lynch once again. Unsure where to find him I went inside the Chapel.

I have never been a religious person, yet anytime I have been inside a church I have al[illegible]ved by the peace and calm that envelops you. Standing in the nave of St Michael's, it was impossible to be unaware of the tranquillity here.

The church was simple in design. The floor, flagstones, and the walls looked like travertine or perhaps marble. Tapestries hung the length of the nave depicting different religious scenes that I did not find familiar.

It was light in here, thanks to a series of stained-glass windows. Like Darkwater, they filtered sunlight wherever light fell, resulting in tiny patterns of what looked like multicoloured fireflies.

It was quiet, and I made my way down the nave towards the altar. There was no one to be found. Was there a room attached to the church where Father Lynch might conduct his business? Failing that, I would leave the building and try his cottage.

I passed a statue of Mary located next to the altar and spotted a door behind the statue. There was a small painted sign that read *Sacristy*. I did not know what it meant, but I knocked on the door anyway.

"Come in." I recognised Father Lynch's voice.

I turned the handle and stepped inside.

This room looked like a place to store implements used in ceremonies. I could see different religious items on top of a large table, various crucifixes, and silver chalices. There was also a stout block of furniture lined with felt, with a beautiful piece of fabric spread out on top of it. It looked like a garment a priest would wear during a religious service.

Father Lynch attended to this outfit. He smoothed out creases, perhaps in preparation to wear the next day when he conducted mass.

He turned and showed surprise to see it was me.

"Mrs Holloway. To what do I owe the pleasure of your visit?"

I did not draw nearer. This man made me uncomfortable and kept me wrong-footed. As a priest and the head of a parish, Father Lynch practised asserting authority and confidence. I was in his territory, therefore the balance swung in his favour.

I reminded myself that I was no shrinking violet, and well capable of speaking to him as an equal. I was not his follower, and I should not allow him to intimidate me.

Coal black eyes regarded me thoughtfully. "Is everything all right at Darkwater?" The expression in his eyes did not change, there was no real concern there.

"Yes. I am here to see if you can spare me some of your valuable time. I have some questions I'd like to ask if you would not mind?"

He pointed to a small table in the corner. "Please, have a seat. I'm more than happy to speak with you."

I took the invitation and sat down. He joined me. I did not like being this close. He leaned forward resting his forearms on the table and steepled his fingers.

"Feel free to speak your mind. You are in the house of the Lord. What can I help you with?"

"I would like to talk to you about what happened twenty years ago on the night my father was accused of killing Keith Delahunt."

He hadn't expected that. He frowned. "My dear, why must you resurrect something that occurred when you were but a child? Do you not think the events bothersome enough they should stay in the past?"

"No," I stated bluntly. "It matters not to me whether it was twenty or thirty years ago. What happened on that awful night set the stage for the rest of my life. I was robbed of a father, and my mother, her husband. I am unconvinced the right person was punished for that crime."

He gave me a thin smile and a pitying look. "I am sure coming to terms with what happened must have been very hard, Claire. 'Tis only natural for you to question something which occurred without your being there, as it were."

"I would expect you to say that, Father. Based upon what you saw that night you believe my father was guilty of murder. But I have read my mother's journals which were quite detailed. I know she was there, that my father arrived after the shooting, and that you were asked not to comment on her presence by my father."

He stared at me, contemplating a response.

I did not look away though I wanted to,

"'Tis no secret amongst your family Jane was there. I agreed not to mention it because of a long-standing relationship I had with your family. Your grandfather, and your father after him, generously contributed to several of our charities, even though they were not practising Catholics. So when Thomas asked me to refrain from mentioning your mother being there that night, I said yes."

"Do you think my father shot Keith Delahunt." I looked him straight in the eye.

He didn't even blink. "Yes," he said. "I don't know how it all happened, or even why, to be sure, but I don't think your mother had anything to do with it. She was in the wrong place at the wrong time. Perhaps Keith did something to put your mother in jeopardy and angered your father. That might be why Thomas felt the need to kill the man."

"You admit to not seeing what happened, and my father maintained his innocence until the end, yet you still felt compelled to testify against him and contribute to the guilty verdict that ultimately got him hung?"

The black eyes narrowed to slits. His mouth tightened. There was no trace of a compassionate priest. I'd made him angry, and I was glad.

"I am not sure what you accuse me of, Claire. But I am offended. I am a man of God, and my vows include those of honesty. I only spoke of what I saw, and answered the questions put to me in a court of law, as truthfully as possible. I do not like your inference." He got to his feet. "Now, I have much to do and I think it best you leave."

I rose. "It is not my intention to be disrespectful. I am sure your vows are very important as is your vocation, Father Lynch, but I would like to point out, though you insist you are honest and truthful, you were nevertheless willing to lie by omission at my father's request. I would not think even in the eyes of the church, you are allowed to select what you lie about."

"How dare you speak to me that way." His jaw was rigid.

"I am not speaking to you in any particular way. I am recounting something that you admit actually took place. That it angers you is not my problem. I cannot control your conscience." I started towards the door. His next words stopped me.

"You are a newcomer here, Claire. It matters not your roots, what counts is time spent. You should be careful how you talk to people, my dear. Someone might take enough offence to retaliate."

I whipped around and faced him. Nervous and unsure, my pulse raced, but my anger superseded every other emotion in that moment. Father Lynch was my adversary. I had sensed it when first we'd met, I just had not been able to give it a name. But there was no hiding behind manners any longer.

"Are you threatening me?"

"Don't be ridiculous." He smiled and I was reminded of a crocodile. "I am a priest. It is not my calling to harm a living soul. I am merely giving you the benefit of some sage advice, Claire. Don't go looking for trouble."

It was my turn to be harsh. "I do not seek your counsel, nor need it, Father Lynch. Oh, and while we are being so frank with one another, I show you respect by calling you by your title, and I would ask you grant me the same courtesy. Let us not pretend to be friends by being familiar. I prefer you not call me by my Christian name as I do not call you by yours."

With that I turned on my heel. Keeping my head high to conceal how nervous I actually felt, I left the room.

I rushed out of the church and, reaching the outdoors, gulped in fresh air. My heart banged against my ribs as though I'd been running. What had come over me just then? I knew the answer. I was tired of subterfuge and dishonesty.

Being a woman, I often encountered people who enjoyed being sanctimonious. Whether from their elevated social status or the fact that they were men and I a lowly female. I did not tolerate it well.

Father Lynch was too big for his boots. I couldn't help but question his actions the night Keith Delahunt was killed. He knew more than he let on about events leading to my father's execution. He was hiding something.

After such a short time of observing his behaviour, I did not care for his assertiveness around my family, and how he took charge of whatever was going on, even when it wasn't his right to do so.

If Uncle Simon and Nanette were involved in a secret religious sect, it was their business ultimately. But if Father Lynch and his group were behind any of the incidents which occurred, specifically what happened to my father, and now Vivienne, then I intended to make it my business as well.

WHEN I ARRIVED BACK AT Darkwater my blood was still up. Frankly, all I'd done since coming to Yorkshire was try and understand what was at work here. I'd thought my greatest challenge would be sharing the same home as Ivan. How ironic he'd be the only person I could confide in, and he wasn't even my own flesh and blood.

On some level the events preceding today had been like the proverbial snowball, starting small and slowly growing larger at every turn. I'd believed coming home to Yorkshire would settle me, provide a foundation so recently lost. Certainly, finding my mother's journals had stirred the pot and awakened my determination to continue her quest and clear Father's name.

Yet that had suddenly become only one of my goals now other occurrences had taken place. It was not my nature to let things go. If something aroused my interest, good or bad, I would have to spend enough time with it before letting slip from my thoughts.

The way Vivienne died just didn't sit right. That the others readily accepted Doctor Tipton's cause of death bothered me more than I wanted to admit. How could a father or a sister be content with one person's opinion? If it had been my daughter, I would have questioned everything about the manner of how they lost their life.

Still brooding, I went up to my room and changed. My meeting on Monday could not come quick enough. I'd be relieved knowing my options regarding where I could choose to live.

As was my habit now, I retrieved my notebook from its hiding place and quickly jotted down my thoughts and opinions from my conversations with Hilary Daly and Father Lynch. Recounting my time with the priest I congratulated myself upon speaking my mind and not letting him browbeat me.

I had made an enemy. There was no doubt in my mind. But at least I recognised it now and did not have to speculate. What really transpired twenty years ago in St. Michael's graveyard? The priest had lied. If he could have helped save my father from such an awful fate, how could he now live with himself? One hoped a man of God would be closer to his conscience than the rest of us. Or did he have more immunity from being judged because of his faith?

And what of the body locked up in the priest hole? Who was that? If it was another man of the cloth, why had his God deserted him in a time of need? Leaving him to die in the very place supposed to keep him safe?

So many thoughts twisted and turned in my head. And with added information from Jack, everything shifted yet again. The necklace I had found was uncommon. Its discovery, along with the tale of a young woman's brother being in Australia, and the recent death of a man from that same country could not be coincidental.

Jack Tibbetts had provided me with potentially important information. But it was all too much for me to sift through alone. I wanted Ivan's help.

I considered my cousin's husband. We made an odd pair, he and I. The children of a murder victim and his supposed killer were never fated to be friends. But I would have taken to Ivan Delahunt no matter the scenario we met in. I liked his steadfastness. Although he'd often seemed moody at the beginning, he was generally in good spirits. An intelligent man, he had the grace to use that intellect in a positive way. Ivan treated everyone as an equal, and I am sure that made him very popular at the mill.

I looked forward to my meeting with the solicitor on Monday with great anticipation. I desperately needed to be busy and not wander aimlessly around this large house any longer. It was disappointing, not having a good relationship with Nanette, or Vivienne, for that matter. How different things might have been if Uncle Simon behaved like a traditional uncle, and if my cousins and I were the best of friends.

My life had been somewhat solitary. It had suited me living that way. With George and Sarah, I'd found true purpose and meaning. Now they were gone I suppose that's what I still sought. My reason to face each dawn had been snatched away from me. I must not blame myself for feeling restless. I was seeking something to replace my loved ones.

Perhaps spending time at Parslow's would be the answer I was looking for. I could sink my teeth into projects that were unfamiliar yet part of my heritage.

I put my notebook away and readied myself for dinner. I would tell Ivan I wished to speak with him, perhaps he'd have time for a conversation in the morning. The family would likely attend mass, and we would have the house to ourselves to talk freely.

I'd feel better having another person know what I'd learned in the course of one day. My head was jumbled. Speaking to him would bring clarity.

Yet I did not doubt my feelings. There was

something unsavoury going on. Whether or not it was linked to the past, I was determined to find out.

Chapter Twenty-Seven

AT DINNER, I FOUND MYSELF alone. Uncle Simon and Nanette were absent. No one seemed to know where they were. I assumed they were paying a call on someone, perhaps Colonel Baldwin? According to Tibbetts, Ivan had taken his own horse to Skipton instead of the carriage and had not yet returned.

As I supped I reflected how odd it was everyone was gone, yet their actual locations were unknown.

It was a quiet meal, other than my occasional conversation with Tibbetts. Tonight I was sick of my own company. After finishing the main course, I asked if I could join him, Mrs Blitch and Mellors downstairs for dessert.

A half an hour passed, and I wished I had eaten all of my meal with them also. Their company was more entertaining than that of my regular dinner partners. Conversation was lively, and even the subject matter far more interesting.

It was refreshing to hear Mellors speak of her father's prize pig, and Mrs Blitch recount her days as a lass. Even Tibbetts spun a few yarns which had us all laughing.

And that was where Ivan found us.

At first, he looked at our motley group in surprise. But in a flash, he joined us, and Mrs Blitch sorted him out a plate of leftovers.

By the time Ivan finished his food, we were all yawning, me being the worst offender. So I bade them all a goodnight, and asked Ivan if he would be at home in the morning so I might speak with him. He assured me he would, and with that knowledge, I went up to my bed.

WHEN I ARRIVED DOWN FOR breakfast the next morning, it was to find Nanette and Simon already gone to church. It was almost nine o'clock and I had slept unusually late. I'd had a dreamless sleep and, waking to the pitter-patter of soft rain on the windowpanes, found myself lulled back into slumber.

Mrs Blitch's scrambled eggs and thick wedges of fresh toast with salty butter and rich damson jam, tasted delicious. I helped myself to a second slice as Ivan joined me.

"Good morning, Claire. I see you are a late starter as well as me."

"I am indeed," I said. "I slept like a log last night and woke up hungry as a bear."

He chuckled and took the seat across from me. He scooped some eggs from the warming pan and helped himself to some toast. I poured him a cup of tea and topped up my own at the same time.

"Were you still awake when the others came home?" I asked.

"Goodness, no. I've no idea when they returned. I went up not long after you and was asleep as soon as my head hit the pillow." He glanced around. "I assume they are gone to mass this morning?"

"I believe so."

He took a sip of tea. "Tell me your plans for the

day. It looks like the rain has settled in, so it will be chilly outside."

"Actually, there are several matters I want to discuss with you, but not in here. I don't want to be overheard."

"That sounds rather ominous, Claire. Where do you want to go?"

"If it wasn't raining, I'd walk down to the cottage. It's such a nice walk and it certainly is private. But I suppose we should just meet in the drawing room after breakfast."

"Has something happened?"

"Not specifically, but I have learned a few things you should know. If that's all right?"

"Of course."

Once we finished breakfast, Tibbetts brought a tea tray into the drawing room. Whereupon he informed us Father Lynch would be joining the family for luncheon, after church.

Ivan thanked him and then we were left alone.

I poured us both a cup of tea. I sat on the sofa and Ivan sat across from me in the armchair. It was peaceful in the room with the soft crackle from the fireplace and the rain tapping the windows. Hardly the setting to discuss murder.

"Well, out with it. What is it you want to tell me, Claire?"

"I had an eventful day yesterday. I went for tea at the Tibbetts residence."

"Ah, yes. I remember you telling me you'd been invited. How was it? I imagine sailors to be such colourful sorts. I'll warrant he had some great stories. What an adventurous life they lead." He suddenly looked thoughtful, and I wondered if he was comparing a mariner's life to his own.

"He did have some tales to tell. But the most interesting part of our conversation was in reference to the necklace I found in the priest hole."

"You don't say? Why would he know about the necklace?"

"I suppose chance is a real thing." I recounted the story Jack had shared regarding his unexpected meeting with an actress named Molly. "It is ironic that he noticed her necklace," I said. But that's not all."

Ivan appeared quite interested in what I had to say. His eyes were very blue today and currently were focused intently upon me.

"Molly, whose reason for being here was never made clear other than her wanting to see my uncle, told Jack about her incarcerated brother, who was then in an Australian jail. She expressed her hopes he would return to England once he was a free man."

I watched Ivan's expression change as the implication of my words suddenly dawned on him. "And you suspect the man who died recently while rambling, could be her brother? Isn't that what they call grasping at straws?"

"You could think that. But isn't it rather coincidental that an Australian man who, according to the people at the inn where he stayed, does not have the appearance of an outdoors person, should happen to be out walking near Darkwater on a chilly autumn day. And that we find a necklace belonging to a woman who was here at this house twenty years ago wanting to see Uncle Simon. You have to agree the odds of Molly having a necklace like the one I found, and a brother like the man who died, all in the vicinity of this house, are slim. Yet that is what happened."

"All right, I'll go along with your theory, for now. Tell me, what do you think this all means? You obviously have drawn some conclusion."

I took a deep breath. I had yet to say this even to myself. "I think the skeleton in the priest hole might have been Molly."

"And this is entirely based on the presence of a necklace?"

"For the moment, yes. But it is also a hunch I have because of the skeleton itself. I can't remember some of my nurses training when we had to study bones. Yet something's been nagging at me since the skeleton's discovery. I've racked my brains to remember what it is. It's a way of telling the gender of a body by their bones. I know there are subtle differences between male and female bones but for the life of me I can't remember what they are. I need a medical encyclopaedia to look up something."

Ivan contemplated my words for a moment and then he grinned. "Wait here," he said. "I shall return momentarily."

I wondered what he was about, but I shrugged and busied myself pouring another cup of tea. I had almost finished it, deciding he had forgotten all about me, when I heard footsteps in the hallway.

Ivan came over to the sofa, then moved the tea tray to one side, setting down a large book on the table in front of me.

"Your wish is my command, Claire." He sounded rather pleased with himself.

I looked at the cover of the book and smiled. It was

a copy of the Encyclopaedia Brittanica, of course.

I gave a wry laugh. "I should have realised there would be one of these in the house with my cousin being so sickly."

He shrugged. "The blasted thing's probably dog eared from all its use."

I pretended to be offended at him for the remark, subtly directed at my cousin and frowned at him. Then I opened the book.

It took me a few minutes to locate the information I searched for. "Here we are," I said. Then I quoted from the book.

'The adult human skeleton has 206 bones, although this number may vary among individuals; a person may have an extra vertebra or rib. Generally, the adult male skeleton is larger and more robust in appearance than the adult female skeleton. An examination of the pelvis can be used to determine the sex of an individual; a smaller pelvic inlet and narrower subpelvic opening indicate an adult male, whereas a larger pelvic inlet and wider subpelvic opening indicate an adult female. The general age of an individual may be determined by skull size, condition of sutures, and an examination of the teeth, as well as by the length of particular bones (e.g., the femur and the humerus) and the degree of ossification (bone hardening) that has taken place between the shaft of a long bone and its end caps.'

"That is still vague," Ivan said. "Do you think you would be able to tell?"

"I'm not sure. But it would be worth checking."

"Didn't Father Lynch already take the skeleton to his church?"

"Yes, the very next day. But I don't know if it's

been buried yet."

"Then we should go and see," Ivan said. "No point in waiting. We know he'll be there as he's conducting mass at this very moment."

I closed the book. I looked down in my lap trying to formulate how I was going to explain my tenuous relationship with the priest.

"I don't think I will be welcome at St. Michael's, Ivan."

"Why ever not?"

"What I haven't told you is I went to see Hilary Daly after leaving the Tibbetts cottage yesterday."

"What has that to do with the priest?"

"We spoke about Vivienne's state of mind over the past few weeks and part of the conversation suggested her connection with Father Lynch was quite deep. In light of that and also because I had my own questions regarding the night my father was arrested, I paid the priest a call."

Ivan's eyes narrowed. "And how did that go?"

Warmth flooded my cheeks. "Not very well, unfortunately. He took offence at my questions and my insinuation that he was not a truthful man."

Ivan's jaw dropped. "You said that to him?"

I nodded.

"My goodness, Claire. I could shake your hand in admiration. I wish I had been there to see the old crow's face. He's not used to anyone standing up to him. He's got them all too scared."

"I've never liked him," I admitted. "And it is mutual. I don't trust him, and I instinctively feel he knows more about the night your father died than he is prepared to say. Father Lynch is the only surviving witness. The constable died, and every other person who was there. He willingly concealed the fact my mother was present even when Papa was found guilty. I should think at such a serious turn of events, all bets would be off, and everyone would tell the truth. Yet he saw an innocent man hang for a crime he did not commit." I looked at Ivan imploringly. "I know this is always a difficult conversation because of the tragic death of your father that night. But speaking with the priest and watching his reaction only strengthened my resolve that the person who shot your father still walks free."

Ivan sat still for a moment. I realised he was trying to absorb everything I had said. My passionate words ignited sparks of energy and suddenly I needed to move. I got up and paced about the room waiting for him to respond.

I had not told him about the secret group named 'The Believers' but wanted to. Yet I'd given my word not to speak of it and felt very conflicted and unsure what to do. However, it was important to share everything I knew with another person. I needed Ivan's insight and opinion.

I returned to my seat and sat down. "There's something else,"

"Go on."

"Mrs Daly eventually relented and spoke openly with me about my cousin. Are you aware of a group that meets at St. Michael's, other than the normal congregation, that is."

"I'm not sure what you mean?" Ivan said.

"According to Mrs Daly, there is a small group who meet with Father Lynch, and they are called 'The

Believers.'"

"What?"

"She would not say much, but it sounds like a select few who are extremely devout, more so than everyone else. Consequently, as well as attending mass, they take time to meet regularly, secretly, where they discuss their beliefs, and worship."

"What does this have to do with anything?"

"Vivienne was a member of the group but, according to Hilary, Vivienne wanted to leave it for personal reasons. When I implied that my cousin had died from another's hand, Mrs Daly looked frightened. Those words changed her demeanour, and all at once she decided to tell me about 'The Believers'. Their secret order."

"This sounds ridiculous, Claire. What are you saying? Don't you think I would know something about a group like this? After all, I've lived here years. If you are trying to make a connection based upon a middle-aged woman's reaction to murder, I'm not surprised she was frightened. She probably thinks there's some lunatic wandering the streets of Starling, thanks to you."

I groaned. "You're missing the point, Ivan. This is a *very* secret group and Father Lynch is the leader. And that is not all." I hesitated.

"Do tell," he said sarcastically. "Next you'll be saying they all think they're descendants of an alien race from Mars?"

"This isn't funny, Ivan. Any order that few have heard of is automatically suspicious in my opinion. You only remain secret if you have something to hide."

"And who else is in this group, then? If it is an

exclusive set up, I'm rather hurt I've not been invited."

"Your wife."

"What? Don't be ridiculous."

"I am not. There are several members of the group, and they include Nanette and my uncle as well."

He looked furious. I believe some of it was embarrassment that he was apparently unaware of his wife's activities that took place right under his nose. I hastened to dispel that feeling.

"According to Mrs Daly, this group has been in existence for a long time, probably before you were even married. If you were a practising Catholic and frequented the church with the family, you might have been made aware of the existence of the group and even invited to join. But I think as an outsider, you are deemed untrustworthy to keep their secret, and therefore have been kept in the dark." Saying the word dark reminded me how I had witnessed his wife sneaking away from Darkwater late at night. I would not tell him this; he had enough to think about as it was.

"I'm sorry." Ivan shook his head in denial. "But this sounds so farfetched. Do you honestly believe I would be ignorant of my wife's activities week after week, month after month?"

"I'm not implying anything bad Ivan. I am suggesting that when you are at the mill during the day, you do not know what Nanette does with her time. And if she went to the group with her sister and father, why would you ever question her going anywhere?"

"All right. If they do attend secretive meetings, what does that have to do with Vivienne's death? There is no direct link as far as I can tell. Think about it. The members are probably all Catholic and local. If they have been meeting for years, why would someone suddenly turn into a murderer? Where is the motive? Being late for a meeting?"

"I don't find your inane comments at all funny, Ivan. Regardless of your finding my ideas unbelievable, you of all people should know murder is no laughing matter."

Just as I'd hit the nail on the head with Father Lynch, so I scored a direct mark with Ivan. His face became stern, his eyes darkened and a muscle in his cheek clenched.

"Look," I said. "Let us not argue or mock one another. I do take this seriously and I thought you respected my opinion enough to keep an open mind. What if this group is so secret, you're never allowed to leave? If that was the case and Vivienne wanted to stop participating, could that have resulted in her death?"

"It sounds overly dramatic to me," said Ivan. "If you think about it, there are probably hundreds of what you would refer to as secret groups that meet under the umbrella of religion. That does not make a group bad."

"I'm not saying that. What I'm suggesting is that this particular group may be different. Perhaps they discuss things of personal or private matters as well as religion. Maybe they take some kind of a vow that they can never stray? I don't know. I'm just trying to think of a motive for someone to poison my cousin. And before you comment, she was poisoned. I'm not going to rest until I figure this all out."

"And where exactly do you plan to start with your sleuthing?"

I flopped back against the sofa. "I would have to attend one of their meetings, I suppose."

"You can do no such thing. Besides, if you and our good priest are now foes, you're not going to be invited. You could throw yourself on his mercy, and say that your soul needs saving?"

"Very funny. Of course I don't plan to go as a guest. I'd want to spy on them. Look, Ivan. I know I am onto something. You promised you'd help me before, will you help me now? Vivienne was your sister-in-law. One would think that counted for something."

Ivan shook his head. "Are you trying to make me feel guilty?"

"Yes."

Much to my surprise he grinned at me.

"You go to any lengths, Claire Holloway. And damned if I don't admire you for it. What is it you want me to do?"

Chapter Twenty-Eight

WE WATCHED PEOPLE LEAVING St Michael's chapel. Some of them paused to bid farewell to Father Lynch and his young deacon. Though Ivan and I stood a fair distance away hidden behind a thatch of large holly bushes, I'd spotted Uncle Simon and Nanette, Hilary Daly and the Tipton family.

Now we waited to see when Father Lynch would leave and what the young deacon might do.

Ivan saw the priest first and gestured in the direction of a small cottage adjacent to the chapel where both of the men must make their home. Deacon Wirral came from around the back, leading a horse and trap to the front. Whereupon Father Lynch climbed up, snapped the reins and headed down the short drive to the road. He would be headed to Darkwater for lunch.

The young deacon then walked back to the cottage and went inside.

"Come on," Ivan said.

We skirted the line of bushes away from the gravel pathway which led to the chapel entrance, instead, coming along the side of the building, out of sight from the cottage.

The chapel door was open, and we went inside.

I led Ivan directly down the nave to the room marked *Sacristy*. But I doubted what we searched for would be there. We were looking for the skeleton.

Father Lynch had taken it away on Friday, and I was counting on the fact that there had not been enough time for him to prepare for a burial.

"There must be a crypt under here," Ivan said as we neared the room where I'd talked with Father Lynch. There was no other door visible. We walked across the width of the nave to the opposite side of the building, past the altar and a large shrine depicting another statue of Mary holding her child. Just beyond were two doors.

"Let's try here," said Ivan. He opened the first to reveal a cupboard, the second, sturdier, was the entrance to a cellar.

Just inside the door at the top of a flight of stairs stood a tall stool with a lamp sat upon it. Ivan lit the wick and then gestured for me to follow.

He closed the door behind us, and instantly we were engulfed it what felt like a tomb. I shivered with cold and smelled damp in the air.

"Use the rope to hold on to," Ivan said, indicating a thick coil fastened to iron rings, secured into the stone wall. Although there were not many steps to descend, they were straight down and steep.

Our progress was slow, for the lamp was not as bright as I would have liked. But presently we reached the bottom of the stairs. Here Ivan spotted another lamp attached to a large hook on the wall. He lit this one also, and the area was suddenly bathed in ombre light.

The crypt was a broad hallway, intersected with stone archway supports. Each side held a row of three rooms. These were more like stalls as none of them were closed in. They appeared to be used for storage.

The first area was quite full, with several crates of

wine, likely used at all the services. We looked at the next two and they had a few boxes scattered on the floor. We turned and walked back in the direction of the stairs passing the other rooms. I paused.

"Look at this, Ivan."

Ivan lifted the lamp higher, and we stepped closer.

In the end room a large stone pedestal and stone sarcophagus stood in the centre of the area. It did not appear to be antiquated, for the stone was clean and not discoloured. On the lid of the coffin, in elaborate, cursive lettering was a name.

'The Prince of Souls."

"Anyone you know?" Asked Ivan, holding the lamp high enough so I could see his face.

"Very funny," I said. "What an odd name. Do you think there's someone inside?"

"Only one way to find out, here." He passed me the lamp and then went to the head of the casket and tried to move the lid. It was obviously quite heavy, but Ivan managed to scrape it partially to one side so we could peek in.

Although our lamp wasn't terribly bright, I held it next to the small opening, standing shoulder to shoulder with Ivan. For some odd reason, my pulse increased, and I was surprised at this, for I had seen many dead bodies in my lifetime.

We peered through the gap.

"It's empty," Ivan stated, and slid the lid back in its place. "That was disappointing. Let's look at the next place." The next area had a table in the centre and nothing else. Once we drew closer, I saw there was something on the table, covered up with a sheet.

"This could be it," I said, unable to hide the

anticipation in my voice. I desperately wanted a closer look at the skeleton, after everything I had learned.

I still held the lamp, so Ivan gently pulled back the cover to reveal the remains of whomever lost their life trapped behind a wall at Darkwater.

I stepped closer, and he took the lamp from me, holding it higher to spread the light farther.

It felt like an intrusion, staring at a pile of bones which had once been a living, breathing entity. I had to remind myself of our good intentions. I began with the skull.

"This person's skull is not large, nor particularly thick," I said to Ivan. "In current times, that would indicate a leaning towards it being female, rather than male. Yet it does not ring so true if these remains are in fact from the sixteen hundreds, for people were much smaller than we are today." I pointed at the forehead.

"From what I remember, the male's brow is often lower and slopes more as well. This one does not appear to do that." I moved lower. "Here, put the light where I can see the pelvic area."

Ivan did as I asked, and he leaned forward with me to peer at the bones. Carefully, I placed my hand over the pelvic bone.

"Look at this, Ivan. Do you see how broad the pelvic area is? In women it has to be because of childbearing." I leaned closer still. I wanted to see the pelvic inlet, the area in the centre of the pelvis. In a male it would be oval, or heart shaped. In a woman if would be larger and round.

"Well?"

I took a deep breath. "I am no expert, but I don't think this is a priest from the Tudor times. I think this is a woman."

In the light of the gas lamp, our eyes met.

"Are you sure?"

"Yes. Look at this." I explained the shape of the pelvic inlet.

"It is circular and wide," he agreed. He looked rather serious. "You think this is the woman with the necklace that Jack Tibbetts talked about?"

"Well under the circumstances, it is a bit of a coincidence, don't you think?"

"Hmm." Ivan looked thoughtful. "We need to properly identify this Molly woman and see if we can trace her. It shouldn't be that hard to find a person in Liverpool, or at least, a record of them. That way, we could rule her out if we found her somewhere?"

It was a sound idea. "Yes. That's an excellent suggestion."

"All right. Then let's get out of here before we're discovered." He moved and I spotted a door at the back of the room, hidden in the shadows.

"Look," I said. "What do you think is in there?"

He glanced over to where I was pointing, and then walked over with the lamp. I followed.

"More than likely another storage cupboard," Ivan said. "Let me see…" He touched the handle. "It's locked," he said, turning to look at me. "Probably where they hide all the gold." Then he grinned at me. "Come on, Claire. Let's get out of here."

We reached the bottom of the stairs, and Ivan snuffed out the hanging lamp. We tenuously made our way back up the steps carrying our light.

At the top, he reached for the doorknob, but it suddenly swung open to reveal Deacon Wirral, looking a mixture of angry and terrified.

"What do you think you're doing here? This part of the church is not open to the public. You have no right to go down there."

Before I could utter a word, Ivan took control of the situation. He extinguished the lantern and placed it back on the stool, then we stepped out into the nave of the church.

"Please forgive us for the intrusion," he said smoothly. "Mrs Holloway and I wanted another look at the skeleton found at Darkwater. We looked for Father Lynch, but there didn't appear to be anyone here." Ivan took a step forward and the Deacon backed away. I didn't blame him. Ivan could be quite intimidating. He was a well-built man of good height, unlike the small Deacon.

"I apologise if we have done something wrong. I assumed that because the skeleton was found on our property, technically it belonged to us. I had a few questions which I thought I might answer just looking at the thing. After all," he smiled, "It isn't every day one sees centuries old bones, is it?"

It was cleverly done. Ivan had quickly asserted authority and ownership, making it very difficult for the deacon to question his presence there.

"We are sorry," I added demurely. "We truly meant nothing by it. I wasn't sure when the burial would take place, so it seemed the best time to come now. Poor fellow. It will be nice when you have laid him to rest." I was surprised how easy it was to be so trite.

"Mrs Holloway, I think it best we take our leave. I imagine Simon will be wondering where we've got to on our walk." He looked at the deacon. "We were actually on our way to Starling and began discussing the old boy down there." He gestured towards the crypt. "On a whim, we thought we'd have a quick look as we were close to St. Michael's. No harm meant."

Deacon Wirral had composed himself. He no longer looked upset. "No harm done either, Mr Delahunt. I heard a noise coming from down there, and it wouldn't be the first time some of our wine has gone missing. We have even caught one of the local beggars sleeping down there."

"My goodness. Well just remember we were not trespassing, and would have asked permission had someone been here." Ivan turned and looked at me. "Shall we go then?"

"Indeed," I replied. "Thank you, Deacon Wirral. The family really appreciates you looking after the poor body."

With that, we left the young man standing by the door to the crypt and made our way back outside. Neither one of us spoke until we cleared the pathway and were back on the road to Darkwater.

"That was exciting," I said walking briskly beside Ivan. "It was quite the adventure. You did a marvellous job with the deacon. I think you frightened him out of his wits."

Ivan chuckled. "Poor fellow. I'm sure he's a nice enough chap. I just didn't want him asking us questions. Fortunately, I've learned how to sound stern from my years working at the mill. But, more importantly, let's discuss our findings. You seem confident the skeleton is female, and therefore if we put the discovery of the necklace alongside it, we can deduce there is a good chance it's the remains of a more recent body."

"That's a fair assessment. We just need to identify who it is. And until we do that, we can't begin to guess how it got there in the first place," I said.

"I wish we could date the bones. We cannot know for certain when the person was interred inside the priest hole, or if they were dead or alive when they went in. Yet I'll admit the necklace you found did look modern."

"Perhaps I could take it to a jeweller and get their impression?"

"What an excellent idea, Claire. Are you still going to Skipton tomorrow?"

"Yes, to meet with Mr Satterthwaite. I'll take the necklace with me and find somewhere it can be valued."

"Once you've done that, come back to the mill and we'll talk more." Ivan abruptly stopped walking.

When I realised, I halted and turned back to face him. "Is something wrong?"

"No. But I want to apologise to you, Claire. Ever since you arrived at Darkwater, you've had doubts about many things that have happened. I've not been as supportive as I should have been. I suppose living here so long, it has all become quite mundane. Making a leap from that to the possibility of murder and mayhem, poison and now skeletons, it's all a bit farfetched. Yet in truth, there is much to your suspicions and, regarding the current situation, I think you might be correct. Something's not adding up with the body being found in the priest hole.

"Considering the history here, starting with what

happened to my father, I agree with you wholeheartedly that it is time to dig into the past once and for all. There are questions that have gone unanswered, and people not held accountable for their actions based on your mother's records. Therefore, let us start now. Get the necklace looked at tomorrow if you can. I intend to use my connections and see if I can find out the full identity of the woman called Molly. If she can be found, I should be able to determine the name of her brother, and we can see if there is any link between him, and the rambler who died recently. Once we have that answer, I think it will open up other questions."

Delighted, I gave a sigh of relief. "Thank you, Ivan. That means a great deal to me. I knew I could count on you. You probably wish I'd never shown up in Yorkshire. I think you led a more peaceful life before I had the audacity to stir up the pot."

We resumed walking.

"I disagree, Claire." We glanced at one another. His eyes were bright yet at the same time intense. "Life at Darkwater has been more than lacking. When you arrived it was as though a small whirlwind whisked through the dark house and blew away all the cobwebs. You are a portent of change. And though I speak for myself, I must tell you how thankful I am you are here."

I was speechless. The sincerity of his words touched me. I did not know what to say in response. I just smiled.

AS LUCK WOULD HAVE IT, we arrived at the exact moment lunch was being served in the large dining room. The heady scent of roast lamb pervaded the entire house and smelled delicious.

Everyone was already seated at the dining table. We walked in together which drew the attention of Father Lynch, Uncle Simon and Nanette. The latter looked displeased. I completely understood as I had obviously been somewhere with her husband.

"Please excuse us," said Ivan as we both took our respective seats. "I made Claire accompany me for a brief walk to Rosell's Cottage. She complained of needing some fresh air, and I persuaded her that the view from the top of the hill was quite lovely."

"That's a horrible place," pouted my cousin. "Why on earth would you take anyone there, Ivan?"

"Don't be cross, Nanette," I interjected. "I bullied him into it. There is a lovely spot overlooking St. Michael's and Starling village."

"There's nothing lovely about that cottage," said Nanette. "It shall always remind me of what happened to that poor girl years ago."

Tibbetts entered the room carrying a platter of meat. He set it before Uncle Simon, so that he might carve and serve, then left.

"Let us discuss something more cheerful," said the priest, who did not look particularly cheery himself. "It is a Sabbath, after all. A time to rejoice in the Lord and contemplate his bounties and blessings."

I contemplated what Father Lynch would think once the deacon told him he'd caught Ivan and myself snooping around. The priest would be displeased, and the notion brought me immense pleasure.

Tibbets reappeared carrying yet another tray, this laden with bowls of vegetables. These he sat in the centre of the table. My stomach rumbled with hunger.

Mrs Blitch's roast potatoes looked wonderful and crispy. Steam rose from sweet English peas, there were fresh carrots drizzled with butter, and a gravy boat full of lamb gravy.

Uncle Simon carved slices of meat and set them on a platter which Tibbetts brought around to each of us, and we helped ourselves.

"Is it not strange us all being here together without my sister?" said Nanette. "I find it awful but life goes on as normal even when something terrible has occurred." She glanced around the table. "Look at us," she said. "We're sitting here helping ourselves to food and behaving as though nothing's changed."

"Nanette," said Ivan. "It is inappropriate for you to speak this way. We are all aware that everything is forever different. What do you propose we do? Refrain from having meals?"

She glared at him. "You have no sympathy for how I suffer, husband. You do not know the depth of my pain."

"Perhaps you are right." His tone lowered. I looked over to see the disgust on Ivan's face as he stared at his wife. "When an individual loses someone they love, it is impossible to measure their grief. You forget, wife, besides Vivienne, I have lost someone dear to me also."

This conversation was becoming dangerously volatile. Fortunately, Uncle Simon decided to speak.

"My daughter has been buried these past five days. There is no question that we feel her loss deeply. Our only solace is she is now with God, and at peace. If she can see us from her heavenly place, I am sure my dearest Vivienne would expect us to carry on with our lives as well as we can." He looked at Nanette. "It pains me to see you suffer and despair. But we must prevail. Live each day fully and with gratitude we have that time. So please, may we now have luncheon together as a family without any contention."

"Well said, Simon," Father Lynch remarked. "You set a fine example to your family by your composure."

Much to my surprise the priest addressed me. "Mrs Holloway, I hear you are bound for Skipton tomorrow? Will you make a day of it while you're there if the weather is fine?"

Why the priest should care what my plans were tomorrow was beyond me. Perhaps he was trying to change the subject and that was all he could come up with. Based on that thought, I decided it wouldn't hurt to converse with him. Though I did not like it.

"Yes, I am going there. I have an appointment, but afterwards I do plan to peruse the shops and then take a tour of the mill."

"Why would you want to do that?" Nanette asked. "I cannot think of anything more tedious than looking at ugly machinery making too much noise. The smell in there is deplorable, and the air terribly unhealthy."

I chuckled. "That is true, but I want to have a better understanding of how the mill operates. It is part of our heritage, after all. Arthur Parslow worked very hard to get the mill up and running."

"Speaking of the old man," said Uncle Simon. "Did I ever recount to you, Claire, the tale of how I came to be part of the Parslow family and the mill?"

"No."

"Then I shall tell you. When I was a young man, I worked the docks at Liverpool as many of us have. Eventually I've got a job on the barges coming down the canal from Lancashire into Yorkshire, which I much preferred.

"On one particular day, we were unloading raw cotton bales from the barge, into the delivery yard at Parslow's. It was a busy afternoon and there were many people around. I heard a loud splash and looked around to see someone had fallen into the mill pond. It was a woman, and she was being pulled under the water by the weight of her clothing and getting very near to the water wheel. Getting caught in the wheel would kill her, knock her out and pull her under. I dived in the water, managed to get a hold of her and pulled her out."

"What a relief," I said.

"She was not harmed, just a little shocked. But not as surprised as I was when I found out her identity. This became abundantly clear when your grandfather came running down the muddy bank. I had rescued your grandmother, Mabel."

I had never heard this story. "What happened next?"

"To thank me, I was invited to their home that very evening for dinner. Of course, I refused. Not because I didn't want to go, but because I had no clothes to wear for such an occasion. But seeing as I too was drenched, Arthur, your grandfather insisted I go straight to his tailor to be fitted for something to wear. My clothes were muddy and sodden. I cleaned up here at the mill, borrowed a pair of old trousers and a shirt, then went directly to the tailors. By the time I arrived at Darkwater Abbey, I look like a new man."

"And then you met Mama," said Nanette.

Simon looked affectionately at his daughter, the image of her long-departed mother. "Yes, my dear. One look at Charlotte Parslow, and I was lost. Never before had I seen such a beauty. Her golden hair was like spun silk, her eyes silver. I was completely and utterly smitten."

"As she was with you, Papa," said Nanette. My cousin's mood had undergone a complete change. Instead of looking angry, she now had a dreamy expression upon her face. I was certain this was a much beloved story.

"I don't suppose Arthur and Mabel were pleased, but Charlotte and I were meant for one another, and we were married shortly afterwards. I never returned to working on the barges, and instead was given a job at the mill. In fact, Claire, it was your father who trained me. He'd married into the family a few years before." My uncle gave a small shrug. "It all seems so very long ago now."

"What a nice story," I said. "I remember my Aunt Charlotte well. She was such a beautiful woman, both in nature and appearance. How Mother loved her so dearly. She would say Aunt Charlotte lit up a room with her presence as would a chandelier. But more than anything, I'll always remember her kindness." I glanced at her daughter. Nanette had not inherited that trait from her mother, far from it.

"People do say I favour her," said my cousin.

"Indeed you do, dearest. You are every bit as lovely." Her father agreed.

I looked over at the priest who had been quiet for some time. "Father Lynch, were you well acquainted with my aunt?"

He put down his knife and fork and patted his thin lips with a serviette. Those cold eyes flickered over my face. “I had that pleasure, Mrs Holloway.” He emphasised my surname, which amused me as I had asked him not to call me by my first name again. The man still thought he could intimidate me. He was wrong.

“Charlotte was a generous woman. She spent a great deal of her time working with those less fortunate. A devout Catholic woman, she always put others first. As you yourself said, one of her greatest attributes was her propensity to be kind. She was also very respectful of her faith and those who practised and believed as she did.”

I decided to fence with the man. His piety was fake. Though I would never be so bold with others who were representatives of their church, this man was the exception. Indeed, I felt more respect for the young deacon than the priest.

“Tell me, Father. Are you of the opinion a person who does not mirror your own religious belief cannot be considered kind, compassionate or generous? Must one use these traits under the label of a particular faith before they are considered justifiably good?”

His face straightened. His eyes grew darker. “Anyone acting kindly to their fellow man deserves praise. Yet with the addition of a strong belief in God, the good an individual does grows exponentially within the hierarchy of faith.”

“So are the rewards of Heaven limited only to those who are good *and* also worship? Or does God in his wisdom think all generosity and kindness enough?”

“Goodness,” remarked Nanette. “You are both talking in riddles and it is quite dull. Can we not speak of something more interesting?”

"What would you suggest?" Father Lynch did not sound pleased with the interruption.

"Oh, I don't know. Let us speak of something cheerful. For it has been such a mournful time here. Papa, let us plan an outing. We have yet to take my cousin to Leeds. Would that not be a wonderful diversion?"

And so the conversation turned to the possibilities of our going to the city. Nanette argued with her father about the activities available there. She favoured shopping and attending the opera, while he preferred the parks and museums. After a few minutes, I lost interest and concentrated on my food. But I felt the object of someone's scrutiny.

I looked up quickly to find a pair of black eyes staring malevolently at my face.

Chapter Twenty-Nine

THE FOLLOWING MORNING I left for Skipton with naught but my own company. Uncle Simon and Ivan had long gone to the mill. Gibbons had returned to collect me in the carriage.

As usual, I had breakfasted alone with only Tibbetts to converse with. I was getting used to his company now I had been in Yorkshire almost a month.

The sky was grey, cold, and periodically spat rain. I dressed warmly in my boots and an overcoat. With a hat and scarf, I would be protected from the weather if I chose to scour the village for a jeweller to look at the necklace, currently tucked safely in my reticule.

Gibbons had not spoken to me, just nodded that massive head as I climbed into the cab of the carriage. The man kept quite a low profile at Darkwater. But then he was separated from the house by a moat, and we did not encounter one another very often.

At length we arrived outside the lawyer's office. I let myself out of the cab without waiting for any assistance from Gibbons, not that I expected it.

The same young clerk greeted me inside the offices of Satterthwaite, Chandler & Humphries, Ltd. It took me a moment to remember his name. Bertram, that had been it. At my use of it the frail looking clerk turned a bright pink. But I think he was pleased to be remembered.

Mr Satterthwaite seemed every bit as jolly as the first time we'd met. This time, he politely got to his feet but stayed his side of the desk.

"Do come in, Mrs Holloway. My, my. What a time your family has had. I am so terribly sorry about your dear cousin, most tragic indeed. So young. My, my. Please, take a seat."

I sat in the same spot as before. "Thank you for seeing me, Mr Satterthwaite."

"Not at all, Mrs Holloway."

"Please, call me Claire."

"Certainly. Now then, how may I be of service?"

"Although you explained my status pertaining to the mill, I had a few other questions to ask."

"I am not surprised. It was a lot for a young lady to take in, all that business mumbo jumbo. Though I must say I was surprised you deferred signing your uncle the rights to manage your affairs. Do you think that wise?"

"I do, as a matter of fact."

His bright blue eyes looked startled, and then he grinned broadly under his grey moustaches. "My, my. You are a young lady who knows her own mind. Far be it for me to persuade you otherwise. It is, however, my duty to explain the seriousness of your ownership of the mill. Your well-being relies upon its success, as does the income of hundreds of families in the area."

"And you think me too inexperienced to run the company?"

Mr Satterthwaite had the decency to flush. "Well..."

"Sir. I can assure you I know what I am doing. I have enlisted the help of my cousin's husband, Mr Delahunt, to assist me. I shall watch and learn from his expertise, until I quickly comprehend the basics of the textile industry. I am a fast learner."

He looked aghast. "But is it not too taxing for a young woman? Being in business—"

"Mr Satterthwaite," I interrupted. "I have been an independent woman for several years. I have worked overseas and am more than qualified to understand the basic rudiments of economics. I've a sensible head on my shoulders and having been employed myself I understand the challenges and rigours of working."

"I see." Clearly he did not. He stared at me as though I were a talking parrot.

"Now then. What I should like to know are some financial details. What should I anticipate regarding my income? After probate etcetera?"

Mr Satterthwaite opened the file laying before him, squinted and then told me a sum that greatly exceeded my expectations.

"Your dear mother was a frugal woman. I have had correspondence from her lawyer in Hampshire. After the sale of the cottage and with her assets you will inherit a lump sum of seventeen thousand pounds, plus, going forward, your share of the mill's profits. You will receive dividends each quarter, starting in January of next year. It will fluctuate depending on the industry but is more than enough for a person to live on, even without your inheritance."

My hand flew to my mouth. I was stunned. "How did Mother have so much money? We did not live like a wealthy family."

"According to her lawyer, she invested heavily and was rather successful, especially in the past five years. You are a very wealthy young woman, Mrs Holloway."

It was a lot to take in.

"When will I have access to these funds?"

"There it gets a bit stickier. You will be paid a dividend, as I said, come January. As for your mother's fortune, probate will take several months, even with a will."

I was crestfallen.

"Don't be alarmed," he said quickly, noting my response. "You may draw from the expected dividends whenever you need money, as the mill is collateral against the credit. I am quite happy to advance you any sum you need for the immediate future."

"I would be grateful for that. Do I need to open a local bank account in Skipton?"

"That would be wise." He studied me for a moment. "You seem a little disappointed in what I have told you."

I nodded. "It is not disappointment in my lot, for I am extremely fortunate and if I'm honest, surprised at the extent of Mother's estate. It is more about my living situation. I am unused to the charity of others and had hoped to secure my own temporary place to live, that is all."

Mr Satterthwaite gave me an apologetic smile. "Why don't I see if we can advance enough for you to lease a small house?"

"Would you?" My hopes leapt. "I would appreciate the help."

There followed a conversation about renting properties and the availability of them in the Skipton area. If the older man thought anything of it, he concealed it well enough.

My next stop was at Barclays Bank in Skipton.

After opening an account, I asked the manager if he knew of a jeweller and was directed to a shop not too far from the mill.

Mr Rosenstein was an elderly man who looked like his name should be Rumpelstiltskin. He was decidedly short of stature, with a crooked back which contributed to his lack of height. His eyes were concealed by thick, bushy white eyebrows, and the hair on his head stood up straight as though he'd been hit by lightning.

"*Kom* in, *mein frau*," he said in greeting as I entered the small shop, detecting a slight smell of cooked cabbage. "*Was* can I *hilfe* you with?"

I approached the counter, where under the glass lay trays of an assortment of gems and baubles.

"I am not looking to purchase anything, but wanted to see if you could value an item for me."

He frowned, probably disappointed there would be no sale.

"I will pay for your time," I said encouragingly.

"Hmph," he snorted, and held out a fingerless, gloved hand, "give here to me."

I retrieved the necklace from my reticule and passed it over. He set it on the counter and poked at it with an overly long fingernail.

"This is nothing," he murmured. "The chain, it is bad silver, and dirty, the pendant…" he held it up, so the light caught the green shamrock. "This pendant, it is painted metal." He handed the necklace back to me as though its presence in his shop somehow cheapened his jewellry collection.

"Can you tell if it is very old, or modern?"

He shrugged. "This kind of thing is what you get from playing a silly game."

"I don't understand."

"You know," he said impatiently. "At the carnival or some nonsense. It is a trinket, worthless."

"But how old do you think it could be?"

"Why you care? It is junk."

I glowered at him. "Please, it's important."

He held out his hand again. "*Kom*, give back to me."

This time he picked up a lens and placed it against his eye. He studied the pendant and then the clasp of the chain. "This kind of clasp is common for modern jewellry." He handed the necklace back. "Twenty, thirty years old, no more."

"Are you sure?" My pulse sped up. This was critical information.

He shook his head. "You ask a question, I give you the answer, and yet you doubt?"

I apologised profusely. "I'm sorry. I mean no insult. It is crucial I have this right."

"Lady, what I say is correct. They changed the way clasps were made forty years ago. This is no older than that."

I gave the odd old man money for his time and left the tiny shop feeling rather pleased with myself.

WHEN I ARRIVED AT THE MILL, I made directly for Ivan's office. He was sitting at his desk, peering through a microscope. But he looked up quickly when I walked in.

I closed the door behind me.

"You look excited," he said. "What have you found out?"

I recounted the tale about the necklace.

He sat back in his chair. "You were right, Claire. My goodness, this changes everything. There's now every possibility it was Molly's body in the priest hole. Well done for acting upon your instincts. My God," he paused, looking thoughtful. "Who the hell would have put her in there to begin with?"

"I don't even want to consider that," I said. "If the woman wasn't dead already…"

"Don't dwell on it," he advised. "We can't change the past, but we can get to the truth. I've already sent word to my contact in Liverpool and asked he enquire about her. He'll start with the dockyard taverns and see if he can get a full name for her. The necklace and her brother being in Australia might help. We'll have to wait a day or two until I hear anything."

A thrum of anticipation ran through me. Finally, we were starting to get somewhere.

"By the way, I have still been looking through the records whenever I have a chance. I have yet to find anything which looks wrong. But I'll keep trying."

"Thank you, Ivan."

He nodded. "Right then." He got to his feet. "Why don't I give you that quick tour of the mill?"

THE ENTIRE BUILDING AT Parslow Mill was a hive of activity, each of its floors devoted to specific tasks in the making of cotton fabric from the bales of raw material which came straight from the docks in Liverpool.

We started on the first floor of the mill which housed the carding machines. Before we went in, Ivan stopped me.

"I'll tell you now because it will be too loud to talk

in there and I'll end up shouting. You probably remember a lot about it since you've been here many times. The carding machines take the cotton fibres and pass it through a series of rollers with varying sizes of metal teeth. This produces a continuous web of cotton which we can then use to spin. We can also create different types of blends by combining different fibres together. Let's go in."

Inside, the noise was deafening. There were six carding machines running the length of the room, and they were massive. I stood back, fascinated as several burly men navigated the fibre through a series of ferocious looking rollers. I recalled Father telling me this was the most dangerous piece of equipment, and workers could get their fingers, hands and arms caught in the metal bristles and ripped off.

We walked past all the machinery, and the men nodded politely to me. Then we left the room and went up another flight of stairs.

"I remember the spinning room," I told Ivan outside the door. "I didn't understand why some of the workers weren't much older than myself. My father tried to explain it to me, but it never made sense. I felt so sorry for them, and I knew they could easily get hurt."

"It is an unfortunate part of our industry, and one I should like to stop. If the workers were paid better wages, their children would not have to earn a living. It's despicable that to some people, the value of a poor person's life is sometimes less than that of a beast in the field. As you know, this subject is a point of contention between Simon and myself. I understand having workers retrieving cotton from underneath the equipment is important. But we need to find an alternative to using children."

I had tremendous respect for Ivan's views on child labour. Working as an adult was hard enough. It was a sad reflection of our society when a child had no childhood.

The noise in the spinning room made it impossible to speak. Row upon row of equipment clattered and chattered. Leather belts flapped and the grinding sound of industrious machinery dominated. In this room, there were many women and several small children. I knew that most of them would be related. Working at the mill was indeed a family affair.

The aisle between each row of equipment was narrow, and I gestured to Ivan that I did not want to stay. The last thing we needed was to get in anyone's way. I know I drew the attention of many workers as they were curious who I was. No one knew me here.

Once we were back in the stairway Ivan asked, "Do you want to go to the weaving sheds?"

"I don't think so. I'm more interested in going back up to the offices. I'd like to get a better understanding of how everything is run." I followed Ivan up the stairs and into his room.

He shut the door behind us and took a seat behind his desk. "May I ask, Claire, how do you see your role here?"

I sat down in the vacant seat across from him. "I don't have any definitive skills in accounting or economics. I do have a great deal of common sense, and obviously, I had to be exceedingly attentive while I was employed as a nurse. I could assist Mary while I learn how the mill works. But I am also very interested in the conditions here. The safety and welfare of our workers is tantamount to the success of any well-run business. I should like to understand how other mills treat their employees and see if there are improvements we could make without undermining the mill's profits."

Ivan stared at me with what I took to be an agreement of my ideas. I do think our opinions paralleled.

"How do you envision Parslow Mill going forward? This place has run very much the same since your uncle took the helm."

"I don't have all the answers yet. But I do believe there is a place for all of us. Your skills are well suited to the shop floor and day-to-day operations. You understand the real function of the mill. You know the equipment, the routine, and the way to get things done. Also, I understand your interest in the future and where the mill is headed. Diversifying is always worth considering as obviously we do have all our eggs in one basket, so to speak.

"As far as my uncle, I am not sure how he will react to my being here. He is used to having full control and not being questioned. Although I respect him as an elder, and for his wisdom based upon years in the cotton industry, it does not make him exclusively an expert. I am sure there are aspects of the business he excels in, and would therefore still be a valuable contribution to the mill as a company. Having said that, I do realise it might take a little time to convince him into accepting me as a co-worker."

"Yes," said Ivan. "That will certainly be an obstacle. Simon is not a modern thinker, especially when it comes to women in the workforce."

"He thinks them qualified enough to operate complicated and dangerous machinery, therefore he will have to get used to us using our academic intellect as well."

A sly grin spread across Ivan's face. I realised this was happening more frequently since the shift in power from my uncle to me had been known to him.

"You're enjoying this, aren't you?" I said.

"I cannot lie. I look forward to change. It has been a long time coming, and it is necessary. Now, what do you want to do next?"

"Actually, while walking around the mill, my father was very close in my mind. It occurred to me Mary might be worth talking to regarding the past. Remember reading in Mother's journal about the mysterious woman named Barbara, who testified against my father and claimed they were in a relationship?"

"I do."

"Mary was secretary to my father then. If there was anything suspicious going on between him and another woman, she would have noticed something."

"Are you going to question her? Do you think she would tell you?"

"I don't know why she wouldn't. Twenty years later it's not exactly raking up the past. In everybody else's opinion the whole incident has been conveniently pushed into the background."

He flinched and I realised my comment had sounded heartless.

"I'm sorry. I didn't mean anything detrimental by that. I just meant there are too many other things people talk about nowadays. All thoughts will be on what has happened to Vivienne, not the past."

I got to my feet. It was probably a good time to end the conversation before I inadvertently insulted Ivan again.

"Thank you so much for showing me around the mill. I'll stop by before I leave."

MARY BUXTON GREETED ME with a friendly smile. "Miss Claire. Why, your uncle never said you were coming for a visit today. But then he's all over the place, what with it being his first day back." She shook her head, and a stray lock of red hair came loose from her tight bun. "Such a sad loss, that. Poor lass."

Of course, she referred to Vivienne. "Yes. Uncle Simon is struggling coming to terms with it. I'm glad he's returned to work. Is he in his office?"

"Aye. But someone's with him, so you'd best wait. Want a cuppa?"

"Thank you, yes."

Before long, we sat cradling out teacups. Mary chatted about inconsequential matters while I sought to find a way in to bring up the past. Finally, I interrupted.

"Mary, can I ask you something about my father?"

She quietened and stared at me blankly.

"When he went to trial, a woman testified against him by the name of Barbara Harding. Had you ever heard that name before?"

She set down her cup on the desk. "Lass, it were a long time ago. You mustn't dwell on the past, 'tis never a good idea. What good does it do?"

"And what harm?" I countered. "Nothing can change what happened back then, Mary. But you must understand that I was a child and not told anything.

Now my mother has gone and there's no one I can ask."
I injected a note of sternness into my voice. She was, after all, my employee now as well. Perhaps she needed a reminder.

"Why should it pain you to speak to me? You have been here longer than most, and your loyalty to Parslow's has been unquestioned. Yet you don't want to help me?" I set down my cup and began to stand.

"Wait," said Mary quickly. "I am sorry, Miss Claire, please, sit down and I'll speak with you."

Satisfied, I did as she asked. "Do you know who the woman was, Mary? If it helps, I can tell you she no longer lives. Neither does either of my parents, so you harm no one."

She relented. "All right, I'll tell you what little I know. This Harding woman, well I never saw nor met her, but I heard your uncle speak of her once or twice."

"To whom?"

"Father Lynch. Likely they were worried about the damage she would do to your father's case."

"Do you remember what was said?"

Mary shook her head. "No. Though I think there was mention of a sick child. Yes, that was it. She were a widow, with a very sick child. She were trying to go to America to get him treatment. I think Father Lynch were trying to raise funds, or something like that."

"Poor thing," I said. I looked at her directly. "Did you suspect my father was involved with another woman? You saw him every day here at the mill. Was he the type of man who paid attention to other women?"

Her gaze lowered and she fell quiet. Then she raised her face. "You father were a good man. He loved you and your mother more than life itself. Don't get me wrong, he were handsome, and there were many a lass who batted their lashes his way. But he didn't see any of 'em."

"Then what did you think when you heard about this Barbara testifying against my father in court? Did you not think it queer?"

"I did. But at the time, I had my own problems. Me mam had fallen ill, and I'd taken off to care for her. I weren't here during the trial, though I followed it in't newspapers like everyone else."

My uncle's door opened, and Father Lynch came out. He seemed as surprised to see me as I was him.

"Why Mrs Holloway, how nice to see you."

I gave a weak smile in return.

"Claire," Uncle Simon came out behind him. "Have you come to see me?"

"Yes, Uncle. If you have a moment."

"Let me get on then," said the priest. "Good day to you all."

Uncle Simon ushered me into his office and directed me to one of the visitor's chairs. Much to my surprise, he took the seat next to me instead of going back to sit behind his desk.

"It is nice to see you, my dear. Have you been shopping in town?"

He still looked rather pale and his eyes not as bright, but at least he had returned to work.

"I've been to visit Mr Satterthwaite," I said. "I had questions about my inheritance and thought it sensible to speak with him."

Uncle Simon looked sheepish. "Did he tell you all you needed to know?"

The way he spoke, I had a feeling that my uncle knew as much about my personal finances as I did now myself.

"Yes, he did. But that's not why I am here. I wanted to talk to you about my role at the mill."

My comment was received with a quick frown, and I knew I trod in awkward territory.

"I know I have expressed my desire to learn more about the mill, but I am not sure you have taken me seriously. Therefore, I want to make it official. I should like to join you here at Parslow's. I am used to working for a living and I'm useless staying at Darkwater every day. I must have a purpose, and mission to fulfil. Learning I'm part owner of the mill, it seems natural for me to take a role in the company."

He did not look pleased. I didn't care. I continued.

"I don't propose getting in anyone's way. I shall be respectful of everyone here and their current positions at the mill. All I ask is for an opportunity to contribute to the business, and time to learn how everything works. I know I am not qualified, but I am intelligent enough to become an asset to our family's legacy."

"And what do you see yourself doing, Claire?" For the first time since his daughter died, he sounded like himself. His colour was high and his eyes bright.

"I should like to study the relationship between the mill and the workers in respect to the conditions here and their safety and welfare."

"I suppose Ivan has been putting silly notions into your head. He likes to think he is such a reformist, but then he does not have to balance our accounts. It is easy to spend money that doesn't belong to you."

His harshness took me aback, but I recovered

quickly. "That is not the case. As a nurse, I was trained to pay close attention to the welfare of others. It is a well-known fact people work in horrible conditions throughout the factories of England. Just as my grandfather pioneered the founding of this mill, bringing work to those living locally, I should like to continue his legacy by making it the best mill. Give a man a good working environment, and he will give you his all."

"It sounds wonderful in theory," said my uncle. "But the bottom line is always about profit. If we wish to continue living at Darkwater, to have servants, to afford our clothes and sustenance, all is reliant upon income. If this was a perfect world, we would not have to think about money. I fear you have an unrealistic ideology."

"Perhaps you are right," I agreed. "There may be a compromise somewhere. But why should it harm anything for me to study and then come up with suggestions of improvement?"

Uncle Simon fell quiet. And then without warning, he got up from his chair and got down on both knees in front of me. Before I could respond, he had both my hands in his.

"My dearest Claire. When you first came back to Yorkshire I was so happy seeing what a delightful young woman you are. I knew of your sorrows but felt such pride in the work you had done with our poor soldiers.

"The day you came home, I was thrilled you were here, but taken aback at the feelings I felt. My affection for you as my niece, was always there. Yet when you crossed the bridge to Darkwater, I saw you for the first time as a grown woman, and you took my breath away."

Revolted, I pulled my hands from his and got to my feet, nearly knocking him over. He recovered and then stood also, and though I moved away he came after me. Uncle Simon reached for my hand, and I pulled it back.

"Claire, I know this has shocked you, my dear, but please, do not be offended. I am only telling you what I feel in my heart."

Disgusted I moved another step back from him. "Please, Uncle. Do not talk to me like this. You're family…like a father to me. I could never think of you in any other capacity. I beg you not to speak of this again, because it makes me very uncomfortable."

It was as though he did not hear me. Uncle Simon took another step closer. He looked crazed.

"But don't you see, Claire. Together, we could form a union that would strengthen your family's heritage. Parslow's would be as one again. And if you and I should have children, they would inherit—"

"Stop," I shouted. "Enough, Uncle. You have lost your mind." The implication of his words made me feel sick. That he would even consider it was abominable.

"Please, Claire. You must give me a chance." This time he grabbed me by the shoulders. Though my uncle was not a huge man there was strength in that grip. I struggled and shouted again for him to let me go.

The door burst open to reveal Ivan standing on the threshold and Mary Buxton right behind him.

Chapter Thirty

"LET HER GO, SIMON," IVAN commanded with authority.

The colour drained from my uncle's face and his arms fell back to his sides. He glanced at me, his son-in-law, and then his secretary. He seemed to shrink before my eyes.

"Forgive me," he muttered. And went back to his desk where he slumped into his chair. "I don't know what came over me. Please, leave me alone."

I hurried out of the room. Ivan came right behind me. I went straight into his office and sat down. My face burned with humiliation, my breathing was rapid, but I was livid.

"What the hell just happened in there?" Ivan asked. "Mary came flying down to my office and said she heard shouting."

I shuddered in revulsion. "My uncle declared his love for me and desired that we marry to strengthen the family business. I stopped him when he began to speak of our children who would inherit."

"Dear God. That bastard." Ivan walked over to a sideboard, and I heard a clink of glass as he poured something from a bottle. He came over to where I sat and handed it to me.

"Here, drink this. It's brandy. I keep it for emergencies."

I downed it in one and handed the glass back to

him. I felt my pulse start to slow and my breathing returned to normal.

"You know it is strange, but ever since I arrived at Darkwater, there have been moments where Uncle Simon made me uncomfortable. I dismissed them as my being too sensitive and unused to his attentions, but now I realise I should have paid heed to my instinct." Much to my dismay I felt tears well in my eyes. It was not sorrow but rage. Angrily I wiped them away with the back of my hand.

"How could he speak to me thus? I know we do not share blood, but we might as well. The man has just lost a child and yet remains fixated on power and wealth." I looked up at Ivan who leaned against his desk staring at me.

"What am I to do now? How can I stay at Darkwater, after what he has said?"

Ivan's hand rubbed against the stubble on his chin. "Unfortunately, there is little you can do on short notice." He walked around his desk and sat down. "To begin with, we can make other arrangements, I'll go to one of the inns here and secure you a room. But it is late in the day and all your belongings are at Darkwater."

"Then what do you suggest?"

"Let me return to Darkwater with you, so you are not alone with Simon. If you can spend one more night there, it will give you time to pack your belongings and for me to make arrangements for you to leave. I'll get you lodgings here in Skipton, and I think you'll feel better about that."

I nodded, dumbly. I would let Ivan organise my situation. Though I was strong enough to stand up for myself, right now I was exhausted. Just for a change, it would be nice to let somebody help.

IVAN SAW ME SAFELY HOME, and I went directly upstairs to my room. He said he would speak with Mrs Blitch, and a dinner tray would be brought up later.

I had no appetite. I busied myself packing my things in my trunk, which Ivan had brought up for me. By the time dinner arrived, I was finished. Tibbetts brought the tray into the room and placed it on the dresser.

He turned to leave and then hesitated. I knew he wanted to say something to me but didn't think it was his place.

"If there is something you want to say, Tibbetts, you are welcome to do so."

"T'aint any business o'mine, Miss Claire. But I'm no fool and I know something bad has happened. Would that you'd tell me." He glanced at my trunk. "Mr Ivan told me you plan to go and stay in Skipton. T'aint right you should have to leave your home. I know you won't tell me, but my guess is Master Simon did somethin' to you."

My glance of surprise gave him the answer he needed. How had he known?

"He's acted strange since you got back here. When his lass died, he went over t'edge. Something's off at Darkwater. What with the lass dying, and them bones being in't cellar. Prap's it's best you go elsewhere for now. I just ask you let me know where you are so I can come and check on you."

My throat felt thick with tears at his kindness. Archie Tibbetts was not only a loyal servant, but he was a true friend.

"Thank you, Archie," I said and gave a feeble smile.

He grinned at me, seemingly pleased at my use of his first name. Then he gave me a nod and went out of the room. I quickly locked the door behind him.

I looked at the food Cook had sent up to me. It was a bowl of thick vegetable soup, a large chunk of crusty bread and a slice of Madeira cake. I tentatively took a spoonful of the soup thinking I would not want to eat, yet one taste of the delicious fare vanquished my lack of appetite, and I tucked in.

I was just finishing the cake when a knock came on my door.

"Who is it?"

"Nanette. May I come in?"

"Just a moment." I put the tray back on my dressing table and unlocked my door.

Nanette flew into my room. She wore a nightgown with a lilac chiffon robe draped about her. How she could dress this way when it was almost winter was beyond me.

"What is this I hear about you leaving?" she said without preamble. "Has something happened I should know about?"

I was not about to tell her the truth. "It was never my intent to stay very long. My plans were to get my own lodgings once I understood my situation regarding the mill. I met with Mr Satterthwaite today, and he tells me I am able to lease a place of my own."

"That is ridiculous. You have a home here with your family. Why would you want to live anywhere else?"

"And you have made me welcome, Nanette, which I do appreciate. However, I have lived alone before, and I am used to being in charge of my own household. So many things have changed in my life recently, I need some privacy to make some decisions."

"But you can't leave me here alone," she said with a cry. "I have already lost a sister, and now you? How can I be expected to stay here by myself with my father and Ivan? It is simply not fair. I am too ill to take care of this house. I do not have the strength to organise affairs and run a household. No, Claire. You have to stay." Her strange eyes filled with tears, and they spilled down her beautiful cheeks.

But I was not moved. There was nothing that would keep me here now.

I took her hand and led her to take a seat with me on the side of my bed. Her skin felt cold in mine and soft as a baby's. The thought crossed my mind that her hands had probably never been in water longer than it took to wash them.

"Nanette. You are an extremely capable woman. You have a staff of three people at your disposal who will take care of the house and everything else. You're panicking unnecessarily because you have also gone through an unsettling time. It's not as if I'm moving to another county. I'm just going to stay elsewhere."

"Ivan said you're going to Skipton."

"Yes. And you may visit me there whenever you wish. It's about time you got out of this house and did something for enjoyment. You can come and spend the day with me, and we can have lunch together, take a walk, go shopping."

A glint flashed in Nanette's eyes. What I said

appealed to her. But I also knew my cousin. Regardless of what I said, she had an innate desire to get her own way, and usually that is exactly what would happen. But not today.

She pulled her hand from mine angrily. "That is no consolation. I'm not a child to be bribed by the promise of a day out." Her voice grew louder. "You're being incredibly selfish, Claire. How can you leave your family in their time of need? You know I still mourn Vivienne, and Father is a broken man. Yet you decide this is the best time for you to strike out on your own? I cannot believe you are being so cruel. Especially when we welcomed you back here with open arms."

I'd finally had enough. I snapped.

"Open arms, you say? That is debatable. Vivienne was miserable at my coming, and although you were kinder, I did not feel you wanted me here either. As for my decision to leave in your time of need, I suggest you take that up with your father. Because it is his unnatural, unwanted attention towards me that forces me to go."

Nanette got to her feet. "What are you saying? I don't understand. My sister was unhappy every day of her life, whether you were here or not. She was discontented and jealous." Nanette moved to stand near the window. She had her back to me while she spoke.

"Oh, and do not think for one moment I was not aware of her interest in my husband. I found it pathetic. She mooned after him like a love-sick schoolgirl. It was utterly embarrassing." She gave a trill laugh. "Of course, I was not threatened. Ivan would never countenance the attentions of a woman like Vivienne. But it did irritate me at times." She turned to look at me.

"As for my behaviour towards you, I made you welcome. I was truly glad you came. It has been more interesting having your company here at Darkwater. After my sister's death, I have relied upon your help these past days. And it has only been days. It is too early for you to leave us." She walked back to the bed.

"My father is a fool. I have watched him with you and seen his interest. You judge him too harshly. He is a man, and men are stupid. They do not think with their heads. They see a pretty object and they reach for it. He means you no harm, nor should you take it that way. You should be flattered. He is a handsome, good person, and many women would welcome his attention."

I got to my feet. "Listen to what you are saying, Nanette. I am not a friend who your father has taken an attraction to. I am his niece. His behaviour towards me is utterly unacceptable. Do you not see how repugnant it is? You do not console me but excuse him." I was incredulous she was so blasé about her father's actions and how it made me feel. "Your father crosses too many boundaries, and I am extremely uncomfortable staying under the same roof as him. Though I am sorry to leave you, especially during this difficult time, I fear I have to do what is best for me, and not you. I'll not be far from here and will always welcome you wherever I stay. But this is my decision, and it is made. All I ask is that you respect my wishes and do not let this come between us."

Her pallid complexion disappeared to be replaced by two bright red spots on her cheeks. Nanette was livid.

"I do not accept this. If you leave Darkwater, Claire, then I shall no longer think of you as family." She stared at me, and I saw triumph glitter in her eyes as she delivered this final ultimatum.

My cousin did not know me very well. I had lived long enough without her companionship, and I would not miss it going forward. I raised a brow and met her stare head on.

"Then so be it," I stated flatly.

A flash of anger shot through her glare. I could sense she wanted to have a last word, but she stopped herself. Nanette whirled around and left my room, slamming the door behind her.

THE REST OF THE EVENING I was terribly unsettled. What a strange day it had been. Uncle Simon had thrown me so off-balance, I hadn't a moment to think about my conversation with the solicitor. But now I did.

Thank goodness I would be independently wealthy. Yet there was a real dilemma. How could I work at the mill with my uncle after what had happened?

I was still mulling over my options when Ivan came to check on me. I invited him into my room, but left the door open for propriety's sake.

He looked tired. I had not considered the day he must have endured, a day complicated by the actions of Simon Manning and from looking after me. Strange how he'd gone from being a potential adversary to my protector of sorts.

Ivan still wore his work clothes, and I wondered if he had gone to dinner with the rest of the family. I didn't ask and honestly did not want to know.

"How are you, Claire?" He looked around the

room. "I see you have packed up your things. I've spoken with Gibbons, and he will take you to Skipton at nine o'clock in the morning. I shall go into work late, so I can accompany you if that's all right?" He explained he'd got me a room at the Duck and Spoon Inn.

I felt a rush of gratitude. "Thank you, Ivan. I should like that very much." He stood awkwardly just inside the door, so I gestured towards the chair by my dressing table. "Please, come in and sit if you've time."

He took a seat, while I perched on the side of the bed several feet away.

"I cannot thank you enough for all you did to help me today. I've been going through it in my mind time and again. It's hard to comprehend what would make my uncle behave so badly."

Ivan shook his head. "I've thought about it as well. I have my own suspicions, but I hesitate to even speak of them for they are malicious in intent."

I frowned. "Then you must tell me. For at this point, I don't think anything would surprise me."

"All right." He gave a heavy sigh. "But remember it is only my theory, and that does not make it true. It's my belief your arrival upset the balance of things, especially at the mill."

"I would agree with that," I said.

"Then, when you denied signing paperwork allowing Simon to continue in his role as executor, it started an avalanche. Consequently, Simon must have felt vulnerable and that his position here would be in jeopardy. Therefore, if he could woo you into a legal marriage…"

I finished it for him. "Then he would gain full

control of the mill."

"And your fortune."

I was puzzled. "Does he not have his own money though? The mill has prospered for many years, and surely he is comfortable?"

Ivan shook his head. "I honestly don't know his financial business, but I do think he has spent unwisely, perhaps made poor investments. I always suspected his business sense let him down, that his judgement is not always sound. But I have no proof, other than your uncle's reputation among his peers within the cotton industry is not particularly good."

Shaking my head, I let out a sigh. "I had no idea. The way Mother spoke of him I believed him to be an astute businessman. She thought so highly of him."

"Well, once we get you into your new lodgings and things are calmer, we'll have time to discuss all of this in better detail later." He gave an encouraging smile which I appreciated. Then added. "By the way, after everything that's happened today I didn't get a chance to ask how your conversation went with Mary, or even if you spoke with her?"

"I did. We shared a cup of tea as Uncle Simon had someone in his office. Father Lynch, to be precise."

"That man spends a great deal of time at Parslow's. Did Mary help at all?"

It took a moment to recall our conversation after the events of the awful day.

"Mary's memory was rather vague, but she remembered overhearing my uncle discussing Barbara Harding with Father Lynch. It was something about an ailing child. Apparently, she was a widow with a very sick son. She needed to take him to America for treatment. This we already knew from the letter recently sent to Mother. But back then, Mary assumed the priest was trying to help raise funds with the assistance of my uncle."

He nodded. "The letter from New York throws some light on this. She admitted to lying in court, but would not name who put her up to it. Yet somehow, the only persons we know connected to her are Simon and Father Lynch."

"Yes, because my father claimed not to know her. It strikes me she would be an easy target if offered enough money to take her sick child to America. Considering all we know about who was in the picture back then, there were not many wealthy enough to buy her off. A mother will do anything to save her child, even if they condemn somebody else."

As I spoke the words I felt a strong conviction. Had I been in Barbara Harding's position, I probably would have done the same thing, anything to save my child. The ache for Sarah suddenly engulfed me, just thinking about another mother.

"This gives us something to work with," said Ivan. "Once you get into lodgings, we'll reassess all we have learned so far. I want to draw up a proper plan of action. There are many irons in the fire. Events of the past still haunt the present, and with the death of Vivienne, life at Darkwater has changed immensely. In some ways, I think it best you don't have to stay here, regardless of what happened today."

"You are right. For some reason, my future suddenly seems so uncertain. Only hours ago, I honestly believed life was beginning to settle down. After the past two years, it was hard to imagine things could be normal once again."

I got to my feet and strolled over to the window. Staring out, I heard Ivan come up behind me. I turned around, not realising how close he was, and my shoulder brushed against his chest.

Ivan looked down into my face. I could not read his expression, but his eyes were dark and moody. For a moment, I stared into them transfixed. A myriad of feelings swirled through me, and I had the sensation of falling, like I was tumbling into the depths of his smouldering eyes. When his head bent slowly towards mine, the breath caught in my throat and my lips parted of their own volition. His warm mouth brushed against my own, my eyes closed, and for a moment, my heart swelled and soared.

His kiss was soft, tender, hungry, and unexpectedly welcome.

For those few seconds, we both escaped from trappings of our respective lives and were simply two very lonely people in need of affection.

There was a sudden clatter in the hallway beyond my open door and we both started, quickly moving apart, each of us unable to look at the other.

"I should go," said Ivan brusquely.

I nodded but did not meet his eyes.

"Thank you for helping me today," I mumbled. It sounded feeble but I didn't know what else to say. My cheeks felt as though they were on fire.

"Don't mention it." He brushed my words off. "I shall see you at breakfast in the morning. I hope you get some rest tonight, Claire."

With that, he hurried from my room. I locked my door and then collapsed onto the bed.

What on earth was I doing? How had I let a man kiss me? I had no business kissing anyone. It was a blatant betrayal of my darling George, and added to that, Ivan was married to my cousin. I was appalled and disgusted with myself.

What a rotten day this had been on all accounts. I was completely at sixes and sevens, my emotions a tangled knot in an intricate web of confusion, all brought about by men.

I was not upset with Ivan for the kiss. I understood it wasn't premeditated, just an impulsive moment after several days of unsettling and disturbing events.

But my uncle? I would never forgive him for behaving the way he had with me. It broke every cardinal rule in my opinion.

Yet the worst of it, the honest truth, was at this particular moment, the person I was most upset with, was myself.

THE NIGHTMARE WOKE ME. This time, as I sank into the depths of the ocean, I looked down to see Uncle Simon pulling me deeper, his hands tight about my ankles.

I sat bolt upright, panting, sweat beading on my brow. I was burning with heat.

I pulled off the covers, and quickly went over to the window, opening it a little wider this time. The night air was sweet and cold, capturing my breath and turning it into a magical mist.

I began to cool off. What time was it? The moon was still bright, so it couldn't be very late. I'd gone to sleep rather early.

I gazed out to the distance. There wasn't much to see as it was black as pitch. I meditated about the days which had passed since first arriving here. All the things that had transpired in such a brief time. How strange life could be, just when you thought you had it sorted out in your mind.

There was a loud snap down in the courtyard. The sound made when a foot treads on a branch or a stick.

All thoughts left my head, and I peered outside, pushing the window farther open still. Would I see Nanette, moving through the bushes with her lantern? Or was it an animal foraging around?

My interest dulled, until I saw a dark cassocked figure walking down the path of the courtyard, heading straight for the moat. The hooded person walked slowly, with no light to show their path.

The hairs on the back of my neck stood straight. Who was this? Immediately, Tibbetts' tale of the ghost of the abbey came to mind. I dismissed it as ridiculous.

As I watched, the figure was swallowed up into the shadows. I stepped back and closed the window. This was my last night here, what did I care what went on in the late night, or indeed if the damn place was haunted.

I returned to bed and snuggled down under the warm covers. I closed my eyes and imagined being at the inn tomorrow.

But try as I might, the image of the lone, hooded figure rose before me. After a few minutes, I threw back the covers with irritation, put on my slippers and robe, and left the room.

I knew it was madness, wandering about Darkwater in the middle of the night. But my curiosity was no friend to me, and I could not resist.

I slipped down the stairs and out the back door into the courtyard. It was quite dark, but I had been down here enough times that it was easy to pick out the pathway and I followed in the same direction as I'd seen the figure.

I thought about Tibbetts' conviction that Darkwater was haunted. The tales handed down through the years about the terrible abbey fire and the loss of those poor monks. Was I considering that is what I'd seen? Hardly. But I also knew it wasn't my cousin, as it had been the previous time I'd come down here.

I reached the edge of the courtyard, where dense bushes marked the start of the slope running down to the water.

I hesitated.

I did not like the thought of getting too close to the moat. Though I had grown accustomed to crossing over the bridge without any misgivings, it was not the same as being near enough to fall in.

The sound of an owl somewhere in the distance interrupted the still of night. And then I heard it. The low sound of a man's voice, singing something quietly. What was it? I listened intently. It sounded like a hymn…

Now the blood in my veins began to pump furiously as my body vacillated between the impulse to run back to the safety of my room or go a little farther into the bushes to see who, or what, was there.

Of their own volition, my feet stepped into the thicket of brush. The sound grew louder still, and as I cleared the brush line at the top of the grassy bank, I gasped at the sight before me.

A tall man, dressed in a monk's cassock, his head bowed, covered with the dropping hood, stood with his hands clasped in prayer, softly singing.

Was this truly a ghost? This apparition was not an imaginary figure; he was there, stood directly in front of me.

Frozen in shock, I tried to formulate something to say to this spectre, this being. But as I opened my mouth to speak, a blinding pain exploded in my head. And the last thing I saw was the ground.

Chapter Thirty-One

MY EYES FLEW OPEN. I GASPED, and my mouth filled with water, thick and nasty as it coursed up my nose, in my eyes.

Where was I? What had happened?

My body slowly started sinking, my gown twisting around my legs, while the cold, icy water pulled me under.

My baby! I had to find Sarah!

At once, I thrashed my arms, my legs. My eyes wide, unseeing in the blackness, my throat gagging with no oxygen, Frantically I turned in circles. Thick rushes, slimy like eels, slithered against my skin. My heart pounded against my ribs. I could not breathe.

And then there was nothing.

"SHE'S COMING AROUND NOW. Careful, prop her head up a little." The man's voice was soft. Who was he?

My eyes flickered open and then I shut them quickly, it was so bright.

"Draw the curtains, Ivan. The light bothers her," said the quiet man.

I heard a swoosh and then opened my eyes once more to find it less painful.

Above me stood a young, bespectacled gentleman, peering intently at my face.

"Mrs Holloway. Do not be alarmed. My name is

Doctor Philip Brown, and I have been attending you since last night."

"Claire." Ivan appeared next to him. He looked worried. "Are you all right? Can you tell me what happened?"

"Happened?" I said drowsily. "What are you talking about?"

"Do not pester her, Ivan. For now, she needs rest."

I fell asleep.

WHEN I WOKE AGAIN, THE bright light was no longer in the room, but a lamp burned on the bedside table. A chair had been placed next to the bed, and in it sat Ivan, his arms crossed, and his head lolled to one side, sound asleep.

I lay still, allowing my thoughts to drift slowly into my mind. Recollection came gradually. Something had happened to me. What was it?

I turned my head and a blinding flash of pain ripped through the back of my skull. I gasped.

"Claire?" Ivan quickly woke up and jumped to his feet. "What is it?" He came to stand beside the bed.

"I am fine, Ivan," I said wearily. My mouth was parched and dry. "I moved and it made my head hurt like the blazes." I looked up at him. "Please sit back down and tell me what this is all about. It makes me dizzy looking up at you."

He complied and poured a glass of water from the carafe on my nightstand. I took it from him and greedily guzzled it down. The sensation of the water sliding down my throat brought a rush of sensations back.

"Did I almost drown?" I asked bluntly.

Ivan sat back in the chair and took the glass from my hand. "Yes, Claire, you did."

"Tell me what happened?"

"You were hit very hard on the back of the head and pushed into the moat."

I gasped with horror, my hand covering my mouth. Finally, I rallied, though my voice shook as I spoke.

"Why would anyone do that to me? Was it a thief trying to rob me? Surely not, for I was in my nightgown and had nothing valuable on me."

"We don't know anything yet. I had just gone down the hall to my room when I heard the back door close downstairs. After what happened to Vivienne, I hurried down to check and make sure it was locked. I looked out the window and thought I saw someone go into the bushes. Thinking it was an intruder, I followed. I hadn't got far when I heard a loud splash of water and knew something had gone into the moat. When I reached the bank, I could barely make out white fabric under the water. I jumped in and pulled you out."

"Good God."

"Thank goodness you were wearing such a light colour, I only just managed to see it under the water's surface. Another minute and you'd have been gone."

I shuddered. "What of my head?"

"You sustained a nasty wound. Doctor Brown put in a couple of stitches, so you'll be sore for a bit. He says you'll be all right, though you'll have a headache for a few days. It was a nasty blow and obviously meant to knock you out cold. Pushing you into the water…"

"Was supposed to finish me off." I turned my head very slowly until I was looking straight at Ivan. "You saved my life," I said quietly. "I would have died if not for you." A tear slipped from my eye, but it was one of gratitude. I reached out one hand towards him. He stared at it momentarily and slowly took it into his own palm.

His skin felt dry and warm. I drew comfort from the sensation of touch and was suddenly not so alone.

He smiled. And it was unlike any of those he had bestowed upon me. For in this smile there was emotion, there was affection. He cared.

My eyes grew heavy. And with the security of my hand in his, I slept.

THE NEXT MORNING, I WAS attended by Doctor Brown. I had been allowed to get out of bed and, with the help of Mellors, had dressed, but as yet I had not left my room.

I liked the doctor. He had an affable demeanour; his softly spoken voice had a calming effect. He spent a great deal of time examining the wound in the back of my head.

"I'm very pleased with the stitches," he said. "There is little irritation to your skin and the wound looks clean. I was concerned about infection due to the condition of the water in the moat. Fortunately, you were not in there very long and I think everything will heal nicely."

He went around the corner into the bathroom and I heard him wash his hands. He walked back into my room wiping them dry.

"I am glad to have met you," I said. "Are you not partners with Doctor Tipton?"

"Yes. He was out delivering a baby when Mr Delahunt came and pounded down the surgery door. He was in a most agitated state, I can tell you." He turned and rummaged in his bag which was sitting on my bed. "Now, let me look in your eyes please."

He held a glass in front of my eyes and peered in each one. "They look clear. I see no trace of concussion, so other than that wound, you are doing exceptionally well. Of course, I don't have to tell you the do's and don'ts whilst you convalesce, because you are a nurse and are well versed in the rules of healing."

His eyes looked large as pennies through the lens of his glasses and were the pale blue of a robin's egg. He was clean shaven, his skin as pink as a baby's. He had plenty of brown hair, but it was so fine it lay flat against his head.

Doctor Brown packed up his bag.

I had a sudden thought. "May I ask you a question?"

He paused and turned to look over his shoulder at me. "Certainly."

"Were you not the doctor in attendance of the rambler who died recently, not too far from here?"

He closed his bag with a snap. "Yes I was. Why do you ask?"

"Am I correct in understanding the man had suffered a seizure, which killed him?" I noticed his expression shift. He did not like my question. Why?

"Yes, that was the cause of death according to Doctor Tipton."

I frowned. "If you were the attending physician, why was the cause of death reported by Doctor Tipton? Surely that would have been your diagnosis, not his?"

The young doctor picked up his bag. I had the distinct impression I was making him uncomfortable. This only served to make me want to ask more.

"As the senior doctor, he would have the final word on my reports. Now, I had better be going on to my next patient. Remember my instructions and get plenty of rest."

"Please wait a moment, Doctor Brown. I hope you do not find me impertinent, but I get the impression you do not necessarily agree with that cause of death. How do you think the man died?"

"Mrs Holloway, I am not at liberty to discuss this with you at all. Your questions are directed at the wrong person. You should be having this conversation with Doctor Tipton."

He gave a curt nod and left the room.

How interesting. Although the young doctor could not speak out against his superior, I was not imagining some sort of disagreement there. If Doctor Tipton's diagnosis was different than his associate's, then what had Doctor Brown's theory been?

Now, more than ever, I was ready to leave Darkwater. It was almost lunchtime, and Ivan had promised to return from Skipton by one o'clock. He would accompany me to my new lodgings. I was still a little lightheaded, and the back of my head and my eyes ached. But the doctor had said I could travel, as long as we were careful.

I took a long last look around my room. My trunk and travel valise were packed. I'd emptied the secret compartment in the seat of the chair and put those items into my reticule which I would keep with me at all times.

Would I ever stay at Darkwater again? It was highly doubtful. Though the place was held in trust by the mill, it would be Nanette's and Ivan's home after my uncle was gone.

I went down the stairs slowly. As the doctor had correctly pointed out, I was knowledgeable enough to know what *not* to do to worsen my recovery.

I went into the drawing room and sat there, waiting for Ivan. I had yet to speak to either of my relatives. If they had attempted to check on me after what had happened, I was unaware. But considering I had been furious with Uncle Simon, and that Nannette and I had words, it was not surprising they had stayed away.

After a short while, I decided I'd feel much better down in the kitchen with Cook and the others. At least they held me in good regard. I made my way down the hall.

Mrs Blitch was at the stove, stirring something in a large pot. She heard me come into the room for she set the spoon down and came over to me.

"Miss Claire? I didn't know thou were up and about. You should be abed after that nasty hit on the head." She pulled a chair from under the table. "Sit you down right here, I'll fetch a strong cup o' tea and a bit o' lardy cake for you."

I didn't argue, and I was feeling a little hungry. I'd been nauseous the day before but thank goodness it had passed.

Presently she brought me my tea and cake, then, like a clucking hen, she looked at the wound at the back of my head.

"Eh," she said. "That's an angry looking cut there. But Doctor Brown's done a good job wi' stitches. With your hair so short, makes it easier for t'wound to stay clean and dry. Do it hurt though, lass?"

"It aches, but I can cope with it."

Mrs Blitch came and sat beside me. "Tibbetts says you're off t'Skipton the day. An' I wish it weren't so, but I think it for the best."

That surprised me. "Why?"

"Somethin's been wrong in this house a while now. With Miss Vivienne gone, things seem a bit worse if you ask me. Your uncle, now he's never mistreated me, but he's been acting funny. It's all to do with that priest, if you ask me. He's got too much sway o'er some of the Starling folk. Best you get away until things settle." Her grey eyes regarded me with fondness. "I'll not tell another, but I'll miss having you here, lass. So I will."

Before I could answer, she was back up on her feet. "Tibbetts," she called out. "Come in here and get you a bowl o'soup, an' be quick about it."

I ate with the three servants, feeling more at home with them than I had the entire Manning family.

WHEN IVAN TOLD ME OUR destination I was rather put out.

"Hilary Daly's house? I don't want to go there. The inn at Skipton is my preference," I said with annoyance. "Please take me there as arranged."

He looked at me sternly from the other seat in the carriage. "No," he said flatly. "Not after what has happened. Skipton is too far away for me to watch over you."

I frowned, which made my entire head hurt. "That was not your decision to make. I have no desire to stay with anyone here."

"You are safer at her cottage than an inn where people can come and go unnoticed. At least humour me with this for a few days while you heal. Claire, you almost died."

His words hit home, and a wave of nausea roiled through my stomach at the memory of being down in the moat and also the motion of the carriage. He must have seen it on my face.

"Besides, a long drive did not seem advisable. Starling Village is close."

He made a good point. Although Doctor Brown had given me permission to travel, each bump in the road resonated as a jolt to my head. But staying with Hilary was not appealing.

As if he read my thoughts, Ivan smiled. "It is not the best solution, I know. But you won't be alone and can stay in your room the entire time if it suits you. Mrs Daly knows you are coming to essentially hide away and she will not bother you."

"Does my family know where I am?"

"Well that would be difficult to conceal, especially with Gibbons driving us here. Now, can we speak of other matters? I have word from my man Dodds in Liverpool who's been enquiring about Molly, our suspected body in the priest hole."

"What did he say?" I asked eagerly.

"That he'll be in Starling tomorrow morning. I shall bring him here and we'll talk to him together."

"Excellent." I was genuinely pleased. It would be nice to think about something else besides myself.

I was at odds really. Deep down I was frightened. After all, an attack had been made upon me, right on the heels of my cousin's death. Why? The only motive I could think of was my position at the mill. How else had I affected another? But who would hate me enough to cosh me on the head and push me into the moat to drown? I shuddered. Not now. I must not think about it now.

At the cottage, Hilary came rushing out of the little house to greet me.

"My dear girl," she said, her eyes raking over me in assessment, "come along. Let's get you inside and up to your room. You must be exhausted."

I flashed a contemptuous stare at Ivan, who merely grinned, and then allowed myself to be escorted into the tiny cottage.

My room was miniature in comparison to Darkwater, yet I found it big enough and pleasantly cosy. The walls were washed in a pale lavender, and the bedcovers were white, with beautiful lacework on the fringes of the pillows. There was a dressing table and mirror, and one nightstand with a jug and a bowl, no private bathroom of my own anymore.

"I know it isn't what you're used to," said Mrs Daly.

"Please," I interrupted. "I slept in a tent for three years. This is paradise."

Her pleasure at my words was obvious, and I felt badly she was worried I would think her accommodation beneath me.

Ivan and Gibbons carried my trunk into the room. With the two men in there as well, there was little space for anyone to move.

Presently, Ivan bade me goodbye, and asked if he might stop by on the way home from the mill. I told him that would be fine, and he set off with Gibbons in the carriage.

A SHORT WHILE LATER, A Constable McNabb came to

the door. Mrs Daly brought him into the parlour and he asked questions regarding what had happened to me the night before. Obviously there was little to tell him. He looked rather incredulous at my mentioning seeing a ghost. I doubted he could do much good anyway. Needless to say he did not stay long.

Afterwards. Mrs Daly and I shared a pot of tea. She abstained from asking me questions, as I'd already been badgered enough. In truth I did feel weary, and my head throbbed. After thanking her for allowing me to stay, I excused myself and went up to my room to lay down.

It was mid-afternoon, and as usual, an October rain threatened. I ignored my trunk, not having the energy to unpack just yet, but my eye roved looking for a safe place for what I carried in my reticule. Nothing suggested itself, so I stowed my bag underneath my mattress, then climbed into bed fully clothed, and promptly fell asleep.

I awoke to the dull murmur of talking from downstairs, and opened my eyes to find it was already getting dark. I pushed back the covers and got to my feet, stretching my arms up to the ceiling. The headache had dimmed, thank goodness.

I surmised the voices must be Mrs Daly and Ivan. I tidied myself up in preparation to join them, left my room and came down the short, narrow flight of stairs.

As I approached the parlour, I paused. The voices were quieter now. A man said a few words in a whispered tone, and my heart sank. It was not Ivan, but Father Lynch. What was he doing here? Should I quickly return upstairs to my sanctuary, or go in and face the man?

It was not my nature to run away from anything. I

steeled myself, straightened my back, and marched into the room.

They had not expected me. Doubtless, they'd not heard me either as they were engrossed in conversation.

They were sitting in two chairs facing one another. On my entering the room, the priest got to his feet, his eyes cold as stone.

"Mrs Holloway, why, how delightful to see you. I hope I did not wake you by my coming?"

"Not at all," I said, joining them and taking a seat at a small table near the window. "Am I interrupting?" I made a point to look at him as though I thought I was.

"No, my dear," Mrs Daly assured me. "Father Lynch wanted to check on you and make sure you were recovering."

He'd already sat back down, but he fastened his gaze on my face. "To be sure I was that shocked to hear about your misfortune. 'Tis the mercy of God you survived my dear."

"Actually, it had more to do with Mr Delahunt. Had he not seen me out there, I'd have drowned." Each time I spoke that awful word, an image of my husband and daughter flashed through my mind.

He did not respond, but his look of disapproval was answer enough.

"Are you settled in?" asked Mrs Daly kindly.

"Yes, thank you. The room is most comfortable."

"It is kind of Hilary to invite you to stay," said the priest. "Although I would have thought you better off with your family, especially after your horrible experience."

"Yet, that is why I left," I said bluntly. "I do not feel safe at Darkwater."

He looked offended, as though I insulted his home, not my family's. "How can you say that, Mrs Holloway? At Darkwater Abbey, you have the protection of your uncle."

"It did not help Vivienne," I snapped.

Mrs Daly gasped at my boldness, and I caught the flicker of contempt that flashed across Father Lynch's face.

Before anyone else could comment, there came a knock on the front door. Mrs Daly's maid answered it and within moments the door to the parlour opened revealing Ivan. I was relieved to see him.

"Mr Delahunt," said my hostess getting to her feet. "Please come in and take refreshment with us. Miss Claire has just joined us."

"And I must be going," said the priest getting swiftly to his feet. "Good evening to you all." He turned to Mrs Daly. "Do not hesitate to fetch me if there is anything I can do to help." With a swift nod at Ivan who had yet to speak, Father Lynch left the room without even looking at me. Instantly, the atmosphere relaxed.

"Let me go and fetch some fresh tea," said Hilary, leaving us alone.

As soon as she left the room I got up and went over to Ivan. "I'm so pleased to see you. I just came downstairs and was surprised to see the priest here." I gestured to the small table. "Come and take a seat with me."

"How do you feel?" he asked as we sat down. "You have a little more colour in your face than you did earlier. Have you rested?"

"I have. I slept most of the afternoon and it did

improve my headache."

"Good. I think you shall be comfortable here, at least for now."

Our eyes met, and I had a sudden recollection of his kiss. After recent events it seemed it was a lifetime ago, like it had happened to someone else. I knew it had been a mistake. Now, after my attack, there were more important issues at hand. I pushed it to the back of my mind where it needed to stay.

"Is there any more news from your contact in Liverpool?" I wanted to talk about something positive instead of dwelling on my situation.

"Dodds arrives in the morning. We are to meet at the inn here, The Ace of Spades, at nine thirty."

"Can you not bring him here? I should like to hear what he has to say myself."

"I considered it, but deemed it unwise," said Ivan. "I would rather we met publicly, especially after what happened to you."

"Speaking of that, do you think whoever harmed me was also responsible for what happened to my cousin?" It seemed likely to me. Although I could not answer what motive there was, it was still too much of a coincidence.

"It is an obvious conclusion," Ivan said after a moment's consideration. "Yet I cannot see a connection, especially when you have so recently come here. Hopefully, Dodds may shed some light on the body in the priest hole. Perhaps it will answer questions which may in turn garner ideas about everything else."

"Here we are." Mrs Daly bustled into the room carrying a tray laden with tea things, along with a plate of small cakes. She set it down on the table where we sat, then poured for us. When she proffered the plate of tea cakes, Ivan helped himself to three of them. He probably was ready for dinner having had a long day taking care of me and going to the mill.

With the older woman present, our conversation turned to mundane topics. I paid scant attention to the chatter, as my mind was absorbed in the imminent meeting between Ivan and his Liverpool contact.

It would be interesting learning what he had to say. Were we on the right track with identifying the skeleton? Because if we were, then someone had put that poor woman in the cellar at Darkwater. With Vivienne's death and the attempt on my life, I grew more convinced we three might be victims of the same person.

But who?

Chapter Thirty-Two

THIS MORNING, I FELT MUCH better. The headache powders from Doctor Brown were most effective, along with a good night's rest.

Given my injury, my recovery moved at a fast pace. I'd hurt myself when brushing my hair, for the wound was easy to clip with the brush. But other than that, I just had a dull ache to contend with.

This morning, I ate breakfast with Mrs Daly before she left to attend to her obligations. This took her away from the cottage, and I was pleased to have the place to myself.

There was a thrum of excitement in my blood today. I glanced at the clock on the mantel. By now, Ivan would be meeting with Dodds. It was terribly frustrating not being able to join them. I'd begged to go along but Ivan had been adamant I keep away. He stated my safety could be at risk.

Of course, he was right. If I had accompanied two men into the inn, it would certainly draw attention. Ivan was a businessman, and it would not be unusual for him to be seen meeting a stranger. Yet common sense did not make it any easier for me sitting alone and speculating.

When the clock struck eleven I had almost worn out the carpet with my pacing. I kept going to the window and peering down the lane for any sight of

Ivan.

I caught myself thinking about him and our unexpected alliance. Who could have guessed he and I would become such friends? Besides George, I'd had no close companions, male or female. There was much to be said of the positive ramifications of friendship. The truth was, without Ivan's help, I would be in the middle of a nightmare.

I heard the front gate swing open and my heart leapt. But it quickly knew disappointment when I saw it was the postman. Another fifteen minutes passed when I saw Annie, Mrs Daly's maid, leave with a shopping basket threaded over her arm.

This was becoming unbearable. It was all I could do not to throw on my coat and run down to the Ace of Spades myself.

Then he appeared. Ivan cut a handsome figure as he came through the garden gate. A tall, well-made man, even in his smart, tailored suit, it was easy to see the strength he carried. He walked with a confident stride. One glance at him said much about his character.

I rushed to the front door and opened it before he had a chance to knock. He stepped across the threshold bringing in the cool air from outside along with him.

Ivan took off his hat and walked directly into the parlour. A fire burned in the hearth and he stood before it warming himself.

I closed the door behind me and rushed over to where he stood. "Sit down," I said taking a seat myself in one of the two armchairs. "You must tell me everything," I gushed.

He did not relax, but sat upright in the chair, his expression giving away nothing.

“Tell me,” I urged. “I am desperate to know what you have learned.”

His eyes met mine and his brow arched. “I’m sorry it took so long, but Ronnie Dodds had much to say.” His face became serious. “Ronnie began his investigation at a police station in Kirby. He asked around at the docks, focusing on the type of establishments where sailors would frequent when they first stopped in port. Jack Tibbetts has a good memory, because Molly was an actress and Dodds eventually found someone who had known her.”

“My goodness,” was all I could say.

“Molly’s surname was Dutton. The person Dodds spoke with was able to tell him the name of her grandmother, who still lives in Kirby.”

This was wonderful news. But I did not want to interrupt Ivan by commenting.

“Dodds went to visit the old lady, who is in her eighties and mostly blind. Apparently, her granddaughter, Molly and an older brother whose name was Lenny, were, in the old lady’s opinion, ‘badduns’. She’d brought them up after they were orphaned, and told a tale of their behaviour being more than she could control.

“Molly had been a prostitute for a short time, and then become an actress. She’d been mixed up with a young man and left home at a young age. Lenny, was in and out of trouble with the police. He left for Australia to evade getting in trouble over something he had done. But not long after arriving in Australia, he was caught stealing cattle and sentenced to many years in gaol.

“However, he wrote faithfully to his sister, using his grandmother’s address. At some point in time, the letters stopped getting answered by Molly. Lenny was unable to investigate why due to being incarcerated. The grandmother could not read or write, and with her impaired vision getting worse over time, didn't bother opening any of the letters."

"Did she still have them?" I could not help but ask.

"She has some letters, according to Dodds. But she is a wily old woman and would not let him see them. She did offer to give them to him for a price."

"What did you tell him?"

"I gave him the money and sent him back to Liverpool. We must see those letters. But it gets more interesting. According to the old lady, Lenny recently returned to Liverpool. He had done his time and was a free man. He arrived in Kirby six weeks ago. The grandmother claims he was obsessed with finding his sister, whose last known whereabouts was in Yorkshire where she had gone looking for a man named Paul."

Excitement coursed through me. We were finally getting answers to some questions. Had we been on the right track the entire time? It certainly sounded as though the skeleton at Darkwater was probably Molly Dutton.

"It has to be her brother who had the seizure and died right before I came here, don't you think?"

"It seems highly likely. There are too many coincidences between what we already know and what he was able to find out from the grandmother. He asked her about the necklace you found. At first she could not corroborate her granddaughter owned such a piece of jewellery. But then she remembered Molly telling her that this fellow, Paul, gave it as a gift to Molly. She also thought it might have been a betrothal gift."

"Molly was married?"

"Dodds has someone checking the registers in various districts in Liverpool, to see if he can find a record of any marriage, now that we have her name. Unfortunately, these things take some time and he wanted to meet with me now so you and I had something to go on."

"My goodness, Ivan. This is a great deal of information to digest. It would be very helpful to know if Molly died of natural causes and was accidentally locked in that priest hole, or if she was killed and hidden there."

"Indeed. It does seem ironic that her brother should come all the way home and then go looking for her in the very area she died."

"Only to die himself from a seizure." A sudden memory flickered through my mind. "It is strange, but I actually questioned Doctor Brown about the Australian man when he attended me the other day. I posed the question why it was Doctor Tipton who reported the cause of death on the death certificate when he was not present and did not examine the patient."

"What did he say?"

"He was not happy I'd asked. His answer was evasive. He said as the junior doctor he would be overruled by Doctor Tipton."

Ivan's eyes narrowed and he stared at me. "What is it you suspect?"

I chose my words carefully. "Initially, nothing. But when Vivenne died, I questioned his diagnosis. If a nurse can recognise a specific poison, the doctor should have identified it immediately."

"Are you insinuating he made a mistake, or that he

did it intentionally?"

"If he believed my cousin had committed suicide and wanted to conceal her manner of death in order to protect the family name, I would accept that. If he had correctly identified the poison it would support that theory. However, claiming she died of a different poison is suspicious. Now, we find out he overruled another doctor's opinion on a cause of death regarding a man we now know as Lenny Dutton. We are not privy what Doctor Brown thinks the man died of, but we can guess he does not agree with Tipton's diagnosis of a seizure. Also, it was put about that Dutton was a rambler. We know for a fact that was not the case. He was here looking for his sister, not knowing she was dead."

"So you think Dutton didn't die from natural causes?"

"Absolutely. If his sister was killed by someone in this area, and then Dutton appears after two decades looking for her, would he not pose a serious threat to the killer."

"Of course. I agree. But I don't see how that ties in with Vivienne or Doctor Tipton."

"No," I reluctantly agreed. "I cannot see a link either. But there must be one. We just haven't found it yet."

The mantel clock chimed the hour and Ivan got to his feet. "I must go. They are expecting me at the mill. Dodds is already on his way back to Liverpool. Tomorrow is Friday, and he's going to see if anything turns up from checking the records. He will return here on Saturday, hopefully with the letters from Molly's grandmother, and more information."

I stood up and followed him to the door. "Until then," he said stopping to look me in the eye. "Please stay inside, Claire. Don't venture anywhere. We still don't have all the answers and if we are only half right, there's a malicious killer living among us. There's a lot to be wary of." He reached out and placed a hand on my shoulder. "I need to know you're being kept safe."

I was taken aback. His hand felt warm against the fabric of my blouse. His eyes, almost dark green in the light of the room regarded me with affection. It touched me deeply. In my current situation, his concern chased away some of the isolation fear had wrought.

"I promise to stay put," I said quietly. "Besides, there is nowhere for me to go anyway. I shall bide my time here, patiently waiting for you to come with the next missive from Mr Dodds. I am disappointed this has stopped me from helping at the mill. I was looking forward to it."

Ivan removed his hand. "When this is all over, I promise you will have more than your fair share of things to do. It would be impossible trying to learn anything in this current situation. Be patient, if you can." With that, he left the cottage.

MRS DALY RETURNED HOME with several tales and bits of gossip about people in the village I did not know. We ate a light lunch together and then I excused myself to go and lie down. Her incessant chatter would not have bothered me before my injury, but with a sensitive head, I could only listen for so long.

At supper that evening. Mrs Daly informed me she was going out. She did not specify her destination, but judging by the guilty look on her face, I knew it had something to do with Father Lynch and The Believers. I was still very curious about this secret society. However, with everything Ivan had told me, my mind was focused in an entirely different direction.

After we had eaten, both she and the maid left the cottage. I slid the bolt on the front door and went back into the parlour. I was not nervous being on my own. Here in the village I felt quite safe. With so many neighbours it would be difficult for anyone to break in and do me harm. Besides, I kept my reticule close and knew my gun was never far away.

What a pity I had not carried it with me the night I'd been attacked. I suppose I'd expected to find my cousin in the courtyard as I had before. How wrong I had been.

I was reading through my mother's journal when someone rapped the door knocker. I went over to the window and peered through the curtains. It was easy enough to see who stood there, even in the dark.

I smiled with pleasure seeing it was young Phoebe Tipton. I hurried to let her in and out of the cold night air.

"Phoebe," I said as soon as she was inside, and the door shut and bolted. "What are you doing out at night all alone? You should not be by yourself."

I let her into the parlour, and she immediately went to sit close to the fire. In the gas-light I was surprised to see how pallid her complexion appeared. Her large brown eyes were as sorrowful as a Basset Hound. Had she been crying?

I took the seat next to her, leaned forward and grasped her hands. They were frozen.

"Phoebe, you look terribly upset. Is something

wrong?" Obviously there was; the girl would not be out at night otherwise.

She blinked and a fat tear rolled down her pale face. "I had to talk to someone. I went to see you at Darkwater, but the butler said you were staying here. He told me not to tell anyone and I promised I wouldn't, but I had to come. Oh Claire, I think I'm going mad."

"What has happened?"

Phoebe pulled her hands away, retrieved a handkerchief from a pocket and blew her nose. "It is my father. He insists I am to join the rest of my family in attending this silly group they belong to."

Instantly I thought of The Believers. I did not want to betray Mrs Daly, so I responded simply, "What group?"

"I am not allowed to say their name, according to Martin. But it's something they've all gone to for several years. You have to be sixteen before you can join, and as I am soon to be of age father says it is time for me to go to the meetings."

My heart sank at the realisation the Tipton family were part of Lynch's sect. I kept my face stoic.

"I can see you do not wish to go, but why are you so upset about it? We all have to do things with our family that we'd rather not. What could be so awful about this?"

She wrung her hands together. "I don't even like going to church, and I cannot stand that awful priest. As if that's not enough, now I'm supposed to go and extra two times a week and listen to him rattle on about who knows what. Father says I have no choice in the matter. Hazel says I should feel flattered that I am invited to join such a select group of people. Honestly, Claire, I'm never going to have any fun."

I did pity Phoebe. Though there were certainly worse things she could be made to do, I understood her dislike of Father Lynch, and could not imagine having to be around the man more frequently. But what was I supposed to say to an impressionable young woman? I could not share my personal feelings about the man. It was not my place.

"Is your father a strict man?" I asked. In truth, I knew very little about Doctor Tipton. He seemed likeable enough, yet I was very suspicious of him after what had happened to Vivienne, and now Lenny Dutton.

She shook her head. "Not especially. But he allows Martin to dictate what happens in our home. Martin can be absolutely beastly."

That surprised me. I remembered the handsome young man who had been so attentive at the dinner we'd held.

"He is the one," continued Phoebe, "Who has convinced our father that it's time for me to join them. I told Martin I would blaspheme in front of everyone if he made me go. He was so angry with me he banished me to my room this past week. I have been locked in there these past three days."

"I am sorry. But I don't think there is anything I can do to help you. This is a family matter. They would not appreciate anyone else knowing their business, Phoebe. When is it you are supposed to go?"

"Saturday night. It is some sort of induction ceremony. Hazel did it a few years ago and I have to wear the same gown she wore. I suppose it must be like a confirmation of sorts. I think it's all rather ridiculous."

"If you think it's silly, then why are you allowing yourself to get so upset about it?"

She blew her nose once again. "I don't know. I think I'm just fed up with everybody telling me what to do. I can't wait until I am old like you, then I will do whatever I damn well please."

Looking at the young woman I suddenly felt rather ancient. I decided to try and reassure her. "Perhaps you will feel better once you get past tomorrow night. Maybe you're just nervous. Could Hazel ease your mind?"

"You must be joking. I can't talk to her about anything. My sister wants to be a nun. I think she'd go to church every single day if she could. She wasn't always like that, though. She changed once she started going to the meetings. If I must go, I hope I don't get boring like she did."

A great sense of relief washed over me. If Phoebe was being snide about her sister, Hazel, it indicated she was going to be all right.

We chatted for another thirty minutes and then I suggested she went home before it got too late. Were I not in such odd circumstances myself, I would have walked her there. Yet the prospect of returning alone concerned me, and consequently I bade her a good evening and watched her walk down the path and out of the front gate.

I returned to Mother's journal. It was strange. Though it had been mere weeks since I had first found the little books, now I read her words with a slightly different perspective. In my short time back in England, so many things had happened that had changed me.

If Mother's commentary had seemed far-fetched initially, I now understood it was not. To read about a murder and my father's subsequent trial, seemed suddenly very real. And after what happened to my cousin and now me, I began to comprehend that anything was possible.

It was almost ten thirty when I heard a light rap against the parlour window. Mrs Daly was finally home. I had not expected her to be gone so many hours and had nodded off to sleep in the armchair. I hadn't wanted to go up to bed because I liked having the front door bolted.

Mrs Daly looked rather done in. We exchanged a few pleasantries and went to bed.

FRIDAY MORNING I WAS UP early and downstairs in the kitchen before Annie had even arrived to start the day. I made myself tea and ate a piece of bread and jam.

My head was definitely on the mend. The stitches were loosening now the skin healed, and therefore did not feel nearly as uncomfortable. My headaches were gone as well.

I had lain awake since the early hours whilst my thoughts catapulted around my mind like flies in a jam jar. Firstly, I was full of anticipation at what Ivan's man, Dodd, would have for us when he ventured to Starling tomorrow. I had every intention of being present this time, regardless of what Ivan thought. I wanted to be part of the discussion.

I could not stop thinking about Molly Dutton. Who was she? How had she ended up being in the priest's hole and who had concealed her being there?

And what about her brother? The fact he died mysteriously, in my opinion, only added to the possibility Molly had been killed by foul deeds. Otherwise, why would Lenny pose any threat? If he had been done in as well, then by whom and by what means?

This threw suspicion upon Doctor Tipton, in turn. For he had overruled Brown's authority and claimed the cause of death as a seizure, which Doctor Brown seemed to disagree with, but could not say why.

Could Molly's death be connected to Keith Delahunt in any way? There was no link between them as far as we knew, except for the time frame. If both deaths had occurred close together, that would be worth looking at, surely? And perhaps the information Dodds would get might throw some light on the timing?

At ten o'clock, Doctor Brown came to the cottage to check my stitches. Mrs Daly showed him into the parlour and left us to put the kettle on.

"Good day to you, Mrs Holloway. Come and sit closer to the window while I look at the wound."

I did as he asked.

He stood behind me and parted my hair. "How are the headaches?"

"Gone," I said. "And the wound heals quickly. I fancy you are a dab hand with your needle and thread, Doctor Brown."

His fingers moved away from my scalp. "I thank you for the compliment, but I should attribute the healing to your good health." He moved away and I turned to face him.

"You are too modest. You forget I know a good doctor when I see one." I stared at him, summoning the courage to speak up. “Doctor Brown,” I began. “The other day I asked you a question regarding a man who died recently of a seizure. I suggested that he might have suffered from something else, but had been mistakenly diagnosed.”

He bristled immediately.

“Not by you, of course,” I added. “But by Doctor Tipton.”

“Mrs Holloway, as I said before, I am not at liberty to discuss—”

“A murder?” I said softly.

His face told me all I needed to know. He blanched, cleared his throat and then picked up his bag.

“Wait,” I said, holding out a hand. “This is no game I play, Doctor. There is reason to believe this person, whose identity is known to me, was no victim of a seizure, and was a victim of a killer. I do not ask you to say anything, but to share with me his symptoms. Surely you can do that? There is no disloyalty in telling a true observation. A diagnosis will always be subjective.”

I’d expected him to push past me and leave. But to my surprise he did not. Doctor Brown spent a moment in thought. Then he looked me straight in the face.

“The patient had vomited, and I believe suffered from organ failure which stopped his heart.”

Poison. The word formed in my mind instantly, and with it an image of Vivienne. I badly wanted to talk to Doctor Brown about his impressions, I was still a nurse after all. But he had already said more than he should.

“Thank you,” I stated, as Mrs Daly bustled in carrying her tea-tray.

“I’m sorry,” said the young doctor. “I cannot stay for tea. I am expected at my next appointment.”

With that he tipped his hat to Mrs Daly and gave me a curt nod as he left the room.

“Well, I never,” Mrs Daly said crossly. “I don’t care for his bedside manner at all.”

Chapter Thirty-Three

IT WAS AS I FINISHED helping Annie put up the remainder of our luncheon in the kitchen, that I heard the unmistakable voice of my cousin. There was a clatter as the front door was closed and the sound of footsteps going down the hall.

Annie glanced at me. "Will I put 'kettle on, miss?"

I nodded and undid the apron tied around my skirt. "Thank you."

Inside the parlour, Mrs Daly chatted amiably with Nanette. They both looked up as I walked into the room.

Nanette got to her feet. "Claire, I hope you don't mind my showing up unannounced. It has been several days since I saw you and I wanted to make sure you were well. I'm so sorry about what happened at Darkwater. Have they caught the villain?"

"Nanette, you know well enough they have not. Your father is the local justice here. With a solitary constable, I do not think much progress has been made at all, although I have only spoken with the man once. But it is nice of you to come and check on me. I can assure you I am healing well and feel fit as a fiddle." I knew my comments sounded glib, but after our last conversation I really didn't care about my manners.

"What a relief." She sat back down again. "Father and I have been worried sick about you. The fact it happened right outside our home is awful. I believe he has put up a reward for the capture of whoever was responsible."

"That is very generous," commented Mrs Daly. "Perhaps it will work. Personally, I find it difficult to comprehend that we have someone so evil living in our midst."

"It is often the person you suspect the least," I added. I glanced at my cousin. "Have you ever had problems with prowlers at Darkwater before?"

"I don't believe so. Why do you ask?"

"It just seems there's been a lot of bad luck there. A skeleton in the priest hole, poor Vivienne, and now me."

"I don't see the connection between any of those events," said my cousin. "Although people will imagine anything if they have a vivid imagination."

"Mrs Delahunt, might I offer you some tea?" asked Mrs Daly. I could tell she was trying to lessen the tension building in the room.

"No thank you. That won't be necessary as I cannot stay very long." Her unusual eyes flickered over to look at me once again. "I hear my husband has called upon you several times since you came to stay with Hilary. Ivan is always most thoughtful when it comes to the welfare of our family."

Obviously this displeased her greatly. With another woman I'd say it was good old-fashioned jealousy when her partner pays attention to another. But with Nanette, I did not really think her jealous in that way. For her, it was all about competition. Even with a tendency towards ill health, she still wanted to manipulate those around her.

"You are correct. Your husband has been most attentive about my welfare. I sincerely appreciate that, especially now I am alone. I know you must be very glad to have him as your partner in life." I amused myself with these comments. They were utter rubbish. Watching my cousin hide her true feelings when she spoke about her marriage was rather entertaining.

Of course, I did not know the truth regarding Nanette and Ivan's relationship. But I was not blind nor deaf. There was no love there, just ownership. My cousin had set her cap for Ivan and had got him. She had a predatory nature, cleverly veiled beneath a needy, sickly person.

"Indeed," she said. "I count myself fortunate having such a considerate husband. But I do ask that your demands of his time are not too great. He has many duties at home and at the mill. He does not have time to play nursemaid to me, even with my ill health. Therefore, I should prefer he left your medical ministrations to Doctor Brown."

And there it was, the warning. Nanette was very upset with me and probably more with Ivan. She was making no bones about her message. Strangely enough, I was not bothered either way. In a normal situation I would never encourage another woman's husband to spend time with me, a widow. But with Nanette, I was more bloody-minded. After our argument the other day, I almost felt pleased she was irritated with me.

"I think you're talking to the wrong person, Nanette," I responded politely. "I cannot control your husband's behaviour, though it has been exemplary. If you don't want him associating with me, I suggest you tell him, not me. Now, if you will excuse me, I must attend to something. Thank you for coming to ensure my wellbeing, Nanette. It was very considerate."

With that, I left the room and both women sitting stupefied. I felt a small buzz of elation; getting the last word against my cousin was no small feat. Her pettiness was annoying. I had far more important issues to think about besides that of a spoiled hypochondriac.

I STAYED UP IN MY ROOM the rest of the afternoon, reading through my notes which by now I almost knew by heart. If Ivan stopped by today, I would go over everything with him. Our conversations were always in brief snatches of time.

Much to my disappointment, he did not come to the cottage. I was anxious to tell him about my visit with Phoebe, and the awful news that the Tipton's were involved with The Believers.

Consequently, I had no way of knowing his plans for the following morning and his meeting with Mr Dodds. My assumption was they would meet at the same location, although I did not know what time. Mr Dodds would have to come in by train therefore he would not arrive too early in the morning.

I wondered if Ivan had gone straight to Darkwater from the mill and been ambushed by Nanette and her foul mood. I'd hazard a guess my cousin would feel unwell this evening in order to keep him home.

As I prepared for bed, I endeavoured to examine why Ivan's situation rankled. Certainly, he had become a friend to me and therefore I cared about his well-being. Yet, knowing myself well enough, I also recognised there was more to it than that. But to delve into my feelings any further was not possible. My heart was owned by my darling George, and to share it with another was the worst kind of betrayal.

SATURDAY MORNING SAW ME up early yet again. I cursed my mind which had not stilled, and kept me awake for hours.

This morning, rain lashed down angrily, pummelling against the muddy streets and drumming the rooftops. I was cross. My intention had been to walk down to the Ace of Spades and wait about, hoping to catch sight of Ivan and his visitor. This would be difficult in such inclement weather.

My plans foiled, I did not know what to do. I couldn't sit here all morning waiting for something to happen.

As my mood darkened, I knew a glimpse of hope when a message was delivered to the cottage before nine o'clock. Mrs Daly was still upstairs and I answered the knock on the door when it came.

It was addressed to me, and I hurriedly tore it open. I almost sighed with relief when I saw the sender was Ivan. In the missive, he apologised for not coming by the previous night and announced his intentions of bringing Mr Dodds to Darkwater Abbey.

He declined to give his reasons, but insisted he would come by the cottage that afternoon once Dodds left for Skipton Railway Station.

Crestfallen, I ripped up the note and threw it into the fire.

I felt like a caged beast. I had come to this house on Wednesday and had yet to cross the threshold out into the fresh air. I was irritable, frustrated, and tired. My life had always been my own, yet since coming to

Yorkshire it felt as though I was someone else's puppet, and this angered me to no end.

When Mrs Daly came downstairs, I was not as civil as I should have been. She twittered about inconsequential nonsense regarding a neighbour, and then a library book, ending with the lack of moisture in Annie's latest baked cake. My patience wore very thin.

I glowered at her across the small dining table. "Mrs Daly. When first we met I considered you a very intelligent woman. You are well travelled and have experienced much in life. Now that I am staying with you, which I greatly appreciate, you have reverted to a matron whose main interests revolve around library books and poorly baked cakes."

I ignored her gasp of outrage.

"You were a particular friend of my mother's, which in itself speaks volumes. I know that is why you offered your home to me for safety, which I thank you for again. However, this is an opportunity for us to get to know one another and to become friends. Yet that is hard for me to do when I believe you are presenting a false persona." I raised my hand in a gesture to halt her protestations. "Hilary, stop being frightened and just be yourself. I know I worried you by asking all those questions several days ago, which has encouraged you to distance yourself. Yet since my cousin died, you have great concerns about The Believers, and I wish you would share the burden and allow me to help ease your mind."

The older woman took a sip of her tea and set it back in the saucer. Our eyes met, and I saw the worry etched on her face.

"Why are you so interested in our group? What

does it have to do with you? You are new here and it really isn't any of your business," she said.

"I understand your thinking that way, but it became my business when my cousin was killed."

"Vivienne died by her own hand."

"She did not," I spoke sternly. "You have been told what to believe."

"By the attending doctor," Mrs Daly stated firmly.

"Has it not occurred to you that he might have lied? Or is everyone in your group incapable of being dishonest?"

"That is very unkind of you to say, Claire. Why would Doctor Tipton lie about something like that?"

"To protect someone else in your order."

This time she looked utterly shocked. I watched her consider the comment and imagined her running through a list of everyone within The Believers to see if they fit the role of murderer.

"Impossible. Our group is based on religious beliefs. To take a life is the worst cardinal sin there is. I may not be able to convince you your cousin died of natural causes, but I can assure you no one in The Believers harmed Vivienne."

"Then why were you so frightened when I first spoke to you about my concerns? You behaved as though my cousin's desire to leave your order put her life in jeopardy."

"That is not true." The words had no passion behind them.

"This is not a situation where loyalties are important. Vivienne's life was taken and I will never believe any differently. Someone also tried to kill me. Is that not enough to make you question everything you know? Or will it take another murder to do that?"

She became very quiet and I realised I had gone far enough. I would not get anything out of this woman. I changed tack.

"Are you attending the ceremony this evening for Phoebe?"

She looked up in surprise. "How do you know about that?"

I shrugged nonchalantly. "I believe this induction to your group carries great significance. Yet it seems a little unfair to indoctrinate someone who has not had the opportunity to make up their own mind."

"She is a child," said Mrs Daly.

"All the more reason to let her mature and make her own decisions."

Two red spots bloomed on the older woman's face and I could tell she'd had enough of my conversation. I got up from the table, gathered my plates and left the room.

I went up to my bedroom until later, hearing the front door open and close, I realised Mrs Daly had left the cottage, and I went downstairs.

It was almost four o'clock in the afternoon. Where was Ivan? I sat down in front of the fireplace and thought about my earlier conversation with Hilary. When we first spoke of my cousin's death I knew she was very worried. What had brought about this change in her behaviour?

Someone had been speaking to her, swaying her away from my suspicions. Were my thoughts known to others? I truly had not considered that. I had not been particularly secretive about my opinions. If the killer overheard my thoughts that would explain why I'd been targeted. Wasn't there always a motive for murder?

When the door knocker sounded I almost jumped a foot in the chair. I hurried to the front door, relieved to see Ivan standing there. I ushered him in out of the rain. He was soaked. His hair wet, and his outer coat drenched.

"Take off your coat," I said. "And come into the kitchen. There's a fire in there."

He followed me into the room which was empty as Annie did not work today. I hung his coat on a peg next to the hearth where it could drip while he went to stand in front of the flames in an effort to dry.

His hair looked darker wet. Ivan ran his fingers through it, until it became tousled, making him look much younger. He shrugged off his jacket and hung it on the back of one of the dining room chairs, then sat down in another and pulled off his shoes and socks. These he carried over to the hearth, setting them down near the fire to dry off.

I put the big metal kettle on to boil and then glanced over where he sat in his shirt, trousers and nothing else. I went into the laundry and took a large towel from the stack which I handed to Ivan back in the kitchen.

As I took out two cups and saucers, and then put tea leaves into the teapot I looked back over one shoulder. "Did Mr Dodds arrive in time to speak with you today?"

"He did. He's gone back to Skipton. His train doesn't leave until tomorrow morning. When you've made the tea, come and sit down and I'll tell you what he discovered."

While I brewed our drinks, I quickly recounted my

visit with Phoebe and the knowledge that her family was involved with The Believers. Ivan was as appalled as I had been.

Presently I joined him at the table. I poured two full cups of tea, strong like Mrs Blitch would make, and added milk and sugar.

"Well?"

"Dodds got the letters from Grandma Dutton." He reached over to the inside pocket of his jacket and pulled out a small bundle of envelopes, tied together with twine, and set them on the table.

"These are all the letters kept by Lenny Dutton from his sister Molly. They are dated from when he was incarcerated, sometime in eighteen-seventy-eight until sometime in eighteen eighty-two when she stopped writing to him."

"The same year your father died," I said quietly. "Another strange coincidence, don't you think?"

Ivan nodded. "Yes. But there is something else written in here that is most interesting." He tapped the pile of letters. "In an early missive, Molly talks about marrying a man named Paul, who bought her a shamrock necklace for their betrothal."

"Good God," I breathed. "So it must be her body."

"It gets better," Ivan said. "In another letter, Molly talks about visiting Starling Village, looking for her husband. She thinks he works at Darkwater Abbey."

"Which ties in with Jack and Archie Tibbetts' story of meeting her at Darkwater. But I thought she wanted to see Uncle Simon?"

"Perhaps she did. This Paul might have worked for him at the mill, or something of that nature."

"Was Dodds able to find out anything at the

Registrar's office?"

"Yes. Molly Dutton and Paul Turner were married in eighteen-sixty-seven, in the Liverpool Registry Office. He is listed as being a dock worker, aged twenty-one and Molly is listed as a dancer, aged twenty."

"So Paul could have ended up here without her, and she came to find him and wound up dead in our priest hole. But what of this Paul? Who is he and where could he have gone? Why didn't anyone notice Molly missing, or come looking for her?"

"They did," said Ivan. "At least her brother did, but twenty years too late."

"This is maddening," I said. "We have so many small pieces of a puzzle, yet nothing to link any of them together." I looked up at him. "There are several potential murders which have been committed. For the sake of argument, let us assume I am right about that. First, it might be poor Molly who was killed. Then, in the same year, your father. Nothing else happens for two decades and then a total stranger dies in the vicinity of Darkwater. Vivienne is poisoned, and an attempt is made on my life." I took a sip of my tea. "What is the connection?"

Ivan let out a deep sigh. "Well, if we assume Paul Turner worked at the mill, then Parslow's would be the common denominator."

"Why would people be killed because of the mill?" I said.

"Other than jealousy, there are two things people kill for. Power and money."

"Your father had an important job at the mill. There was talk he had taken money. And though the books were found to be altered, it was never proven he did anything wrong. Then the finger was pointed at my father, and an invented paramour which we now know was fake. If Paul Turner was employed there, perhaps he had something to do with money being stolen?"

"Or knowing who took it," Ivan stated.

"How does that tie in twenty years later?"

"What if Lenny knew something and had come here to see someone, maybe even blackmail them?" said Ivan.

"I'll go with that theoretically. But how do you connect Vivienne and me?"

His eyes narrowed. "It's still the mill. You and the Manning girls are the sole proprietors. If any of you die, the ownership is divided between the survivors."

"What if Nanette and I die? Who inherits?"

"Simon."

We stared at one another for several moments.

"Simon would never harm his daughter. Besides," I said. "He already has power and money as it is."

"Until you came along." Ivan's face grew angry. "Simon was trying to get you to marry him so he would have full control of the mill."

"As despicable as that sounds, Ivan, it's not murder. I don't think my uncle is a killer."

"Probably not. But whatever this is about has something to do with the mill, I'm convinced."

"I think you're right."

The sound of the front door opening interrupted the flow of conversation. "It must be Mrs Daly," said Ivan. He got up to retrieve his shoes and socks and quickly put them back on, then slipped on his jacket in case Hilary came into the kitchen.

"Claire," she called. "Where are you?" Her voice sounded panicked.

"In the kitchen, Mrs Daly. We're in here."

The woman who flew into the room looked nothing like the one who had left a few hours ago. Mrs Daly was soaked to the skin. Her hair was a wet mess, spilling out from underneath her hat.

"Come by the fire," I said, getting up and going over to her.

Ivan placed a chair in front of the blaze and she obligingly sat down. Her lip trembled and her hands were shaking.

"What is it?" I asked softly, kneeling beside the chair. "Has something frightened you? You look scared." Had she been targeted as the next victim?

Mrs Daly turned to me, and her eyes were wild. "You have to help her," she said, her voice tight with hysteria.

"Help who?" I asked, as Ivan came over to stand behind me.

"I'm not going to be a part of it," said Hilary. Grabbing my hands, she shook them violently. "I shan't do it. Even if there's trouble."

"What are you talking about?" I asked. "You're not making any sense at all. Ivan, can you get her some sherry from the parlour, please."

He went immediately, coming back with a glass of dark liquid. Mrs Daly took it without protest and drank the entire contents in one gulp.

I took the empty glass from her hand.

"Now," I said. "Take a few deep breaths and compose yourself. We are here to help you, so don't get hysterical. Speak calmly so we understand what you need us to do."

The older woman nodded. She took several long, slow breaths, then she looked straight into my eyes.

"You have to save Phoebe," she said, "He's going to rape her tonight."

Chapter Thirty-Four

IVAN AND I WALKED TO St. Michaels, under cover of darkness, leaving Mrs Daly with a neighbour. Thank goodness the rain had finally stopped, so at least we were not weighed down with umbrellas and raincoats. Ivan carried a large iron crowbar. I was uncertain if this was a weapon or a tool. My derringer was in my coat pocket.

"Are you sure about this?" Ivan asked as we reached the outer perimeters of the church.

"Absolutely," I said without hesitation.

We had no idea what we were about to come up against, but it was imperative we act, and act now. After Mrs Daly had blurted out what was getting ready to happen at The Believers meeting tonight, we had no choice but to help.

Ivan had sent word to Dodds, who was staying in Skipton, and to Archie Tibbetts before we left for the church. But we daren't wait for their arrival as timing was of the essence.

It was easy to see the entrance to the church as a light burned outside the main door. As before, it was left unlocked, and we went inside as quietly as we could.

Several candles were lit in sconces running the length of the nave, their light so weak it gave the church an eerie atmosphere.

“Come on,” said Ivan. We followed the same path we had taken before, until we reached the door that led to the cellar.

The church had been lit; so was the stairway. I let Ivan go ahead of me and followed him down, holding onto the rope bannister. I shivered. Was it from the cold, damp air, or fear? There were just the two of us, after all.

The crypt was festooned with candles, forming a straight line either side of the passageway, illuminating a pathway to our destination. We passed under the stone arches until we reached the area where we’d seen the strange sarcophagus.

And there it was, surrounded by even more candles, flickering in the cold air. Tonight, the top of the casket was festooned with thick garlands of ivy, like shiny green snakes slithering all over the lid of the coffin and wrapped about it like a scarf. On the floor below, scattered like confetti around the plinth, were flower petals. Yet all the decorative elements did nothing to soften the dark foreboding I felt in my heart.

I read the inscription as I had the last time we were here.

‘The Prince of Souls.’

I gave an involuntary shudder and moved into the neighbouring area where poor Molly had been laid out. But we did not stop to look at her this time, though it appeared she was still there, under the white sheet. We passed by, heading straight for the door we’d seen tucked away in the back.

It was easy to navigate tonight, as everything was lit by candles. I assumed this was all part of the disgusting ceremony that was about to start.

Nearing the door, I suddenly heard a soft echo of voices, and my heart picked up speed as we drew closer.

We both pressed our ears against the old wooden portal and listened. It was hard to hear anything. The stone walls down here were so thick, they trapped the sound within. But I could distinguish some sort of chanting going on.

Ivan looked at me. “Are you ready?”

I nodded, trying to calm my nerves. We had talked at length about what we could do, which we realised was not much because we’d be outnumbered. But at the very least, if we could interrupt their ridiculous ceremony and get Phoebe out of harm’s way, then we would call it a success. I only wished we had more help. But who could we trust?

Ivan turned the door handle. It was locked. Then he took a step back, fitted the crowbar’s end between the edge of the door and frame, and pulled. I could see the strain on his face as his teeth gritted and his whole body shuddered. The mechanism of the ancient door was solid, but the wood was not. Suddenly the area supporting the lock gave a crack, splintered, and fell apart. Within moments, Ivan managed to prise it open.

We rushed through the doorway, descended three broad, flagstone steps, then ran down a narrow hall towards the haunting chants coming from somewhere close by. Rounding a corner, we stopped in amazement.

We were inside a small chapel, with no pews or windows. In its centre, surrounded by several people, stood a raised stone altar, bearing the figure of a woman lying prostate and not moving. Phoebe!

I watched in horror as a tall man dressed in a gold

gown and mask pulled the unmoving girl's legs to slide her closer to the end. He raised up her white gown as he fumbled with his clothing.

I screamed. "No!"

He froze.

The chanting ceased abruptly.

Figures gowned and masked, standing in a protective semicircle around them, turned to see who had interrupted their worship.

Automatically Ivan and I moved towards the altar. It was like something out of a bad dream. We pushed through the congregation. Some garbed in black gowns and black masks, a few dressed in red. No one tried to stop us.

Ivan reached the altar and gave the man in gold a hefty shove so that he stumbled and fell backwards. I quickly went to Phoebe. The girl was out cold. She had obviously been drugged, but her breathing was steady although very slow.

"What the hell do you think you are doing?" Ivan shouted at the man who was being helped up from the ground by two of his followers.

"You are not welcome here," a familiar voice growled back at him, tainted with a slight Irish accent.

Ivan stepped forward and with one tug yanked the gold mask away from the man's face.

Father Lynch stared back at him, black eyes blazing with hatred. "Get out of my church this minute," he said. "You have no right breaking into a private ceremony."

Ivan took a step closer. "And you have no right forcing yourself on an unconscious girl. How dare you."

"Ivan," I called to him, concerned he was going to do something physical. There were at least ten of them here, and we were far too outnumbered to start a fight. "Please come here and carry Phoebe. She is in no fit state to walk."

"Leave her alone." The voice came from someone dressed in black. I recognised it immediately. It was Martin Tipton, Phoebe's brother.

"She is going with us." Ivan quickly came to the altar and scooped the young girl into his arms as though she weighed nothing.

"We are taking her," I said. "And if you try to stop us, I'll see you all in gaol."

I became aware that everyone in the room had moved a little closer. I looked at Ivan to follow his lead. We needed to leave this place quickly. The atmosphere shifted ominously. The hair on the back of my neck stood up in warning.

"Put the maiden down." This from another dressed in black whose voice was slightly familiar. It was Constable McNabb. The very man I suggested we send to for help. Thank goodness Ivan reminded me we were not sure who belonged to The Believers. He'd been right.

A surge of anger rose through me. I looked around at grown men and women dressed in their ridiculous gowns and masks, then at the limp body of a young woman in Ivan's arms.

"You should be ashamed of yourselves," I said loudly. "You gather here in secret and take advantage of an innocent girl, all in the name of some pseudo religion you have made up. You are cowards, all of you. Hiding in the dark like rats and cockroaches, concealing your identity because you know, deep down, what you are doing is wrong. You disgust me. Now let us leave with Phoebe or there will be more trouble than you know. Do not think for one moment we have not informed others of our location. If you do anything to harm us, they will know who to look for."

It was a blatant lie. The only people who knew where we were was Mr Dodds, if he got Ivan's message, and the Tibbetts brothers, if they'd received the note we'd sent earlier.

Father Lynch drew himself up to his full height. "Leave our maiden here and get out of my church."

Ivan let out a laugh and stepped down from the altar carrying Phoebe. He turned his back on the priest. "Come, Claire," he said. "Let's leave this den of iniquity and these idiots to worship that evil man. It turns my stomach just to look at all of you."

I began to walk away with Ivan right behind me when several of the black clad figures blocked my way. I glanced around quickly. Those dressed in red had swiftly moved back. It was then I realised that they were probably the women, our aggressors garbed in black were all men.

Ivan stepped around to be in front of me. "Move," he ordered the five men blocking our path.

One of them laughed. "I don't believe you are in a position to give any orders."

As if one body, they all stepped closer. For the first time that evening I knew real fear. I stepped closer to Ivan's back and wrapped my fingers around the gun in my pocket.

A loud voice suddenly rang out.

"Master Delahunt mebbe in no position to order

you, but we are."

Jack Tibbett's voice soared through the room and was music to my ears.

The men whirled to see not just one, but three figures standing in the entrance, two armed with pistols pointing straight at Father Lynch and the mob.

Ivan roughly pushed his way through the men with me practically attached to him. When he got to the doorway, he gently settled Phoebe in a half-seated position on the floor, leaning against the wall, then took one of the pistols from a man who I assumed was Mr Dodds, and levelled it on the priest.

"Take off your damned masks," he growled menacingly. He was livid.

There was a stunned silence. Ivan took another step forward. "Do as I say, or I'll shoot him."

I watched as collectively, the heads turned to look at one another. I could imagine their panic at this moment. Good. They deserved it.

The first to pull off her mask was Hazel Tipton. No surprise there. The next person was unknown to me. The third was Mary Buxton, and I gasped in surprise. How could she bear witness to this abomination? Some of the men were taking off their masks as well. Martin Tipton, his father, the doctor. Then Jeremy Rotherham, and the constable. Only two people remained masked. The woman had moved closer to stand between Father Lynch and the masked man.

They remained still.

"You heard what I said," Ivan commanded once again. "Take them off."

Almost in perfect unison, the two slowly lifted their masks up, and it was then I wanted to be sick.

Uncle Simon at least had the decency to look ashamed. While his daughter, my beautiful cousin, and Ivan's unhappy wife, scowled at us with unadulterated hatred.

Chapter Thirty-Five

WE TOOK PHOEBE BACK TO Mrs Daly's cottage. If I had my way, she'd never go home to the Tiptons again. I was both sickened and appalled by what had almost happened tonight. The poor girl was still drowsy when we put her to bed. But I felt confident she would be fine after a sound night's sleep.

After settling her and seeing Mrs Daly off to bed, I rejoined Ivan in the parlour, where he paced like a panther, speaking with Mr Dodds on what should happen next.

"Gentlemen," I said. "It is very late. I think you should have this conversation in the morning."

Ivan took a seat, dwarfing the flowery Chesterfield armchair, while Mr Dodds, a charming man with a fine set of moustaches, looked equally uncomfortable in the matching chair.

Mrs Daly had asked them both to spend the night in the cottage, although they would have to be content with pallets on the floor, which they both were happy to accept. I planned to sleep in the room with Phoebe. And so it was we all had some semblance of rest.

SUNDAY BROUGHT BACK the weak autumnal sun. Phoebe woke with a start, and I watched the girl blink several times, trying to come to terms with where she was.

"It's all right," I said, getting up and going to sit on the side of the bed. "You are staying with Mrs Daly and me. We brought you here last night, but you won't remember as you had been drugged."

Phoebe raised her hand to her forehead. "I feel quite groggy." Her eyes suddenly filled with tears and she looked at me with an expression of fear. "Did…did that awful man do anything to me?"

I quickly placed my hand on hers. "No, he did not. Ivan and I arrived there before anything happened. Unfortunately you had already been given something to make you sleep and that is why you don't have any recollection of it." I hesitated to ask her the next question, but we needed to know. "Phoebe, did they tell you what was involved in the ceremony?"

She wiped her eyes. "Father did. He told me I was to be a spiritual bride of the Prince of Souls."

That name…it was the one we saw on the stone tomb in the crypt.

"Who is that?" I asked.

Her eyes grew round. I knew she was too frightened to say.

"Father Lynch," said Mrs Daly as she stepped into the room. "He is the leader of the order and decides all we do there."

"Will you tell me about it so that Phoebe doesn't have to?" I asked.

"Yes," the older woman agreed. "Let the young lass rest."

IVAN AND MR DODDS WERE busy in the kitchen cooking sausages and a pan of scrambled eggs. My hostess and I smiled at one another at such an unusual sight. Each man wore one of Annie's aprons.

I put the kettle on, and Mrs Daly saw to slicing up a loaf of bread. We'd take a tray up to Phoebe afterwards. I believed she would sleep another few hours yet.

Presently, we four assembled at the table. Ivan poured everyone a cup of strong tea and we ate. The food was surprisingly good.

"Mrs Daly is going to tell us about the practices of The Believers. She will explain the ritual we stopped last night, and its significance." I looked across at her and gave the woman an encouraging smile. "Go ahead if you will."

Mrs Daly nodded. "The Believers began many years ago, long before I moved back to Yorkshire. Father Lynch was a follower of a group called The Agapemonites. A religious order led by a man named Henry Prince.

"Henry Prince was a reverend in the Anglican Church, who parted ways with them due to some of his beliefs being considered too radical. It is so with our order, only our leader being Father Lynch, is a priest in the Catholic Church."

"What has this to do with Phoebe?" Ivan interrupted.

"Let her speak," I said.

"Henry Prince eventually took his congregation and built not only a church, but a compound where they all lived together. This has always been the goal of The Believers. But it takes time and money to accomplish and consequently we have continued to meet at St Michael's until our own church can be established.

"Women are allowed to join the group after the age

of sixteen, because they must be of childbearing age to be a believer."

"Why?" asked Mr Dodds.

Mrs Daly let out a long sigh. "In the beginning, I think it was so people in the congregation could marry and keep the group pure. But last night was something entirely different. Father Lynch, whose Believer name is the Prince of Souls, was to take a virgin to begin a new line of descendants directly connected to him."

"That's disgusting." I put my fork down. My appetite had disappeared.

Mrs Daly flushed bright pink. "The Prince of Souls mates with all the younger women within the group; it is the only way they may become a Believer, and they are always willing." Her eyes looked up and directly at Ivan.

"All the women?" he asked through clenched teeth.

She nodded, knowing exactly who he referred to.

Ivan's cutlery rattled as he threw it down on the plate. Abruptly he got to his feet, his chair falling back and banging on the stone floor.

I leapt up and placed my hand on his forearm. "You cannot lose your temper now. Certainly, you can go and plant your fist in that pompous man's face, but he would heal. It is wiser to think first, Ivan. There are far worse punishments we can give him. For now, you have thwarted an unspeakable act. Please, sit down and let us understand everything before we take action."

Reluctantly, Ivan picked up his chair and sat back down.

"Mrs Holloway has the right of it, Ivan," said Mr Dodds in a kind voice. I liked him very well. His brown eyes put me in mind of a faithful labrador. Seeing him with the Tibbetts brothers last evening was a moment I shall never forget.

"The priest is a sly fellow," said Dodds. "Using faith as his weapon, he has the charisma to hypnotise many good people into doing things of his choosing. Sounds to me like he's set himself up to be something like a king of his own little country, be it a church and a compound and not much more than that. It's always about power. What a nasty piece of work."

"I doubt he's feeling powerful this morning," said Ivan, his voice deep with anger. "What do you imagine his congregation are thinking now they are discovered?" He directed this at Mrs Daly.

"Some, like me, will be finished with him. I do believe they questioned his intent with that young girl. But others will feel no different. Doctor Tipton has always been greatly under the Prince of Soul's influence. As for your father-in-law and your wife, they are considered high priests, the second in command of our order."

"Good God," said Ivan.

I felt terribly sorry for him. This was horrible enough, but for him, and him alone, it was personal. How would I have felt were it George? Horrified, sickened, and humiliated. That his wife participated in this was awful enough; that she had lain with Father Lynch was too revolting to contemplate.

And what of the parents involved? How could my uncle Simon stand by and watch not just one daughter, but two be abused? Doctor Tipton, he had done the same. Fathers were supposed to protect their children, and both of these men exposed them to the worst kind of man. In my mind, Father Lynch was a beast and an evil rapist. The cowardly men who had stood idly by and watched were perhaps even worse.

Mrs Daly continued to educate us on the subject of the secret cult. She explained that though she was uncomfortable with the physical acts between the Prince of Souls and the female congregation, she also recognised they were adults who knew their own minds. There was also much promiscuity between some of the younger members. But she could not condone forcing a girl to participate. She had finally had enough.

Ivan eventually began taking notes. I knew he planned to go to Leeds and speak with the Bishop about what had gone on in Starling Village. Surely Father Lynch would be removed from the parish and punished severely. Better that than Ivan taking it into his own hands.

We finished breakfast and cleared off the table.

LIFE HAD TO CONTINUE, regardless of what had happened last evening. Mr Dodds prepared to return to Leeds. Mrs Daly agreed Phoebe should stay on at the cottage, we would have to share a room, which was fine by me.

Mrs Daly warmed some food and took a tray up to Phoebe. I bade farewell to Mr Dodds, and saw him out the front door. I went back into the kitchen where Ivan readied himself to return to Darkwater Abbey.

"I wish to join you there later today," I told him.

"No," he said quickly. "You have no business coming to that house. The people who live there are evil, and I am beginning to think may have played a part in what happened to you and even Vivienne."

I had already drawn the same conclusion. "I am not

scared of them, Ivan. With you there, and Tibbetts, I feel safe. But I have questions which require answers, and not just about last night."

His troubled eyes stared unflinchingly into mine. Our strengths and stubbornness evenly matched, neither one looked away.

Then without another word, Ivan stepped forward and took me into his arms. His hungry mouth claimed mine, his hands, one pressed against my back, the other around my shoulders, pulled me hard against his chest, until we were almost one.

There was no tenderness there. It was pure desire, anger, and frustration all together. My mind fought against responding while my body made a traitor out of me.

Suddenly he ended the kiss and abruptly let me go. We stared at one another, panting like dogs, his eyes looked almost black.

"I'm sorry," he said, his voice thick with emotion. "I should not have done that." Then he turned and left me standing there, my lips swollen and my heart pounding.

Chapter Thirty-Six

AFTER IVAN LEFT, I REFUSED to think about his kiss. Yet it would not leave my thoughts. What on earth was I playing at? Murder and mayhem surrounded me and all I could think of was a kiss?

Disgusted with myself, my irritation galvanised me into action. I hastily scribbled a note to Mrs Daly and Phoebe, took my thick coat from the peg in the hall, slipped the derringer in my pocket and left the cottage.

The sun was bright in the afternoon sky, but the wind had a mean bite wherever it encountered naked skin.

I walked down the lane in the direction of Darkwater. There were few people about as they were probably home eating a hearty Sunday roast, or drinking down at the pub.

When I neared St. Michael's, I kept my eyes on the road ahead. It would be hard to step foot in that place again after witnessing Father Lynch and his wicked deeds.

Darkwater Abbey came into view, and I felt such a pang of sadness, it took my breath away. Such a beautiful old house, yet it harboured ugliness in the form of murder and wrongdoing. The ruin of my father, the deaths of Keith Delahunt, Vivienne, Lenny and Molly Dutton, and now my narrow escape, what a legacy there was attached to the old place.

I crossed the moat. Surprisingly I did not fear being close to it as I'd expected. I'd almost drowned in the weedy depths, but I'd survived. Because of Ivan, I had triumphed over death. Water had failed to claim me twice in my lifetime. I was finished being frightened of it, once and for all.

I did not knock when I reached the old door, I stepped inside without fanfare. But Tibbetts must have heard me, for I saw him coming down the hall.

"Miss Claire." His voice was full of concern as he rushed towards me. As he neared, I reached out my hand and grasped his. He was taken aback by this show of affection.

I shook his hand heartily. "Archie Tibbetts. Thank you for coming to our rescue last night. We were in a fine pickle, until you and the others showed up."

"Ee, but it were dangerous, right enough," he agreed.

I let go of his hand and smiled. "The world has gone mad, Archie. Well, my family has, anyway."

"Have you come to see your uncle?"

"I have. Is Mr Delahunt home?"

"He were, but then he took a horse and went to Skipton."

I was astounded. "To the mill?"

"He didn't say, miss. Just that he'd be back shortly."

My heart sank. Now what? Was it safe being alone? As if he knew my thoughts, Tibbetts spoke up.

"Don't you worry none, miss. Mr Delahunt told me to keep an eye on you should you come here. They'll not touch a hair on your head, my word on it."

"Thank you, Archie," I said. "I'm going into the

drawing room. I'll wait there to speak to my uncle."

"He's already in there," he said quietly. "Be careful, miss. He's in a right way. I'll stay close."

Uncle Simon sat in his armchair nursing an empty glass. As I walked into the room, he almost dropped it, recovered, and then glowered at me.

I did not speak, but went to sit on the sofa, where we could face one another.

He looked dreadful. Not the healthy exuberant man I'd seen on my return here a month ago. His face was ruddy, which made his eyes look bluer. He looked exhausted.

"I'd like to know what is really going on at Darkwater," I stated. "What is your true association with Father Lynch and his secret society."

"Don't call it that," he said angrily. "The Believers are more than that."

"Rubbish," I snapped. "Grown men and women prancing about in gowns and masks are no better than children at play."

His eyes turned cold. "You'll show some respect for your elders, Claire."

"Like you respected Phoebe?"

He flinched.

"How could you be party to what Lynch planned to do? She's still a girl. You had no right to—"

"Enough," he said, abruptly getting to his feet. He went to the port decanter and poured himself another glass. "You know nothing about our group. We would never hurt Phoebe. She was being gifted love by the Prince of Souls and our congregation."

"You are deranged," I said. "An innocent girl was going to be raped by a lecherous, disgusting man, hiding behind the camouflage of a priest. You have all been utterly duped."

Uncle Simon shook his head and returned to his seat. "Say what you like, Claire. We have committed no crime. Phoebe was there under the supervision of her father."

"Phoebe was drugged and held against her will."

At this, Uncle Simon raised his eyebrows, shrugged, and then took a drink.

I studied him. He was the epitome of a weak man in my eyes. A respected member of the community, an industry leader, and a sick, pathetic follower of a twisted cult.

"Tell me. If you think The Believers are so exceptional, explain why that is? Why would you associate with them?"

He gave a soft chuckle. "My dear niece. One cannot possibly sum up such a wide subject in a sentence or two. But I shall tell you this. Many of us are tired of living in a world so tainted and spoiled. Tired of fighting to make a living, being subjected to life's difficulties alone. Yet in our group, we had formed a new family, related not by blood, but by beliefs. You see, Father Lynch, once a simple Catholic priest had received a message from God. Like Moses, he was to lead new disciples to join together and form a new society. When the Rapture comes, we will be taken first, for God has named our leader a Prince of Souls. Through our devotion and prayer, we are cleansed, pure, and shall ascend."

"I don't think Moses, or God approves of kidnapping and rape," I said. "And much as I respect any person's religious beliefs, whether I share them or not, what you speak of is complete nonsense. If a Rapture were to occur, I don't think a group of Starling villagers with deviant desires will be the first on God's list to ascend. You are mad, the lot of you."

"Says a woman of loose morals." Father Lynch's voice came from behind and I turned to see him walk into the room. I was filled with such a wave of loathing, it boiled under my skin.

"Coming from you, that's pure hypocrisy," I said. "You have used your position to abuse the good people of Starling. I wonder what your God really thinks about that."

The awful man had come into the room and stood behind my uncle's chair. He meant to intimidate me, but I did not fear him.

"Then it's time you left, Claire." Nanette joined us. She took the seat next to her father.

Now there were three of them before me. Rats back in their nest. Three people who were, in my opinion, quite mad.

"Tell me," I said. "Does God condone you committing murder?"

A gasp left Nanette's lips. "How dare you."

"What are you talking about?" asked Uncle Simon.

"Your daughter," I stated. "Did you know Doctor Tipton lied about Vivienne's cause of death? She did not take an overdose of morphine. She was poisoned with potassium cyanide."

"That is ridiculous," Uncle Simon said. "Why, Father Lynch and Doctor Tipton assured me—"

"They lied. Vivienne was murdered, because she wanted to leave The Believers. But she was scared there would be recriminations, which there were." I looked at the three of them. The only person showing any type of emotion was Uncle Simon. The other two were both impassive.

Father Lynch moved away from Simon's chair and strolled to the fireplace, where as usual, the fire warmed the room. He placed his arms behind his back and regarded me.

"I knew you were trouble the day you arrived at Darkwater. You're just like your parents. You can't keep your nose out of other people's business. You've done nothing but snoop since you got here." He moved a few steps closer. "Some of us have worked very hard these past years to better our lives, be good citizens, and create an order where people can live in peace and harmony. We have diligently saved monies to build our own private sanctuary. A place for us to live and worship. A home for—"

"What rot," I said, unable to listen to another word. "You have hoodwinked gullible people into thinking you are some type of messenger from God. I don't know what bible you have read, but I don't believe any version condones the behaviour you have exhibited. I thought celibacy a most important vow of a Catholic priest. Yet you, *Father* Lynch, have used your congregation as surely as they worked in a brothel."

"How dare you speak to me like that." He rushed towards me, his face red with rage, his hands balled into fists.

"Don't touch her," Ivan bellowed from the doorway, Archie at his side.

The priest stopped in his tracks. Ivan marched into the room, walked up to Father Lynch, grabbed him by the scruff of the neck and threw him down to the floor.

Chapter Thirty-Seven

"IVAN, DON'T HURT HIM," shouted Nanette. She flew from the chair and dropped to the ground next to the crow-like man who was still recovering from the shock of Ivan's attack.

Uncle Simon, half-drunk, looked bewildered. His eyes darted from one of us to the other, as if he could not process all which occurred.

I was on my feet. "Who poisoned my cousin?" I demanded. "For I know it was one of you." My gaze settled on the priest. I was convinced it was his doing. "Did she threaten to tell the Diocese about your little group? Were you frightened what the bishop would do when he found out about your depraved actions under the guise of the Catholic church? You wanted to silence her, didn't you? You were terrified she would expose your secrets and destroy all you were working towards."

Nanette and Lynch had got to their feet, and I watched in horror as she placed her arm around his waist and leaned the other against his chest.

"Shut up, Claire," she hissed. "You are ruining it, can't you see. Oh, why couldn't you just stay away? We didn't want you here, you and your skulking about, always sad because of your stupid husband and baby dying." She gave a strange laugh. "Don't you see? They died because they didn't matter. Only the pure matter."

She gazed up at Father Lynch. "The Prince of Souls shall lead us into harmony. We, the anointed, the favoured. No one can take that from us. Not you, not Vivienne."

The penny dropped. "You killed her, didn't you? You administered cyanide to you sister on the night of the party, when you insisted she go up with you to bed." I moved closer. "Vivienne threatened to take away your future with The Believers, to expose what you really were, a delusional woman in search of the attention and admiration you never received in your home. You saw yourself as an elevated member of your cult, for that is what it is. And Vivienne was going to ruin it all, wasn't she, Nanette?"

I was mere feet away from her. Her eyes were bright and crazed. Those peculiar eyes of different colours.

Suddenly she screamed and threw herself at me. But I was ready. I kept my feet steady and as she reached me I grabbed a handful of her hair and pulled her head back. Her nails raked across my face, but I was the stronger. Years of nursing would always trump a woman who had lain in bed most of her life.

"Get off her," Ivan commanded, plucking his thrashing wife away from me. He held her back flat against his chest while her legs kicked uselessly in the air. She was wild with anger, her language foul.

"You bitch!" she yelled as tears streamed down her face. "You betrayer. I'll kill you!"

"Like you did Vivienne?" I retorted.

The screaming immediately stopped, and Nanette went very still. Slowly, a wicked smile spread across her face, a sight I shall never forget for it was so malicious, so evil, so mad. Then she gave a chuckle.

"It was only a little drink. It made her fall asleep forever."

"What?" Uncle Simon leapt from his chair. "What are you saying, Nanette?" He reached her and looked imploringly into her face. "You did not…you could not…tell me the truth, my darling."

"Oh, shut up, Father." Nanette did not even sound like herself anymore. "Vivienne was such a pain. Always moping about, fawning over my husband, whining and complaining about looking after me. Me! When I am her priestess, and it was her duty to serve me and my prince. I was glad to get rid of her."

Uncle Simon reached back and delivered a hard slap to his daughter's face. Though it must have stung, Nanette did not even flinch, but laughed at him. He stood stock still and stared at his daughter as if he'd never seen her before.

Then his shoulders sagged, they began to shake, and he started sobbing. Slowly, he went back to his seat and collapsed in the armchair. "Dear God," he muttered. "What have I done?"

"Be quiet," snarled the priest. "This is no time to lament. Pull yourself together, man."

My uncle looked over at the priest. He looked like a broken man. "You did this," he said to Father Lynch. "This all began because of you."

"Keep your mouth shut, Simon," growled the priest.

Ivan stood holding Nanette and I sat watching the scene unfold in complete shock.

"Tell me," I said to my uncle. "It is over. Your daughter has killed her own sister, and all because of this dreadful man. Please, for your own sanity, tell us the truth."

"Be careful," threatened the priest. "I am not the only one with secrets to tell."

"I no longer care," said my uncle, looking distraught. "You made Nanette attack her cousin, but how could you order her to take the life of her own sister?"

I gasped. Nanette had tried to kill me? But then how could that surprise me now.

"Your hands are not clean, Simon. Do not cast the first stone," said the priest.

"Don't preach to me, you bastard. I thought you were my friend, my mentor, my leader. Yet you turn my daughters against each other? After all I have done for you, given you."

"Shut up, man," Father Lynch roared. "Let us discuss this by ourselves, not in front of these people."

But my uncle was not to be silenced. He had reached the end of his tether, a place he would never return from.

"Though I have been a member of The Believers, and I am not proud of some of the things I have done in my lifetime, I would never condone murder. That my own child could kill her sibling is completely beyond my comprehension. I am ashamed of my connection with Father Lynch, and I hereby renounce my membership from The Believers. I am beyond worrying, keeping all these ugly secrets. They have worn me down these twenty years."

"What?" I said. "Twenty years? What are you talking about?"

Uncle Simon gave a long sigh. "I have been the

primary financial backer of our Society since its inception. I have provided funding for The Believers' sanctuary, which we started building three years ago."

"How have you managed that?" asked Ivan. "That would be quite an undertaking."

"With money from the mill," I interjected. "And judging from what I learned when I spoke with Mr Satterthwaite, I don't think my mother was ever paid her rightful stipend. I think Uncle Simon made false reports with the help of Mary Buxton. He has committed fraud."

"It is true," said my uncle. "At first, it was all going towards our future plans for The Believers. But then he started blackmailing me."

"Enough, you fool," shouted the priest. "You had better shut up or you'll regret it."

Much to my surprise, my uncle ignored him. He kept his eyes on me. "I have listened to this man for a very long time now. Under his advice, I have made terrible mistakes. I wish I could turn back time and start all over again." He turned his face and looked at the priest. "It's over, Lynch. You shouldn't have had my daughter killed." Ignoring the priest's protestations, Uncle Simon looked back at me.

"My name is Paul Turner. And I was married to a woman by the name of Molly Dutton. She ran off and left me not long after we married. I worked at the Liverpool docks and ultimately ended up in Skipton. I'd had a spot of bother at home and used the name Simon Manning in order to get work. The story I told you about how I met my darling Charlotte is absolutely true. I fell madly in love with her.

"We wanted to wed, and although I tried

everything, I could not locate Molly to divorce her. Marrying into your family, Claire, was a once in a lifetime opportunity. I was not about to lose that chance. So I married Charlotte."

"You committed bigamy," I said.

He nodded. "I am ashamed to say I did. My only excuse is how much I loved your aunt. I couldn't bear to lose her. Your grandfather would never have let her marry a divorced man. Charlotte had become a devout Catholic and it would go against her beliefs."

"Let me guess," said Ivan, still firmly holding onto a more passive Nanette. "Molly came back."

Uncle Simon took a sip of his drink. "I don't know how she found out I was in Skipton, but she did. She came to the mill and threatened to expose my secret. I paid her off and she left."

"I will not listen to any more of this nonsense," Father Lynch said and made to walk towards the door.

I pulled the derringer from my pocket and pointed it in his direction. "Get over there," I said. "Don't give me an excuse to shoot you, because I'd love nothing more than to pull the trigger. And you know I am not bluffing."

His eyes narrowed, his lip curled, but he moved back to stand in front of the hearth.

"Go on, Uncle."

"A year later, Molly came back. This time, she went to the mill, but I was in Leeds for the day. Instead, she spoke with Keith Delahunt and told him who she was. Molly had become a drunk. She was in a state when she got there, so Keith didn't take her seriously at first. Then she came to Darkwater, but luckily no one was here except Tibbetts, who took her to his father's cottage where they sobered her up. Once she left there, she came back to find me at the house." He finished the rest of his drink, swallowed and chewed his lip.

"We had a terrible argument. In a fit of anger I hit her. She fell down, banged her head and stopped moving. I panicked. I knew my family would be home soon, so I took her body and put it in the cellar and then went to see Lynch. He said we should hide her in the priest hole and then plaster it up. We did it together that very night without anyone seeing. Then afterwards, when one of the servants finally noticed the change in the cellar, I said it was done to strengthen the foundation of the house. They were never the wiser."

"I found the necklace you bought her. It was there with her skeleton."

"Dear God," he said. "I'd forgotten all about that shamrock necklace."

"What happened then?"

My uncle glanced over at Ivan and then back at me. "Keith Delahunt confronted me. He'd already been snooping through the books and was suspicious I'd been taking money. Luckily for me, Thomas always defended me. He didn't believe I was capable of theft. After Molly spoke with Keith, Father Lynch told me we had to do something; otherwise the future of The Believers would be in jeopardy. He said he had spoken with God and had a plan."

"To murder my father," said Ivan, his voice deep with malice.

My uncle nodded. "Lynch said it was the only way to ensure no one would find out about my first wife. If I was convicted as a bigamist, I would lose all claim to the mill, and there would be no money for the order."

"How does my father come into this story?" I asked. "If he always defended you, what changed?"

"Keith gave me one day to tell Thomas the truth about what I'd been doing, and about Molly. Thomas was in Leeds on business but was expected back that evening. I sent a note to both men and asked that they come to the churchyard. The one to Keith was signed Molly, the one sent to Thomas was signed Barbara."

"Why Barbara?" I asked.

"So we could have a witness to testify against Thomas. She would say they were in a relationship which would give him a motive to steal money and cause harm to Keith, the one person who would notice money had been stolen."

"But my father would not even know her name. Why would he go and meet someone he didn't know?"

"Because she wrote it was a matter of life or death, and Thomas was a good man. He would have gone just to ensure nothing was wrong. Especially for a woman, even if she was a frightened stranger."

"Except my mother saw the note first and became suspicious. So she went in his stead." I couldn't believe my mother's words were coming to life in this very room.

"Yes. Everything went wrong when she was the one who arrived at the cemetery. But we had come too far now, and Keith would have exposed our secret."

"So, you shot my father in cold blood, and then pinned the blame on a man who'd done nothing but good, and called you friend?" Ivan's voice sounded ominous.

At this, Uncle Simon burst into tears and buried his head in his hands, all the while mumbling, "I'm so sorry, I am so sorry. Please forgive me."

"You can come in now, Sergeant Morris." Ivan shouted the words loudly and suddenly a uniformed man entered the room, with four constables behind him. I now understood why Ivan had gone to Skipton. Thank goodness he'd the foresight to think ahead.

The man in charge had a round face, decorated with thick, bushy sideburns and moustaches. Stout, built like a bull, he directed his men. One of them went to Nanette, placed handcuffs on her wrists as she screamed abuse at him, then led her out of the room.

Ivan glanced at the policeman. "Sergeant Morris, were you able to listen to the conversation in its entirety?"

"Aye, I did." He stepped towards my uncle, a pair of handcuffs in his hand.

"Wait," said Uncle Simon. "I'm willing to take the blame for everything I have done, but I will not see this man," he pointed towards the priest, "get away with murder. He has blood on his hands just as much as I do. He is the person who has directed everything I have done because he would profit from my success. This pious man administered poison to a man named Lenny Dutton who came here looking for his sister. This man instructed a member of our congregation, Doctor Tipton, to lie about the cause of death and say he died of a seizure. Today I have learned the doctor committed the same fraudulent activity on my own daughter."

"He's been a very busy priest," said Sergeant Morris clicking the handcuffs on my uncle. He yanked him to his feet as another of the constables handcuffed Father Lynch.

"Just a moment," Uncle Simon said as he was led

away. “There’s one more secret you haven’t been told.”

“Keep your mouth shut you coward,” growled the priest.

“Ask him about Lucy. The Rosell girl who was murdered years ago, just after the good father came to Starling village. He told me what he did to her. He doesn’t remember saying anything because he was drunk. But that girl died at his hands.” Uncle Simon was led away. Behind him the constable pushed Father Lynch forward. As he reached me, he stopped and looked at my face.

“You’ll go to hell for this,” he said scowling.

I smiled and tucked my gun back into my pocket. “Perhaps. But I won’t be arriving there as quickly as you. Now you’ll know how my father felt.”

With that, they all left the room, leaving Ivan and I standing as still as statues, all words gone.

In the silence, we turned to face one another, and much to my surprise he did not look angry. His eyes, blue with sadness, were full of tears.

I felt my own running down my cheeks. I opened my arms, and he came towards me.

Epilogue

Saturday, January 13th—1903

WHAT IS IT ABOUT THE start of a new year which brings hope?

I didn't know the answer, yet I felt a renewal in my heart which gave me the sense that in time, things would be right once again.

I was never more glad to see the end of the last year. One of heartache, trouble, and awful turmoil.

The day Ivan Delahunt and I learned the truth about his father's death, and my father's unwarranted conviction, was truly a life changing event. Placing blame on the right shoulders regarding wrongs committed in the present was most gratifying. Yet clearing my father's name and punishing the true villain of Keith Delahunt's untimely death settled a heavy unrest I had not realised I carried.

And the day my uncle, my cousin, Father Lynch and Gibbons were arrested, I cried myself to sleep. My tears were not solely in sadness at the unnecessary loss of the people who perished and those who would die for their crimes, but mostly for my parents.

I cried for the loss of Thomas Shaw, a man considered to be good and kind by all who knew him. That he should suffer the indignity of a hangman's noose I should never quite get over. I wept for my mother, Jane. She, whose unwavering love for her husband never faltered. That she lived her life constantly grieving for him—desperate to clear his name.

I was not religious, nor had I ever been. There were so many facts contributing to my belief system which I myself did not quite understand. But if our souls really did go into the heavens, then I wished with all my heart my parents were together now, and somehow knew the truth had finally come to light.

If my cousin had not killed her own sister at the instruction of Father Lynch, Uncle Simon might never have broken down and been so willing to tell all he knew, even with the threat of death for his punishment. He also admitted to burning Mother's journals in the fire once he knew of their existence.

Nanette had been committed to an asylum. So many stories of her antics came to light in due course. She had been extremely promiscuous. It was common for Nanette to sneak away from Darkwater at night for assignations with others from the order, including the Tipton men and Rotherham. I had been a witness to one of her escapades the night I'd seen Nanette crossing the moat. The so-called ghost I'd seen previously was in fact Jeremy Rotherham, who'd paid a call to Nanette's boudoir.

In retrospect, examining what I knew of my cousin, it was not too surprising she was quite mad. She'd become completely under the control of the man she called the Prince of Souls who had promised her she would be beside him in ruling their new community.

THE BUILDING WHICH HAD been financed by my

family's cotton mill, unbeknownst to us, was put up for sale even though it was not quite finished. The money collected from the sale was mine, or should I say belonged to the mill, which I now owned in its entirety.

Mr Satterthwaite, ever helpful, had become my financial advisor in every sense of the word. I trusted him completely, and he guided all my decisions.

Mary Buxton and Doctor Tipton were both convicted of falsifying records. Martin Tipton was suspected of suppling the potassium cyanide used to kill Vivienne and the Australian, but it had yet to be proven. Gibbons would serve time for helping to dispose of a body, namely moving Lenny Dutton out onto the road from where he had died in the drawing room of Darkwater Abbey.

Archie Tibbetts told the police he thought he'd seen the Australian go across the moat to Darkwater the day his body was found, but hadn't paid much attention. He'd heard the man had died and accepted the cause of death like everyone else. When pressed why he'd kept this information to himself, Archie admitted it was because he'd been in his cottage with Susan Mellors. He didn't want anyone to know they were stepping out together in case they 'got the sack'.

The other members of the congregation were not liable for any crime committed. They were bystanders and did not personally break the law. However, the newspapers somehow received a list of their names and made them public. Therefore, Constable McNabb lost his job, and Hazel Tipton joined a convent somewhere near Manchester. The Tipton family were no longer in Starling Village, with the exception of Phoebe.

Dearest Phoebe had become a younger sister to me.

I rented a small house close to the mill, and she had come to live with me. With Mary Buxton gone, Phoebe now took up a position as secretary to me at the mill. I expected her future to be bright, and ultimately not in Skipton. But this would put her in good stead should she decide to go on to university or live elsewhere.

I refused to live at Darkwater Abbey. For me, memories of my family home would never be good. But I had plans for the old house and its future. After lengthy discussions with Mr Satterthwaite, I had also spoken with both the Tibbetts brothers, Mrs Blitch, and Mellors, who was happily engaged to dear Archie.

Though my nursing career had ended with the loss of my husband and daughter, there was still within me a desire to help people with ill health, especially those who could not afford medical treatment. I would make Darkwater Abbey a hospital. And the servants already there would be critical to its success.

It would not be a large endeavour but could be utilised by people living locally and working at my family's mill, and other mills too. I hoped to get funding from other leaders within the textile industry to help the people we relied so heavily upon for our livelihood. The hospital would be named the Thomas and Jane Shaw Hospital.

With the help of Mr Satterthwaite, an appeal to the courts was launched to clear my father's name. Once the legalities were settled, his body would be exhumed and brought back to Starling, where he would be interred with his darling wife in the Parslow family vault. Mother had already been brought here, and once her husband joined her, we would have a memorial service for them both.

Molly's remains, and the body of her brother, Lenny, were already buried at Starling's church, just down the lane from Mrs Daly. Hilary made a point of keeping fresh flowers on both their graves.

All this had been accomplished without Ivan's knowledge. He had left Yorkshire only a few days after learning the truth about his father's death. I had encouraged, practically persuaded him to take as much time as he needed to get away from everything.

I remembered him talking about his desire to travel, and how he had married instead and not had a chance to be on his own out in the world. He had worked so hard for my family, only to be repaid by losing his father and then living with the man who had been responsible for that murder. I know his mind was in turmoil and he needed time to think everything through.

He had been gone more than two months now. It was strange not seeing Ivan at the mill. Thank goodness he had trained his supervisors well enough that everything ran smoothly most of the time.

I had received the occasional letter from different locations. His last missive had come from Scotland of all places. Ivan had travelled vastly in Europe, as far as Gibraltar. Perhaps his being in Great Britain indicated he was thinking about returning soon.

How would I feel about that? It was something I contemplated often. During the day I was extremely busy, but the evenings were quiet and before I went to sleep I found myself thinking about our relationship.

We had never repeated our kisses. It was hard imagining they ever happened. What we had between us was difficult to define, but I took great comfort knowing Ivan was the dearest of friends and the best confidante I could have.

I liked living in Skipton. Phoebe and I had settled into a comfortable routine. As young as she was, I am sure she grew bored at times for her social life was sadly lacking, but I think she welcomed it as she healed from her own awful experience.

Phoebe was in Starling Village with Mrs Daly today. It was my opinion Hilary fulfilled the role of mother Phoebe had long been denied. It was of mutual benefit, for Hilary had no children herself.

I was in an odd mood. So many of my plans were starting to take on their own life. I was now able to delegate responsibilities to those more skilled than myself. Word had spread about my intentions of a hospital near Starling, and there was much local interest.

Doctor Brown offered to assist me by interviewing a doctor and three or four nurses. He and I had become fast friends over the past few weeks. He'd been relieved to finally share the truth of what had happened with Lenny Dutton.

The young doctor was engaged to be married and had expressed an interest in taking a lead role at the new hospital. We were still discussing the terms.

I sat in my kitchen drinking my second cup of tea. I spent a great deal of time in here, preferring it over the drawing room as it was warm and cosy.

One of the mill workers whose lungs were troubled, likely from the fibre at the mill, had accepted a job as my cook.

Marion Walters was in her mid-thirties and dependent on her family now she could no longer work at Parslow's. She enjoyed cooking and lived close to my house. Therefore, she came most days to prepare food for Phoebe and I to eat once we were finished at the mill.

I had just polished off a piece of lemon drizzle cake, my very favourite. I finished my tea and set the cup and saucer in the sink. I looked up and gazed out of the window.

My house was very basic. One in a line of terraced homes situated close to the centre of town and built not long after the mill opened. Most of the street's inhabitants worked at Parslow's.

I did not plan to make this my permanent home. I didn't enjoy being surrounded by so many people. Living in Africa had made an impression on me insomuch as I became used to living in less populated areas.

January was such a cold month. It was easy to stay indoors when it looked so bleak outside. All the trees had shed their leaves and shivered under the bitter wind. I peered out at the street. The front of the house had no garden but opened straight onto the pavement. There were carts and carriages passing down the road and people going about their business, but it was Saturday, and no one was in a big hurry.

I saw someone walking along the pavement across the street and they caught my eye. It was the walk. As though they favoured one leg over the other. A tall man in a dark overcoat and a black hat.

Ivan.

I stood rooted to the spot while he came up closer. He glanced at the numbers on the front doors and then looked across the street, realising he was on the wrong side of the road. He was level with my house when he crossed over.

At once I was aware of how I looked. My hair was still too short to wear up or to be fashionable. I wore a dark green skirt and a cream-coloured blouse, with a warm cardigan that matched my skirt. I quickly chastised myself for being so concerned with my appearance. What difference did it make?

I opened the door just as Ivan raised his hand to rap the knocker. For a long moment we just stared at one another as though we were both surprised to be there. He looked different. He'd obviously been in warmer climes because his skin had the healthy glow from the sun which made his eyes brighter.

"You have shaved off your moustache and beard," I said. The lack of facial hair made him look younger.

"And hello to you too, Claire." He grinned broadly and his teeth gleamed in contrast with his sun-darkened skin.

I laughed nervously. "I'm sorry. Please, come in."

Ivan stepped inside, and I closed the door behind him. He stopped to let me pass so I could show him where to go and I led him into the small drawing room.

"Have a seat," I said, turning to crouch by the fireplace and stoke the coals. It would only take a moment to get the fire going once again. I got back up. "Would you like a hot drink?"

He shook his head. "Actually, a brandy sounds better. You don't have any do you?"

I smiled. "What a question. Of course I do. I'm a nurse. Though I keep it purely for medicinal uses."

This made him laugh. "Mrs Holloway, you are never short of an answer, are you?"

I was already at the sideboard pouring us both a small glass of brandy, even though it wasn't even lunchtime. "It's true, I do often get the last word."

I took a seat on the sofa as Ivan had claimed the only armchair. I took a sip of my drink. "Welcome back to Yorkshire, and to the cold weather."

He grinned. "After a week in freezing Scotland, this feels almost warm."

"Was it snowing there?" We had our fair share of snow in the Dales, but the highlands usually had the worst of it.

"Enough that I thought I was at the North Pole."

"It certainly didn't do you any harm," I said. "You still have a nice tan to your skin and look very well. I, on the other hand, have turned the colour of milk."

"You certainly look more like an English woman than you did when we met several months ago. But you look very well, Claire. Living here suits you." He sat back against the chair. "Tell me. How have you been? You didn't say too much in your letters."

"Terribly busy. But in a good way. I have much to share with you about all the changes which have taken place in your absence."

His face grew serious.

"Not at the mill," I quickly reassured him and his face relaxed. "Well, except I have hired Phoebe Tipton as our secretary." I had said 'our' which might be presumptuous. For all I knew, Ivan might want to live and work elsewhere.

"Phoebe? What an excellent idea. She's living with you, then?" He looked around as though expecting to see some sort of evidence.

"Yes, it's been a wonderful solution to both of our

predicaments. We seem to rub along well together, at least for now. She is still so young and needs the stability of a home. Phoebe sees quite a bit of Hilary Daly, which has turned out to be a good thing."

"Is she here now?"

"No. She's gone to Starling to visit Hilary. She'll be back in the morning." I looked at him, finding it difficult to come to terms with the changes in his appearance. It was Ivan, and yet…

"You're staring at me, Claire."

"Sorry. It's just strange to see you clean-shaven."

"Do I meet with your approval?"

I tilted my head contemplating the answer. "You certainly do."

We both fell quiet. What was wrong with us? We had always found so much to talk about before.

I cleared my throat. "When did you arrive in Skipton?"

"Last night. I've taken a room at the Bear and Whistle on Stembridge Street. I didn't want to go to Darkwater Abbey."

I nodded in understanding. "Have you had time to think about your plans? By that I mean do you still want to stay at Parslow's?"

The few letters I'd sent had not been detailed, due to the fact I was unsure Ivan would receive them as he was not in one place for very long. I'd wanted him to stay apprised and kept informed about the legalities regarding the mill. He understood I was now its sole owner.

"I have had plenty of time to think about the future. But I would rather discuss that topic later if that's all right with you?"

"Of course," I said automatically, but my stomach lurched in anticipation he was going to tell me he was leaving.

A knock sounded on the door. I set down my glass. "I don't know who that might be?" I excused myself and went to answer the door.

It was Doctor Brown. He carried a small bouquet of flowers in his hand and I bade him to come in. When we entered the drawing room, Ivan was already on his feet, hat in hand.

"Ivan. I believe you remember Doctor Brown. He attended me when—"

"I remember," he said sternly and then held out his hand. He glanced at the flowers.

The men shook, but Ivan's mood was changed. I was not surprised when he announced he was leaving.

"Must you?" I pleaded. "I have so much to tell you." I did not want him to leave yet.

Doctor Brown looked at him and then back to me. "I can come back," he said awkwardly.

"That won't be necessary," Ivan said curtly. Then he put on his hat, said goodbye and went on his way.

MY MEETING WITH DOCTOR Brown lasted longer than expected. He had brought a stack of letters from a number of doctors and nurses who had applied for positions at Shaw Hospital. He wanted my opinions of a select group of them, which I was happy to give. Then he went happily on his way to meet with his fiancée and her parents for dinner. The flowers were for her, of course.

Once he'd gone, I was suddenly at a loss what to do with myself. My mood was strange.

Why had Ivan left so quickly? We'd barely had time to talk, and he'd whisked himself back to his rooms. His manner had been odd.

Then it came to me. The man had been travelling all over Europe. A handsome man, one soon to be divorced, he would have attracted the attention of many women on his travels.

This caused a strange feeling in the pit of my belly. One I did not care for. Was I jealous? I laughed out loud. How utterly ridiculous. Ivan was my friend, almost like a brother. Well not in the true sense of the words because we had kissed twice.

That last kiss. I touched my lips with my fingertips and remembered the passion which had blazed between us, only for a moment. I thought about the day my family were arrested, how we'd held on to one another as though we couldn't stand up alone.

And then I thought of George. How his beautiful eyes would soften with love when they looked into mine. How his arms would hold me in my sleep at night.

And I began to weep. Because deep in my heart I wanted to fall in love with Ivan Delahunt, but by doing so I'd be betraying the husband I had adored.

That evening, I read through every missive I had ever received from George. They had come with the other items which had been stored when I'd left Hampshire. I'd never taken them to Darkwater. It would have been too soon for me to read them.

I read, late into the night. Each letter, I lovingly placed back in its envelope and back into a small tin where they were kept, along with a few other special keepsakes.

Here were George's cufflinks and his regimental medals. A lock of his hair, and Sarah's, folded in a piece of lace. With these were Sarah's first little bootees, Mother's surviving diary, and lastly, Molly Dutton's shamrock necklace.

This tin held my past. Each item valuable in its own way. I replaced the lid and put it back in the top drawer of my dresser.

That night I dreamed I walked through the Dales. The grass was thick and the colour of emeralds, with tall brown reeds bending in the breeze. The sky, cerulean blue and the clouds beautiful puffs of cotton.

In the far distance, I saw a tall, sandy haired man, gently holding a baby in his arms. He stood completely still and then after a moment, he lifted one arm and waved to me. Then slowly, he turned and began walking away, until little by little, he became a tiny speck on the horizon.

And then he was gone.

I woke drenched in sweat, my face wet with tears, a sob in my throat and a sense of such desperate loss. But as I lay there, thinking about the dream, I finally understood.

****

I'd never been to the Bear and Whistle pub. It was quite new, in comparison to the other inns in town, and situated on the edge of Skipton.

It was late on Sunday morning, and I could smell the roast beef cooking in the pub's kitchen, ready for the onslaught of customers wanting a delicious Sunday roast and all its trimmings.

I stopped by the bar and enquired about Ivan's room and was told Mr Delahunt was on the second floor at the end of the hall. If the barman wondered at my visiting, he did not show it.

The staircase was wide, and the hall well-lit from large windows at either end. I walked to the last room at the end of the corridor, took a deep breath and knocked.

I heard footsteps, and then the handle turned, and the door opened.

"Claire?" I must have been the last person he expected to see standing there.

"May I come in, Ivan?" I asked.

His brow furrowed. "Of course." He stepped back and I entered.

The room was spacious, with a bed, dressing table and cupboard. The bed was made, and the curtains wide open, allowing the light from outside to come in. It was warm in here, the fire flickered nicely and there was a pleasant aroma of citrus.

"I'd offer you a seat," Ivan began. "But as you can see, there isn't one."

He stood in front of the door, and I walked over to the window. I turned to face him.

"Why did you leave so quickly, yesterday?"

He leaned back against the door and crossed his arms. "You had company, and I didn't want to be in the way."

"Surely that was for me to decide. I didn't want you to go. You'd only just arrived."

He shrugged. "I don't think your friend was particularly pleased to see me there."

"Doctor Brown isn't my friend. He is a colleague."

Ivan gave a curt laugh. "A colleague of what exactly? Do you mean he's a doctor and you are a nurse? Or has he now become an employee of the mill?"

"Neither," I said with annoyance. "He's helping me with one of my projects."

"I see. How fortuitous he knows what they are. I have yet to learn. But then as you said, there have been changes in my absence. Am I to assume that Doctor Brown is one of those changes?"

I stared at him dumbfounded. "You were jealous."

He said nothing for a moment. He still had not moved. "And what if I was?"

His words sank in. Everything around me suddenly stopped. I heard the ticking of a clock somewhere in the room. The soft hum of activity downstairs. The sound of my breath as my heart began to beat harder.

Our eyes met.

His, a mixture of warmth and passion and…love?

We stood as if frozen and the moment grew long. The tension between us becoming palpable and still we stared at one another, our gaze locked as one while we uttered not a word.

I loved him.

Whether it be right or wrong, wise or foolish, there was nothing to be done about it.

And then Ivan uncrossed his arms. This time, it was his turn to reach out towards me.

I ran into his embrace.

His arms wrapped around my waist while I grasped his strong, broad shoulders. Ivan stared deep into my eyes, and I fell into the depths of his.

Then his hand raised to gently lift my chin. Slowly, he tilted his head to one side. I closed my eyes, my lips parted, and then I sighed as his mouth touched mine.

The kiss was warm and supple, his lips toying with

mine as though learning their contours, their taste. His arms again encased me within their strong grip and pulled me close until I was pressed against the firmness of his chest.

His mouth plundered my own. Between us I felt such energy, a hunger borne of loneliness, sadness, isolation and the need to be one. His hand pressed against the back of my neck, and he pulled me closer still, while my fingers raked against his back, relishing the feel of his muscles, hard underneath my palms.

Ivan pulled away gently, but barely an inch from my face. His eyes blazed with desire and I saw the mirror of my own reflected there.

"Do you want me to stop?" he said, his breath laboured.

I answered him with a kiss.

WE WERE MARRIED SIX months later. Phoebe was our bridesmaid and the Tibbetts brothers our witnesses. Jack had retired from the navy and now worked at the new Shaw hospital in Starling with his brother Archie, whose wife Mary, expected their first child. Hilary Daly was the administrator there, working for Doctor Brown and his compatriots.

Ivan agreed to run the mill so that I could focus upon several issues that warranted change. I no longer wished to employ children, yet understood their need for income. It would be a challenge to find the right solution, but I was determined to try.

WE WERE ON OUR WAY BACK home after spending a short week in the Lake District for our honeymoon. We would live in my small house to start with, but there were plans to look for a larger place, perhaps one with room for a family. I'd even suggested the Rosell place as I'd always been drawn to it.

As we reached Skipton, I asked the carriage driver to take an alternate route to our home, one which would take us past the mill.

"Why are we going this way?" Ivan asked when the driver veered away from our turn into town.

"I want you to see your wedding gift," I said, unable to hide my smile. I had planned this for weeks and been assured it would be completed in our absence. I couldn't wait to see Ivan's reaction.

The carriage turned down the cobbled street to the mill. I opened my window to peer out and smiled in delight. There in the distance was the old brick building my grandfather, Arthur Parslow had built. As we drew closer, I rapped on the ceiling of the cab.

"Please stop."

The carriage came to a halt.

"What are you doing?" Ivan was puzzled; one eyebrow arched.

"Humour me," I said. "I want you to see your wedding gift."

I opened the cab door and climbed out first, closely followed by my new husband. He stepped out onto the cobbled street, and I took his hand in mine.

"Look," I whispered.

His gasp of shock brought tears to my eyes. It was not much, but I knew this would mean more than any monetary gift could bring. It would never change the past, but at least it could honour those who had fallen.

We stood side by side and stared at the mill.

This was the place which had brought us together.

Here we would work hard so all might prosper. For both our families had instilled not only the desire to be successful, but to acknowledge those who worked along with us.

High up on the building was the new sign, painted bright green, the letters bold and bright.

'Parslow & Delahunt, Cotton Mill'—Spectemur Agendo.

'Let Us be judged by our Acts.'

About the Author

Jude Bayton is a Londoner, who currently resides in the American Midwest. An avid photographer and traveller, Jude enjoys writing about places close to her heart. To keep up with her latest releases and her monthly blog, subscribe to at judebayton.com

Find Jude Bayton at:
judebayton.com
Facebook: Jude Bayton
Twitter: @judebayton
Email: author@judebayton.com

Other Books

By Jude Bayton

The Secret of Mowbray Manor
The Secret of Hollyfield House
The Secret of Lorelei Lodge
The Secret of Pendragon Island
The Secret of Jacaranda
The Secret of Witch Haven Lane

Made in the USA
Las Vegas, NV
05 June 2025